CW00336410

THE QUEEN'S PAWN

A Jayne Robinson Thriller: Book 4

ANDREW TURPIN

The Write
Direction
Publishing

First published in the UK in 2023 by The Write Direction Publishing, St. Albans, UK.

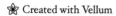 Created with Vellum

WELCOME TO THE JAYNE ROBINSON SERIES!

Thank you for purchasing *The Queen's Pawn* — I hope you enjoy it!

This is the fourth in the series of thrillers that features **Jayne Robinson**. Jayne is formerly of the British Secret Intelligence Service (the SIS, or as it is often known, MI6) and is now an independent investigator. She has strong connections with both the CIA and MI6 and finds herself conducting deniable operations on behalf of both services.

The **Jayne Robinson** thriller series is my second series and so far comprises the following:

1. The Kremlin's Vote
2. The Dark Shah
3. The Confessor
4. The Queen's Pawn
5. The Dam Keeper (due to be published mid-2023)

My first series, in which Jayne also appears regularly, features **Joe Johnson**, a former CIA officer and war crimes investigator. The Joe Johnson books so far comprise:

0. Prequel: The Afghan
1. The Last Nazi
2. The Old Bridge
3. Bandit Country
4. Stalin's Final Sting
5. The Nazi's Son
6. The Black Sea

If you enjoy this book, I would like to keep in touch. This is not always easy, as I usually only publish a couple of books a year and there are many authors and books out there. So the best way is for you to be on my Readers Group email list. I can then send you updates on the next book, plus occasional special offers.

If you would like to join my Readers Group and receive the email updates, I will send you, **FREE** of charge, the ebook version of *The Afghan*. It forms a prequel to this series and to the Joe Johnson series, and normally sells at $4.99/£3.99 (paperback $11.99/£9.99).

The Afghan is set in 1988 when Jayne was still with MI6 and Joe Johnson was still a CIA officer. Most of the action takes place in Pakistan, Afghanistan and Washington, DC.

To sign up for the Readers Group and get your free copy of *The Afghan*, go to the following web page:

https://bookhip.com/RJGFPAW

If you only like paperbacks, you can still just sign up for the email list at the above link to get news of my books and forthcoming new releases. A paperback version of *The Afghan* and all my books is for sale at my website, where you will find large discounts on bundles of my books. I can currently ship to the US and UK:

https://www.andrewturpin.com/shop/

Or if you live outside the US and UK you can buy them at Amazon.

Andrew Turpin, St. Albans, UK.

DEDICATION

To my wife Jacqui, who very sadly and unexpectedly passed away at the age of 61 on Christmas Eve 2022 as this book was being finalized. She was in Cape Town, in her beloved homeland of South Africa, on a trip to visit her mother and family. Jacqui was the architect of our family, a dedicated mother to our two children Alexa and Ross, and a very talented marathon runner and long distance cyclist. She was a great blessing to all of us and will be very deeply missed.

"And you thought that Ukraine is so simple. Ukraine is great. Ukraine is exclusive. All the rinks of history have passed through it. All kinds of tests have been tested on it. It is hardened by the highest hardness. In the conditions of the modern world, it is priceless."

— Lina Vasylivna Kostenko, a Ukrainian poet, journalist, writer, publisher, and former Soviet dissident.

PROLOGUE

Monday, September 19, 2016
London

The two-hour surveillance detection route on foot through Hampstead Heath and Highgate was nothing new for Ed Grewall, but despite having done hundreds of them over his long career in different parts of the world, he still resented the time lost while walking, standing, loitering, and watching.

They were two hours he would never get back, essential to his work as they were.

Grewall's stride lengthened as he made his way up Swain's Lane, a narrow street lined with tall brick walls that split the east and west sections of Highgate Cemetery.

As there was nobody in sight, Grewall changed his appearance a little for the third time on his SDR. First, he put on a pair of brown-rimmed glasses, then a woolen hat, and finally a black scarf.

Then he continued into what had once been Highgate village but now formed part of North London's urban sprawl.

A slight drizzle began to fall from the late afternoon skies as he turned left onto South Grove at the old village center. There he stopped, took out his phone, and sat on a low stone wall outside a church.

After his lengthy SDR, the CIA's Moscow chief of station was confident he had no tail, no coverage. This was not the Russian capital, where a suffocating surveillance team from the Federal Security Service, the FSB, tracked his every step.

However, he would not take any risks, and the pretext of being on the phone allowed him to make one final check before going to his destination.

A lady was walking two dachshunds. An old man shuffled along with the aid of a walking stick. Three teenage girls laughed as they took turns to light cigarettes. The driver of a black taxi sat in his vehicle in a parking bay, window down, music blaring as he waited for customers. Nothing out of the ordinary.

After a minute, Grewall ended the charade and replaced his phone in his jacket pocket. He continued westward along South Grove for a hundred yards or so toward Highgate Hill.

The oligarch he was due to meet, a multibillionaire, owned an enormous mansion that was set in twelve acres of landscaped grounds and was worth more than £40 million. It was only half a mile away in Hampstead Lane.

But they weren't going to meet there. Instead, they had set the rendezvous for a much more modest house, a three-bedroomed brick Edwardian terraced property.

The house's existence had come as news to the CIA, who thought they had records of all the man's properties. But not this one. It had since emerged that he had bought it anonymously through an offshore company registered in the Bahamas and never lived in it.

The message suggesting they meet there had come from

an unknown Russian burner phone to a British burner phone that Grewall kept for such purposes.

It had come as a surprise. Grewall, a Moscow veteran who at forty-nine was the Agency's most productive recruiter of assets in the Russian capital, had given up on this man after their initial brief encounter three years earlier at the city's legendary Central Chess Club. Now the oligarch had got in touch again, out of the blue, with the suggestion that he had something important to convey.

A meeting in Moscow was out of the question, given the level of surveillance Grewall was currently under. It would have been too difficult and extremely risky. Instead, he suggested that the man meet one of his colleagues from the CIA station in London. But the oligarch was insistent. He only wanted to meet with Grewall. So, they decided to do so in London instead.

Grewall wiped a hand across his five-day gray stubble, which stood out against his dark skin, a product of his half-Indian, half-white American parentage. He stopped and surveyed the target house, only forty yards away, across the other side of the street.

White net curtains masked all the windows facing the street—two on the ground floor, three on the first floor, and one in the attic. The white front door, tucked inside a porch, was shut, and there was no sign of movement. The house looked exactly as it had on the three previous occasions when Grewall had driven past it that week.

He checked his watch. It was 4:48 p.m., precisely the time scheduled for the meeting. Grewall, like many of his colleagues, avoided arranging meetings with assets at predictable and obvious times on the hour or half hour.

He crossed the street, walked past the privet hedge that marked the boundary of the property, and up the short path that led to the front door.

The house was old, but unlike the neighboring three properties on the terrace, which had old-fashioned wooden front doors and windows, this one had steel and PVC fittings.

The security was more modern, too. Beneath the porch, on the wall to the left of the front door, was a black box with a numeric keypad, a small screen, and a sensor panel. From his pocket, Grewall removed a small key fob he had received by courier two days earlier and raised it to the sensor panel.

There came a discreet beep from the black box, and a message flashed up on the screen: ENTER PIN.

He tapped in the five-digit number that had come with the fob, which he'd memorized. "Make it look like you live there," the message had said.

There was another extended beep and a click, and the door opened an inch inward.

Grewall took a handkerchief from his pocket and used it to push the door fully open. By habit, he always tried to avoid leaving fingerprints in a strange property. He then stepped into a hallway with black-and-white floor tiles and closed the door behind him. He stood still for a moment.

Silence.

"Pyotr," Grewall called softly, questioningly.

No response.

The house owner, Pyotr Fradkov, had come to prominence in the years after President Vladimir Putin's rise to power in 2000. Originally a senior officer in the KGB, the security and intelligence agency of what was then the Soviet Union, he had amassed his fortune from ownership of Russia's largest cell phone operator, MetroPhone. The stake had been acquired under dubious circumstances as a result of the president's largesse.

"Pyotr," Grewall called again, louder this time.

Still no reply.

Grewall scratched his thinning, short-cropped gray hair.

The stairs rose ahead of him to the right, but he ignored them and padded down the hallway toward the rear of the house. The first two doors to his left were closed, but the third was wide open.

It led into a kitchen with a gray-tiled floor and granite counters. There were sliding doors that led to a small patio and garden.

A few dirty plates, cups, and glasses stood on the counter along with a half-empty bottle of wine and a jar of ground coffee next to an electric kettle.

But there was no sign of Pyotr Fradkov.

Grewall walked to the counter, took out his handkerchief again, and felt the kettle through it. It was cold.

He turned and went back to the hallway. Still using the handkerchief, he opened the first door to his right, which turned out to be a small bathroom, so he moved to the second, nearest to the front door.

The door creaked loudly as he opened it.

The first thing Grewall saw was a wooden coffee table in the center of the room with a chessboard standing on it, a game half completed.

The second thing was the slumped figure of Fradkov, lying sprawled on the carpet between the coffee table and a sofa, his face as gray as the skies outside and utterly still.

My God.

Grewall took a couple of steps nearer. There was a large pool of vomit on the carpet next to Fradkov, with more vomit down the front of his sweater and splattered on the sofa. A large wet stain had spread over the crotch of his beige trousers, and spittle covered his lips and dribbled down his chin.

A half-full coffee mug stood next to the chessboard on the table just in front of the Russian, and another, also half-full, was on the other side of the table, in front of an armchair where, presumably, the oligarch's opponent had been sitting.

Grewall knew there was no hope for his asset. The Russian was unquestionably dead.

"Shit," he muttered to himself. He felt his stomach flip over.

Instinctively, Grewall took a step backward, reached into his back pocket, and removed a pair of thin rubber gloves, which he put on.

He glanced around, looking for anything that might be useful. Fradkov's laptop, his phone. But there was nothing in sight, and he didn't dare search Fradkov's pockets.

He needed to get out of the house.

What substance they had used was anyone's guess, but given the Kremlin's history of poisonings and Fradkov's appearance, he knew there was a chance he too was now humming with radioactivity.

PART ONE

CHAPTER ONE

Monday, September 19, 2016
Amsterdam

Jayne Robinson heard her phone vibrate in her handbag on the bedside table but ignored it.

Instead, she remained exactly where she was for several moments, as did Joe Johnson. Their lips locked together, tongues touching lazily. It was her favorite time, the few minutes after they had just finished making love. The pleasure chemicals rushing through her body left her feeling relaxed and satiated.

He was too close to focus on his features properly, and she didn't try, rather enjoying the blurred image of his face a few millimeters above hers and the warmth of his chest pressing on hers.

"I love you—and I loved that," she said as Joe finally pulled back.

He raised himself on his elbows, then dipped his head and kissed her again before finally rolling off her and across the queen-sized bed. "Why is it always better on vacation?" he asked. "And I love you too."

Jayne remained where she was. She flicked a hand through her dark hair and gazed at the wooden beams high above her head. Their top-floor junior suite in the College Hotel was in the roof space, so the external wall sloped at a steep angle with the window inset into an alcove.

They were only five days into their three-week break. It had so far included a short visit to London, where they stayed in Jayne's old apartment near Tower Bridge, before continuing to Amsterdam yesterday. It was a rare opportunity to take a long trip together away from their home in Portland, Maine, where Jayne had moved a couple of years earlier to be with Joe.

Joe's daughter, Carrie, a political science student at Boston University, was due to fly in to join them on Saturday and to stay for their final twelve days. Peter, who was Joe's eighteen-year-old son, had remained at home.

Carrie was visiting primarily to carry out research for a project on New Amsterdam, the fifteenth-century Dutch settlement in North America that was later renamed New York City when the English seized it in the 1660s. But research aside, the trip also meant some family vacation time. Jayne, who got on well with Carrie, had also developed quite an interest in the formative years of the United States and was looking forward to seeing her.

Furthermore, the College Hotel, an elegant nineteenth-century brick building, was Jayne's favorite place to stay in one of her favorite cities. It was a two-minute walk from the nearest canal and had a choice of nearby coffee shops, bars, and characterful restaurants. The vacation was shaping up nicely.

Jayne glanced at the clock on the wall. "How about a quick shower, then downstairs for cocktails before dinner?"

Joe grinned. "Sounds good. Shower together?"

"I'll soap you all over."

"Slowly, yes." He had a glint in his eye.

Jayne reached out with her left hand toward her handbag, intending to grab the phone inside it, but Joe quickly slapped her wrist playfully.

"Leave it alone. Later," he said. "You're like an addict waiting for their next fix."

"You don't know what I was going to do."

"I know exactly what you were going to do. I heard it buzz—just like you did," Joe said.

"Okay, okay."

Jayne knew he was right. Cell phones could be a real issue. They made life both easier and more difficult. She knew that too often she prioritized dealing with incoming messages above conversing with the people she was physically with. She put it down to working in the security and intelligence business, where time was often critical. But maybe there was something in his comment about addiction.

She turned her focus back to Joe. "Go on, shower time. Turn the hot on first."

He smiled. "I think you need cooling down, not warming up."

Half an hour later they were sitting at a table on the terrace bar, both clutching V2C Classic gin and tonics with ginger, lemon, and juniper berries. The evening was warm, and the terrace was busy.

Jayne took a sip from her drink. "This gin is different. I like the juniper taste."

"It's a pleasant variation," Joe replied, glancing at his phone. "I've just got a text from Peter."

"Is he okay?" Jayne asked.

"He's fine," Joe said. "Think he's enjoying being in charge, with no adults around and looking after Cocoa. Just listed all the tasks he did in the house today and detailed their longest walk."

Jayne smiled.

Cocoa was Joe's chocolate Labrador. Peter liked taking him for walks around Back Cove, the inlet off Casco Bay on Maine's Atlantic Seaboard, just down the street from their house in Portland.

It was then that Jayne remembered she had her own message to check and took out her phone. It was on her Signal encrypted messaging app. She tapped the screen.

The message was not from one of her stored contacts, but it showed the sender's number, which began with a +7 dialing code, and a profile, which had no photo and just the initials VU rather than a name.

"Russia," Jayne murmured. "Who?"

She tapped on the message, which was short.

Fradkov plans to defect but may be in danger. FSB may know. I have information. Can you get to Moscow? Do not reply this number. Use SRAC.

Jayne exhaled and glanced up at Joe. "From VULTURE," she said in a low voice.

"It's from her?" He raised an eyebrow.

She nodded. "Signal. Looks like a burner account. Why? Must be very urgent." She held out the phone so Joe could see the terse message.

"Fradkov?" he asked, also lowering his voice. "He's the cell phone guy, right? He owns MetroPhone."

"He does," Jayne said as she put the phone on the table. "But I know nothing about this defection she's referring to. Is he defecting to the UK or the US? And where? She doesn't say or doesn't know. Either way, doesn't sound good if VULTURE thinks he's in danger."

Two years earlier, she and Joe had recruited VULTURE, the code name for Anastasia Shevchenko, to work for the

CIA from her position inside the SVR, Russia's foreign intelligence agency.

Shevchenko, a deputy director in charge of the SVR's Directorate KR, counterintelligence, was the CIA's biggest asset inside Russian intelligence. She was based at the SVR's headquarters building at Yasenevo, south of Moscow.

"What are you going to do?" Joe asked.

"I'd better pass this to Vic." She paused. "More likely it's the CIA he's defecting to. If I'm wrong, I'll let Nicklin-Donovan know."

Vic Walter was the CIA's deputy director for operations. Since leaving Britain's Secret Intelligence Service, better known as MI6, four years earlier, Jayne had worked freelance for him on a number of deniable jobs. Several had been carried out in partnership with Joe. She also continued to work occasionally for her former MI6 boss, Mark Nicklin-Donovan, who was now director of operations and deputy chief of the entire service.

Joe leaned back in his seat and sipped his drink. "Sounds like VULTURE wants you to go to Moscow."

"Well, that's not happening—not after the year I've had. Anyway, we're on vacation. She'll have to talk to Ed Grewall or someone else at the Moscow station."

There was a brief silence.

Joe pursed his lips. "The problem is, she'll probably only want to meet you," he said eventually. "And I hope whatever she's got won't be wasted. Not after everything we went through while recruiting her."

Jayne knew precisely what he was referring to. Joe's children, Carrie and Peter, had been kidnapped while on vacation in France by the Russians prior to them trapping Shevchenko in Washington, DC. It was only after they turned Shevchenko that she gave them the information needed to exfiltrate the

children from the Black Sea area where they had been trans-
ported and held captive.

And Joe was also correct about Shevchenko not wanting
to meet anyone else. Jayne was the only one the Russian
seemed to trust. But she needed to accept that Jayne couldn't
do it every time. She would inevitably need to meet with
others too, and Grewall was a real professional.

"It won't be wasted," Jayne said. "Ed would bloody well
make sure of that. VULTURE needs to build a rapport with
him, too."

However, it was one thing to plan such a rapport, quite
another to deliver it. Recently, the level of paranoia and
surveillance among the Russian security and intelligence
community had grown significantly. As a result, it was exceptionally difficult for anyone at the CIA's Moscow station to
get face-to-face time with Shevchenko or any other asset.
The FSB, responsible for domestic intelligence and security,
had mounted blanket surveillance of all known Western intelligence officers and embassy staff. Moscow station staff had
found that breaking the shackles was almost impossible. It
was currently just too risky to meet people.

True, Jayne had managed an undercover foray into Russia
to meet Shevchenko the previous year, using false identities
and disguises. With Shevchenko's help, she uncovered a
potentially devastating plot to fix the United States presidential election. However, the meeting with Shevchenko came
extremely close to being blown. It also resulted in the death
of a CIA officer stationed in Moscow who, after diverting the
attention of a FSB surveillance team away from Jayne and
Shevchenko, was mown down mercilessly by their patrol car.

Since then, the expected level of intelligence flowing to
the West had proved a mirage so far. In fact, the message just
received was the first hint of anything of substance for
months.

There was another pause.

"You know," Joe said, "during the last few years, this business has gotten harder—and I don't just mean more difficult. I mean, more cynical, more cutthroat, more lacking in respect between us and our rivals."

"True."

"There used to be more respect among management for those in the field," Joe said. "Less willingness to hang people out to dry if things went wrong. Now there's a blame culture, and it's always passed down the chain from the suits to those doing the dirty work."

"That's why I'm happy not to be a suit anymore," Jayne said.

"I know." Joe tipped his head back. "At one time, two rival intelligence services wouldn't shoot each other. We knew where we stood thirty, twenty, or even ten years ago. If we got caught, we were usually allowed to go home quietly. Now? No way."

"It's Putin who's to blame," Jayne said. "He's led the change in culture, and Langley's had to follow suit."

Joe was correct. Jayne sipped her drink, then picked up her phone, logged onto the secure messaging app she used with Vic, and began to type.

See message below from VULTURE. Clearly something important. Can Ed make contact asap and try to meet VULTURE soonest. PS am on vacation in Amsterdam with Joe.

Then she copied and pasted Shevchenko's note into the message and pressed send.

CHAPTER TWO

Monday, September 19, 2016
London

"As one of our Founding Fathers pointed out, united we stand, divided we fall," President Stephen Ferguson said. "The Russians will drive their tanks through the cracks between us and the Germans and the French." He pushed his chair back from the circular elm table, stood, and walked to a large portrait of Margaret Thatcher that hung over the marble fireplace.

Vic Walter, the CIA's deputy director for operations, watched as the United States president jabbed his index finger at the picture of the former British prime minister.

"She wouldn't have taken this shit from Putin," Ferguson said. "She'd have brought the French, the Germans, and the rest of them into line and made them take a tough stance."

The current prime minister, Daniel Parker, who had remained seated, watched Ferguson, his lips pressed together. "She'd have tried. But yes, I agree, Stephen, the Europeans are bloody annoyingly soft on Russia. Nothing changes. Like you Americans, we've been warning them about the dangers for decades. But I'm not sure that telling Merck and his friends that in public is going to achieve anything. In fact, it could have the opposite effect."

Erich Merck was the man who had served as German chancellor for more than a decade, at the apex of European politics.

Ferguson marched back to his seat at the table in the first-floor study at Number 10 Downing Street, caught Vic's eye, and momentarily rolled his eyes.

Sitting opposite Parker was Mark Nicklin-Donovan, director of operations and deputy chief at Britain's Secret Intelligence Service, otherwise known as MI6, and his boss, Richard Durman, chief of MI6, widely known simply as C. Next to Vic was his boss, the director of the CIA, the barrel-chested figure of Arthur Veltman.

Vic pushed his wire glasses up his nose. He had watched the president become increasingly frustrated over the past couple of years after Russia had first seized the iconic Crimean Peninsula from Ukraine, and then began a war in the Donbas region of southeastern Ukraine by providing paramilitary backing to separatist pro-Russian forces there.

The president's irritation was understandable. Vic too had often pointed out to anyone who would listen that several European nations had indeed been far too soft on Russia for too long. And increasingly, they had ingratiated themselves even further with the Russian president by buying vast quantities of Russian gas through a new subsea pipeline under the Baltic Sea, called Eurostream One, built with the seal of approval and help from the German government and the involvement of German companies.

Vic had seen the numbers. Germany bought about a third of its total gas requirements from Russia, worth about eight billion euros a year, plus fourteen billion euros worth of oil. France bought about two billion euros of gas and five billion of oil a year.

These gas purchases had helped fill Putin's bank accounts and bankrolled his military aggression toward Ukraine.

But despite Russia's seizure of Ukrainian territory, the German government now seemed certain to issue construction permits for a second massive gas pipeline along the same route from Russia, dubbed Eurostream Two.

"Going soft on Putin is going to lead to disaster," Ferguson continued. "Next thing, he'll be trying to invade the entire country. After Ukraine, maybe Poland, or Finland. And he'll be doing it with the profits from his gas sales to Germany, as well as to France, Italy, and Austria. We need to be sanctioning Putin, not bankrolling him. Even my son can see that—and he's no politician."

Ferguson's son, Arnie, in his twenties, was a water sports instructor. Vic had met him and his sister Laura, an officer in the US Army Corps of Engineers, a couple of times at White House social functions.

Ferguson tapped his forefinger on the table and eyeballed Parker. "And I need to tell you, Daniel, your open-door policy toward Putin's oligarchs is further greasing the wheels of the massive theft that has gone on in Russia. Billions and billions have been stolen from the Russian people and put into the back pockets of these people—and they're using it to buy up houses and businesses in London. Your country is providing the bank accounts, the vast houses, the country estates, harbors for their yachts, and the access to British companies that permits them to launder the money. It has to stop. It's enabling them."

Parker blinked. "And you, Stephen, are not doing such things? Is that what you're telling me?"

"Not so much anymore. We are changing. You must do the same."

The six men sat in silence for a couple of seconds.

The only sound was the gentle ticking of a carriage clock that stood on the mantelpiece below Thatcher's portrait.

Vic had been to Downing Street a few times previously and always felt as though he was stepping back in time when he crossed the threshold. The room they were sitting in was referred to as the Thatcher Room by staff, because she had used it as her private office while in power.

The study, decorated in a style that hearkened back to a bygone era, was lined with ornate white bookshelves, their ancient contents protected by wire mesh doors.

Vic's phone vibrated in his pocket as a message arrived. He knew who it likely was but left it until the meeting had finished. Ferguson and Veltman wouldn't mind if he checked it, but it certainly seemed rude to do so in front of Parker and Nicklin-Donovan. It could wait.

Ferguson cupped his chin with his hands, elbows resting on the table, and surveyed his two British hosts from beneath bushy eyebrows.

"I'm going to tell Merck we're going to sanction the German, Russian and French companies building that damned Eurostream Two pipeline," Ferguson said. "We're going to just stop doing business with them. Period. And I'm going to ask him to tell them to stop working on it until Putin has backed out of the Donbas and Crimea. We're just feeding the beast if we let him continue."

Parker nodded immediately. "I was going to suggest the same thing myself."

Again, Vic's phone vibrated in his pocket as a second message arrived. Again, he ignored it.

The two national leaders had arranged this discussion at

Downing Street to work on tactics and strategy ahead of various crucial meetings that were coming up.

One of these was a North Atlantic Treaty Organization summit, primarily to discuss Russia, starting on Monday, October 17, in Warsaw. Both Ferguson and Parker, keen to show global leadership, were planning to call for stronger sanctions to be imposed on Russia, its banks, and its businesses.

Vic knew the support of Germany and France would be critical to achieving that at NATO. Therefore, a prior meeting was arguably even more important—it was a more informal gathering between Ferguson, Parker, Erich Merck, and the French president, Pierre Martinez, scheduled in Berlin for the day before the summit began. The plan was to get the German and French leaders on board ahead of the NATO meeting.

The informal meeting was also due to include the leaders' key intelligence chiefs. Vic, Veltman, and Nicklin-Donovan would be there, together with Norbert Wessel, the president of Germany's foreign intelligence service, the Bundesnachrichtendienst, or BND, and Jean Revel, head of the French military intelligence service, the *Direction du Renseignement Militaire*, the DRM.

Even before that, though, Ferguson and Vic had also scheduled a separate visit to the Ukrainian capital, Kyiv, to meet with the Ukrainian president, Pavlo Doroshenko. Ferguson was keen to show support to Doroshenko in the face of Russian aggression. He wanted to expand an existing commitment to directly supply Ukraine with a variety of military equipment, training, intelligence, and other assistance.

Ferguson and Parker's Downing Street meeting continued for another twenty minutes. When it finished, Vic and Veltman left the two leaders, who were having an informal lunch together, and were shown out of the building by Nicklin-Donovan and Durman.

It was only when they were in an unmarked CIA car on the way back to the US embassy, which was still at Grosvenor Square prior to its upcoming move to Nine Elms, that Vic checked his phone.

He tapped on his messages app and keyed in his security password and PIN.

The first message was unexpected. It was from Jayne Robinson. Vic scanned down it.

So, VULTURE knew about Fradkov defecting. Interesting, Vic thought. But a chill ran through him as he read the sentence about potential danger. He would need to call Jayne about that. He exited the message and tapped on the second one.

This was the one he had been expecting and was from his colleague, Ed Grewall.

But the contents—short, blunt, and to the point—were not at all what he had anticipated.

Vic stared at it.

Target dead. Could be nerve agent or radiation, based on his appearance. Leaving now. Will call asap.

It suddenly felt as though the bottom had dropped out of Vic's stomach. Grewall had assured him the rendezvous was watertight.

"Shit," Vic said out loud in his usual low, gravelly voice. He glanced sideways at Veltman, who was leaning back against the headrest, his eyes shut, clearly taking a moment to decompress after the intensity of the Downing Street meeting.

"Take a look at this," Vic said, his voice tense. "From Ed. Fradkov's dead. He never got to speak to him. Sounds like he's been poisoned."

"*What?*" Veltman's eyes flicked open and his head jerked forward.

Vic nodded and passed the phone over to his boss.

Veltman took it, squinted at the screen, and shot up in his seat. "Bastards. How the hell did that happen?"

"And that's not all," Vic said. "Check the message above it. It just came in from Jayne Robinson. It seems VULTURE knew Fradkov was defecting and was in danger."

Veltman tapped on the screen and scrutinized the message. This time, his head rocked back. "Sonofabitch. Too late."

* * *

Monday, September 19, 2016
London

Vic Walter stood, walked to the fourth-floor office window, and stared out over the green trees, lawns, and symmetrical pathways of Grosvenor Square below. Tourists were taking selfies in front of a ten-foot bronze statue of former president Ronald Reagan that dominated the southwestern corner of the square, right in front of the United States embassy.

It had been a long five-hour wait, and dusk was drawing in. There was still no word from the team of specialist doctors who were testing Ed Grewall for a variety of radiation and chemical exposures in a secure medical facility down in the first basement of the embassy. Vic had seen some of the equipment, which included a dosimeter and a Geiger counter.

Vic turned to Arthur Veltman, whose office they were in.

"Ed must be shitting himself," Vic said.

He could only imagine the state that Grewall was in as the tests continued. If Pyotr Fradkov had been killed by some kind of radioactive poison, such as polonium-210, then Grewall could be contaminated too, even if he hadn't touched the body. On the positive side, he hadn't reported feeling unwell, nor had he vomited or even had a headache.

"If it wasn't polonium, it was Novichok," Veltman said. "Those guys have no imagination." He sat in his swivel chair behind his large mahogany desk, his mouth set in a grim line.

"Let's just wait for the teams to report back," Vic said. "Another coffee?"

They had already drunk three cups, but Veltman nodded, picked up his phone, and asked his secretary to bring two more cappuccinos.

Another team, from Britain's Security Service, better known as MI5, was at Pyotr Fradkov's house on South Grove. They had sealed off the area, working alongside the Metropolitan Police. A rapid-response unit from Porton Down, Britain's biological and chemical research establishment, a two-hour drive west of London, had arrived and was conducting tests on the house and the body.

There had been no sign of Fradkov's phone, laptop, or wallet at the house. The assumption was that whoever had murdered him had taken them.

Vic had received a call from Grewall just as they were arriving at the embassy. By then, the Moscow station chief, knowing that he could have been contaminated, had sensibly gotten himself away from passersby and was waiting in a deserted parking lot next to St. Michael's church, a hundred yards along South Grove.

Vic had then alerted Nicklin-Donovan at MI6 and his counterpart at MI5, the deputy director general, Harry Buck. They immediately activated crisis plans designed to deal with exactly this type of eventuality.

Two CIA medics picked Grewall up in a special unmarked private ambulance kitted out for such circumstances, complete with a stretcher, IV drips, and an array of other equipment in the back.

Apart from ensuring Grewall's safety and condition, Vic's and Veltman's other priority was to prevent any media leak about the incident for as long as possible. Inevitably, news of Fradkov's death would emerge sooner rather than later, but it was critical that the CIA's involvement remain secret.

Thankfully, Nicklin-Donovan, Buck, and the Metropolitan Police commissioner, Sir Richard Blackthorn, were fully aligned with the need for secrecy.

But what they were less comfortable about was the fact that neither Vic nor Veltman had informed any of them about the operation that Grewall was running with Fradkov. The unwritten protocols that existed between international intelligence and security services said that if they were active on another service's turf, their counterparts should be informed. So often, though, practical and security considerations made it very difficult.

As a result, Vic had been forced to listen to lengthy tirades from both Buck and Blackthorn. All he could do was apologize, claiming the need for security as his defense. However, Nicklin-Donovan had been more understanding, having many times crossed the same boundary himself.

Senior officers from MI5 and the police were also in the medical facility downstairs, trying to question Grewall as the tests continued.

The coffees arrived, along with a plate of cookies. Vic and Veltman returned to their seats at the circular meeting table in the corner of the office.

Vic had just taken a sip from his cup when there came a sharp knock at the door. It opened, and there stood Grewall, his shoulders slumped, his normally immaculate hair tousled, and his brow creased. Even his dark skin looked a little pale. He was carrying a coffee in a takeaway cup and was wearing jeans and a black sweatshirt that looked a couple of sizes too large.

Vic scrambled to his feet. "Ed. Are you all right, buddy?"

Beside him, Veltman also stood.

"I got the all-clear downstairs," he said. "They think it was Novichok, but it's going to take some time for Porton Down to confirm that. Nothing radioactive, anyway. It's not polonium. And it didn't touch me."

"That's a relief," Vic said. "At least from your viewpoint. This is a mess. We need the Brits to put out a media statement immediately. They've got to make clear it's the Russians who killed him; otherwise, the Kremlin will announce it first and accuse the Brits of doing it, and probably us as well. Hopefully, MI5 and Downing Street will get on that."

"Good point," Veltman said. "I'll get Durman to put some pressure on MI5."

Vic took a couple of steps toward Grewall. "How do you feel, Ed?"

Grewall shrugged. "Like shit, actually. But not ill, if that's what you mean." He patted his jeans and sweatshirt. "They took all my clothes and my shoes for testing, gave me this crap to wear."

"Take a seat. You look exhausted," Veltman said. He pulled a chair back and indicated toward it, then sat back down himself, as did Vic.

Grewall walked to the table, took a seat, sipped from his drink, and exhaled through pursed lips. "Shit, he was a mess."

"Any idea how long he was dead by the time you arrived?" Veltman asked.

Grewall gave a slight shake of the head. "The techs will give us an estimate. I would guess a couple of hours at least. The kettle in the kitchen was cold. His skin was gray."

Vic took another sip of his coffee. "Obviously done by another Russian. But who? And why?"

The Moscow chief of station sat back in his chair. "He was halfway through a chess game. Both of them had been drinking a mug of tea or coffee. So you have to assume it's someone he knew well—unless the chess game was mocked up afterward." He creased his face, as if in pain. "I'd guess the Novichok, if it was that, went into his mug."

"Did you know he played chess?" Vic asked.

Grewall nodded. "That's how I met him. At the Central Chess Club—I showed it to you once, remember? I'd gone there to watch a Candidates Tournament final, the winner to challenge the world champion, Magnus Carlsen."

Vic had indeed driven past the club in Moscow a few years earlier with Grewall, an enthusiastic chess fan and player, who had pointed it out. It was an elegant two-story nineteenth-century mansion with a white-and-yellow frontage that faced onto Gogolevsky Boulevard, near to the American embassy.

"So, how did he make contact?"

"He caught my eye in the lounge, then spoke to me in the bathroom, passed me a phone number on a piece of paper, and told me to message him on his Signal account."

That seemed acceptable to Vic. Signal was seen as a secure messaging option, with end-to-end encryption. It was fine for short messages with no sensitive content.

"But you'd met before? It wasn't completely out of the blue?" Veltman asked.

Grewall nodded. "We'd met at a couple of business events and had spoken briefly, also once at a diplomatic party."

"And you know nothing of why he wanted to meet you?" Vic asked.

"I got nothing in advance," Grewall said. "That was the point of the meeting. All he said was that it was about Ukraine and that it was bigger than I could imagine."

"Bigger than you could imagine?" Vic repeated, staring at

Grewall.

The Moscow station chief nodded.

Veltman leaned forward. "Was he going to defect, do you think?"

Grewall shrugged. "No idea. Maybe, or maybe he would let us recruit him. One of the two. We didn't quite get as far as discussing that, as you can see."

Vic creased his brow. "Someone in Moscow must have realized what he was going to do."

"Which is odd," Grewall said. "He was a pro. Nobody gets as rich as he has done in Russia, and in favor with Putin and the upper reaches of the Kremlin without being street smart and ruthless—and extremely careful."

"But such people have many enemies," Vic said.

There was silence for a few seconds.

"So who else would know what he was going to say? Who would he have told?" Vic asked. "What about his wife? Who are his friends? What's his power base in the Kremlin? Does he have a direct line to Putin?"

"He has a few other oligarch friends," Grewall said. "And a few chess friends. I don't know about a hotline to Putin, but he is supported by the Kremlin, or he has been until this happened. Medvedev liked him. He might have confided in his wife, but we can't easily ask her."

Dmitry Medvedev was the Russian prime minister and previously the president from 2008 to 2012.

Vic stood, adjusted his glasses, and walked to the window again. It was dark outside now, and the Ronald Reagan statue was bathed by floodlights. He turned.

"We need to chase this," he said, catching Grewall's eye. "It's not every day we get some oligarch wanting to talk to us about something so sensitive he gets himself killed over it. And Ukraine is a hot potato. He must have had something major to give to us."

Grewall stroked his chin. "Indeed."

"The other channel we need to pursue is VULTURE," Veltman said. "Vic had a message from Jayne Robinson earlier. She received a message from VULTURE saying she'd heard about Fradkov defecting, and that he was in danger. Obviously, this came too late."

Veltman motioned to Vic, who took out his phone and showed Grewall the message from Jayne.

"What are your communications with VULTURE currently like?" Vic asked Grewall. "I'm concerned that we don't lose her—which might happen if we don't keep the relationship going."

"We exchange very brief SRAC messages every couple of weeks," Grewall said. "That's about it. I know we need some face-to-face time with her, but it's been almost impossible."

Shevchenko had a short-range agent communication system, or SRAC, in place that enabled her to wirelessly send electronic messages or files from a small hand-held transmitter to a base receiver that Jayne had buried a year and a half earlier among bushes in a park only seventy meters from her apartment in Moscow. Shevchenko could also collect messages in the same way. All she had to do was walk within twenty meters of the receiver and press a button on a transmitter carried in her pocket.

The system operated using transmissions of up to three or four seconds. The short range and the brevity made them almost impossible to detect, unlike cell phone communications. But although the system was useful, it wasn't a substitute for having a live conversation with an asset when there was something significant or complex to discuss. There was also a real need to maintain personal relationships with assets, who could feel very isolated without at least some human support.

"VULTURE obviously wants to meet Jayne," Vic said. "I'll

speak to Jayne and see if she'll do it. Then you can let VULTURE know via SRAC, as she suggests."

Veltman leaned back in his chair. "The only other alternative is VULTURE gets herself out of Russia on a pretext. Surely she can manufacture some counterintelligence investigation that needs to be done in the Helsinki *rezidentura*, or Kyiv, or Athens or somewhere. Then we could try to meet with her there. Or is Kruglov keeping them on a tight leash?"

Maksim Kruglov, the SVR's director, was known to be strongly focused on counterintelligence. It was another reason why information had been difficult to come by. Vic knew well that potential assets inside the Kremlin and other Russian organizations were often too scared of being discovered to consider betraying the Motherland.

Grewall drained his coffee and put the cup on the table. "You're correct, Arthur. VULTURE hasn't been outside Russia since she started that counterintelligence chief's job. Kruglov is keeping her too busy, it seems. And he's a suspicious bastard. He's got his own small personal counterintelligence team inside his office who watches everyone. We need another way."

"All right. I'll contact Jayne," Vic said. "She's in Amsterdam on vacation. I'm due to fly to Berlin tomorrow afternoon, so I can divert and meet her. And I think you'd better get back to your hotel, get a shower, some dinner, and some rest. We can talk again here in the morning."

Grewall stood and nodded at Vic and Veltman. "See you in the morning, then. The MI5 team wants another debrief first thing."

Grewall made his way to the door, opened it, and walked out.

When he had gone, Vic looked at Veltman and raised his eyebrows. "Here we go again," he said, a tired note in his voice.

CHAPTER THREE

Tuesday, September 20, 2016
  Amsterdam

They were halfway through their first drink on the College Hotel terrace when Jayne's phone beeped. She glanced at it.

En route. Will see you in your room 20 minutes. Pls confirm.

She looked over the table at Joe and held up her phone. "That's Vic. Twenty minutes. In our room."

"This'll be the end of our vacation," Joe muttered. "Or at least the end of yours. Enjoy that drink—I guess it'll be your last here."

Jayne didn't reply. Joe had been making similarly downbeat comments ever since Vic informed her the previous evening that he would stop in Amsterdam to discuss the VULTURE message.

She sent a quick confirmatory message back to Vic. Ten minutes later, when they had both drained their glasses, they made their way back upstairs.

Vic turned up right on time, as was generally the case.

Jayne let him in and closed the door, having carefully checked that nobody was loitering in the corridor.

Vic looked a little more anxious than usual, which Jayne guessed was likely because he was uncertain of what kind of reception he was going to get.

"Jayne, Joe. How's it going?" he began. "I know what you're thinking, and I'm sorry to intrude on your break, but—"

"You're sorry to intrude?" Jayne interrupted, lowering her voice and adding a note of sarcasm. "But you've obviously flown here to do exactly that."

Vic gave a stifled attempt at a laugh. He glanced around at the hotel room. "The problem with you two is you're too good to ignore. There is something I couldn't discuss on the phone. I'm really sorry—I hate to do this."

Jayne gave a sharp nod toward the interior of the room. "Course you do. Take a seat. Let's hear it."

While Jayne and Joe sat on a long orange sofa beneath the window, Vic perched opposite them on an armchair.

He lowered his voice. "I'll get to the point. Look, the message that you received from VULTURE mentioned that Fradkov may be in danger, right?"

Jayne nodded.

"She was correct about that," Vic said. "But unfortunately, the message came too late. Fradkov was killed in London."

Jayne felt as though someone had just punched her. "*Killed?*"

Vic nodded. "He was supposed to be meeting Ed Grewall. But he was dead when Ed turned up. You hadn't heard because the Brits haven't issued any statement yet."

"When did this happen?" Joe asked.

"Yesterday morning. It's Novichok."

Jayne stared at Vic. "I know Fradkov owns MetroPhone. He's been a Kremlin favorite. But no longer, obviously."

"It seems not."

"So why have they turned on him?" Jayne asked.

Vic shrugged and explained in some detail about the meeting Fradkov had been due to have with Grewall. "He was going to tell us something important about Ukraine. We have no idea what. I'm assuming the Kremlin found out somehow and got there first. But I'll tell you this—it was carried out by a professional. No bungling."

"How did they do it?" Joe asked. "Was there a break-in? Any CCTV images?"

"It seems quite the opposite of a break-in. Fradkov was apparently playing chess with whoever did it."

"Chess?" Jayne raised an eyebrow.

"Yes. He must have known them well."

Jayne let out a low whistle. "Bastards." She knew how Novichok worked—the muscle paralysis, including the heart and lungs, the vomiting, diarrhea, and foaming at the mouth, followed swiftly by the inevitable heart attack or suffocation.

"And as for CCTV," Vic said, "there's none on the property. It wasn't Fradkov's main residence. It appears he only used it for occasional meetings. Police are trying to get footage from nearby properties, but nothing so far."

"What about DNA or prints from the house?" Jayne asked.

Vic nodded. "The techs have found hairs on the chair where the likely killer, the other chess player, was sitting. They are doing an analysis. We'll get the results soon, I hope. There were also prints, but whether they will help, I don't know. You don't need me to tell you it depends on whether they're in the police database so they can get a match. If it's a Russian, that's highly unlikely."

There was a long pause as Jayne eyed him carefully. "So what, exactly, are you here for, Vic? It's not just to tell me that a Russian oligarch has died in London."

"You assume correctly," Vic said. "You might also assume that we were extremely interested in hearing whatever he was going to tell us. And I was—"

"I'm not going back into Russia, if that's what you're about to ask me," Jayne said, eyeballing him.

Vic returned her gaze from beneath lowered eyebrows. "After Fradkov's killing, I had a long discussion with Ed. As you know, he and his Moscow team are under the heaviest surveillance we've ever seen from the FSB. But your message from VULTURE is the only lead we've got. If she doesn't know who killed Fradkov, and what he wanted to tell us, maybe she can find out. Now, since you were last in Russia, which was what, a year and a half ago, we—"

"Seventeen months, actually." She could have told him the precise number of days.

"Okay, seventeen months," Vic said. "Since then, because of the oppressive coverage, neither you nor anybody else has had face-to-face contact with VULTURE."

"An enormous waste of a great asset," Jayne said. She had a strong respect for Shevchenko, whom she saw as like-minded and similarly skilled to herself.

"Precisely," Vic said. "And that's before we mention the large retainer we're paying her for no return. Anyway, if you're willing, I agreed with Ed that we should try to somehow arrange a face-to-face meeting for you on this, despite the risks. It's too complicated to discuss by other means."

Jayne pressed her lips together. "VULTURE needs to build up a relationship with someone else besides me, Vic. It's not good for her to only have one key point of contact. I could get hit by a bus tomorrow."

Vic threw up his hands. "I agree with you. That's what Ed would like to do. But I don't want him to have a face-to-face with VULTURE now, not after what happened to Fradkov. The FSB will likely know what he's doing, and have a target on his back. And I can't send anyone else from Moscow station for the same reason. We're short of time, Jayne. This is urgent."

Jayne exhaled vigorously. She knew Vic was correct.

"And if you were VULTURE, who would you trust?" Vic continued. "She won't want anyone new if it can be avoided."

That was the issue, and Jayne had to accept it. Ever since she and Joe recruited Shevchenko in Washington, DC, she had felt a close affinity with the Russian. Their mutual bond had deepened during Jayne's subsequent foray into Russia, when Shevchenko had not only helped her flee the country and the clutches of the FSB, but helped her obtain critical information about the Kremlin plot to fix the US presidential election.

"So what do you want to do, then?" Jayne asked, with a note of resignation in her voice.

Vic folded his arms. "Ed will arrange for a short message to be left on VULTURE's SRAC asking if she will meet you if you're okay with that."

Jayne shrugged. "Does it need to be now? Can't we let the dust settle?"

Vic shook his head. "We have no time. Ferguson is eager to ramp up international pressure on Putin over the Crimea invasion and what he's doing to eastern Ukraine, and so is Daniel Parker. There's a NATO summit next month, at which Ferguson will call for tougher sanctions against Russia. Before that, he and Parker have scheduled a meeting with Erich Merck and Pierre Martinez, because they want to get Germany and France onside. If Fradkov had something critically important to give us, Ferguson wants that information before the summit. I'm going to try to speak to the BND head Norbert Wessel when I'm in Berlin and persuade him how important it is."

Jayne knew Wessel at the BND, having worked in

Yugoslavia at the same time as him many years earlier. She nodded. "Wessel's a good operator."

"He is. I did initially wonder if Fradkov's information was related to Operation Pandora," Vic said. "But I think it must be something else. I don't see how Ukraine would fit into Pandora."

Operation Pandora was a broad, long-running Kremlin umbrella program, comprising active measures and individual operations to infiltrate and destabilize the United States at political and corporate levels over several years. Jayne and Joe had first got details of it from Shevchenko.

Jayne knew that what Vic was saying made considerable sense, despite her irritation. But the practicalities bothered her. She caught a glance from Joe, who was looking equally concerned.

"I don't see how she can easily get inside Russia again after last time," Joe said. "She must be at the top of their wanted list."

Jayne had foiled too many Russian operations, of which the plot to fix the US election had been the most critical.

Vic breathed out heavily. "There is a possible way. Ferries run into St. Petersburg from Helsinki and other Scandinavian cities. In fact, you can get into St. Petersburg by ferry for a seventy-two-hour tourist visit without a visa, although I don't think we'll do that. The ferries are lower key than Moscow's airports. Less scrutiny."

Jayne was well aware of the ferries and the lower intensity of security checks. "I know they're encouraging tourism that way. But Shevchenko is in Moscow, Vic, not St. Petersburg."

"I know. So use the high-speed train." Vic paused. "Look, Jayne. It's up to you whether you do it. But you're the one who's closest to VULTURE. And I know the president would like it if you went. And of course, we'd put in place a range of solid exfil plans in case things go south. You've got enough new legends. We'll get the visas put into your passports. We can make it happen."

She did indeed have new identities, known as legends, and matching passports, all acquired over recent weeks after her old ones had been blown. Would that be enough, alongside a few simple but effective disguises? CCTV facial recognition systems in Russia still weren't properly integrated with the FSB and police databases, which also helped.

Jayne sat back on the sofa, trying to look at the situation objectively. What chance would she realistically have of discovering what Fradkov had been intending to pass on to Ed Grewall? The odds had to be against her—but then again, it felt that had often been the case throughout her career.

Vic's phone pinged. He picked it off the table and studied the screen.

"Shit," he said.

"What?" Joe asked.

"Looks like the Russians have preempted us. Usual disinformation ploy." Vic read from his screen. "A story's running on the Russia Today website. The Kremlin has accused MI5 of murdering Fradkov in London and then trying to cover it up by keeping silent." He banged his fist on the arm of his chair. "I knew this would happen if the Brits didn't announce it. Now the Kremlin's on the front foot. So, so predictable."

He held up his phone so Jayne and Joe could see the story.

Jayne could feel the familiar swirl of anger rising inside her.

No longer was it anger at Vic for interrupting her holiday with Joe, but fury at yet another astonishing example of the murderous Russian leadership carrying out another horrific killing on foreign soil and then twisting the truth about it.

It had happened so many times before.

She could recall at least a dozen examples of similar killings of Russians overseas since Alexander Litvinenko was murdered with polonium-210 in London in 2006, including those in Austria, the United Arab Emirates, and Turkey. Most were shot dead. Some had been poisoned. There were many more murders of dissidents carried out inside Russia.

Insiders who worked against Putin received no mercy.

Jayne stood and walked to the window.

The truth was, after the battles she'd had over the past few months, she was feeling utterly war-weary. That feeling contributed to her hesitation.

Down below, two blue-and-white electric trams rumbled past in opposite directions along the twin tracks in the center of the street. Some friends on bicycles rode past, laughing at each other. A couple kissed on a bench. Another walked past them, hand in hand.

Amsterdam was a city of cyclists and lovers.

It was tempting to turn down Vic's proposal. The break from assignments and the time with Joe like this was doing her good. But another Russian had died, and he had been prepared to run the risks of providing vital intelligence to the West.

Fradkov hadn't decided to meet with the CIA for financial reasons—he was a very wealthy man. He had done so, almost certainly, out of principle and because he disagreed strongly with the actions of his government and his president. He paid for it with his life.

Jayne knew she couldn't allow that to happen in vain.

She glanced at Joe, who gave a slight shrug and an almost imperceptible nod of the head. He was obviously thinking along similar lines to her.

"I can stay here with Carrie for the second half of the trip," Joe said.

Vic's gaze swung to Joe, then Jayne.

Jayne pressed her lips together. That would be an obvious solution. Carrie could still do her research work and have some quality time with her father. Meanwhile, Jayne could meet Shevchenko. But she would like to stay here until Carrie arrived to make the most of her time alone with Joe, which was a rare luxury. An extra few days wouldn't make much difference to the Shevchenko meeting.

Jayne turned back to Vic and leaned against the wall, her arms folded. "I'll be honest, I was looking forward to a family vacation here. It's been a long time coming. I see the urgency in what you and the president need, so I'll do what you're asking. But that said, I'm staying here until Saturday and I'm not budging on that. I'll finish out the week and be here to greet Carrie on Saturday and spend the day with her. Then she and Joe can stay on together."

Vic spread his palms wide. "So you'll do it after Saturday? We can plan for next week?"

Jayne shrugged. "I guess that's what I'm saying, yes. Reluctantly."

"Thank you, Jayne. I'm grateful for that. Really, I am. I'll inform Director Veltman."

Jayne paused. "And those ferries from Helsinki to St. Petersburg. How often do they sail?"

CHAPTER FOUR

Thursday, September 22, 2016
Moscow

The heavy twin wooden doors to President Putin's personal office swung open. Anastasia Shevchenko watched as one of the president's aides, wearing a white shirt and black waistcoat, stood there, eyeing her and the other three men who were waiting outside.

"The president will see you all now," the aide said, stepping to one side to allow the group to file into the inner sanctum past two unsmiling bodyguards.

The entrance was formed of two sets of paneled and soundproofed doors with a kind of airlock between them, forming an additional line of protection and privacy for the president.

Shevchenko, one of several deputy directors at the SVR, Russia's foreign intelligence agency, hung back a little to allow the men to enter first, then followed her boss, the ape-like director Maksim Kruglov, into the room.

She knew the men would feel obliged to take seats nearest to the president at the polished oak meeting table, allowing her to keep a more comfortable distance.

Putin sat motionless, his palms facedown at the head of the rectangular table, scrutinizing the group one by one through laser-like blue eyes as they filed in. His index finger tapped on the wooden surface.

Tap, tap, tap.

It was his tell.

Putin was anxious.

Shevchenko, who headed Directorate KR, the SVR's external counterintelligence arm, watched as Kruglov, his fleshy neck wobbling, sat down next to Igor Ivanov, known as the Black Bishop of the Kremlin and one of Putin's closest advisers.

To Putin's right, as Shevchenko had expected, sat the two people whom she privately termed the silent twins—they came to the meetings and sat next to the president and listened carefully, but rarely spoke unless asked to do so.

The first of them was Kira Suslova, a striking woman with shoulder-length black hair. Like Ivanov, Suslova's official role was as a top-level adviser to the president. The difference was that she was more than an adviser; she was a friend of Putin's, a relationship that went back a long time. Shevchenko knew they had worked together in East Germany with the KGB during the 1980s and in St. Petersburg in the mayor's office in the 1990s.

Rumor even had it that Suslova was more than just a friend, if the whispers of overnight and weekend trysts at the president's various residences were to be believed. Of course, nobody ever dared to talk about their relationship openly.

One thing was clear, though: Suslova was a rung above everyone else present in the game of career chutes and ladders over which Putin presided. But unlike the others, she never seemed to slip down the chutes.

Sitting next to Suslova was the other silent twin, Gennady Sidorenko, with his protruding blue eyes and large paunch. He was chief of the specialist small counterintelligence team, known as DX, that was based inside Kruglov's office and was quite separate from Shevchenko's department. Sidorenko, a notorious sadist, had also recently been ordered to operate from the Kremlin for three days a week, working closely with Putin and Suslova, no doubt on whatever secret projects they needed him to carry out.

It was no surprise to Shevchenko to see Suslova and Sidorenko already seated at the table as the rest of them entered. There had obviously been a pre-meeting.

Shevchenko stepped onto the ornate Bokhara carpet that lay beneath the table, pulled out a padded chair, and took a seat to the president's left, farthest away from him and next to Kruglov.

The aide left the room, pulling both sets of doors shut behind him as he departed.

Shevchenko glanced around the president's second-floor office, in the northwest corner of the Kremlin's three-story Senate Palace building. The light from a pair of ornate chandeliers above reflected from Putin's bald head. The walls were lined with oak panels, with matching wood used for the table, bookcases, and a door to a small sitting room.

Behind the president, at the far end of the room, was his desk, also made from matching wood. A smaller square table was placed in front of the desk for one-to-one meetings, a few of which Shevchenko had endured. The windows looked out over the Kremlin's huge defensive walls into Red Square, and just down the corridor outside were Josef Stalin's former living quarters.

"You will know by now that we have dealt with the threat

to Operation Imperiya and, by so doing, have protected some of our most important assets," Putin began, without bothering to greet his subordinates. "Pyotr Fradkov made a foolish choice, and he has paid for it. It will stand as a warning to anyone else who considers doing anything similar. Wealth and status are no protection." He glanced sideways at Suslova, as if to exempt her from the comment, then eyeballed each of the others.

Kruglov nodded vigorously in agreement. On the other side of the eight-seater table, there was also a nod from Nikolai Sheymov, director of the FSB, the Federal Security Service, responsible for intelligence gathering inside Russia.

Sitting between Sheymov and Putin, Suslova and Sidorenko both sat silent and motionless, as usual.

"The operation in London was an outstanding piece of work," Putin said. "There will be an appropriate reward for that." He paused and gave the faintest glimmer of a smile. "I understand he was terminally checkmated."

Shevchenko noted Putin didn't name the person who had carried out the hit on Pyotr Fradkov. The president compartmentalized everything, allowing only a select few to know what operations were currently underway. It was an old habit born of his KGB background. As a result, despite her counterintelligence brief, Shevchenko knew there were operations of which she was unaware, neither their codenames nor their details.

However, Shevchenko had to admit that the job on Fradkov had been more successful than other recent botched poisonings on foreign soil.

"The surveillance team in London also did an outstanding job," Putin continued. "We know Fradkov was about to pass information to the CIA. Those files and documents were retrieved before that could happen, along with his laptop and phone."

The president paused and surveyed the others around the table. "However, we all know the Americans and the British will not let this pass. They will know they have missed out on something significant. Our high-level assets in the West need to remain secure. Increase surveillance of the known American and British intelligence people and embassy employees in Moscow. I want the city watertight. We all know one CIA asset was found in Moscow last year. I don't want to see any complacency."

There were nods around the table.

Shevchenko had become aware only two days earlier of what the relatively new Operation Imperiya was, and her ears also pricked up at the mention of Russian assets in the West.

She was certain she knew the code names of the assets he was referencing, of which there were two, and the name of the operation to handle them. She had glimpsed an operational file on Suslova's desk a week earlier while she popped out to speak to her assistant, but hadn't dared look inside.

Strict compartmentation of information meant Shevchenko had not been given their identities, as there was no clear need for her to know them.

Finding out that detail would not be easy—that was underlined by Putin's reminder that the Kremlin needed to remain vigilant against Western penetration. It made Shevchenko resolve to keep her guard up and not take unnecessary risks. She had come very close to being uncovered once before.

However, since seeing the file, Shevchenko had known she needed to do something.

She had to pass on the information she'd discovered to Jayne Robinson, as it was significant enough. It would give Robinson a starting point.

Shevchenko had also learned a few days ago—too late, it was now clear—about the risk to Pyotr Fradkov.

It had been the final impetus for her to take the risk of messaging Robinson a few days earlier. Given the urgency of the warning, she'd used a burner phone rather than the much slower SRAC method, which relied on someone collecting the message and then relaying it accurately and in a timely way.

Shevchenko refocused on the meeting.

Putin was pointing a finger at Sheymov. "Nikolai, ensure your border guards are alerted about the mounting risks. I don't want any Western intelligence people sneaking in through our airports."

"Yes, sir," Sheymov said.

The president's finger swiveled and pointed this time at Shevchenko. "And you, do you think, as counterintelligence head, you can actually avoid anyone leaking all of this?" The eyes were unblinking, the sarcasm heavy.

"I am confident we can, sir," Shevchenko said, trying to project as much assurance as she could. "As you say, sir, we uncovered a CIA mole in our ranks last year, although he then fled. I'm as certain as I can be that there are no more."

It was Shevchenko's role, as head of foreign counterintelligence, to ensure none of her colleagues were supplying information to Russia's enemies.

Ironic, therefore, that she had personally ensured that Pavel Vasilenko, the CIA mole who had been working for the Americans, had escaped Russia alongside Jayne Robinson. That then gave Shevchenko a convenient scapegoat for the leaks she herself had provided that torpedoed Russia's attempts to fix the US presidential election.

"Let's hope there aren't anymore," the president immediately responded, his laser eyes still fixed on Shevchenko. "If there are, it is *your* responsibility to catch them —understood?"

"Of course, sir."

"You know the price of failure."

Shevchenko felt her scalp prickle as she nodded.

It was completely characteristic of the president, a former KGB intelligence officer himself, to pay very close attention to the activities of his intelligence agencies. This type of threat was nothing new from Putin, whose face remained as inscrutable as ever.

But Shevchenko couldn't avoid the feeling of fear in her stomach. She knew firsthand how excruciating it could be if the president or one of his henchmen put someone under the microscope. Though she had been cleared less than eighteen months ago after briefly falling under suspicion, that was only after an exceptionally painful and invasive series of interrogations and investigations in Moscow's notorious Lefortovo prison.

She had been ultracareful in her communications with the Americans as a result, so much so that contact had been virtually non-existent until now.

Responsible for catching myself. How Kafkaesque.

Finally, the president turned his gaze away from Shevchenko, and his head swiveled to Ivanov. "Igor, do you have anything to add?"

Ivanov, a black-eyed former officer with Russia's GRU military intelligence unit, had previously been deputy prime minister but had since been put in charge of special operations at the Kremlin. He had most recently been tasked with implementing Operation Imperiya, as well as Operation Pandora. He sat up straight. "The job in London was well done. I believe it will ensure the security of Operation Imperiya, and, as you say, sir, it will protect our assets."

Obviously Ivanov knew who these assets were too, Shevchenko pondered.

She glanced around the table. There were glass-like expressions on the faces of Sheymov and Kruglov, but that meant nothing: both men were masters of the poker face. Deception and falsehoods ran red through their veins.

Shevchenko noted that even among this elite group, Ivanov did not use the codenames of the key assets, let alone their real names. Not that she ever expected him to make such a slipup. She needed to work out a way of finding out the real names without leaving her fingerprints behind.

The FSB chief, Sheymov, leaned forward and spoke to the president. "Sir, the only thing to add is that our post-operation surveillance in London showed that the CIA officer who was due to meet Fradkov is known to us—he is Edward Grewall, the chief of station here in Moscow. He was seen entering Fradkov's property some hours after the execution and then leaving again soon after, presumably after finding the body. He, of course, immediately alerted his colleagues and police, and since then the property has been swamped with investigators. We have continued surveillance, but we are being very cautious. However, our suspicions about Grewall were confirmed. We are continuing to keep an especially close watch on him, and likewise with those he comes into contact with and works with at the CIA."

Dermo.

Shevchenko knew she would need to take extreme care for her planned covert meeting with Jayne Robinson, scheduled for next week. She was certain that Robinson must have been coordinating with Grewall and Vic Walter ahead of her trip into Russia.

Putin nodded. "You have my authority to take whatever means necessary."

Everyone knew what that meant, and Sheymov nodded. "Of course, sir."

Putin gave a sharp nod, then looked at Ivanov. "And what do our foreign accounts total now?"

Shevchenko had a quiet bet with herself that Ivanov

would know the number. She guessed it was the first thing he checked every morning on waking.

Sure enough, he responded immediately. "Our foreign currency reserves currently stand at 551 billion dollars, sir."

Putin viewed that sum as his cash pile to fund Russia's armed forces.

The president gave an almost imperceptible nod. "And our daily oil and gas sales to Europe and Turkey?"

Ivanov cleared his throat. "They are still averaging about six billion rubles a day for gas and ten billion for oil, sir. Sales volumes remain good."

Shevchenko knew from countless conversions in her head over the years that that was roughly $100 million a day for gas and $160 million for oil. Everyone at the Kremlin thought in dollars just as much as rubles because international sales of oil and gas funded pretty much everything Russia did.

"We need to maintain that," Putin said. "We have tanks and soldiers to pay for." For the first time during the meeting, he gave a hint of a smile. The numbers were good.

The president glanced around the table. "We are done now. You can all go."

As she stood to leave, Shevchenko caught Suslova's eye. As was often the case, she just looked back at her from beneath her long black fringe but didn't speak.

That was typical of her. Suslova knew everything but said nothing. Unlike the others, she seemed to have no need to curry favor with the president, to prove herself, or to impress.

Shevchenko now had a decent list of items to report back to Jayne Robinson the next day.

But there were also a few critical pieces of missing information—not least the names of the assets in the West.

And she was unsure how, or whether, she could safely get them.

CHAPTER FIVE

Tuesday, September 27, 2016
St Petersburg

Jayne zipped up her waterproof jacket, slung her small backpack over her shoulder, and pulled her black cap over her hair, which was now platinum blonde and straight, thanks to the high-quality wig she was wearing. Then she exited the twin-bed cabin, made her way along a long corridor, and joined the line of people disembarking from the Princess Anastasia, the enormous eleven-deck cruise ferry on which she had traveled overnight from Helsinki.

It was peculiarly appropriate, she reflected, that the ship she had sailed on to enter Russia bore the same name as her key asset inside the country, Anastasia Shevchenko.

As Jayne made her way down the gangway, past clusters of red, blue, and white balloons, she glanced toward the sprawling dockyards, with their yellow gantry cranes, power station chimneys, railway sidings, and container ships. Most were concentrated around the mouth of the River Neva to her right.

It was nine o'clock in the morning, and the air felt distinctly chillier here than when she had boarded the ferry in Helsinki the previous evening. Ahead of her, the sculpted gray concrete facade of the Morskoy Vokzal passenger terminal, a 1980s Soviet-era building, towered above the quayside.

She followed the other passengers along the quay and into the terminal, and tried to relax as she joined the line for customs and immigration. The journey so far had been straightforward, and the vessel, while showing its age, was comfortable enough for an overnight trip.

Jayne adjusted her cheap gold-rimmed glasses, which were purely for disguise and had no prescription, and removed her British passport from her pocket. The passport, in the name of her recently acquired new identity of Ashima Caire, looked as though it had been used regularly. It bore stamps, all fake, from a handful of countries, including Norway, Sweden, Canada, and Italy.

The passport and disguise items had been supplied by the wizards in the CIA's Office of Technical Services, known to everyone at Langley simply as the OTS. The passport gave her birth date and place as March 6, 1962, in Bombay, India. If interviewed by border guards, she would tell them she was born of British parents and was currently working in London as a self-employed financial adviser. In her wallet, she also carried two fully working credit cards in the same name, a bank card, a British driver's license, and a library card. All the documents were sourced to a house owned by the CIA in East London, coincidentally only a mile or so from her actual London apartment. Her Ashima Caire identity, which was properly backstopped, also included fake social media accounts, including Facebook and LinkedIn.

Hidden in the thick bottom lining of her backpack were two more British passports in other false identities, Polish-British travel consultant Cara Budz and Czech-British accountant Karina Horowitz. Both identities included credit cards and driver's licenses, all supplied by the OTS following her last operation. Given the short notice for this job, she was thankful that she had taken the precaution of obtaining the new legends, as Langley called the false identities, well in advance.

All the passports also contained false Russian tourist visas, allowing a stay of up to thirty days. They had been inserted into the passports the previous morning by a CIA tech officer at the station in London.

The cover story she had prepared was that she was taking a break from work to backpack around Scandinavia and was staying with a friend in Helsinki. She had made a spur-of-the-moment decision to do a side trip to see St. Petersburg, as she had never visited Russia. She was traveling light, with only a laptop and a few belongings, having left most of her stuff in Helsinki.

To help allay any suspicions at passport control, she had used the shipping company website to book a hotel for the first two nights, although she had no intention of using it. She also had on her phone the hotel booking confirmation, together with details of a booking for an official guided tour around St. Petersburg, which she also had no intention of attending. On the ship, she had filled in the mandatory two copies of an immigration card, with all her passport, home address, and hotel details.

Slowly, the line of people inched forward toward the row of passport control booths at the back of the immigration hall. Jayne estimated there had been well over a thousand people on the ferry. It was going to take some time to process them all.

Having been through a similar process with false documentation many times, Jayne consciously tried to relax and reduce her level of anxiety. She checked once more that there was no obvious sign of surveillance beyond the uniformed security men who were stationed around the terminal. It wasn't them she was concerned about, it was the possibility of a plain-clothes officer who was focused on her alone. There were none, as far as she could tell.

There were the inevitable cameras positioned around the terminal, too, but she could do nothing about them.

Finally, she reached the front and was beckoned forward by a bald, middle-aged man in a blue uniform shirt and tie.

"*Dobroye utro*," Jayne began. *Good morning.* She was fluent in Russian but didn't want to appear so. However, she did want to give the impression that she was trying.

However, her attempt fell on stony ground. The officer gave her a glance but made no reply. Rather, he focused immediately on her passport, which he flicked through slowly, and then fingered the main page that included her photograph, followed by the visa page.

"From the UK. Why are you here?" he asked eventually in stilted English, fixing her with his dark eyes, his mouth a straight line.

"I am on vacation," she said.

"How long?"

"Only a few days." She smiled at him. "Not long enough."

There was no smile in return.

"You are staying only in St. Petersburg? No travel elsewhere?" he asked.

"That's my plan, yes."

"You have a hotel booking?"

She showed him the confirmation for the Hotel Rimsky-Korsakov, the three-star hotel that she had booked.

"What will you do here?" the man asked.

*Why is he going through these details? He didn't do so with the
previous two passengers.*

"I have booked a tour around the city," she said. "I'm
looking forward to it."

"Which tour company are you using?"

"I am with City Bus Tour."

He looked up at her from beneath lowered eyebrows.

Finally, the passport officer returned one copy of the
immigration form to her, along with her passport. "Hand in
the immigration form when you leave. You may go," he said,
indicating with his thumb behind him where she needed to
head next.

Jayne knew from the latest CIA report that although
there were large numbers of CCTV cameras in the main
Russian cities, facial recognition was still a work in progress.
The FSB's border guards, who ran immigration controls at
Russian airports and seaports, were testing some facial recog-
nition systems, but this was still at a trial stage.

Rather, the FSB relied on human intelligence gathering.
Any sign of suspicious behavior, passports, or documents that
triggered any concerns would be reported upward. They
would have informers not just at the ports but at most of the
hotels and taxi companies. Indeed, there were clear signs that
the government was planning to make it compulsory for taxi
companies to share passenger data electronically with
the FSB.

Jayne's concerns at this stage lay not so much in the
quality of her false documents or the effectiveness of the
disguise she had deployed, but the possibility of being tripped
up by some employee with little better to do than look for an
excuse to pick up the phone to the FSB.

Jayne made her way through the customs green channel
without interference. She then continued to the bus stop at
the rear of the passenger terminal, where she quickly found a

taxi to take her to the hotel, a six-kilometer journey away, across the River Neva in the city center.

An hour later, after a tortuous registration process at the reception desk of the Hotel Rimsky-Korsakov, details of which Jayne knew would be transmitted directly to the FSB, she finally made her way up in the elevator to her third-floor room.

The hotel, near to St. Petersburg's historic Mariinsky Theatre, was a four-story stone building that was modernized inside and was comfortable enough. It was built around an internal courtyard that served as a parking lot, accessible by car through a central arch.

After a shower, Jayne put on a blue sweatshirt and jeans. She rearranged the bed covers to make it look as though she had been sleeping, hung a 'Do Not Disturb' sign on her room door, and turned on the television, which she tuned to a Russian news channel. She also boiled the kettle in the room and made a coffee, from which she took a few sips and left the half-empty cup on the bedside table.

The quick introduction to the hotel given to her by the manager on registration told Jayne that the ground floor café had its own external door onto the street.

She took out her phone, logged onto her secure messaging app, and sent short missives to Vic and to Ed Grewall, who had flown back to Moscow.

St. P lovely. Heading out now. Hope to visit the theatre tomorrow.

As arranged, Grewall would know from the text that she was about to head to the train station. He would instruct one of his team to leave a message on the SRAC for Anastasia Shevchenko, informing her that the meeting scheduled for the following day in Moscow was still on.

Jayne put on her reversible full-length raincoat with the navy blue showing on the outside. She pulled her backpack over her shoulder and headed for the rear staircase. She then slipped down to the café and past a handful of people drinking morning coffee and out of the hotel. From there, she walked to a bus stop next to the Mariinsky Theatre, a block and a half away, checking as she went to ensure she had no coverage from surveillance officers.

Jayne then caught a blue-and-white number 22 bus to the grand Moskovsky railway station in Nevsky Prospekt. She was booked under the second of her false identities—Cara Budz —on the one o'clock Sapsan high-speed train that would whisk her the 650 kilometers to Moscow in a shade under four hours.

As the final part of her transformation from Caire to Budz, she found a narrow alley off a side street near the station, where once certain she was alone, she pulled a curly blonde wig from her bag and exchanged it for the straight blonde wig she had been wearing. She also removed the gold glasses and replaced them with a black-rimmed pair. Now her face matched her second passport photo. Finally, she turned her raincoat inside out, transforming it into a beige version.

Jayne guessed it was possible that once the hotel realized Ashima Caire wasn't using the room she had booked, they might inform the FSB.

But that would take quite some time, and there were no rules compelling her to sleep in the room. By then she would hopefully be in the Russian capital under a different identity and with a different appearance.

CHAPTER SIX

Tuesday, September 27, 2016
Moscow

Colonel Leonid Pugachov removed a pack of LD cigarettes from his jacket pocket and offered one to the man on the other side of the wooden desk, his boss, the director of the FSB, Nikolai Sheymov. It was always a good way to keep him happy.

Sheymov took one, as he always did, and picked up a gold metal lighter from his desk. He struck it and used the flame to light first his own cigarette, then Pugachov's.

It was the way the two FSB veterans bonded, over shared cigarettes. It was probably the only thing they had in common, but it usually facilitated an amicable conversation.

The price that Pugachov paid for his smoking habit was that his white mustache had become yellowed with nicotine, and his teeth had yellow stains. He also had a persistent cough and struggled to catch his breath on the stairs.

"What progress have you made?" Sheymov asked. Behind

him on the wall were two black-and-white photographs of previous occupants of his director's office: Yuri Andropov and the legendary Lavrenty Beria—Stalin's enforcer and the architect of numerous bloody purges. Both had been chairmen of the FSB's predecessor secret police organizations, the NKVD and KGB. Sheymov clearly enjoyed the historic notoriety of his director's position.

Pugachov placed a slim cardboard file on the desk. "Some progress, sir. We have continued to tail Edward Grewall. He has now returned to Moscow, and we have him under twenty-four-hour surveillance here. Before he left London, we know he met with the CIA deputy director, Victor Walter, and also with other members of the CIA station in London, as you would expect."

"Remind me who your asset is in London?"

"It's STRIPES. She's a secretary on the top floor at Grosvenor Square who has access to calendar appointments, travel arrangements, and other administrative items. She sees a lot."

"You need someone higher up the food chain than that," Sheymov snapped.

"We're working on it. But this secretary is currently applying for a post as personal assistant to the US ambassador in London. That will greatly increase her access, if successful. We are doing all we can to help her get the post."

"I hope so. Are you confident you have listed everyone Grewall met?" Sheymov asked. His thin frame, gaunt face, and dark circles beneath his eyes suggested that decades of stress, smoking, and a tendency to skip meals when busy were taking their toll.

"We believe so."

"And what about those people? Walter and the others. Do you believe they are currently investigating the Fradkov operation, and if so, do they have assets on our side who they are talking to?"

Pugachov was the FSB's head of counterintelligence, a role into which he had been promoted by Sheymov more than eighteen months earlier. Like others in counterintelligence roles, of which there were many, his key task was to locate those Russians who had turned traitor and were selling the Motherland's secrets to foreign agents.

He nodded. "It is inevitable they'll investigate—they will want to know what Fradkov was going to tell them."

"So what is Grewall's and Walter's strategy, do you believe?" Sheymov asked.

Pugachov shook his head. "I don't know. I've told you already that Walter flew to Berlin via Amsterdam last Tuesday. He stopped in Amsterdam for a few hours. We are still trying to find out who he met there and where he went, and what he is now doing in Berlin. I have people in Amsterdam and Berlin who are working on that."

Sheymov sat back in his chair and took a deep drag from his cigarette. "Progress is slow, Leonid. The president will be impatient."

"The president is always impatient."

"But if we don't get results, we will feel the pain," Sheymov said. From behind his rimless glasses, his eyes stared unblinkingly at Pugachov. "I told you what he said at the Kremlin meeting last Thursday. He wants anyone who represents a threat to his plans to be traced and dealt with. He said he wants us to take a ruthless approach if needed."

"What are his plans?" Pugachov asked.

Sheymov shrugged vaguely. "He didn't go into detail. You know how everything is need-to-know with him."

Pugachov's phone vibrated in his pocket. He took it out and scrutinized the long message that had just arrived. A jolt went through him.

Surely not.

"What is it?" Sheymov asked.

"My asset in Amsterdam has reported back," Pugachov said. He glanced up at Sheymov. "When Walter traveled there last Tuesday, he apparently visited that British woman, the former MI6 officer, Jayne Robinson. The one who caused us those issues last year after she sneaked into Moscow on a false ID."

"Apparently?" Sheymov asked, a note of skepticism in his voice.

"Walter went to an Amsterdam hotel and disappeared upstairs. We hacked the guest list and found that Robinson was staying there. Can't be any other reason."

Sheymov stared at him. "Doesn't necessarily mean anything. What's she doing in Amsterdam? Maybe working on an operation."

"Don't you think it's a bit too coincidental? Walter visits her the day after Fradkov is killed in London. She then checked out of her hotel on Saturday and flew back to London."

There was a thoughtful expression on Sheymov's face. "So Robinson checks out four days after Walter's visit. Doesn't look that urgent. And now? What's she doing?"

"We don't know," Pugachov said.

"Get the team in London to find out, then. And if you think she might come back here, then put the Border Service on alert. Send out her description and photo."

Pugachov sat back in his seat. "Last time she was in Moscow, we were this damn close to nailing her." He held up his thumb and index finger, a fractional gap showing between them. "And I'm certain she's got a contact somewhere here. Probably a highly placed one. We could have got the traitor that night too—but they got away as well."

"You'd better not screw up again," Sheymov said. He

CHAPTER SEVEN

day, September 27, 2016
loscow

made her **way** along platform three at Moscow's
gradsky rail **station** and out through the exit area,
d by security guards. The building, a copy of the
ovsky station **at** the other end of the line in St. Peters-
might be the **oldest** station in Moscow, but the trains,
ing arcade, **and** ticket hall areas were very much
y-first century. This was an advert for the new Russia.
little to her **surprise**, after a careful passport check
boarding, **there** was minimal scrutiny on the actual
ther than regular patrols by staff through the carriages.
w, in line with her usual operational behavior, Jayne
turned to look back behind her, never hesitated, and
made eye contact with any of the railway staff or police
s in the shopping mall or the booking hall.
passed the ATMs, the KFC restaurant, the coffee

stabbed an index finger in Pugachov's direction. "The president will personally disembowel both of us if that happens."

Pugachov pressed his lips together. "That's why we've
been so thorough in our surveillance of the British and Americans since then. That's how we know Grewall rushed straight
back to Moscow. Why rush back?"

"Good question."

Pugachov pulled at his mustache. "You know, Grewall and
Robinson have worked closely together in Moscow before.
Maybe the plan is to do so again. It might explain their move-
ments. Maybe he was in touch with her agent."

Sheymov inclined his head to one side. It was his usual
way of indicating that he thought someone had a good
point.

Pugachov stood and pushed his chair to one side. "I'd
better get going with this. Let me talk to London."

He headed out the door and went to the elevators. The
idea of walking up to the sixth floor of the old gray-and-
yellow granite Lubyanka building was just too much. Better
to risk being trapped in a broken-down elevator—something
that had happened to him more times in this ancient building
than he could remember.

When he reached his office, he shut the door behind him,
lit another LD, and sat at his battered old desk.

The office reeked of stale sweat, nicotine, and floor
cleaner. There were no pictures on the walls or indeed any
other decoration. Pugachov had always thought he was likely
not going to be occupying the room for long enough to make
it worth putting them up.

But despite his self-doubts, at sixty, he was driven by a
steely determination, an obsessiveness, and a survival instinct
that had seen him navigate an entire thirty-five-year career of
backstabbing by colleagues and rivals in other services. The
experience might have completely whitened his hair, which in

the long-distant past had been black, but hadn't blunted his drive.

His phone pinged as a notification popped up from the secure messaging app he used to communicate with his case officers overseas. It always amused him that the United Kingdom and the United States appeared to underestimate the threat posed by his rapidly growing cohort of operatives and assets in those countries.

Everyone in the West seemed to assume that the FSB was purely focused within Russia. They couldn't be more wrong.

Over the past five years, numbers in the UK employed by the FSB alone had more than quadrupled, and he knew his rival service, the SVR, had many more, as did the military intelligence service, the GRU. And Pugachov knew for a fact that out of the 56 staff members at the Russian embassy in London, 26 were now operatives from all three of Russia's intelligence agencies. In the United States, there were about 150 spies working under the guise of diplomats.

Pugachov tapped in his private key to access the message, which he saw was from an officer in London who was handling the secretary in the CIA station. He scanned down the contents.

STRIPES confirms Victor Walter now in Berlin, Edward Grewall returned to Moscow, Jayne Robinson flew yesterday to Helsinki. No details yet on reasons for movements. Will advise further as appropriate.

Well, Pugachov was already aware of the first two developments. But the third, regarding Robinson, was new. That was interesting. Why the hell would she be flying to Helsinki so quickly after arriving back in London from Amsterdam, and what was she doing there?

Pugachov tapped his cigarette on his large ashtray, which was already full of old butts. After knocking off the surplus ash, he took another long drag.

Instinct told him that there was onl_ Robinson would be in Finland.

She was about to enter Russia by the back Maybe she had already done so.

Suka. Bitch.

He picked up his desk phone and called his most trusted colleague inside the FSB anc business when it came to surveillance.

shops, and a MetroPhone shop, part of the group owned by the late Pyotr Fradkov. There she finally did stop, took out her phone, and used a pretend call as an opportunity to check behind her for any sign of coverage. There seemed to be nobody coming to a sudden halt, ducking behind pillars, taking an interest in a window display, or otherwise looking less than purposeful.

Jayne continued through the exit and out into the expanse of Komsomolskaya Square, which also housed two other railway stations. From there, she walked northwest past the Botanical Gardens and the Moscow Cathedral Mosque.

There, she found a fast-food shop, where she visited the bathroom and again changed her clothing and wig, turning herself into a brunette in a gray sweatshirt. Eventually, she arrived at Sushchevskaya Ulitsa, a busy residential street about three and a half kilometers northwest of Leningradsky station.

In the old days of the Cold War, it would have been almost impossible for the CIA to operate a safe house in Moscow, such was the level of scrutiny of any Westerner. Now, one of the front companies that the Agency operated in the Russian capital, a small travel business, owned two apartments, ostensibly for the use of visiting executives. One of those apartments was allocated to Cara Budz.

The safe apartment was on the second floor of a seven-story building in Sushchevskaya Ulitsa. It overlooked a small park in the Tverskoy District and was a few minutes' walk from Mendeleyevskaya station on the Moscow metro's Serpukhovsko-Timiryazevskaya line.

Jayne keyed in the PIN she had been given to open the security door on the ground floor, then made her way up the stairs to the apartment, where she used another PIN to get in.

The apartment, like most safe houses she had used, was furnished in a spartan style with well-worn secondhand furniture and was painted plain white throughout. There were no pictures or any other decorations. However, there was plenty of food in the fridge, some coffee and tea, and a couple of bottles of wine. In line with Jayne's request, there was also a selection of women's clothing and shoes in the wardrobe, allowing her options to change her appearance.

There was no time to waste. Jayne plugged in her laptop and got to work.

She tapped out a brief message on her secure link to Ed Grewall at the CIA station to confirm the meeting details for Shevchenko, asking him to arrange for it to be sent on to Shevchenko's SRAC receiver in the park.

In Moscow. Site BUZZARD Thursday 00:21–00:27. Confirm.

There was no need to say who was requesting the meeting or who it was with. Shevchenko would know—Jayne was the only person she would meet. The window for the meeting was the usual six minutes, which was enough to allow for any important information to be passed over and for a discussion of the kind that was impossible via SRAC. Any longer and the risks would become proportionately greater.

Site BUZZARD, which she and Shevchenko had intended to use the previous year but had been unable to do so, was a pair of benches in a leafy, secluded park off Ulitsa Mishina street. It was near a kids' playground in a residential district consisting mainly of apartment blocks, with paths, side streets, and alleyways providing escape routes if required. The meeting time in the dead of night was perfect. Grewall's team had confirmed there were working streetlights in the vicinity, but they clicked off automatically at midnight.

And by the early hours of the morning, the hope was that most FSB officers would be home in bed rather than on surveillance operations.

Site BUZZARD was approximately a forty-five-minute walk from the CIA safe house, which Jayne intended to extend to at least three hours to allow for a surveillance detection process. She could not afford to run any risk of being followed and identified, as that would mean a very uncomfortable spell in one of Moscow's notorious prisons, if not worse.

For Shevchenko, the risks were even greater. If she were identified as a traitor, the penalty would almost certainly be death. Jayne knew that most likely, Shevchenko would be sent to Lefortovo, the prison east of the city center that was normally the destination of anyone who spied against the Kremlin. It had an exceptionally gruesome reputation for being the final resting place of such offenders. Usually, their fate was sealed by a bullet in the back of the head in one of the many basement torture suites.

The stakes could hardly be higher.

Next, Jayne dispatched a secure, encrypted message to Vic Walter to confirm her arrival at the safe house. She also wanted to confirm the planned exfiltration arrangement he had put in place, using Route Yellow One. It involved a pickup by a high-speed helicopter from the village of Kalinovka, a short distance inside Russia from the Ukraine border. She hoped it wouldn't be necessary and that she would go undetected in Russia and could simply retrace her steps through St. Petersburg and out to Helsinki. But experience told her that little went to plan on such operations.

To her relief, within ten minutes, she received replies to both her messages.

Grewall confirmed the message would be transmitted to Shevchenko's SRAC within the hour, and regular checks would be made for replies from her. He also stated that two of his countersurveillance officers would be near site BUZZARD for ten minutes before and after the scheduled meeting time with Shevchenko. That was reassuring. Jayne knew Grewall was not always in favor of using CS because of the risks that they might attract attention, but the last time she had met with Shevchenko in Moscow, they had saved her skin.

Then Vic responded to say that Route Yellow One was confirmed if required.

Jayne went to the main bedroom, pulled aside a chest of drawers, and found the safe built into the wall behind it, as Grewall had directed. She tapped in the security code, opened the door, and removed the 9mm Walther PPS and three spare magazines that Grewall had left for her. She carefully checked the pistol, which, like most CIA weapons, was well maintained.

Then she made herself a coffee and stood by the living room window, scrutinizing the street below through the white net curtain. One of Moscow's ubiquitous blue-and-white electric trams came to a halt at a stop near the apartment. A crowd of passengers bustled off.

She kept watching for a further half hour but saw nothing that caused her any concerns. Grewall's team had chosen the safe house well. The street was busy enough to provide good cover when Jayne needed to head out for her meeting. She wouldn't be easily noticed.

But on the other hand, she knew only too well that it also made life easier for anyone tailing her. There had been no sign of that so far, but the only way to operate in Moscow was to stick to Moscow Rules. Those were the ground rules adopted by the CIA during the Cold War for those operating in the capital. The list was quite long, but the most important of them in Jayne's mind were to keep her options open, assume nothing, and listen to her gut feeling, her personal radar, which was usually reliable.

That was why she had made multiple arrangements with

Ed Grewall to extricate herself, and Shevchenko, if necessary, from site BUZZARD if anything unexpected happened.

But now, for the next twenty-four hours, until she could begin her surveillance detection route, she needed to sit tight.

CHAPTER EIGHT

Tuesday, September 27, 2016
Moscow

Leonid Pugachov walked into the cramped meeting room that he had commandeered in the same corridor as his office and took another drag from his LD cigarette. At the desk nearest to him was his trusted lieutenant, Roman Gurko, who was studying his laptop screen, his face bathed in a ghostly white light from the glow. He also had a cigarette stuck between his lips.

"See something?" Pugachov asked.

Gurko straightened his lean frame. He remained silent for a few seconds as he scrolled down his screen.

"Possibly," he said eventually. He removed his cigarette from his mouth and stubbed it out in an ashtray. "I've got the St. Peter Line ferry's passenger manifest, Helsinki to St. Petersburg, for last night. There are very few solo women on it who match the age group we're after. Only four, actually." He pointed to the screen.

Pugachov took three steps forward and crouched down so he could see the screen.

Gurko had on the screen a list of the passengers on the overnight ferry that had arrived in St. Petersburg that morning. He had filtered out all passengers apart from the ones he had pinpointed.

"These are the four," Gurko said, stabbing his index finger at the screen. He then toggled to another screen. "Now, look at the list of hotel bookings in St. Petersburg for tonight. I've cross-checked all of them. All four are booked into hotels, all different. But there's a red flag against this one, Ashima Caire, who checked in but apparently hasn't been seen at the hotel since lunchtime, according to the manager."

"So where's she gone?" Pugachov asked.

Gurko shook his head, causing a lock of his slicked-back dark hair to flop sideways. "I don't know. She's not boarded any flights or trains out of St. Petersburg, at least under that name. So unless she's found herself a guy in a bar and gone back to his place, I'd say—"

"She's moved on elsewhere under a different name?" Pugachov interrupted.

"Yes, and the guys are checking the manifests for the trains and flights out of St. Petersburg now." Gurko waved a hand toward his three colleagues, who were all focused intently on their computer screens.

"Guys, do you have anything yet?" Gurko asked them.

The FSB could get access to all passenger bookings on planes and trains, both government-owned and private, across Russia, via its proprietary Magistral database system. Gurko could use the system to get a real-time view of all tickets purchased, listed by either passenger name, journey, or mode of transport, right across Russia.

One of the men, the fresh-faced Yacov Denikin, looked up. "I've got the trains. Fifty-six women traveled solo on the afternoon services to Moscow. Forty-five of them are Russian citizens. Eight of the others are checked into Moscow hotels. That leaves three foreigners on the loose." Denikin glanced at his computer screen. "I'd say we're looking for one of those three. Got to be."

Pugachov nodded. The process of eliminating suspects in this way was a familiar one that the team had gone through many times before. "You may be right. Good work. Let me have a look." He walked around the desk and looked over Denikin's shoulder at his screen.

"What are the dates of birth of these people?" Pugachov asked.

Denikin clicked on a tab, and the relevant data appeared in a column down the right of the screen. Pugachov bent down to look at it.

"Two of these are in their twenties and thirties, according to Magistral," Pugachov said. He placed his finger on the screen and traced it down over the names. "It won't be them. Robinson is older—she's over fifty."

"What about this one?" Denikin asked. "Cara Budz, a travel consultant. Aged fifty-five. Polish-British dual nationality."

Pugachov's eyes widened a little. "That's more like it. Can we get video of her from the train cameras?"

Denikin nodded. "I've got her seat number. I'll get the video off Russian Railways."

"Quick as you can then," Pugachov said.

Denikin began to tap at his keyboard.

Pugachov walked back around the table and stood next to Gurko. He glanced at his watch. "It's now gone eleven, and the ship on which these people arrived docked at nine this morning. That's fourteen hours. Too long. Even if we're on the right track—which is a big if—and both these women, Caire and Budz, are actually Robinson, she could be anywhere by now. She's bound to be in disguise. And the chances of finding her are not good."

Gurko turned his head and glanced up at his boss. "You're taking a very pessimistic view, Leonid."

"I've learned to be pessimistic." Pugachov walked out and went to fetch another coffee. He'd been in the office since before eight that morning and could feel his eyelids sinking.

While he was at the coffee machine, his phone vibrated in his pocket. He took it out and checked the encrypted message. It was from Sheymov.

Can you give update on the witch hunt? Suslova wants to know urgently, and to be kept up to date in real time on all developments.

Pugachov grimaced. This was getting worse. Why was Suslova putting this operation under the microscope? He had to assume it was because Putin was breathing down her neck. If something big was happening at the top level and the president had even a vague suspicion there might be a Western spy in the Kremlin, he'd be hyperfocused on it. He decided to wait and reply later, once the team had done this phase of their work.

By the time he returned to the meeting room, Denikin had a somewhat grainy video running on his screen of the interior of a carriage on the one o'clock Sapsan train from St. Petersburg to Moscow. As he approached, Denikin tapped his keyboard, and the image froze.

"That's Cara Budz," Denikin said. "It shows her getting on the train. I've cross-checked the seat numbers to make sure."

The woman, who was making her way down the aisle, had curly blonde hair and black-rimmed glasses, wore a blue sweatshirt and jeans beneath a beige coat, and had a small backpack slung over her shoulder.

"Let the video run," Pugachov said.

Denikin tapped the space bar, and the video played. It

showed Budz walking with a languid stride, checking the number next to a pair of seats, and then removing her coat and taking her place.

In the top corner of Denikin's screen, in a separate small window, was one of the many still images the FSB had of Robinson from over the years, mostly dating back to her time as an officer with Britain's Secret Intelligence Service, or MI6. It showed her with dark hair and without glasses.

"Possibly Robinson," Pugachov said. "She's done disguises before. Anyway, Budz is the only obvious candidate. I remember the way Robinson walks—a bit catlike, quite fluid, athletic, if you know what I mean. It looks like her. Play the video again."

Denikin played the film of Budz again. "I see what you're saying," he said.

"Now we need video of this Budz woman at Leningradsky station after she gets off the train," Pugachov said. "Can you get on to that? We need to know where she goes."

"Sure. Will do."

* * *

Wednesday, September 28, 2016
    Moscow

The white wig, circular wire glasses, beige scarf, old brown woolen coat, and matching knitted hat had been a staple of Major General Anastasia Shevchenko's disguise portfolio for several years now. They gave her the look of a working-class housewife and went well with the hunched shoulders she had perfected and could maintain for several hours if needed.

However, on virtually all previous occasions that she had deployed them, they had been used on foreign soil to protect her from scrutiny by intelligence services run by Russia's enemies.

The items were laid out ready on Shevchenko's bed. Tonight, the disguise would ensure her secret life remained secret from her own countrymen, if any were watching.

Some people at sixty, a milestone she had passed a few weeks earlier, would be genuinely white-haired, stooped, and well past their best.

But minus her disguise, Shevchenko ensured that she remained almost as fit as she had been two decades earlier. Even her black shoulder-length hair had only a few flecks of gray.

It took a lot of work in the gym to ensure she maintained that condition, but it had been worth it. On more than one occasion, it had enabled her to run for her life.

She padded across the living room of her two-bedroom apartment on the fifth floor of a building in Ulitsa Seregina street, northwest of Moscow's city center, practicing the walk she would use. As she went, she checked in the full-length mirror on the wall. Her hunched gait looked about right.

The apartment overlooked Petrovsky Park, where the CIA's SRAC base transmitter unit was located. On the far side of the park, she could see cranes towering over the new stadium that, when finished, would form a much-improved base for her beloved Dynamo Moscow football team.

Soon, she would set off on foot for the designated meeting point, code-named site BUZZARD, where she would hold a six-minute rendezvous with Jayne Robinson.

The meeting location was just a kilometer and a half to the east, beyond the stadium. But Shevchenko intended a much longer route of perhaps two and a half hours, during which she would check for certain that she had no surveillance, no FSB officers on her tail. It was something she was an expert at and was another reason she needed to remain fit.

Shevchenko walked through to her spare bedroom, which she used as an office. There she sat down and, yet again, mentally ran through the key talking points she needed to communicate to Jayne. This was going to be a critical meeting, with a lot to say and little time to say it. There was much she knew, but also much she didn't.

CHAPTER NINE

Wednesday, September 28, 2016
Moscow

It had taken longer than Pugachov had hoped to set up a dedicated connection between the video streams from Moscow's network of 170,000 street CCTV surveillance cameras and the secure server belonging to his team. That was nothing new, though. In theory, video should be available almost in real time. But as usual, there had been a few technical issues, which in his experience was code for drunken or lazy staff in the Department of Information Technology, whom he had to cajole into action.

In the end, he'd given the DIT team a rocket and told them they would earn a negative mention in his report to the FSB director if they didn't move faster.

Anyway, by lunchtime, he and Gurko were once again buried in their laptops, using two new analysis tools that were still under wraps in their trial phase but which promised to be game changers for the FSB, once proven.

The first of the tools, facial recognition software, had been widely publicized by the Kremlin. The software could compare photographs of individuals held in the FSB or police databases against images from any of the surveillance cameras mounted on buildings, lampposts, and traffic lights, as well as on trams, buses, metro stations, and train carriages.

When fully operational, it would provide an automatic link between the cameras and the database, the developers had promised the FSB. The system would enable the team to pinpoint a particular person's location swiftly. It would instantly compare all live feeds from the city's cameras and flash up the names and locations of targets. It would be extremely difficult to avoid detection because the sheer volume of cameras now in operation meant that the vast majority of the city was now covered. Furthermore, the facial recognition system would work even if the person's face was partially obscured by a face mask, scarf, or sunglasses, for example.

Unfortunately for Pugachov, the process during this trial phase was far more labor-intensive.

Currently, it required the target person to first be located manually, and then comparisons could be made with a known photograph or video in the database.

Well, Pugachov had images of Robinson. There were some already held by the FSB, and they also had the video from Russian Railways of the woman calling herself Cara Budz.

But they didn't yet have images from Moscow's streets to compare them with.

The second tool, in Pugachov's limited experience of using it, promised to be even more of a breakthrough. Gait recognition software, introduced only a few months earlier and so far kept a close secret, enabled the team to identify individuals from the way they walked, moved, and used their arms and hands in certain ways. It also matched body shapes to photographs and video held in databases. It allowed an identification even if the person's face was turned away from the camera lens.

The gait recognition system would also be useful if the target was not near a camera and facial recognition was not yielding results, as it worked at distances of up to fifty meters. It also could not be fooled by a target trying to walk differently by, for example, hunching their back, limping, or splaying their feet outward, because it instantly analyzed all of a body's features.

The only issue was that the gait recognition system was also not yet automated against the database and was currently slower than Pugachov would have liked. It required video, rather than simply still images, and it took about ten minutes to analyze an hour of footage.

The FSB was not hampered in its use of such systems by the cumbersome privacy laws in Western countries that sometimes rendered them less useful than they were capable of. There were no such obstacles in Russia.

By midafternoon, Pugachov was on his second pack of LD cigarettes and his third cup of strong black coffee, watching as Gurko, Yacov Denikin, and his colleagues worked away on their laptops.

Gurko, whom Pugachov had brought to Moscow the previous year from a role based in St. Petersburg, was concentrating on the previous day's recorded feeds from the vast array of cameras mounted in and around the Leningradsky railway station.

He had already manually run the facial recognition tool against more than eighty possible candidates. But each time a fresh image popped up into the analysis box in the app on his laptop, after a few seconds, a message in red capitals appeared across the bottom.

NO MATCH.

Denikin and his colleagues were having a similar lack of success in their task of analyzing the live video feeds. There was no sign of Budz—or Robinson—today. She was either staying indoors or had somehow avoided detection by the CCTV network.

Nevertheless, Pugachov had ordered the head of his surveillance division to put four teams on standby, each comprising a high-powered unmarked car containing three armed officers. Another car and driver were also on standby, ready to whisk Pugachov and Gurko to any location in Moscow, if required.

Gurko sighed, reached for his pack of cigarettes, and lit another. He turned around and caught Pugachov's eye.

"Keep going," Pugachov said. "We haven't got time to waste."

Gurko said nothing but turned to his computer and dragged the next image he had pinpointed for scrutiny into the analysis box.

Seconds later, there was a ping, and a message in green popped up.

85% MATCH.

Pugachov took an involuntary step forward. "Who's that?"

He stared at the screen. The image, taken as a still from a video sequence, showed a woman with curly blonde hair, a blue sweatshirt, a beige raincoat, and a backpack over her shoulder walking past a KFC outlet at Leningradsky station. She was heading away from the platforms in the direction of the station exit. Though she looked nothing like the images of the dark-haired Robinson, the hair, coat, and backpack were a match for Cara Budz.

"Not a hundred percent match," Gurko said. "But close."

"Get the video clip and run the gait analysis on her," Pugachov snapped.

Gurko tapped on his keyboard and toggled to the gait app, where he cued up the video segment, which lasted for about fifteen seconds.

After the video had run through, there was what seemed like an interminable wait. The laptops supplied by the FSB were all equipped with a minimal memory capacity to save money. That meant any app requiring video processing ran at very slow speeds.

Finally, another notification popped up.

95% MATCH.

Gurko removed his cigarette from his mouth. "Got the bitch," he said, his voice level and utterly devoid of emotion.

"Right, now hunt her down. Track where she goes."

That proved less than easy, but over the following three hours, the two FSB men pieced together the route taken by Robinson the previous afternoon as she made her way on foot through the area northwest of Leningradsky station. She was caught by a series of cameras, including those near the Botanical Gardens and the Cathedral Mosque.

The task was delayed significantly when Robinson at one point disappeared into a restaurant. It took a while for them to realize she had reappeared through a different door, this time as a brunette and wearing a gray sweatshirt.

Every so often, Pugachov dispatched a brief update on progress to Sheymov, including links to the videos they were using to track Robinson's movements. He had no doubt that his boss was passing the information on to the Kremlin, probably to Suslova, maybe even to Putin. There was much at stake here. He could not afford to make a mistake.

Finally, they discovered a camera mounted on a lamppost in Sushchevskaya Ulitsa, near Mendeleyevskaya metro station, had captured Robinson as she disappeared into a large apartment building.

"It'll be some kind of safe house," Pugachov said.

He glanced at his phone. It was 10:41 p.m. They had been working for ten and a half hours to get this far. It was dark outside, which would not help them as the CCTV network became of more limited use, unless the cameras were in areas that were well lit. Success here was going to require some old-fashioned tradecraft.

Pugachov turned to Gurko. "Come, let's get out on the street. Yacov can track the bitch with gait recognition from here and direct us on the radio. We'll get four teams up there, cover all the streets around the building, then flush her out."

He called Denikin around to look at Gurko's screen, gave him the street address and coordinates for the apartment building where Robinson had gone, and instructed him to focus his analysis on the live camera feeds in that area and to use the FSB's city residents' database to pinpoint which apartment was the likely safe house.

Then he took out his phone, called his surveillance team chief, and ordered him to get his four teams at strategic points around the apartment building. He also instructed him to have the car allocated for him and Gurko to be ready in the Lubyanka's underground parking lot in ten minutes.

Then Pugachov returned to his office and took his Makarov semiautomatic, a holster, and a spare eight-round magazine from his desk drawer. He checked to make sure the chamber was empty and the safety was on, then clipped the holster to his belt, pushed the weapon into it, and headed down the stairs to the parking lot with Gurko, who also carried a Makarov. As he went, he called Sheymov and gave him another update.

This operation was going to show the high value of the asset that had been carefully cultivated inside the CIA's London station, as well as the technology that was now helping Pugachov to combat the forces lined up against him. Given that Pugachov had played a major part in both developments, he couldn't help anticipating that once Robinson was trapped, along with the traitor whom he guessed she was meeting, there would be a reward heading his way soon.

* * *

Wednesday, September 28, 2016
   Moscow

A shaft of moonlight glinted between the blinds of the second-floor office, just down the corridor from President Putin's, in the Kremlin's Senate Palace building. The light caught the face of Kira Suslova as she padded toward the window, the intelligence report she had just finished reading in her hands. She gazed out over Red Square.

Suslova liked to imagine how a previous occupant of the room next door, a certain Josef Stalin, would have proceeded. Thinking back to all the reports she'd received over the past few days, there seemed little doubt in her mind.

Suslova turned and faced her visitor, Gennady Sidorenko, who was seated in an armchair next to the ornate fireplace.

"I think we give Peskov the green light. I've seen enough," she said, waving the report from the FSB director Nikolai Sheymov in the air.

She didn't particularly like Sidorenko, who always came across as a vicious character who enjoyed inflicting pain on others. His counterintelligence role, with its need for a certain ratlike cunning in hunting down traitors, seemed to suit him. But she knew he didn't like her either, and resented her ruthlessness, her ambition, and the way she sometimes used her sexuality to the best advantage in the Kremlin career stakes.

Sidorenko leaned back in the red-covered armchair,

placed his hands behind his head, and nodded. "A green light for both recommendations?"

"*Da*. Yes. Green light for both."

Suslova walked to her desk, on one end of which there stood an exquisitely carved ivory chess set and board, made from the tusks of an elephant that she had shot while on a trip to Zimbabwe a few years earlier.

She sat down, opened her laptop, and scrolled down the list of Sheymov's previous reports.

They all seemed conclusive enough.

But she had no confidence that the FSB would deal with the situation to guarantee the outcome she wanted. Indeed, sometimes they screwed up spectacularly.

"I'll call Peskov now," she said.

Suslova picked up the encrypted desk phone, dialed a cell phone number, and waited.

When it was answered, she paused for a second before speaking.

"It's FERZ."

FERZ was the Russian name for the queen in a chess set. It was the codename that Suslova sometimes used when calling her operational subordinates, even on a secure line.

"You have instructions?" said Andrey Peskov, the man at the other end of the line.

Peskov was the best in the business—a sublime tracker of people, clearheaded and ruthless during operations.

"Yes, I do. Execute Operation Scorpion," she said.

"Understood."

"And then I may have another operation for you," Suslova said. "But first, get Scorpion done. Then we talk."

"Of course. Understood."

Suslova replaced the handset, folded her arms, and looked at Sidorenko. "It's happening," she said.

CHAPTER TEN

Wednesday, September 28, 2016
Moscow

Line Nine on the Moscow metro, often referred to as the Gray Line but officially named the Serpukhovsko–Timiryazevskaya line, had served Jayne Robinson well by 11:45 p.m. She had been along most of its forty-one-kilometer length and through five of its twenty-five stations by the time she finally walked off the platform at Dmitrovskaya station, past a bas-relief depicting the 1941 Battle of Moscow.

There was no special reason to choose this metro station, as it was just as far from here to site BUZZARD as it was from her safe house. But that wasn't the point. The rationale was to spend a long time on the move to flush out any tail.

After her four-and-a-half-hour surveillance detection route—much of it on foot—she had traveled from one end of the Russian capital to the other and was confident she was black, with no coverage, no FSB officers tracking her.

She made her way up the escalator, through the entrance

hall with its brown marble floor and walls, and out into the moonlit expanse of Butyrskaya Street, next to a small mall.

Jayne had left the safe house at seven o'clock, her Walther stuffed into her belt beneath her jacket and taking her small backpack and all her belongings with her. Her aim was to appear like a typical tourist, wandering around the city and seeing a few sights. She had placed her phone into a Faraday pouch—a small fabric wallet lined with layers of metalized material that would block all radio signals and prevent the device from being tracked.

She was now feeling quite exhausted, as was usually the case at the end of a surveillance detection route, or SDR as she and colleagues usually termed it. The exercise was even more mentally tiring than it was physically, as she could not afford to let her concentration slip even for a moment. Yet she needed to appear completely relaxed and to behave normally.

All that was left now was a two-and-a-half kilometer walk from Dmitrovskaya along a zigzag route to site BUZZARD, which was just three hundred meters from the Dynamo Moscow football stadium.

Jayne set off at a brisk pace, never looking back, trusting the process that had got her here. Her feel for the street and scent for trouble had rarely let her down over her thirty-year career.

She had memorized the route that she had discussed with Ed Grewall and didn't need to refer to the maps app on her phone. She'd also memorized the emergency escape plan should anything happen during the meeting. Grewall would wait one street away in a car at a point that would give easy access onto Moscow's ring road, where it would be easier to speed away to safety. That, however, was a last option. Hopefully, it wouldn't come to that.

Jayne glanced at her watch. She was exactly on schedule for the meeting at twenty-one minutes past midnight.

She continued through the residential area past an array of almost identical gray concrete apartment buildings.

The moon was bright and almost full and threw shadows from the trees that lined most of the street. A completely dark night would have been better, but there had been little flexibility over timing. At least the street lights were off, as expected.

Eventually, Jayne walked around yet another apartment building, this one with a dentist and pharmacy on the ground floor. There in front of her was the children's play area with its swings, jungle gym, and slide. It was nicely shielded from the street, Ulitsa Mishina, by trees and bushes.

Next to the swings were the two benches where she was due to meet Shevchenko in precisely one minute.

The street was completely silent now. Only a few of the apartment windows had lights showing. Most residents here were working people who needed their sleep.

There was no sign of the two countersurveillance officers Grewall had put in place, but Jayne didn't expect to see them. They would remain unobtrusive, looking for trouble on her behalf.

Jayne made her way to the bench and sat down, her senses now in full overdrive. She could feel her adrenaline pumping, but despite that, she remained calm. She had been in this situation many times.

She placed her bag on her lap, keeping hold of the strap. As she did so, she scanned the path to her left, which entered the playground on the far side, where she expected Shevchenko to approach from. The only illumination came from the moon and the occasional apartment with its lights on.

To her right, heading back the way she had come around

the side of the apartment building behind her, was the route she would take to get to Grewall's car if the shit hit the fan.

A light came on in a first-floor window of the apartment building on the far side of the playground.

The silhouette of a woman appeared at the window, peering out.

Was she looking at Jayne?

Could she see her in the dark?

It was impossible to tell.

The woman disappeared, and the light went out. A dog barked in an apartment somewhere behind Jayne.

She glanced back at the path and caught a hint of movement in the shadows. Two seconds later, a dark figure appeared, walking steadily in her direction.

Anastasia Shevchenko.

Despite the hunched shoulders and the slightly shuffling gait, Jayne knew it was her.

She sat upright as Shevchenko walked up to the bench and sat at the far end, a meter away. Shevchenko's white wig hair protruded from beneath a woolen hat. The disguise was good. She looked as if she were seventy years old and had not aged well.

"Hello, Jayne, good to see you again," the Russian said in her accented English, her voice low. "Did you travel safely?"

Always the routine checking, the need to know the other's status.

"Good to see you too after so long. And yes, I traveled well. I have walked for more than four hours," Jayne said. "I'm black. And you?"

There was a slight chuckle. "*Bozhe*. God. Long, but not that long. Two and a half hours. I'm confident."

"Good."

Shevchenko finally glanced at Jayne. "We have much to talk about and not much time. Let's get started."

* * *

Wednesday, September 28, 2016
Moscow

The splintered door slammed back against the wall with
tremendous force as Pugachov's men burst their way into the
apartment. But it took only a few seconds for the FSB counterintelligence chief to realize that the second-floor apartment, in a building in Sushchevskaya Ulitsa, was empty.

He swore quietly at Gurko and the surveillance team
leader, who were both standing next to him, as the men filed
out again. There wasn't even a toothbrush there, only some
milk in the fridge, bread, and tins of food. Robinson had gone
and likely wasn't coming back. But he knew they hadn't
missed her by too long.

"She must have gone to meet her traitor," Pugachov said.
"No other explanation at this time of night."

Gurko nodded. "She wouldn't have risked coming to
Moscow for any other reason, and she wouldn't have left here
for any other reason."

Pugachov slammed his fist on the wall. "She's meeting the
bastard tonight, then she'll run out of the country. We've not
got much time left. Come, let's get out of here."

As the three men were heading back down the stairs,
Pugachov's phone rang. It was Denikin, back at the
Lubyanka, his tone of voice terse.

"We got lucky with gait recognition. It picked up
Robinson leaving Dmitrovskaya station," Denikin rapped
out, his voice staccato. "We've confirmed it's her. That was
thirty minutes ago."

"Keep checking," Pugachov snapped. "Give me updates as
soon as you've got them. We're heading there now."

Pugachov turned to Gurko and the team leader. "Quick, we need to get to Dmitrovskaya."

He ran down the remaining flight of stairs and out of the building to his car, parked at the curb, Gurko just behind him.

CHAPTER ELEVEN

Thursday, September 29, 2016
Moscow

"First, our next meeting," Jayne said. It was a core element of the tradecraft she employed that details of the next encounter with an asset should be the number one item on the agenda. "Are you likely to get to the West in the foreseeable future?"

It would be far easier if they could meet in some European capital rather than inside Russia.

Shevchenko shrugged. "I will advise via SRAC if so. But let's assume not. Shall we say two months from now at site ROBIN?"

Site ROBIN, which had been established between Ed Grewall and Shevchenko, was just to the east of Moscow's city center.

Jayne nodded. "But I need to tell you now, for meetings in Moscow, it isn't always going to be me who meets you. The risks are mounting. We got away with it last time, but I must be on the FSB's watch list. If anything else goes wrong, we'll need to change things." She glanced at Shevchenko, looking for a reaction.

Shevchenko grimaced, but nodded. "Understood."

"Good," Jayne said. "Anyway, for now, it's site ROBIN on November 29. Now, what do you have for me?"

"I know of two top-level, highly compartmented operations that are being run by the Kremlin," Shevchenko said without hesitating, her voice little more than a murmur. "Operation Imperiya and Operation Peshka."

"Peshka? Pawn? As in chess?" Jayne asked. She was fluent in Russian but wanted to confirm.

"Yes."

"What are they?" Jayne's eyes scanned the park and the street beyond, behind the trees. There was a need here to concentrate on what Shevchenko was telling her and to memorize it all, but also to remain focused on her surroundings, watching for signs of danger.

Shevchenko frowned. "Putin is planning a follow-on to the invasion of the Crimea and the deployment of troops in the Donbas. My understanding is Imperiya will be a full-scale invasion of Ukraine."

Jayne's scalp tightened. "A full-scale invasion of Ukraine? *Seriously?*"

This was massive.

"Not this year, maybe not next year, but soon. It will follow a steady buildup of troop levels near the Ukrainian border, which Putin will try to characterize as a routine military training exercise. Of course, that will fool nobody."

"Bloody hell," Jayne muttered. "He won't get away with that, though. The West won't let him."

"You think so?" Shevchenko raised an eyebrow. "I'm not so sure."

"You're thinking of the gas and oil?" Jayne asked.

Shevchenko nodded.

Jayne knew that 40 per cent of Europe's gas requirements came from Russia. Most countries depended on Putin for gas and oil—including Greece, Germany, the Czech Republic, the Netherlands, Austria, Italy, and France. She and Vic both agreed that was why the reaction to the invasion of the Crimea and the Donbas was muted. Nobody wanted to risk Putin cutting off their gas and oil supplies.

But Jayne felt a full-scale invasion would be different. The West, despite having protested and having imposed some limited sanctions, had failed to do anything more significant partly because those parts of Ukraine were seen almost as a gray area geopolitically, given the large number of Russian speakers there. That was not true for the whole of Ukraine, however.

"Ukraine is different from the Crimea and the Donbas, though," Jayne said. "But let's move on. What is Peshka?"

"Well, Putin apparently has at least two high-level assets in the West," Shevchenko said. "They are helping him prepare the ground for an invasion of Ukraine—they are code-named ILYA and ALYOSHA."

"ILYA and ALYOSHA? The bogatyrs? The legendary Russian warriors?"

Jayne had read about them in a book on medieval Russia she had borrowed a few years earlier. A bogatyr was like a knight-errant in Western Europe.

Shevchenko nodded. "You know your stuff." There was a note of approval in her voice. "And the operation to run ILYA and ALYOSHA is Operation Peshka."

"Who are these assets?" Jayne asked. "Where? Are these new?"

Shevchenko spread her hands wide. "That is the problem. I have no idea of their identities. The Kremlin has sewn this up tighter than a, how do you say, a duck's ass. It is compartmented and impossible to penetrate—at least, not without me running huge risks. All I know is that he has two moles in place."

This sounded worrying.

"Don't put yourself at risk," Jayne said. "We need you. Who in Moscow is handling these people?"

Again, Shevchenko shook her head. "I think it's not being done from within the SVR, otherwise I'd probably know about it. It may be from directly inside the Kremlin. I got a glimpse of a file about Peshka on the desk of Kira Suslova—ex-KGB, and Putin's special adviser. She may be running the operation."

"I know of her. The chess woman." As a highly capable player in her younger days, Jayne was aware of Suslova's background, not just as a key figure in the Russian intelligence community but as a chess champion decades prior. She had been an international grandmaster who beat many of her male counterparts. But Jayne had never had any direct dealings with her.

"Yes, the chess woman," Shevchenko said. "She's dangerous—always has been, ever since her time as governor of St. Petersburg, when she worked with Putin, and going even further back with him, to East Germany. Putin and Suslova are close—even rumored to be lovers. Suslova is at the heart of most of Putin's secret and most strategic operations. She sits at the top table, alongside Igor Ivanov and that bastard Gennady Sidorenko—who put me in Lefortovo last year. If it's not Suslova who's running Peshka, it's one of those other two. But I think it's her."

Jayne exhaled. All three of the Kremlin names Shevchenko had mentioned were seen as formidable opponents at Langley and at MI6's headquarters at Vauxhall Cross. This was all new material that would undoubtedly cause a large explosion at both the White House and Downing

Street, never mind the Ukrainian capital Kyiv. It had been well worth the trip to Moscow simply to get all this.

"And there's something else," Shevchenko said. "Suslova is also trying to become the next president of the International Chess Federation, FIDE. Russia has held the FIDE presidency since 1995, and Putin doesn't want to relinquish it when the current president's four-year term ends. FIDE is already tied hand in glove to the Kremlin, and Putin wants to take even more of a stranglehold and to use it even more for political purposes. Chess is Putin's Trojan horse, and he wants Suslova to drive that."

Interesting.

Jayne was aware of the political battles that occurred to secure the top job in world chess, the presidency of the International Chess Federation, often referred to by its French name, the Fédération Internationale des Échecs, or FIDE for short. But she hadn't been closely tracking chess news recently.

"Does she stand a chance?" Jayne asked.

"She does. Though for certain she's only doing it to do the president's bidding."

Jayne would need to think through all this later.

"And should we assume all that you've just told me is connected to the murder of Pyotr Fradkov in London?" Jayne asked.

In the apartment building opposite, the same light that had gone on earlier flicked on again, and the same woman appeared in silhouette. Shevchenko also noticed it and paused before answering.

"I think he was about to pass details of these operations and assets to your service," Shevchenko said. "The Kremlin obviously realized that."

"Did you know Fradkov?" Jayne asked.

"I met him a few times through work, and his wife, Maria.

Most recently a year ago. But they weren't friends. Not people I could call up and chat to."

"How did the Kremlin find out Fradkov was going to leak this material?" Jayne asked. "And if he had the details of these operations, how did he get them? He was a cell phone oligarch. He wasn't part of the Kremlin inner circle."

"How did he get details of the operations? I have no idea. But even if Fradkov wasn't part of the operational inner circle at the Kremlin, he had connections, as you'd expect with his wealth. He was one of Putin's *siloviki*. He was ex-KGB, like Putin and many of the others."

The moon went behind a cloud and the night went suddenly darker. Shevchenko glanced around her, checking the gloom. Over in the apartment building, the woman's silhouette disappeared and the light in her apartment went out again.

"Is there a way of finding out what those details are and how he got them?" Jayne asked.

Shevchenko threw Jayne a sideways glance. "You think I should go and ask? It might not help my chances of reaching old age."

Jayne nearly smiled. "No. But who can I ask?"

"You could try Fradkov's wife, Maria," Shevchenko said. "They've been together a long time. I know he confided in her—the only problem is I don't know what."

"How do you know he confided in her?"

A faint trace of a smile crossed Shevchenko's face. "Because I interrogated her for two days after her husband's death. I was told to do it for counterintelligence reasons—and because I knew her. The FSB also interviewed her separately before I did, but they got nothing. They passed her on to us on the instructions of the Kremlin."

"So she admitted her husband had confided in her? How did you get that from her when the FSB didn't?"

"I have my methods," Shevchenko said, again with a faint smile. "Sometimes it pays to persuade rather than bully. She didn't really admit it, but she left me in no doubt."

"Does Kruglov know?"

Shevchenko shook her head. "I omitted that from my report. I knew she might be useful to you."

"But she refused to say what he had confided?"

Shevchenko nodded. "I didn't push it too hard during those interviews. I thought I could go back to her privately another time, when the dust settled, and have another conversation. But I don't know when I'll get the opportunity, and actually, it would be far less risky for me if you speak to her. She might be more willing to tell you than me, to trust you, given that her husband was intending to inform your station chief."

Jayne never ceased to be surprised at Shevchenko's ingenuity, but she felt a spike of concern at the risks she had clearly taken.

"Where is Maria now, then?" Jayne asked. "Still in custody?"

"They let her go—I know that because I signed her release papers. She told me she was planning to leave her home in Moscow and was going to stay with her sister, Olga Sidorova, in Belgorod, near the Ukraine border. I have the address. That's something else I didn't include in my report, by the way."

Shevchenko recited an address for Maria Fradkova's sister in Belgorod, together with brief directions, and instructed Jayne to memorize it, which she did.

From somewhere distant, behind the building opposite, there came the sound of a car, followed by a slight squeak of brakes, then silence as the engine was switched off. A dog barked twice, a deep throaty echo in the darkness.

Both Jayne and Shevchenko listened without speaking for several seconds. But there were no more sounds.

"One thing I don't understand," Jayne said. "Why did Fradkov want to pass this information to us about Putin's plan for Ukraine, assuming that's what it was? Ed Grewall arranged it, but we never got an explanation why."

Once again, the moon threw its silvery light across the park. Shevchenko's face took on a slightly eerie two-tone appearance, half in deep shadow.

"One motivation may have been Fradkov's two adult children—he has a boy and a girl," Shevchenko said. "They're both in their twenties and live and work in Ukraine, in Kharkiv, where they run a business together. I understand they are not fans of Putin. They moved out of Russia for that reason. If Putin decides to invade Ukraine, as I suspect may be the case, then they would both be in the firing line. Kharkiv, as you doubtless know, is near the Russian border." Shevchenko shrugged. "But that's another question for Maria. Ask her. Perhaps there were other reasons her husband wanted to turn informer."

Jayne glanced at her watch. They had just gone past their allotted six minutes on the bench. It was time to wrap up.

"Is there anything else you need to tell me?" Jayne asked. "Is anything imminent with Operation Pandora?"

"Nothing imminent, I believe, but I expect Pandora to activate again soon. There are other things, but we don't have time. We must go. You have the key points. I will try to find out more by next time. Site ROBIN."

A slow, metallic squeaking noise broke the silence, like a rusty hinge opening.

Jayne looked up at the apartment building opposite to the north, trying to locate the source of the noise. She sensed Shevchenko doing the same.

But then came a flash from somewhere halfway up the building, and a tremendous bang.

What—

The next thing Jayne knew, Shevchenko's head exploded in a fountain of blood and flesh at the other end of the bench.

The Russian's body catapulted backward and her arms and torso, now lifeless, sprawled halfway over the backrest of the bench.

Her head was almost entirely missing.

Fuck.

Jayne threw herself sideways off the bench, pulling the bag she was holding with her, just as another deafening gunshot echoed around the playground. She banged her shoulder painfully on the ground but managed to roll over a couple of times, leap to her feet, and sprint to her right, while vaguely aware that the round had just destroyed the trash can right behind where she had been sitting.

Then another earsplitting whip-crack sounded as a third shot ripped through the gloom.

CHAPTER TWELVE

Thursday, September 29, 2016
Moscow

It was 12:27 a.m. by the time Pugachov and Gurko arrived at the GPS location sent to them by Yacov Denikin from the FSB's offices. Three backup cars with more armed FSB officers were a couple of minutes behind them and were due imminently.

Pugachov, who was behind the wheel, turned off the engine. "Let's go," he muttered.

He got out of the car, shut the door, pulled his Makarov from its holster, clicked off the safety catch, and looked across at Gurko, who also had his pistol ready.

"Watch for countersurveillance," Pugachov said. "They may have someone."

Gurko nodded, and the two men walked toward the apartment building. Behind it, according to Denikin, was the children's playground where Robinson was located—most likely with her asset.

Denikin had informed them that gait recognition analysis on video received from a camera on the side of the building nearest to the playground had given an 85 percent match with Robinson.

Footage of another person, for whom no match had yet been established, was now going through the computer. Facial recognition analysis had not delivered a result because it was too dark.

Pugachov flattened himself against the wall of the building and inched his way toward its front, Gurko just behind him.

He paused at the front corner. Ahead of him to the south were swings, a jungle gym, and a slide. And there, only fifty meters away on the far side and partly in shadow, were two figures sitting on a bench, just about visible in the gloom. Behind them loomed another apartment building.

Pugachov turned to Gurko. "That must be them," he murmured. "We'll get round the rear of the other building and take them from the back. We can't go from here—they'll see us coming, or countersurveillance will and warn them."

Gurko nodded. "Backup will be here in a minute, anyway. We'll take them from the rear. Backup can approach from the front."

Pugachov nodded. As he did so, there came a metallic squeak from somewhere above.

He glanced up but could see nothing.

Pugachov was just about to move when there came a flash and the loud crack of a high-powered rifle.

"*Dermo*. Shit," Pugachov muttered involuntarily as he ducked down against the side of the building. His first thought was that someone was opening fire on them. "What the hell was that?"

Next to him, Gurko pointed. "I don't know, but someone just took out one of the people on the bench."

Pugachov looked up to see one figure on the bench sprawled motionless. The other person was throwing themselves to the ground just as there came another flash from above and a second earsplitting gunshot.

Pugachov saw immediately that the shot had missed. The person jumped to their feet and sprinted off in the opposite direction. It looked like a woman. Was that Robinson?

"Let's go. After them," Gurko hissed as he pointed toward the fleeing figure.

"No! We'll get hit." Pugachov's immediate thought was that if they ran across the open playground, they'd be next in the firing line for whoever had the rifle.

Then there was another bang as a third gunshot echoed across the playground.

* * *

Thursday, September 29, 2016
Moscow

Jayne sprinted around the corner of the apartment building, past two cars, and across a stretch of grass beneath some trees.

In the distance, she heard a squeal of brakes and someone screaming.

She then ran across a pedestrian crossing and beneath more trees next to another brick apartment building, just as a car turned a corner with a screech of tires and accelerated at high speed past the crossing.

Jayne knew exactly where to go. She had memorized the escape route.

After another fifty meters, she saw the black Audi A4

parked at the end of a side street, in the gloom beneath a tree.

Jayne ran up to it, flung open the passenger door, and climbed in. Grewall immediately started the engine.

"I heard gunshots," he said. "What's happening?"

"It's all gone to shit," Jayne said. "Go! Go now!"

Grewall accelerated down the street toward the ring road. He didn't turn his lights on until he passed a multistory parking lot and did a right turn onto the ring road, heading west.

"So, what the hell?" Grewall asked.

"VULTURE was shot. Killed," Jayne said. "They just missed me. They must have tailed one of us somehow. God knows how. I was certain I was clear."

Jayne turned and scanned the street behind them, fully expecting to see an FSB pursuit car screaming after them. There was none visible, but that meant little. The ring road was crawling with traffic cameras, and Jayne knew the FSB didn't need human eyes on them to track their route.

"Where the hell was CS?" Jayne asked. "I never saw them."

"They were there, behind the apartments west and east of the site. Couldn't have spotted the gunman—or didn't have a chance to warn you."

"Useless. The gunshots came from the building to the north."

"VULTURE is definitely dead?" Grewall asked, disbelief coloring his voice.

"They blew her head off. High-caliber round. The shot that missed me destroyed a trash can behind us."

"That doesn't sound like FSB."

"No. You're right." Jayne welled up as an image of Shevchenko's body flashed across her mind. But Grewall was correct. Such a hit wasn't in the FSB's usual playbook. Their modus operandi was normally to capture their target, torture them, and extract information. They generally used handguns, not sniper rifles.

"You sure you were black?" Jayne asked.

"I'm sure. I got out of my apartment through the underground boiler room and an alleyway near some lockup garages."

"Good. I got a ton of information from VULTURE before it happened. She told me to go find Fradkov's wife in Belgorod."

"Belgorod?" Grewall asked, glancing at her. "That's half a day's drive away."

"I know," Jayne said. "Where's the car swap point?"

"Another kilometer," Grewall said.

"Okay, let's swap first, then I'll explain it all."

They continued on the ring road at speed, through the four-lane tungsten-lit tunnel that ran beneath Leningradsky Avenue. As soon as they emerged at the other side, Grewall steered off the main highway down a narrow side street and came to a halt behind a gray Toyota Camry sedan, opposite a park near the Nordstar Tower.

"That's our change car," Grewall said. "Let's go."

"Cameras?" Jayne asked.

"It's a blind spot," Grewall said. "We've checked."

Jayne nodded, and they both jumped out and ran to the Toyota. Grewall started it up, did a U-turn, and accelerated back onto the ring road once again.

"So, what did VULTURE say?" he asked.

Jayne finally gave him a brief account of the conversation she had with Shevchenko and her recommendation to meet with Maria Fradkova at her sister Olga's house in Belgorod.

"Bottom line is," Jayne concluded, "VULTURE's just tipped us off on a likely invasion of Ukraine sometime in the future and two high-level moles in the West—bloody *two*. She didn't know who they were or who runs them. Just had code-names—ILYA and ALYOSHA."

"Holy shit," Grewall said. The Moscow station chief was visibly trying to contain himself as he drove. "We need to get all this to Vic ASAP in case anything happens to us."

Jayne remained silent for several seconds. "And I'll have to tell Vic I've lost him his biggest asset in Moscow—how could that happen? I was certain I was black, and so was VULTURE."

"Don't blame yourself. It's not your fault."

Jayne shrugged. The truth was, she had no idea.

"I hope not," she continued. "But it feels like it's over before we'd even begun with VULTURE. I had a vision of running her for the next decade—our greatest penetration of the SVR. I don't know how I'm going to give Vic the news. What a bloody, shit-awful disaster. They'll be bouncing off the walls at Langley."

She banged her head back against the headrest and closed her eyes momentarily.

"Don't let it be in vain, then," Grewall said. "You got what she wanted to tell you. Make it count. Do it for her."

He was right. She would make it count, although precisely how was far from clear. But first, they had the small matter of getting to Maria Fradkova—there was no question they had to give that a try, given the information from Shevchenko. Then there was the exfiltration out of Russia to manage.

One step at a time, Jayne told herself. That's what Mark Nicklin-Donovan had always drummed into her.

"What now, then?" Jayne asked. "Direct to Belgorod? We can't go back to the safe house. It's likely compromised."

"We don't have much time before they shut this city down," Grewall said. "They'll have roadblocks on the main routes out of town in no time. I say we get on the road to

Belgorod immediately—we need to get to Maria before the FSB put two and two together and get there first."

"It must be a ten-hour drive." Jayne tried to calculate the distance in her head. "It's near the Ukraine border."

"Maybe more than ten. We can't take the motorways or toll roads. Too many cameras. It'll have to be the scenic route —I know the way. I went there last year. But we can get a head start before it gets light. If we can get past Vnukovo Airport, there are far fewer cameras on the rural roads, if any, and very few police patrols. We'll be more than halfway by dawn. You'll have to share the driving, though. I'm probably as exhausted as you are right now."

Indeed, Jayne was feeling exhausted. But she knew he was right.

"Do you have the exfil transmitter?" she asked.

He pointed to the glove box, which Jayne flipped open. Inside was a military-grade SARBE personal locator beacon, a small black device not much larger than a pack of cigarettes, with a flexible antenna. The device was designed to securely transmit location coordinates via satellite to Vic Walter, to the CIA station in Kyiv, and to the Ukrainian army helicopter team, based near Kharkiv, who would be responsible for the exfil operation. Jayne had used a similar device on previous escapes.

"Good." She placed the transmitter in her backpack and closed the glove box again.

Jayne knew she would now need to take the risk of sending Vic an encrypted message to tell him to expect the Route Yellow One helicopter exfil point to be somewhere near Belgorod. The city was roughly two hundred kilometers to the south of the original designated spot at Kalinovka but was an equally short distance over the border from Ukraine. It was better she sent such a message from Moscow rather than while en route to their destination, just in case her phone's location was logged by the FSB.

As Grewall accelerated away, she removed her phone from its Faraday pouch, switched it on, and tapped on her secure communications app.

CHAPTER THIRTEEN

Thursday, September 29, 2016
Moscow

Andrey Peskov swore softly and clicked on the safety of his Hungarian Gepárd GM6 Lynx semiautomatic sniper rifle. He removed the chunky magazine, which still held two of its original five large .50 BMG rounds, and retracted the barrel, which reduced its length to less than a meter. He then replaced the black weapon in its carry case and clicked the lid shut.

With a squeak of metal on metal, he then closed the fourth-floor apartment building landing window, through which he had just fired. Finally, he took out his phone and tapped on a secure number.

"FERZ here," said Kira Suslova when she answered the call.

"It's DOBRYNYA," Peskov said.

"Well?" said Suslova.

"Operation Scorpion is done. The SVR woman is dead. I was a minute or two late getting here. I suspect they had been talking for a few minutes."

"And the English bitch?" Suslova sounded anxious.

Peskov hesitated. "Missed, unfortunately. She ran."

There was a silence at the other end of the line. "*Dermo.* Shit. So it's not done. That is not good news. I will need you to get after her once we know where she's gone."

The moonlight through the window glinted slightly from Peskov's bald head. "No problem," he said. "Let me know once you've found out more. The FSB is outside now. I need you to call Sheymov and tell him to clear the path for me to leave. Trouble is the last thing I need. I'll need to know the name of whoever is in charge of the team out there."

"*Da.* Understood," said Suslova. "Give me two minutes. I will message you when all clear. You did a good job tracking Shevchenko without detection and taking her down—"

"Just doing what you're paying me to do."

"But Robinson was a bad miss," Suslova added. "A terrible miss."

"Apologies."

Peskov ended the call. A stocky, muscular man in his mid-forties, he was dressed in plain green battle fatigues. There were two patches sewn onto the upper right arm of his shirt. The first was circular and showed a grinning skull and the words 'PMC Vagnar Group.' The second, lower down the arm, carried the company motto in Russian: *Death is our business and business is good.*

Vagnar was a private paramilitary company whose existence was denied externally by the Kremlin. By keeping it separate from the mainstream Russian army and security forces, it could be compartmented more easily.

It amounted to the president's personal army, a group of

mercenaries, which he used to further his foreign policy objectives.

Owned by Yuri Burlakov, one of Russia's most secretive oligarchs, it comprised about a thousand soldiers and was growing fast. Vagnar only recruited the best people.

It wasn't very often that Peskov missed when given two targets in a static position.

But the Englishwoman had moved far faster than he had expected once the first shot struck its target.

He cursed inwardly as he waited on the landing of the apartment building for a reply from Suslova, staring out across the playground.

From outside came the sound of wailing sirens. Peskov watched as a group of four FSB men charged across the playground and disappeared around the side of the apartment building opposite, in the direction Robinson had run. Another cluster of officers stood near the kids' slide, conferring and gesticulating. Behind them, the bloody corpse of Anastasia Shevchenko lay sprawled on the bench where she had been sitting.

A few minutes later, Peskov's phone vibrated as an encrypted message arrived.

Clear to leave. FSB leader is Colonel Leonid Pugachov. Further instructions to follow. Pursue Robinson.

Peskov stood and stared at the screen for a moment.

Pugachov. There was a name from the past.

He picked up the rifle case and headed down the staircase to the ground floor, where he opened the door and stepped outside.

Standing a few meters away was Pugachov, a man who he had occasionally come across previously when Peskov was still a colonel general in the Spetsnaz, or special forces, of Russia's GRU foreign military intelligence organization.

It was there that Peskov had acquired the tool kit that had just enabled him to deliver Operation Scorpion—the elimination of one of Russia's most highly placed traitors. His time in the Spetsnaz included sniper training and street surveillance skills.

Peskov stood still and nodded at Pugachov. "Leonid. It's been a long time."

"It has." Pugachov pointed an accusatory index finger at him. "*Svoloch*. Bastard. You have just completely screwed up my operation. You realize we were about to arrest both of them? Now one's dead and the other's run for it. What the hell are you doing here?"

Peskov had been expecting this. "I was following my orders. That's all."

"Whose orders?"

Peskov shook his head. "Too many questions."

Pugachov pointed at the grinning skull badge on Peskov's upper right arm. "I see you've joined the private sector."

"Well spotted." There was no need for Peskov to elaborate. The Vagnar Group badge, which he was obliged to wear against his better judgment, told its own story.

"So, you're working directly for the Kremlin."

Peskov didn't reply. It was a statement, not a question.

"Who in the Kremlin?" Pugachov persisted.

Another silence.

Pugachov rolled his eyes.

"It's probably best if we don't get into an argument," Peskov said. "We may need to cooperate now. I've just been told to hunt down Robinson. I'm assuming you probably have been too."

"As soon as the office gets onto the camera feeds and works out where she's gone, yes," Pugachov said. "Maybe this time you'll allow me to bring her in. She will have a lot of valuable information—and I'm going to enjoy extracting it from her as painfully as possible when we get her back to the Lubyanka."

Peskov pressed his lips together. "I suspect your job will be to find her. Mine will likely be to kill her."

PART TWO

CHAPTER FOURTEEN

Thursday, September 29, 2016
Moscow

All four Moscow passenger airports, as well as the main train stations, were temporarily closed by FSB director Nikolai Sheymov as soon as he heard of Robinson's escape.

Meanwhile, Pugachov forced himself to put aside his anger, and confusion, at the assassination of the traitor whom Robinson had been meeting—confirmed by fingerprint analysis to be SVR deputy director Anastasia Shevchenko—and the subsequent failure of his operation.

Instead, he put his mind to organizing an extensive nighttime search for Robinson.

Pugachov was as certain as he could be that Robinson would not attempt to flee through the airports or train stations. She had proved herself far too much of a professional in the past to get caught in rat traps like Sheremetyevo, Domodedovo, Vnukovo, or Zhukovsky airports.

In any case, there were only a handful of flights and trains out of Moscow between one and six in the morning.

Instead, Pugachov raced back to the Lubyanka and focused his attention on what he viewed as the likeliest, quickest, and most flexible means of escape: the highways.

Pugachov woke up five of his staff at home and ordered them into the Lubyanka office to work on the search alongside himself, Gurko, and Yacov Denikin.

Pugachov then called the Moscow Police night duty chief at his headquarters a kilometer north of the Lubyanka, briefed him, and asked him to alert all patrols to be on standby once they had identified the target vehicle.

It didn't take long to identify the car. There were relatively few vehicles on the streets at 12:30 a.m., and video from the surveillance cameras quickly pinpointed a black Audi A4 seen leaving the area near the apartment buildings where Shevchenko had met Robinson.

Close-up images of the car identified Robinson in the front passenger seat, with the unmistakable figure of the CIA's station chief Edward Grewall at the wheel. That triggered an explosion from Pugachov, who had issued strict instructions to his team to keep Grewall under constant surveillance, day and night.

From there, track-and-trace software, utilizing the license plate, enabled them to follow the Audi westward around the third ring road to where it turned off near the Nordstar Tower.

But after passing the tower, it vanished from view and failed to reappear on the next set of cameras farther down the street.

Pugachov swore loudly. "It can't just disappear."

"It has," Gurko said.

"Well, get someone down there and find it. They must have dumped it in a camera blind spot or something."

Eventually, a Moscow Police patrol found the car at the side of the street. Sure enough, it was positioned between cameras. It then took another forty-five minutes to establish that a gray Toyota Camry sedan had appeared on the camera at the entrance to the ring road next to the Nordstar building a couple of minutes after the Audi had exited it and gone off-camera.

It was obvious there had been a change of vehicle in the blind spot. A standard but smart move by the CIA team. But thankfully, the Toyota's license plate was identifiable on the video footage. A quick trawl back through video showed the Toyota heading southwest out of Moscow on the M3 highway.

The initial suspicion was that it was heading for Vnukovo International Airport, a major base for private planes. But the car shot straight past the airport off-ramp and continued southwest toward Kaluga.

By that time, it was almost four in the morning and Pugachov was having difficulty keeping his eyes open. The battered old sofa in his office was becoming a great temptation.

But he forced himself to continue. He knew how dire the consequences would be if Robinson escaped from Russia and it emerged he had been sleeping.

The problem the team now faced was that Robinson and Grewall could be anywhere. They'd had a three-and-a-half-hour head start. And although Pugachov knew there were more than fifteen thousand traffic cameras across Russia with license plate recognition capability, the vast majority were in the cities and on the toll motorways, where they were used to collect fees. He also knew from bitter experience that outside the main cities, and particularly if a target was using a minor highway, the chances of successfully tracking a vehicle were far lower.

Pugachov called the MVD federal police night duty desk at the force's monolithic headquarters building near Gorky Park, south of the city center. He requested that an alert be sent to all regional police offices to hunt down the Toyota. He then sent a similar alert to all the regional FSB offices.

But despite a continued frantic trawl by the FSB team through the camera feeds on the M3, there were no further records of the Toyota's license plate after it left the Moscow oblast. The federal police also found nothing from initial checks on their system.

"Maybe they've changed cars again," Gurko said.

"Maybe," Pugachov said. "Or more likely, it's just that there are no cameras because those corrupt bastards in the Ministry of Internal Affairs have siphoned all the budget into their own bank accounts. And there's no police on duty."

The situation was a standing joke in the FSB.

The shortage of police outside Moscow, following cutbacks of about a quarter of the force in a reorganization a few years earlier, was one of Pugachov's biggest irritations. It had caused him significant problems in several previous investigations.

Pugachov instructed his team to continue pressurizing regional police in the direction the Toyota was last seen traveling. Then he grabbed a black coffee, called Gurko into his office, and shut the door.

"The big question is, where is Robinson headed?" Pugachov said as he lit the last LD cigarette left in his pack. "Did she get what she needed from Shevchenko and is she now heading out of Russia? Or does she need something more and is she therefore staying?"

"If our Vagnar Group friend took down Shevchenko before the end of the meeting, there's a chance Robinson didn't get all she wanted," Gurko said. "They didn't have long together. A few minutes, that's all."

"True, but we have to assume that people of her and Shevchenko's experience and caliber would have exchanged the critical information immediately in case something happened," Pugachov said as he blew a long stream of smoke toward the ceiling. "However, let's assume she's in Russia because she wants to find out what information Pyotr Fradkov was going to give the Americans. And let's also assume Shevchenko wasn't able to give her everything she needed to know. Who else might she try to contact?"

Gurko shrugged. "Someone else close to Fradkov. Someone he might have confided in. One of his close business associates. His wife maybe—but our foreign intel guys interviewed her, didn't they?"

Pugachov nodded slowly. "Fradkov's wife, Maria, was interrogated by our team after his death and was also interrogated for two days by SVR counterintelligence. She passed two polygraphs—no lies registering. Her house was searched from top to bottom. She knew nothing about her husband's links to the West, it seems, and nothing about what he was going to pass on to them. So we let her go, and so did the SVR." Pugachov threw a glance at his colleague. "But who do you think was in charge of interrogating her at the SVR and who made the decision and signed the papers to let her go?"

There was a pause before Gurko answered. "You're not telling me it was Shevchenko."

Pugachov inclined his head to one side. "*Da*. It was."

"*Dermo*."

"The border guards are tightening up all the border checkpoints, so Robinson's got no chance of getting across anywhere," Pugachov said. "But until we locate her, let's bring Maria Fradkova back in here."

"Where is she?"

"I assume she's at home," Pugachov said. "In Moscow.

Curious, the Toyota now appears to be heading southwest and away from her."

Gurko scratched his chin. "True. But I say nevertheless, bring Maria back in."

"Agreed. Let's get a team there and fetch her."

* * *

Thursday, September 29, 2016
    Berlin

"They've killed VULTURE," Vic said, his voice low. The darkness of his bedroom in the CIA safe house in Berlin perfectly reflected the subject of his call to the CIA director, Arthur Veltman.

"*What?*" Veltman muttered. "You can't be serious?"

The response down the secure line from Veltman, who was still working at the Agency's London station, had a real edge to it.

"Sniper," Vic said. "Took her out during the meeting. I've just had an exchange of messages with Jayne Robinson."

There came another expletive from Veltman. "Who screwed up? Jayne or VULTURE? What about CS?"

"No idea what happened. Jayne doesn't know. She said they were both black. She'd done a long SDR. Countersurveillance was there, but wrongly positioned, it seems."

"What about Jayne? Is she okay?" Now Veltman's voice sounded electrified as the reality sank in. "How the hell did this happen?"

"Jayne was almost taken out herself," Vic said. "But she got away and is on the run with Ed Grewall. We've got an exfil plan to get them out of Russia. But VULTURE suggested she try to speak to Pyotr Fradkov's wife first, on the basis she might know some of what her husband was going to tell us. She's apparently in Belgorod at her sister's place—Jayne and Ed are going there."

There was a pause. "So Jayne got some intel from VULTURE?"

"She got quite a lot," Vic said. "I don't have all the details, but it wasn't good news. For one, apparently, the damn Russians have got two very high-level assets in the West—and have had them for a long time."

"What assets in the West?" Veltman demanded. "First I've heard of it. On our side of the Atlantic? Not in the Agency, don't tell me that, dear God."

"We have no idea who or where, Arthur. VULTURE didn't know. But she believes that was the information Fradkov was going to pass on to us before he was killed. His wife now appears to be our last hope."

Vic paused. "I have to tell you there's more. The Kremlin is planning a full-scale invasion of Ukraine."

Veltman cursed again. "The president will just love this. It'll go down like a storm at the Berlin and Warsaw summits."

Vic passed a hand over his face.

"First we lose Fradkov," Veltman said, "and then we lose the best asset we've had inside Russia for years, decades. What the hell?"

Vic grimaced. "Well, Jayne is trying right now to salvage what we can from it. And we're changing the exfil to Belgorod accordingly."

"It had better work. She's no doubt got the entire FSB on her tail, and she's trying to reach the wife of a guy who's been taken out under our noses in London. She's got the odds stacked against her."

"So what do you want me to do?" Vic asked.

"I don't know. Sounds like everything depends on getting to Fradkov's wife and your exfil to work. But I know that if you and Jayne don't turn this around by the time Ferguson goes to Berlin and Warsaw, the president's reaction will not be predictable. I'll likely be out of a job. Possibly you too."

Vic exhaled. "You're right about one thing, Arthur. That was when you said the odds were stacked against her."

CHAPTER FIFTEEN

Thursday, September 29, 2016
Kursk

"We need to change this car," Jayne said as she steered the Toyota along the flat M2 highway, with a single lane in each direction, lined on both sides by sprawling agricultural fields.

Between them, she and Grewall had driven through the night for seven hours, taking turns to nap when they weren't driving. There was still at least another two hours to Belgorod, and they were now approaching the city of Kursk—the largest population center they had passed since leaving Moscow.

There were likely to be more police patrols now as the day shift officers came on duty, and maybe cameras too, as they drew closer to the city.

"We've been lucky to get away with it this far," Jayne continued. "But now it's getting much riskier."

"I agree," Grewall said. His face looked ashen in the early morning light.

"We need something that'll give us cover if we approach Maria's sister's house," Jayne said. "Something that won't arouse attention."

"What are you thinking?"

Jayne remained silent as she drove, trying to get her brain into gear. It was a battle against the fog of tiredness that was threatening to overwhelm her. "A delivery van, maybe. Or a utility vehicle, like an electricity or gas company truck. Or a builder's pickup."

"That could work."

They continued for another fifteen minutes. Now they were on the western fringes of Kursk, but the highway remained fairly unmodernized. The blacktop was worn and potholed in places, and there were no cameras visible. Jayne felt pleased they had avoided the toll roads farther north.

To the right of the highway ahead of them was a long rest area with picnic tables for drivers to stop and eat. There was only one vehicle parked there, a white Transit van marked with the purple-and-gray insignia of Rostelecom, which Jayne knew was one of the biggest state-owned phone companies in the country.

"What about that?" Jayne asked, slowing sharply as she approached the rest area. She pointed at the van.

"What? We take the van? Are you kidding?"

"Why not? We're in enough trouble as it is if we get caught. Might as well double down. We won't get pulled over by police driving that, would we? It won't raise any red flags if we go through a set of cameras."

Grewall grunted. "It will if it's reported stolen."

"Come on, Ed," Jayne said. "If we deal with the driver properly, it won't get reported stolen for hours. Enough time to get us to Belgorod and out again."

"What do you mean by deal with the driver?"

"Tie him up," Jayne said. "Leave him in the Toyota. Give

him some cash for the inconvenience. I remember Joe doing that once before in Russia."

She braked to a halt at the northern end of the rest area. The van was another fifty meters farther on.

There was silence for a couple of seconds. "All right," Grewall said. "Let's do it."

"Where shall we put the Toyota?"

Grewall pointed to a farm track just beyond the rest area that led into a large clump of trees. "We can dump it down there out of sight."

Jayne nodded, drove slowly toward the telecoms van, and parked a few meters behind it. She took her Walther from beneath her seat, racked the slide to chamber a round, and clicked off the safety. Grewall took his Beretta and a reel of duct tape from the glove compartment.

A solitary car hummed past on the highway, heading southward. A minute later, a large truck came the other way.

They both got out of the car and Jayne looked carefully in both directions. There was no more traffic. She glanced at Grewall, who nodded.

They walked together up to the van driver, dressed in a navy-blue company jacket, who had his back to them and was sipping a coffee he had poured from a flask. A half-eaten sandwich lay on the wooden picnic table.

"Excuse me, can you help us?" Jayne said in fluent Russian. She held her Walther unobtrusively at her waist but pointed it directly at the man.

He turned around and saw the gun, then noticed that Grewall was also holding a pistol. His eyes widened, and he dropped the coffee cup, which spilled over his jacket. "What are you doing?" His voice rose sharply, and he raised his hands reactively above his shoulders.

"I apologize for this," Jayne said. "But we need to borrow your van for a few hours."

"You can't take my van," the man spat. "I'm working." His eyes flitted between Jayne and Grewall, a note of panic in his voice.

"Just give me the keys," Grewall said, also in Russian. "Do it very slowly." He held out his hand.

The man looked at him, fury in his eyes. "You bastard. That's my van. That's my work. How I feed my family."

"You'll get the van back. And we'll give you some cash," Jayne said.

The man exhaled and rolled his eyes, a resigned look on his face. He lowered his right hand, dipped it into his pocket, and handed over his van keys to Grewall. He then raised his hand again.

"That's good," Jayne said. "Now, get in our car. I need you to look after it while we're using the van. And put your hands down, but keep them where we can see them." She didn't want to unnecessarily attract attention from passing motorists.

The man shook his head but stood, his shoulders droop-ing, and lowered his hands to his waist. He obviously knew he had no choice.

Jayne indicated with the barrel of her Walther toward the Toyota. "Get in. Front seat."

The man walked slowly to the Toyota. As he did so, a semitrailer chugged into view on the highway, belching black diesel smoke from its exhaust.

The van driver raised his hands right above his head again.

"Shit," Jayne snapped. "I said put your hands down and get in." She held her gun to her side, out of view of the passing truck.

The man lowered his hands again and got into the front seat.

Jayne climbed into the rear seat and jammed the muzzle of her Walther against the side of the van driver's head.

Grewall got into the driver's seat, started the engine, and drove slowly down the dusty farm track. The clump of trees lay about a hundred meters away on the left. He tucked the car in behind some bushes, out of sight of the highway.

A few minutes later, the driver was trussed up and gagged with duct tape in the trunk of the Toyota. Jayne pushed a bundle of rubles into his jacket pocket.

"I apologize," she said. "We'll have you released in a few hours." They would have to make an anonymous call to the police once they were safely in Ukraine.

The man grunted, unable to speak, and stared at her as she lowered the trunk lid and clicked it shut.

Jayne took her small backpack and the SARBE exfil transmitter from the car, while Grewall stuffed their other belongings into a plastic bag. He then locked the car and placed the keys on top of the front driver's side tire.

"Let's get the hell out of here," he said.

They walked back down the farm track to the rest area, where Grewall unlocked the van and they climbed into the cab, with Grewall behind the wheel. Two sets of clean coveralls, identical to those worn by the driver, were hanging on hooks behind the passenger seat. A pair of yellow safety helmets were in a cardboard box between the seats.

"Put the coveralls on," Jayne said. "We need to look the part."

Grewall nodded, grabbed one of the garments, and put it on. Jayne did likewise, although it felt at least two sizes too large for her, whereas Grewall's fitted perfectly.

"It'll do," she said.

"Good. Next stop, Belgorod," Grewall said as he started the engine, slipped the van into gear, and steered back onto the highway.

Two hours later, they turned into Ulitsa Mikrorayon, a street south of Belgorod on a recently built housing development, comprising apartment buildings on one side and large detached houses on the other.

"Shevchenko said it was on the corner of another street, Volnaya Ulitsa," Jayne said as she scanned the street ahead. "That's it." She pointed to a large, single-story, brick house with a brown-tiled roof, a garage, and a rear garden enclosed by a wooden fence. A black BMW station wagon was parked in the front driveway. Clearly, Maria Fradkova's sister was doing well enough, albeit not quite as well as her sibling, a billionaire by marriage.

The house looked no more than five years old, as did the other properties on Volnaya Ulitsa, a wide, tree-lined street with a grassy central island. Several of the cars parked on driveways were new. This was a neighborhood occupied by affluent professionals, unlike many of the run-down suburbs they had passed.

"Park in the street, next to the house," Jayne said. "We need to look like we're visiting on a proper telecoms job."

Grewall turned left into Volnaya Ulitsa and braked to a halt outside the property.

"Let's go," Jayne said. She grabbed a yellow protective helmet from the box and handed the other to Grewall.

* * *

Thursday, September 29, 2016
Moscow

The call from the MVD federal police duty desk at Gorky Park came as Pugachov was sitting in his office, sipping yet another black coffee, with a fresh pack of LDs next to him.

The desk officer passed on a report received from the regional police headquarters in Kursk, where a truck driver had reported a possible kidnapping or hijack at a rest stop west of the city. A man with his hands above his head, possibly the driver of a Rostelecom van, was being hustled into a gray Toyota.

Pugachov jerked up in his chair, despite a numbing tiredness that had left him struggling to think properly. After several hours of nothing, was this the breakthrough?

At last.

There was no license plate number for either the Toyota or the van, the officer said, but Pugachov didn't need one. This had to be Robinson and her colleague Grewall. Kursk was in the direction they had been traveling, and the timing fit with a drive from Moscow.

"Tell the desk in Kursk to do an urgent trace on the Toyota and the van," Pugachov snapped. "Arrest the woman and the man. We are heading there as soon as possible."

Of course, there had been zero sightings of the Toyota on traffic cameras since those near Vnukovo Airport on the M3 hours earlier, because there were no cameras farther west. Police patrols had also come up with nothing, probably because they were all tucked up in their stations for the night, likely swigging vodka. And now, it had come down to a passing truck driver who had his eyes open at the right time. This was typical.

He called Gurko to his room and quickly briefed him.

A minute later, another call came in. This time it was from the FSB team who had gone out in search of Maria Fradkova at her home in Moscow. After taking Maria's housekeeper into custody and applying some pressure, it emerged that she had traveled to Belgorod to stay with her sister Olga Sidorova for a few days. The team had the address.

Pugachov then made several more calls. The first was to the FSB's Aviation Department. He wanted a high-specification Mil Mi-8 attack helicopter, armed to the teeth with a machine gun and 57mm rockets, to be made ready on the octagonal helipad on top of the Lubyanka building to take him and Gurko to Belgorod. He calculated that if the pilot pushed the Mi-8, capable of doing more than 250 kilometers an hour, they should get there in just over three hours.

The second call was to the head of the FSB's regional directorate in Belgorod, Nikolai Zinichev, instructing him to have a car and driver ready to meet the helicopter on arrival at a point next to Maria's sister's house. Furthermore, Pugachov ordered that two armed backup units should surround and raid the house and arrest all occupants. A hunt should also be launched for the Rostelecom van that Robinson was suspected of stealing and the gray Toyota.

Pugachov then called Nikolai Sheymov and briefed him on developments. He put the phone on speaker so that Gurko could hear.

"I need to know what to do about that Vagnar sniper, Peskov, who took out Shevchenko," Pugachov said. "Do we have to take him with us to Belgorod?"

"No," Sheymov said. "I've had a message from the Kremlin telling me he won't be involved in this operation any further. They didn't say why."

"Good. What about Robinson and Grewall? Kill or arrest?"

"Preferably arrest. But if you can't, just do what you have to do," Sheymov said. "The president wants to make an example of them on television. He's planning to lock them up in Lefortovo, and he wants us to give them a grilling, a going-over. I'm looking forward to that. Bring them back here. That's plan A. But you're authorized to have a plan B, just in case."

Pugachov ended the call, then grabbed his coat and emergency travel bag. "Come on," he snapped at Gurko. "You heard what the boss said. Get your stuff. Let's go."

* * *

Thursday, September 29, 2016
  Moscow

Kira Suslova made her way to the temporary office that had
been allocated to Andrey Peskov on the ground floor of the
Senate Palace building at the Kremlin.

She closed the door and shook hands with Peskov.

"You did a good job with Operation Scorpion," Suslova
said, waving a file that she had been carrying. "*Suka*.
Shevchenko was a bitch. A traitorous bitch. Just bad news
about Robinson."

Peskov nodded in acknowledgment of the compliment
and indicated to her to sit on a small sofa that was placed
against a wall.

"A bitch indeed," he said as he sat opposite her in an
armchair. "You're correct. It was unfortunate about Robinson. She moved like lightning. It seems the FSB is still scram-
bling around trying to locate her."

Suslova nodded. "I have heard in the last ten minutes that
they have received some information. It seems Robinson may
be headed for Belgorod, where Pyotr Fradkov's wife, Maria, is
staying with her sister, apparently. Robinson will surely try to
speak to her."

Peskov sat up. "Really? Do you want me to go there and
finish the job?"

Suslova shook her head. "No. The FSB director assures
me that his men are on the case. Instead, I have another task
for you. Some preparation work for a backup plan in case the
FSB screws up again, which is likely."

"And what is that?"

Suslova had learned long ago that it was a good idea to be

ahead of the game in the Kremlin and to have plans B, C, and D ready in case there was a problem with plan A. It was a good way to take the credit for correcting other people's failings.

She opened the file she had brought, removed a sheet of paper, and handed it to Peskov. "Now, this is what I want you to do. Listen carefully."

Suslova began to rattle through a lengthy set of instructions.

CHAPTER SIXTEEN

Thursday, September 29, 2016
Belgorod

A slim woman with gray hair tied back in a ponytail stood in the door and looked alternately at Jayne and Grewall, an expression of distrust written across her bony face. "I'm not expecting any telephone people here."

"Are you Olga Sidorova?" Jayne asked in Russian. They had decided Jayne should lead the conversation initially to establish some woman-to-woman trust.

"I am."

"We are not telecoms engineers," Jayne said. "We're friends of your sister Maria's husband, Pyotr. I've come from London, and we work for the organization he was meant to be meeting there when he was killed." She indicated to Grewall next to her. "This is the colleague he was due to meet with. I understand Maria is here, and we would like to speak to her, urgently."

Olga took a step backward and her eyes darted right and left, scanning the street. "You're telling me you're CIA?" she asked.

She knows.

Jayne gave a slight nod, fully aware as she did so how much of a risk she was taking. But there was no alternative.

Olga scrutinized both of their faces, her expression saying she was having difficulty deciding what to do next.

"I promise you, we were on Pyotr's side, and we're on Maria's side," Jayne said.

"You realize you might get us both killed," Olga said. "Or at least thrown in prison. You're impersonating telephone engineers, and you're spies. If the FSB come here, we're all finished."

A voice came from behind Olga. "Who might get us killed?"

A woman appeared who had a similar bony face as Olga, but with her hair hanging down. This was, without question, Maria.

Olga turned to her. "These two say they're CIA, who Pyotr was meant to have met in London."

Maria stared at them. "Are you? And how are you going to prove that? Do you have some ID?"

Jayne nodded. "We have ID. I assume you're Maria, and I'm very sorry for what happened to your husband. I'm Jayne Robinson, and this is Ed Grewall. We're taking a risk coming here, we realize that, but we need to speak to you."

"And what makes you think I want to talk about my husband?" Maria asked. There was a more than slightly hostile edge to her voice.

Now Jayne could feel her anxiety levels rising. They had already been standing on Olga's doorstep for a few minutes. The longer they remained there, the more likely they would be spotted by a neighbor or passerby. Informing to the police or the FSB about anything or anyone unusual was still a reflexive instinct among many Russians who had grown up during the Soviet era.

Maria glanced sideways at her sister, who gave a faint nod.

"You can have two minutes," Olga said. "But first prove who you are."

Jayne took out her phone, tapped on her secure documents app, keyed in a passcode, and showed the two women a scan of her genuine British passport. Grewall did likewise with his US passport.

Maria stood, hands on hips. She gave a curt nod. "All right."

"Can we go somewhere safe to talk?" Jayne asked. "I don't mean inside the house, as I believe there's a chance your security forces, the FSB, might turn up here. I don't want to talk in our van either, as that may have hidden microphones. Can we drive somewhere safer and talk in the open air? Or can we talk in your car?"

The two sisters exchanged glances again.

Olga put a hand on her sister's shoulder. "You can't talk in the car, Maria. I suspect it has also been bugged. Everything is bugged in this country. And she might be correct about the FSB coming here, and—"

"Can we go somewhere a little farther south toward the Ukraine border?" Jayne interrupted. "We might need to get across it in a hurry—a helicopter is coming for us. The closer we are, the better."

Again, the sisters looked at each other.

"What about the lane at the back of the White Bullet?" Maria asked her sister eventually. "It is secluded, and away from the highway."

Olga nodded. "Good thinking."

"What is the White Bullet?" Jayne asked.

"A restaurant about twelve kilometers from here, toward

the border. There is a narrow lane at the back of it, past some woodland. We can park there out of sight and talk among the trees."

"Is the land flat, so a helicopter could land to fetch us?"

Maria nodded. "It is very flat, yes. Farm fields."

Jayne looked at Olga. "Could we follow you in our van first? We borrowed it, so I don't want to leave it here, as it will likely land you in trouble. Can we dump it somewhere, then you take us the rest of the way?"

"Yes. There's a hotel and a restaurant on the way with a big parking lot. We'll leave the van there."

"Good," Jayne said. "You and Maria can leave us at the helicopter pickup point after we have spoken. We will then need to get out, fast."

Jayne paused as a thought crossed her mind. "Before we leave, do you have any of your husband's electronic devices, his laptop or phone? They were gone from the house where he was killed in London."

Maria shook her head. "Nothing like that. He kept no work papers at home either. I would let you see them if I did. The Kremlin probably has them now."

"I'm sure that's true. I had to ask."

Olga nodded. "Wait. I will get the car keys."

She disappeared into the house, then returned a few seconds later. "Follow us," she said.

* * *

Thursday, September 29, 2016
Belgorod

.   .   .

The Mil Mi-8 attack helicopter clattered southeast, helped by a strong tailwind that propelled it at high speed east of the city of Kursk.

Pugachov glanced to his right at the Kord 12.7mm heavy machine gun mounted in the specially widened starboard-side door. At the front, there were also two forward-firing UPK-23-250 pods with rapid-fire GSh-23 twin-barrel guns.

On both sides of the helicopter, the starboard- and port-side stub wings each carried launchers holding four AT-6 Spiral semiautomatic radio-command anti-tank missiles with an effective range of about five kilometers.

This helicopter, specifically requested by Pugachov, had been acquired by the FSB from the Russian military and had previously seen service in Chechnya and against Islamic terrorist groups in the troubled North Caucasus region.

It was a fearsome machine whose shape always reminded Pugachov of a giant hornet.

Not long after the FSB chopper crossed the regional border from Kursk oblast into Belgorod oblast, flying at only a thousand feet, a call came in for Pugachov on the secure radio. The caller was Nikolai Zinichev, head of the FSB's regional directorate for Belgorod.

"Sir, our armed units have just raided Olga Sidorova's house," Zinichev said.

"Do you have them all in custody?" Pugachov snapped.

"No, unfortunately not. The house was empty. No car in the driveway. No sign of your targets."

"Well, find them," Pugachov ordered. "Question the neighbors. Ask if they've seen the Rostelecom van."

"We're doing that right now," Zinichev said.

"By the time we arrive, I want those targets located, and I want the GPS coordinates," Pugachov said. "We will fly directly to them and give them an experience they won't forget."

"Yes, sir. One of my teams has found the driver of the van, however," Zinichev added. "He was tied up in the trunk of the gray Toyota, which we found near Kursk."

"Good work," Pugachov said. "Now do the rest."

"Sir, I will call you immediately if we have any update," Zinichev said.

"Do that," Pugachov said. He ended the call.

CHAPTER SEVENTEEN

Thursday, September 29, 2016
Belgorod

Olga parked her BMW off the heavily potholed single-track lane and switched off the engine. She signaled to Jayne, who was sitting in the rear seat with Grewall, to get out of the car.

Jayne did as asked. She hadn't spoken a word since they had left the Rostelecom van in the parking lot of the Rezidentsiya hotel, about three kilometers south of Olga's house. Hopefully, if the van was found there by the FSB, it might trigger a search of the hotel and buy them some extra time.

To Jayne's relief, the land here was indeed flat, as Maria had said. It would make it easy for the exfil helicopter to land. However, the downside was that apart from a wooded ridge on the horizon, there were few hills to shelter an incoming chopper from radar scanners.

Jayne removed the SARBE exfil locator transmitter from her backpack and handed it to Grewall, who activated it to send their precise location to the Chuhuiv Air Base near

Kharkiv, seventy-five kilometers south, where the Ukrainian Air Force team responsible for the exfil should pick it up. The device operated on a 406 megahertz frequency, using short, random-burst encrypted transmissions, which ensured a very low probability of detection.

While he was doing that, Jayne sent an encrypted message to Vic.

Confirm exfil ASAP. Getting briefing from target now. Have activated location transmitter.

The exfil arrangement had been put together by Vic's team together with Valentin Marchenko, a Marlboro-smoking man with a gray goatee who was an assistant director of the Foreign Intelligence Service of Ukraine, the SZR. Jayne and Grewall had both worked with Marchenko on a previous operation that had also involved Joe Johnson.

The arrangement with the SZR was in part a quid pro quo in return for the extensive range of weaponry, military equipment, and training that the United States had provided to Ukraine, including Javelin anti-tank missiles, Firefinder missile detection radar, Humvee armored vehicles, and night-vision goggles.

Jayne walked with Maria, Olga, and Grewall into the thick trees, where she and Grewall both removed their Rostelecom coveralls and pushed them under a bush.

Then they all stood in a small circle. It was hardly a relaxed situation, but they had little option. "What do you want to know?" Maria said. "And how did you know I was with my sister?"

Before Jayne could answer, her phone vibrated in her pocket. She took it out and read the incoming secure message from Vic.

Exfil confirmed. ETA 18 minutes. Be ready. Good luck.

Jayne pushed the phone into her pocket and folded her arms. "We were told to come here by someone I believe you know, and who your husband knew—Anastasia Shevchenko."

"Anastasia Shevchenko?" There was a note of confusion in Maria's voice. "But she's from the SVR. You've spoken to her . . . how?"

"She was a source of mine," Jayne said.

"A source? Was?"

Jayne paused for a couple of seconds. "Unfortunately, she's also been killed. Shot by someone from your Russian security services last night, just as I was speaking with her."

"Oh my God," Maria's eyes widened. "Another one. She was one of the better people who interviewed me, quite easy-going. She let me go, eventually." She glanced sideways at her sister, who was clasping her hands tight together.

"I desperately want to get to the bottom of all this," Jayne said. "The key to it all is what your husband wanted to tell us. So do you know what he wanted to say? Did he confide in you?"

Maria grimaced and looked down at the ground. Jayne thought she was going to burst into tears, but she gathered herself.

"He told me very little," Maria said. "It was better I knew nothing, he thought, because that way I wouldn't get into trouble. He had a secretive life. He was a businessman, yes, but he behaved like a spy much of the time."

There was a certain edge to her voice, a definite note of something that sounded like dislike or contempt.

Jayne felt a spike of anxiety. "Did he not say anything about the Kremlin having spies in Western intelligence services, or who was handling them? Or about an operation to invade Ukraine?"

Maria fiddled with the strands of hair that were hanging down to her chest. "I got no details, though I was vaguely aware. I overheard things."

Jayne rocked back on her heels. Was this tortuous trip to Belgorod going to be a complete waste of time?

"Your husband was a businessman," Jayne said. "He didn't work for the FSB, or the SVR, and wasn't in the Kremlin. So how did he get this information?"

"From someone he was close to—but shouldn't have been close to." Maria shook her head as she spoke.

"Who?"

"A woman at the Kremlin. One of Putin's puppets. Kira Suslova."

"He got that information from her? How?" Jayne's initial reaction was one of surprise.

Maria's face crumpled, and she closed her eyes briefly, as if in pain. "Because he was having an affair with her."

There was a brief silence. Jayne could almost feel the embarrassment radiating from Maria.

"I'm sorry to hear that," Jayne said. "It must have been very difficult. Can I ask how it started?" Perhaps Pyotr had been carrying out espionage work for the Kremlin after all and was planning to operate as a double agent in the West.

"Was he working for her?" Grewall asked, a distinctly cynical note in his voice. Clearly, he was thinking the same as Jayne.

"I don't think so. Not in the sense you mean, no," Maria replied. "Not spying for Moscow."

"Then how?"

"Chess." Maria almost spat the word. "They played each other at chess. That's how it started. They are, or were, both very good chess players."

Jayne and Grewall remained silent.

"I tried to stop the affair many times, but he just continued," Maria said, again looking at the ground. "To be honest, I should have left him a long time ago, but here in Russia it's not so easy, and he had a huge amount of money to make life difficult for me if he chose to do so. I know she was confiding in him, because I saw messages that I shouldn't have seen."

"All right. So, despite being very close to Putin's right-hand woman, Pyotr decided to leak information to us. Why?"

"He secretly hated Putin, for multiple reasons. First, he didn't like what Putin's done to our country, even though he became incredibly wealthy because of that man. That's one reason."

"That's a motivation," Jayne said.

"Yes. But there is another. Putin has also been close to Suslova for a long time. They go a long way back. I know he is an admirer of Suslova—likely more than just an admirer. And recently, Putin was trying to force Pyotr to sell his stake in MetroPhone to Suslova at a large discount. It was robbery, quite honestly. Pyotr refused."

Jayne nodded. It sounded like a common tactic by the Russian leader. "So Putin was trying to win favor with Suslova? It was a gift of sorts?"

"I believe so."

"And would that be a motivation for Pyotr to turn traitor against Putin?"

"Of course."

A thought occurred to Jayne. "Would Putin have known about the affair?"

Maria shook her head. "I doubt it. Suslova is still standing, isn't she?"

Jayne nodded. That made sense.

"But there is a third reason Pyotr came to you," Maria said. "Our son and daughter both live in Kharkiv, not too far over the border from here. If Putin invades Ukraine, as seems likely, they'll be in the firing line."

"They wouldn't return in that case?" Jayne asked.

Maria shook her head. "Like many young people here, they don't like Putin. That's why they left. We let them go. A few years ago, there was little difference between the two countries, but Ukraine is a very different place than Russia these days. Forward-thinking, modernizing, increasingly Europe-oriented. The young people like it. There's no future for them here, and Pyotr and I know that, deep down. If we weren't so tied to Russia, we'd have gone too. But Pyotr's wealth stemmed from Putin's patronage. If he turned against us, all that would disappear."

What Maria was saying about their children corroborated what Shevchenko had suggested might be Pyotr's likely motivation.

"So do you believe that Suslova somehow found out that Pyotr was going to give us the information?" Jayne asked.

"I believe so," Maria said.

"And then she had him killed?" Grewall asked.

Maria gave a slight nod and clasped her face in her hands. "That would make it easier for her to get her hands on MetroPhone too. I am not in a position to stop her against Putin's wishes."

"Bloody hell." Jayne felt a spike of adrenaline rush through her. She guessed that Suslova, despite their affair, would have put surveillance on Pyotr twenty-four hours a day the minute she developed the slightest suspicion.

Jayne folded her arms again. "So to get the answers to our questions, and to get what Pyotr was going to tell us, we need to get them out of his source, his killer, who you're telling me is probably Suslova."

Maria shrugged. "I can't see any other way."

"Any suggestions about how we get to her?" Jayne felt suddenly despondent. With Shevchenko alive and operating inside Moscow, they might have had a chance, albeit a slim one. With her dead, that was no longer an option.

Maria gave a short, sarcastic laugh. "You won't get to Suslova. Never. Not in Russia. She's a professional, a hard woman. She's Putin's protégé. They're out of the same KGB school."

"So what, then?" Jayne asked.

"You'll have to get her to come to you somehow. Get her to come to the West, and then find a way to apply leverage."

"How can we do that?"

"I do not know."

There was silence for a few seconds.

Bloody hell.

Jayne exhaled in frustration. "All right. Thank you, Maria. This has been more helpful than you realize. Let me take your phone number and email in case I need to contact you, and perhaps your sister's details too, just in case. And I will give you my details in case you think of anything else you think is worth telling me—especially regarding any leverage over Suslova that you might recall later."

She tapped the details into her phone as the two women recited them and then gave them each a scrap of paper with the number of a burner phone, but not her name.

Jayne glanced at her watch, then at Grewall. "We must let these two go now. They've been here long enough."

She took a step forward and shook Olga's hand, then held hers out to shake Maria's.

But Maria just stood there. "Can I come with you? I've been through hell here. I want to get out of Russia, but they won't let me go. And if they find out I've been helping you, I'll be sent to Lefortovo. Killed, most likely."

Jayne hesitated. She should have expected this. "Where will you go?"

"My children are in Kharkiv. I have nothing left in Russia apart from possessions and money. They don't matter—not anymore."

Jayne pointed toward Olga. "What about your sister?"

Maria looked at Olga, who held out her hands, palms up.

"I'm in a different situation," Olga said. "My husband hasn't been targeted by the Kremlin. And my children are here, not in Ukraine. I couldn't go, although I would like to."

Jayne calculated quickly. There should be room on the chopper. "Do you have a passport with you?" Jayne asked.

Maria shook her head. "The FSB confiscated it. They don't want me to leave the country."

There seemed no option.

"All right, Maria, you can come," Jayne said. "Olga, you'd better leave quickly. Get back to your house and get your head down."

Olga placed both her hands on her sister's shoulders, then hugged her hard. "If you want to go, then go. Be with your kids. Be free. I'll see you soon, I'm sure. I love you, sister."

The four of them walked out of the trees toward the BMW. Olga and Maria hugged again, then Olga climbed into the driver's seat. A moment later, she had disappeared out of sight down the lane.

Then, suddenly, there came the distant and faint but unmistakable high-speed clattering of a helicopter engine.

Jayne stood still, listening and scanning the sky ahead of them toward the Ukraine border to the south.

"Where the hell's that coming from?" Grewall asked.

It was then that Jayne realized.

"Shit. It's behind us," she yelled as she turned around. "Get back in the bloody trees."

* * *

Thursday, September 29, 2016
Belgorod

. . .

The Mil Mi-8 helicopter swept south of Belgorod and banked to the left in a long sweep of the stretch of mainly flat countryside sandwiched between the city and the Ukrainian border.

"We stay in this area," Pugachov ordered the FSB pilot over his intercom. "We sweep this territory until we get a positive ID from the ground team."

"*Da*. Roger," the pilot said.

Pugachov's gut feeling was that they needed to be somewhere in this location, ready to pounce if their targets were spotted on the ground. He assumed Robinson and Grewall would try to get across the border, either by land or by air, once they had reached Maria Fradkova, and this was the nearest obvious point.

He looked out the window as the chopper slowed and hovered. Below was a stretch of woodland and a single-track road that passed through fields to the M2 highway that ran south to the Ukraine border. He tried to get his bearings. "What's that building down there with the parking lot?" Pugachov asked the pilot.

"The White Bullet restaurant, sir," the pilot responded.

Pugachov's secure phone rang. It was Zinichev again.

"Sir, we have eyes on Olga Sidorova's BMW. It's near the house, sir. A patrol spotted it and a surveillance car is pursuing it right now. We're assuming Sidorova and her sister are in the vehicle. We have also located the stolen Rostelecom van in a hotel parking lot near the house."

"Good work," Pugachov said. "Any sign of Robinson and Grewall?"

"We think they're not in the BMW, sir. Unless they are hidden in the trunk or on the floor out of sight. We're searching the hotel."

"Detain the women and check. We need to know where Robinson is, urgently—we will get the women to tell us. We will track back in the chopper and land near the house. I can do the interrogation when I arrive."

"Understood, sir," Zinichev said.

Pugachov ended the call and barked instructions to the pilot to head to Olga Sidorova's property on Volnaya Ulitsa in Belgorod.

CHAPTER EIGHTEEN

Thursday, September 29, 2016
Belgorod

Jayne, Grewall, and Maria ducked down behind a large bush as the helicopter roared low over the woodland, then banked off to the east toward the White Bullet, its engines throbbing. This was definitely not their exfil aircraft.

She looked at Grewall. "Has to be FSB or police."

He nodded but said nothing.

The helicopter slowed and began to hover a few hundred meters away, somewhere near the M2 highway. This was not a good sign. Jayne braced herself for any indication that it was going to land nearby, images of a shootout in the woodland going through her mind.

But moments later, the chopper moved off northeast, back toward Belgorod.

Grewall checked the locator transmitter.

"Working okay?" Jayne asked. She glanced at her watch. More than sixteen minutes had passed since Vic had given her the eighteen-minute estimated arrival time for the exfil helicopter.

"Yes, all good."

Jayne left unspoken her fear of what might happen if the exfil chopper arrived while the Russian aircraft was still in the vicinity.

But over to the east, the sound of the Russian helicopter grew fainter as it moved away.

Jayne again checked her watch.

The exfil was due right now.

Immediately ahead of them was a patchwork quilt of arable wheat fields of the type that were ubiquitous in Ukraine—the breadbasket of Eastern Europe. Grain from here was shipped all over the world.

The harvest had been brought in several weeks ago, and most of the fields now comprised just short, golden stubble where the combine harvesters had done their work. To the right was a long, broad strip of brown land that had already been plowed.

On the far skyline, where the land rose in a ridge, was another area of dense woodland. A line of high-voltage electricity pylons ran east to west across the fields, parallel with the ridge and the horizon.

Suddenly, Jayne caught the faint sound of another helicopter.

"Hear that?" she murmured to Grewall.

He gave a slight nod, then pointed south. "There. Just come over the ridge."

Jayne squinted and stared, and then finally she saw it. A black speck was briefly visible against the sky as it flew over the ridge to the south. It then dropped and flew against the backdrop of the brown plowed strip below the horizon. It was only visible because it was moving, drawing rapidly closer at high speed.

She walked out from behind the bushes, followed by the other two, keeping her eyes on the helicopter.

"Bloody hell, it's low," she said.

"Avoiding the radar," Grewall said.

The aircraft was heading directly toward them, guided by the precision transmitter Grewall was holding.

Jayne watched as it climbed a little, vaulted over the electricity pylons, then dropped back down to what looked like an altitude of no more than fifty feet as it hammered toward them.

"Let's get out there," Grewall said.

Jayne followed him across the lane and onto the stubbled field beyond.

The chopper finally slowed to a hover about a hundred meters away and slowly descended. The downwash from its rotors blew clouds of dust and wheat chaff in all directions.

The chopper settled on the field. As Jayne had expected, it was a Mil Mi-24 Hind attack helicopter, built by the Russians but widely used by the Ukraine military. The aircraft's hull was painted in a desert tan-and-green camouflage pattern, but Jayne could not see any identification markings. There were rocket launchers beneath each stub wing and what looked like a Yak-B Gatling machine gun protruding from beneath the front cockpit.

Immediately, the hydraulic cabin door to the rear passenger compartment swung open and a man wearing a khaki uniform and peaked cap jumped down, holding a rifle. He ran straight toward Jayne, Grewall, and Maria, who walked to meet him.

"Ed Grewall, Jayne Robinson?" he asked.

"Yes," Jayne confirmed. Grewall did likewise.

"I am Petro. Ukraine army military intelligence. Copilot of this chopper." He pointed at Maria. "Who's this? I was told to expect two, not three."

"Maria Fradkova. She's just given us crucial help with our exfil and is providing much important intel. She needs to come with us—her life is at risk if she stays. I assume you have room on the chopper?"

A look of annoyance crossed Petro's face. "If necessary. But you need to warn us in advance about these things. You can't just start bringing extra people ad hoc."

Grewall nodded and held up the transmitter. "We apologize. But thank you. You found us," he said.

"Come, quickly," the officer said in stilted English. "We must go."

He turned and jogged back to the helicopter, Jayne, Grewall, and Maria close behind him. He then waited as Jayne clambered onto the step. Another khaki-clad officer hauled each of them up into the surprisingly large rear compartment, which had two rows of bench seats facing back-to-back.

"Sit next to each other. Fasten your seat belts," the officer said. He picked up three wireless headsets with microphones and handed one to each of them. "In case we need to talk."

Petro climbed into the chopper and pushed a button that closed the door.

Immediately, the engine volume rose as the pilot increased the revs.

The second officer took a seat next to Jayne, Grewall, and Maria as they strapped themselves in.

Petro walked through a narrow central gangway that joined the cabin and the passenger compartment and took a seat next to the pilot. Both were visible from where Jayne was sitting. She knew from her experience as an MI6 officer in Afghanistan, where she had helped the Afghans to shoot down Russian Mi-24s with Stinger missiles, that the copilot also acted as the front machine gun operator.

The engines cranked up another few notches, and the

chopper began to move forward across the stubble field. The rear of the aircraft rose a little off the ground, the nose tilted forward, and then they were airborne.

The Mi-24 accelerated with surprising speed for such a large helicopter and headed back directly south, the way it had come, so low that Jayne felt they were almost touching the ground.

Jayne felt the aircraft lift as they vaulted the power lines. Then, as it settled back down again, a loud triple beep came over the headset.

"We have company," a voice said in her ear, presumably the pilot's. "Ahead of us, eleven o'clock. Three hundred feet higher."

Jayne heard Petro swear in Ukrainian, and she was suddenly pushed back hard into her seat as the chopper accelerated.

She glanced out the port windows, which her seat faced toward, but could see nothing.

"Who is it?" Jayne asked.

"Russian Mi-8 chopper," Petro replied. "Probably FSB."

Shit.

"We saw a chopper earlier," Grewall said through his headset. "It circled near where you picked us up, then headed off east. Might be the same one. Probably looking for us."

"We are a lot faster than an Mi-8," Petro said. "But we have to get past it first."

He paused. "It's coming down at us. We may have to take it on. Brace yourselves. We're going up."

Jayne grabbed the vertical steel pole that held the seats in position as the helicopter climbed sharply and banked to the port side, leaving her stomach feeling as though it had been left behind.

Suddenly, there came a low-pitched rat-tat-tat from the front of the chopper.

Jayne leaned forward and peered down the gangway to the cockpit. Petro was hunched forward, concentrating intensely, firing his front Gatling gun.

But then, above the noise of the Gatling and the Mi-24's twin engines, Jayne heard a series of loud thuds from the front of the aircraft.

The helicopter juddered and there came a loud whistling and a rush of air through the cabin.

There was no mistaking what had just happened.

"*Layno*. Shit," Petro yelled. "We have been hit."

Then came more thuds, followed by a sharp crack at the front of the chopper. The Mi-24 lurched to the port side and tilted at an angle of about forty-five degrees, leaving Jayne feeling as though she was falling out of her seat into an abyss.

Two large holes were visible in the windshield in front of the copilot, with cracks stretching out in all directions like a spiderweb.

* * *

Thursday, September 29, 2016
    Belgorod

"Got the *bljad*, the sonofabitch," the copilot of the FSB Mil Mi-8 said over the intercom. "I hit his cockpit."

"Good. Now finish the job. Take him down," Pugachov said, his voice level and unemotional. "Fire again. We've got one chance."

"As soon as I can," the copilot said.

The pilot banked to port and headed straight for the larger Ukrainian Mi-24, which was no more than three hundred meters away.

As soon as his chopper was on an even keel, the copilot,

sitting next to the pilot, reached forward. Using the nose-mounted GSh-23 twin-barrel guns, he again opened fire on the aircraft that Pugachov was convinced contained Jayne Robinson and Edward Grewall.

"Got him again," the copilot said. And indeed, the Mi-24 did appear to yaw a little to starboard now.

But then the target chopper immediately recovered and launched into a high-speed dive that took it back down to treetop level. It headed off in a southerly direction, toward Ukraine.

"Chase the bastard," Pugachov urged, his voice rising sharply. "Don't let him get away."

Pugachov knew that the larger helicopter could outrun the Mi-8, given the chance, as it was simply faster. The only hope they had of taking it down was to hit it hard and quickly.

They had received an urgent radio call from military air traffic control in Belgorod ten minutes earlier, reporting that a helicopter had crossed the border from Ukraine into Russian airspace. It was traveling at high speed and at very low altitude. For that reason, it only registered on the Belgorod radar screens at a late stage.

Instinctively, Pugachov knew this was an exfil operation to get Robinson and Grewall out of the country. He had ordered the pilot to abort the landing he was about to carry out at an open space near Olga Sidorova's house, where her black BMW was now parked, together with two FSB cars. Officers were holding Olga inside the house but reported that there was no sign of Maria Fradkova.

Pugachov could only assume that Maria was with Robinson and Grewall and was about to flee the country.

They'd flown back at top speed toward the M2 and the White Bullet restaurant, where air traffic control reported the Ukrainian helicopter to have headed. En route, the air traffic controller told them that the target chopper had dropped off the radar screen altogether for about two minutes, presumably when it was picking up its passengers.

"Can we use the missiles?" Pugachov asked as he craned his neck from the seats in the rear compartment, trying to get a glimpse of the chopper they were pursuing.

"They're anti-tank guided missiles. But with a bit of luck, they could work against a chopper—if we get a hit, they'll take him down for sure."

Pugachov nodded. "Do it."

"Of course, sir."

The pilot followed the Mi-24 into a steep dive.

As soon as the larger chopper was in his sights, there was a flash from beneath the stub wings on either side as the copilot unleashed four of his AT-6 Spiral guided missiles, two from each wing.

Pugachov watched as the missiles streaked toward their target, now about a kilometer ahead.

* * *

Thursday, September 29, 2016
Belgorod

"Incoming missiles," said the copilot over the intercom. "Get over the ridge. Fast."

It seemed to Jayne that the Mi-24 virtually scraped the trees as it hauled itself over the wooded ridge, then went into a shallow dive on the other side and simultaneously banked sharply to starboard in a bid to avoid being hit. Now they were over a railway line, the M2 highway to their port side.

There was a continual, extremely loud whistling noise from the two holes in the cockpit windshield.

Jayne again clung to the pole with her left hand and the edge of the seat with her right. She glanced sideways at Maria, who was hanging on desperately to a pole on the other side, her knuckles white, sweat droplets visible on her forehead.

A second later, there was an audible whoosh from above, like a small jet had just flown past. Jayne guessed it was the missiles.

"Bastards have missed us," Petro said. "Thank God for the ridge. Now run for it."

"Going to stay at low level," the pilot said. "We're well ahead of them now. They won't get eyes on us down here. Not too much farther to go now."

The chopper straightened, then accelerated again and hammered on south, still at little more than treetop level. It tracked the railway line for a short distance, then passed over more plowed fields and a village.

Jayne's stomach felt as though it was located somewhere in her throat. She hoped that the pilot was correct and the immediate danger was past. She had to admire his skill. Despite the damage up front, he had kept his aircraft under total control.

A few minutes later, Petro's voice came over the intercom again. "We're over the border."

"Will he try to chase us into Ukraine?" Jayne asked.

"He can try. He will regret it," Petro said. "Our air force is on standby. He'll be a sitting duck for our fighter jets. But anyway, he's not fast enough. This old girl can do over three hundred and thirty clicks an hour. The Mi-8s are a hundred kilometers an hour slower."

Not long after, Jayne felt a tap on her shoulder from the officer sitting next to her.

"That's Kharkiv," he said, pointing to starboard. "Chuhuiv Air Base is five minutes."

Jayne gave him a thumbs-up.

Sure enough, the helicopter continued southeast, then slowed to a crawl soon after. It hovered and descended slowly to the Chuhuiv helicopter landing pad, next to the main apron. A row of other Mil-24s stood nearby.

As the chopper's doors opened, Jayne exhaled vigorously in relief. Next to her, Grewall gave a thumbs-up and then squeezed her wrist. Maria was looking more than a little worse for wear, sweat dripping off her forehead and her skin ashen.

Jayne grabbed her backpack and followed Grewall, Maria, and the officer out of the helicopter. By this stage, she felt so tired that it seemed as though her head was enveloped in a kind of fog.

Grewall, who looked as drained as she felt, caught her eye. "Are you all right?" he asked.

She shook her head. "Not really."

Jayne knew she was functioning purely on adrenaline, and there was a certainty that quite soon, now that she was out of Russia, she was going to simply cut out.

She hardly noticed the pale September sun, veiled a little by hazy cloud, that greeted them as they walked across the apron to the small terminal building. To their right, a row of Ukrainian military fighter jets was parked, awaiting action.

Another white-knuckle trip to Russia was over. This time, it had left her feeling more than a little bereft.

Yes, she had gained information and a lead from Maria. However, she had no clue where she would start in trying to gain access to Kira Suslova, let alone obtain the kind of leverage that she needed.

And in the debit column, she felt she had lost the CIA's biggest asset in Moscow for many, many years.

Anastasia Shevchenko was completely irreplaceable in terms of asset value. But beyond that, Jayne felt that she had developed a real bond with the Russian from the encounters she'd had with her. She recognized a kindred spirit in her—a high-class, relentless operative but with a human touch.

The image of Shevchenko's body, blown apart next to her on that bench in Moscow, was one that she knew would never leave her.

How she was going to begin to explain it to Vic Walter was quite beyond her. She still didn't even know what had happened.

Petro led her, Grewall, and Maria through the chipped, dirty double doors that led into the terminal building.

The terminal appeared straight out of the Soviet era, where it had belonged until 1991 when Ukraine won its independence after the old USSR was dismantled. The decor looked fifty years old, the walls were filthy, and the tiled floor was cracked.

But the difference was that this was Ukraine, a country where the leadership valued the personal freedom of its citizens, not Russia, where quite the opposite applied. It was a friend to the United States and the UK, not an enemy.

What a difference a few kilometers of land could make.

Jayne took out her phone and tapped out a short, secure message to confirm that she had arrived safely in Ukraine along with Grewall and Maria Fradkova. At last, she had at least some good news for Vic.

She knew that Vic and President Ferguson would now be in Kyiv, the capital of the country in which she was now standing, for their meeting the following day with President Pavlo Doroshenko.

Maria caught Jayne's eye. She was looking a little better now. "Thank you," she said. "You don't know how much it means to me to have got out."

"I can imagine," Jayne said. "I've been in tight spots in Russia several times."

There was something that had crossed Jayne's mind during the flight, but she hadn't had a chance to ask Maria until now. "You probably tried to keep an eye on your husband's phone calls, given the circumstances," she said. "Did you ever see a phone number for Suslova by any chance?"

Maria smiled for the first time since they had left Belgorod. "Actually, yes. I did. I went to some trouble to get it. I thought it might be useful if things turned nasty with my husband." She took out her phone, scrolled through her directory, and showed it to Jayne, who tapped it into her own phone.

"Thank you."

Maria nodded. "There is one other thing I thought to mention now," she said, stroking her chin. "I've been thinking of anything else helpful I could give you. There was a conversation I overheard my husband having with someone a few months ago. I suspected it was with Kira Suslova just because of the familiar way he was speaking. They were discussing how to pay someone. I don't know who or what for. But I heard him suggesting money should be taken from the chess account. He didn't clarify what he meant, but the caller obviously knew."

"The chess account?" Jayne asked.

Maria shrugged. "That's what he said. I'm sure he meant a bank account."

"Interesting. What do you think it might be?"

"It was the first time I'd heard him refer to it, and I don't know what it is. But as I told you, I do know that Suslova was big in the chess world, and he often played her at chess."

Jayne's thoughts flashed back to what Shevchenko had told her about Suslova plotting to secure the FIDE president's role.

Jayne touched Maria's arm. "Thank you. Your information

has been very useful. Now we need to arrange for you to see your children—you've got a lot to discuss."

Her phone vibrated in her pocket as a message arrived. She took it out to find a reply from Vic.

Good to hear. Pls fly direct to Kyiv. Need you for Doroshenko meeting tomorrow and for debriefs with me and Ferguson.

Jayne closed her eyes momentarily. Vic would have to wait for a while. She needed to sleep.

When she opened them, a man with a graying goatee was standing in the doorway. She recognized him immediately. It was Valentin Marchenko, assistant director of the Foreign Intelligence Service of Ukraine, the SZR.

The last time Jayne had seen him had been more than two years earlier in Athens, when she, Vic, and Joe Johnson held a covert meeting with him before another undercover operation into Russia. The actual operation primarily involved Joe rather than her, but he hadn't changed much. He still had a Marlboro stuck between his lips, as she remembered, and a pen in his shirt breast pocket like a taxi driver.

"Jayne," he said, taking a step in her direction. "Good to see you."

"Valentin," she said. "I wasn't expecting an SZR reception committee. Good to see you too." She introduced Maria and Grewall.

Marchenko shook her hand, but the thin smile on his face didn't last for long.

"We need to get you out of here," he said to Maria. "The Kremlin's tentacles spread far in this part of Eastern Ukraine. You're not safe, even over the border. There are pro-Putin separatist militias, some of whom have Russian military backing. We have a safe house for you."

"But my children are in Kharkiv," Maria said.

"We know that. We'll arrange for them to come to you."

Marchenko beckoned to Jayne. "Come. I'm taking you all

to Kyiv. We have a private jet waiting." He pointed to a Cessna a hundred meters farther down the apron. "We need to make sure you're at the meeting with Doroshenko tomorrow, Jayne."

"You know about that meeting?" Jayne asked.

Marchenko nodded. "Of course. I'll be at it."

CHAPTER NINETEEN

Friday, September 30, 2016
  Cape Idokopas, Russia

The sun was close to setting across the Black Sea to the west as Kira Suslova strolled across the marble terrace to the white stone balustrade that bordered it. A shimmering pathway of gold ran across the water from the western horizon to the beach below her.

Putin's Palace, as she always thought of it, was a place of dreams. When here, she sometimes thought back to the drabness and poverty of Dresden in the 1980s when she and the president had first met and worked together as lowly intelligence officers.

The low point had come in December 1989 when they were targeted in their local KGB offices by East German protesters. The protest, a few weeks after the fall of the Berlin Wall and the beginning of the end for the Soviet Union, had eventually dispersed after she and Putin warned the demonstrators they would be fired on if they entered the building.

They had both come a long way since then—geographically, politically, and economically. From Dresden, they ended up in St. Petersburg, where they both held increasingly responsible roles in the mayor's office. After that, Putin had somehow been catapulted up the political career ladder, and he had dragged her along in his wake—all the way to the Kremlin, where he had taken over as president in March 2000 from Boris Yeltsin.

Suslova placed both hands on the balustrade, leaned forward, and gazed across the landscaped gardens and wooded slopes that led down to the beach.

She had been a fairly regular visitor during the construction of the enormous complex on Cape Idokopas, a heavily protected seventy-four-hectare site near the village of Gelendzhik, in the Krasnodar Krai region. Nobody was permitted to discuss the cost, but Suslova had seen spreadsheets that told her the construction bill was around 100 billion rubles, or $1 billion, almost all of it plundered and squeezed from various government funds.

Now she was able to enjoy the palace building and its facilities, which included an underground ice rink where she loved to skate and where the president sometimes played ice hockey. There was an arboretum, a helipad, and an amphitheater as well.

There was, of course, a price attached to such privileged access—a high one. It was utter loyalty and round-the-clock availability to the president. He treated her not just as a professional slave in her capacity as a political fixer, a manipulator, and a ruthless international problem-solver but as a sexual convenience too, when it suited him. It had been like that for more than two decades. As soon as her divorce was finalized, after just five years of marriage, it started.

Had she been complicit in this? She found it difficult to be clear in her mind. It was complicated. True, once the relationship began, the rewards and power that came with it were very nice. But she knew that if she had spurned the president or ended it, she would have been finished at the Kremlin, career over. She would have been back to a shitty little apartment somewhere on the fringes of Moscow—or worse, maybe even forced into exile somewhere remote. So she had felt there was no choice. He had control over her. It was a conditional affair.

These days, now that she was in her late fifties, she was less in demand in bed as he tended to pursue somewhat younger women, but he still valued her other professional skill sets, which were extensive.

Suslova glanced at her watch, a Patek Philippe that Putin had given her on her fiftieth birthday. It was time to go to the president's office for the scheduled meeting, which she knew would be a difficult one.

Another cost of the access she had was having to put up with the president's anger whenever things went wrong, as they sometimes did. On those occasions, it was like dealing with a complete stranger.

Again, very tricky.

She made her way across the terrace to the double-height oak doors, slipped through into the grand hallway, and then walked down a long corridor with a marble floor and gold light fittings. At the far end, past the music room, the ballroom, the cocktail hall, the hookah bar with its ornate pipes, and the reading room, was another door with two guards standing outside.

The guards nodded but didn't interfere as she went to the door, pressed a buzzer, and entered when a green light appeared. They knew her well.

The president, his adviser Igor Ivanov, his personal coun-

terintelligence chief Gennady Sidorenko, and the director of
the GRU, Colonel General Sergey Pliskin, were seated with
the FSB director Nikolai Sheymov at a circular oak table
when she walked in.

The circle of hell.

If Putin forced his senior team to fly from Moscow to his
Black Sea palace for a meeting around this table, it was rarely
to congratulate them.

The five men didn't bother greeting Suslova when she
entered, but she was used to that. She didn't greet them
either. She often had to deal with them in the course of
Kremlin business, and while they cooperated with her to her
face, she knew they disliked having such a powerful female
rival in the president's palace.

"We seem to be suffering from one amateurish screwup
after another," Putin said as Suslova took her seat. "Between
you and the FSB, I don't think I'd trust you to take down a
spiderweb, let alone a CIA operation."

He eyeballed first Suslova, then Sheymov, from beneath
his eyebrows, his forehead creased.

"I'm sorry you feel that way, sir," Suslova said. "I did
arrange the termination of one of the most highly placed
assets the Americans or the British have recruited inside
Russia for many years. Anastasia Shevchenko could otherwise
have continued to do an enormous amount of damage."

Suslova had been expecting at least some recognition for
the operation conducted in partnership with Sidorenko that
had eventually uncovered Shevchenko's deceit. After covertly
tracking the SVR counterintelligence deputy director's movements for several months as part of routine monitoring, they
had realized she sometimes took an evening walk through
Petrovsky Park, across the street from her apartment. Acting
on a hunch rather than proof, they'd decided in the last few
days to carry out an all-night sweep of the park along her

usual route, using a team with metal detectors. The search uncovered a lot of rubbish, but also a small rectangular steel SRAC transmitter device buried behind some bushes next to a wall.

They had downloaded copies of SVR files from the SRAC that could only have come from Shevchenko. The SRAC was left in position to avoid suspicion, but surveillance on her had been stepped up. There was no doubt about what she'd been doing, and once she'd gone to meet Robinson, the decision to assassinate her had been a straightforward one.

Peskov had tailed her, then executed her.

Putin banged his right fist on the table. "But that Robinson woman not only escaped the hit in Moscow, she has now got out of Russia. And who knows what Shevchenko told her before she was terminated, or what other contacts inside Russia she might have given Robinson. For all we know, she's provided her with other assets inside the Kremlin. The instruction was to take down both of them. I am trying to plan major operations and your incompetence is threatening to torpedo them before we've even started. Now we have a new situation facing us."

There was a short silence.

"What is this new situation, sir?" Suslova asked.

"Nikolai's men have reached a new level of incompetence," Putin snapped, throwing a poisonous glance in Sheymov's direction. "Robinson and the Moscow CIA station chief, Grewall, appear to have smuggled Pyotr Fradkov's widow out of Russia with them. I'm assuming they have not carried out such a high-risk move out of the goodness of their hearts. They will have a damn good reason for it. God knows what information she's giving them." He stabbed a white, bony index finger in Sheymov's direction. "I won't forget this."

Pliskin, never one to neglect an opportunity to stab the

director of a rival intelligence service in the back if he had the
opportunity, slowly nodded his mane of silver hair in
agreement.

"But I thought Maria Fradkova was cleared?" Suslova
asked. "She was put through the countersurveillance wringer
in Lefortovo. She passed polygraphs."

"Indeed, she was," Putin growled, his voice now oozing
menace. "But tell me this—who the hell was carrying out the
interrogation in Lefortovo and who cleared her? And who
signed the papers to have her released?"

Nobody spoke.

"I'll tell you who," Putin continued. "It was Anastasia
Shevchenko. So exactly how thorough do you think that so-
called interrogation was? How sound a decision was it to have
her released? And what do you imagine would have happened
to any useful information extracted?"

Another silence.

Now Putin's face, normally marble white with his skin
stretched across his cheekbones, had taken on a distinctly
purple tinge. "We need to give Maria Fradkova another, much
more thorough and much more persuasive interrogation," he
said, his tone low and menacing. "We need to resolve this
mess. I need you to devise a way to get that woman back into
Russia, where we can deal with her properly. And I also want
Jayne Robinson dealt with permanently—she's done enough
damage to the Motherland. If she does have more assets
inside Russia, thanks to Shevchenko, she's a major risk to us.
End her."

The president looked around the table, eyeballing them
one by one.

Nobody responded.

The priorities were obvious. Suslova failed to see how
Maria Fradkova had been allowed to escape Russia—it was
beyond her. The bunglers at the FSB had much to answer for.

When Putin's gaze reached Suslova, she leaned forward. "I do have ideas about how to achieve what you need, sir."

"What ideas?"

"Sir, I need to talk to someone who can help deliver this. I will keep you updated as soon as I'm in a position to do so."

The fact was, she had already dispatched Andrey Peskov with a specific set of instructions. But the last thing she wanted to do was show her hand in this meeting, not with three other self-interested buffoons who would likely steal her idea and claim the credit. They had done it before. And they clearly had no ideas of their own; otherwise, they would have said so.

Putin inclined his head a fraction and stared at her, unblinking. "Very well. You had better make sure it works, then."

"I will, sir."

"And what is the latest with FIDE?" Putin asked. "That needs to happen. I hope you are focused on it."

The FIDE international chess federation presidency was another one of Putin's pet projects, which he was watching closely. Suslova knew he saw her candidacy as a perfect vehicle to raise Russia's profile internationally and as a Trojan horse for all kinds of espionage and political lobbying operations.

But it was also for other public relations reasons. He'd be able to falsely claim that his country was taking bold steps to empower women if she had the FIDE top job. That was another reason he had handed Suslova an extremely large budget for lobbying and bribery purposes to ensure it happened.

"I am working hard on that, too," Suslova said. "It is going to plan so far. There are still many more national chess federations whose votes I need to secure, however."

"Such as?" Putin asked.

"The Philippines, the United Kingdom, France. And several others."

"Make sure it happens," Putin said.

"It is a matter of time, I believe," Suslova said.

"And I assume that Operation Peshka continues to run smoothly?"

Suslova pressed her lips together. She could see the president visibly bracing himself for any kind of negative response. "All is well with that operation from my perspective, sir."

The president glanced around the rest of the table, gave a curt nod, and sat back. "That's all. Get out, all of you."

CHAPTER TWENTY

Friday, September 30, 2016
  Kyiv

"I apologize for all this old Soviet stuff," Pavlo Doroshenko said, as he waved a hand around his enormous gilded office in the Presidential Office Building at 11 Bankova Street.

The presidential suite, a rabbit warren of corridors, offices, and reception rooms, occupied the entire fourth floor of the white stone building. Bankova Street was closed off at both ends by security barriers and a battery of guards.

Jayne glanced around at the old-fashioned green leather chairs, the parquet floors partly covered by yellow-and-red carpets, and the green curtains, green leather tabletops, and green marble pillars. There were crystal chandeliers and too much bling. It was, she silently agreed, all somewhat tasteless.

"It's not symbolic of the future," Doroshenko continued in a bass voice as he tapped his hairy fingers on the oak meeting table. "We're headed toward Europe and the United States now, not Moscow."

"Glad to hear it," Ferguson said from his seat opposite the Ukraine president.

"And achieving that will take some effort," Doroshenko said. "So the décor and furniture are not our top priority. We are occupied with dealing with the threat we face from the east—something I understand you are now well acquainted with, Jayne."

He turned to Jayne and scrutinized her, a quizzical expression on his creviced face, his coiffured steel hair swept back over his head.

Jayne, Vic, and Marchenko had been asked to attend the first part of the meeting between Doroshenko and Ferguson to brief them on the information gained from Jayne's short, fatal meeting with Anastasia Shevchenko and the additional details obtained from Maria Fradkova. Ed Grewall had been left out of the meeting and remained at the CIA station, on the top floor of the ugly new concrete US embassy building on Sikorsky Street, on the western side of Kyiv.

"You could say I'm acquainted with it, sir," Jayne replied. "We were chased over the border yesterday by an FSB gunship helicopter. I'd like to thank your people for getting us out safely. The helicopter pilot did a superb job."

Doroshenko nodded in acknowledgment. "I gather it was a little fraught. I'm glad you all made it intact." He paused for a few moments, then continued. "Anyway, we have a long agenda, so let's move to the business at hand. Tell us what you learned in Moscow."

Jayne had earlier spent an hour at the Kyiv CIA station discussing the Moscow trip with Vic and what they should disclose to Doroshenko. They had then briefed President Ferguson.

"There are two important operations underway at the Kremlin that I was told about by the asset just before we lost her," Jayne said. "Both are highly relevant to you. The first is code-named Operation Imperiya, the second is Operation Peshka."

"What are they?" Doroshenko asked.

"In summary, Operation Imperiya involves a planned full-scale invasion of Ukraine."

Doroshenko creased his forehead and stared silently at Jayne for several seconds.

"*Pizdets*. Shit," he said eventually. "It doesn't surprise me. We had heard rumors. The very name—empire. What crap. When?"

"Not immediately," Jayne said. "The name implies restoring territory lost when the Soviet Union was dismantled and must go beyond Ukraine, although this is the first country in danger. My source's understanding was that it is not scheduled to happen this year, or even next, but sometime relatively soon. There will be a steady but large buildup of Russian troops near your border before that happens, dressed up as a training exercise."

Doroshenko snorted, and his face visibly colored. "How reliable is this information?"

"My asset is, or rather was, very well placed."

"Putin is losing his mind," Doroshenko snapped. "He must be insane if he seriously thinks he has a chance of successfully taking over this country."

Ferguson leaned forward. "Well, he is probably calculating that he's taken the Crimea off you without much opposition. And he's getting his claws into Eastern Ukraine too, the Luhansk and Donetsk regions. So why not the entire country?"

Jayne was a little surprised that Ferguson was being so forthright. He almost sounded provocative. She certainly wouldn't have made such a comment.

Doroshenko gave Ferguson an angry look. "Crimea is different—it has many ethnic Russians," he said. "In 2014, many of our service people there, especially in the navy, defected to Russia once the annexation began, from the leadership downward. It made it impossible to defend. The rest of Ukraine is not pro-Russian like that—if Putin thinks it is, he is gravely mistaken. Also, thanks partly to the weapons and the training that you and other Western countries are providing, we are far better equipped and far better motivated than Putin thinks. We are well positioned to teach him a lesson he will never forget if he is foolish enough to try a full-scale invasion of our country. His is the arrogance of an old KGB officer. Anyway, the rest of Europe would not just stand by and let it happen—and neither would you." He pointed his index finger at Ferguson.

There was a conviction in Doroshenko's voice that left little doubt he meant what he said.

"The Russian army is nearly three times as large as yours," Ferguson said. "We in the United States will support you further—I've already said that. But as for other European countries, how certain can you be about that?"

"I'm certain," Doroshenko said.

Jayne hesitated. She always found it difficult to argue with those at the presidential level but often forced herself to do so if she was certain they were not taking everything into account.

"My asset in Moscow made a very good point about Europe not allowing it," Jayne said, looking directly at Doroshenko. "I asked her that same question. She pointed out that forty percent of gas consumed in Western Europe comes from Russia. The likes of Austria, France, Germany, Greece, the Netherlands, and others are up to their necks in Russian gas—if they fight against Putin, they might be cut off and the lights might go out. That would not be a vote winner. So although you might be right about European countries not allowing it, I would not take it for granted. You might want to carry out some lobbying work to get them on your side."

"Noted," said Doroshenko, with a nod.

Ferguson glanced sideways at Jayne, then at Vic. "Go on, tell President Doroshenko about the other matter."

Vic placed both hands on the conference table and looked at Doroshenko. "Sir, Jayne was briefed by her source in Moscow that the Kremlin has at least two highly placed, very important assets in the West who are helping him prepare for an invasion of Ukraine."

Doroshenko leaned forward and stared at Jayne. "Who?"

Jayne glanced at Ferguson and Vic. It suddenly crossed her mind that they might believe Doroshenko himself was one of the assets.

"That's what we'd all like to find out," Jayne said. "My asset did not know. All we have is their code names—ILYA and ALYOSHA."

"The warriors," Doroshenko murmured. "Did your asset know who is the spymaster handling them?"

"One strong possibility is Kira Suslova," Jayne said. "There are others, of course."

Doroshenko glanced at Marchenko. "Hmm. Suslova. We've got to know a little more about her recently."

Marchenko nodded. "She's tried more than once to bribe our chess federation president to vote for her as FIDE president."

"We're aware of the FIDE campaign," Jayne said.

"She owns a lot of property across Europe, we've discovered," Marchenko said. "And she tries to hide it. She has a mansion here in Kyiv worth more than a billion hryvnia—that's nearly forty million of your dollars. She's got others in Switzerland, Monaco, Spain, and elsewhere. The one here is held through an obscure network of offshore companies, but we know it's hers. We suspect that her other properties are also likely to be held through such companies."

"A familiar story," Vic said.

"Where's the money coming from?" Jayne asked.

"That is what we would like to know," Marchenko said. "It must be from the Kremlin, somehow. But the question is whether it is coming with Putin's approval or not."

"You think she might be siphoning it from somewhere that is not approved?" Jayne asked. Now her radar was fully on.

Marchenko stroked his goatee. "We think so."

"Could be leverage to use against her," Jayne said.

"Exactly."

Doroshenko clasped his hands on the table in front of him. "What you have told us is interesting and important, Jayne. Thank you for your work. We know the risks you took."

He turned to Marchenko. "I want you intelligence people to pursue the leads you have urgently. I don't need to tell you how important it is that we uncover these Kremlin agents."

"I agree and I would like to add my thanks too," Ferguson said. "Please keep us updated on progress."

He glanced at Jayne and Marchenko. It was a clear signal for them to leave.

They both rose, shook hands with the others, and made their way out. Vic remained behind for the second part of the meeting, at which ongoing US military aid to Ukraine was to be discussed. Indeed, he was planning to remain in Kyiv for the following days to facilitate further discussions between the US and Ukrainian teams.

An hour later, in her ninth-floor room of the Fairmont Grand Hotel, overlooking the Dnieper River in downtown Kyiv, Jayne sat back in her chair, enjoying the view through her open balcony door, a gin and tonic in her hand.

First, she had a short phone call over a secure connection with Joe, still in Amsterdam with Carrie, who was making good progress with her research.

Jayne had called Joe briefly the previous night to let him know she was safe. Now she gave him a brief update on what had happened in Russia, including the fate of Shevchenko, whom he had played a key role in recruiting for the CIA. She could hear the shock in his voice at the news, but they could not have a detailed conversation, as he was in a public café with Carrie. They agreed to talk again the following day, and Jayne ended the call.

At last, she had time alone to think.

Doroshenko had impressed her. A statesmanlike figure, he was fiercely nationalistic, anti-Russian, and focused on maintaining his country's independence, achieved in 1991.

Their discussion about Suslova had been enlightening. One thing that had struck her even more than the revelations of her extensive property ownership was Marchenko's comment about Suslova attempting to bribe the Ukraine chess federation president into voting for her. If she'd done that with one country's federation, then she had likely done it with others, too.

Her thoughts went to her old childhood chess sparring partner in Nottingham, Nick Geldard, with whom she had several battles over the board as a young teenager. That hadn't lasted long, as he was far better than she was, despite her father's attempts to coach her. Although he was a slightly eccentric character, like many chess players, she had something of a crush on him. But there had been no reciprocity, so no romantic side to their friendship ever developed.

Nick had then become a leading grandmaster who, in his thirties, twice reached the semifinals of candidates tournaments for the right to challenge for the World Chess Championship title. Jayne recalled him losing to the same man on both occasions during the 1990s—Wolfgang Paulsen, the top-ranking German grandmaster.

Despite never quite qualifying to play for the world title, Geldard was ranked number three in the world at his peak and had a glittering chess career.

Now fifty-five, born only a month before Jayne, Geldard was director of international chess at the English Chess Federation, for whom he also acted as the delegate to FIDE. Jayne knew he had represented the English Chess Federation at various FIDE international congresses to elect the organization's global presidents in the past.

Geldard was a rarity in the chess world in that he had become rich through the game and the high profile he had achieved, thanks to various business ventures once his top-level playing career was over. Jayne knew he had also inherited well from his parents, who had made a fortune after selling their house-building business.

Jayne took a sip of her gin and tonic and gazed across the river. Several tourist boats were passing up and down, showing visitors the sights.

Surely Geldard must have come across Suslova. Maybe she had tried to corrupt him and the English federation, which was struggling financially and organizationally, like many across the world, a likely target for a temptress with a bundle of dollar bills. Unlike the game in Russia, there was no state funding, and corporate sponsorship was difficult to get.

Jayne hadn't spoken to Geldard for at least three years. Perhaps now would be a good time to renew an old friendship. There was a risk involved in what she was considering, but maybe he might have ideas about how she could reach Suslova.

She took out her phone and searched for his number.

CHAPTER TWENTY-ONE

Monday, October 3, 2016
London

Jayne stood in the hallway of Nick Geldard's six-bedroom brick detached house on Bolingbroke Grove, across the street from Wandsworth Common in southwest London.

She mentally compared it to her own more modest two-bedroom apartment a few miles northeast, near Tower Bridge. His place must have been worth at least six million pounds.

In his front garden, next to a fish pond, he had an enormous ornamental chess set on a fifteen-foot-square board made from white and black granite squares.

Geldard proudly showed her another more normal-size set, but vastly more valuable, that he kept in the largest of his three living rooms, next to his home cinema room. Somewhat to Jayne's disgust, the pieces were all made from antique African ivory, but given that she wanted him in an amenable mood, she kept her views about elephant hunting to herself.

On a shelf were two large black-and-white action photographs of Geldard playing chess. The first showed him deep in concentration, contemplating a move during one of his losing candidates tournament semifinals against Wolfgang Paulsen, a tall man with a thin face. The second, also of a game against Paulsen, was in a more informal setting. Both men were smiling, and some spectators were holding large beer glasses, while other chess games were going on in the background.

"Where's that second photograph?" Jayne asked.

"A chess club in Kreuzberg, in West Berlin," Geldard said. "It was 1988. I made a guest appearance. That was the first time I played Paulsen. The second time, it was a little more serious."

"Are you still playing much?" Jayne asked.

"Of course, though nothing like as much as I used to. My FIDE rating is 2602—well off my best, but not bad for my age. I'm ranked two hundred and sixty-something in the world still."

"Impressive at your age," Jayne grinned.

Geldard smiled. "You're not doing badly at your age either."

They decided to take a walk across the common rather than sit inside, and they strolled north along a path that led toward Clapham Junction railway station.

Geldard started by giving Jayne an update on his two children, now both in their twenties, and his ex-wife, now living in Madrid.

"How are Joe and his kids doing?" Geldard asked. "Are you settled over in Portland now?"

Jayne and Joe had had an enjoyable night out with Geldard four years earlier in London, and the two men had got on well. She gave him an update on their current situation and described how the family holiday in Amsterdam had been interrupted by work, without mentioning Fradkov's killing or the trip into Russia.

"I'm glad things are going well, despite your disrupted vacation," Geldard said. He stopped and straightened his wiry frame. "But I'm assuming your visit here today isn't entirely social," he continued, eyeing her through his rimless glasses. "Is there something you need?"

"There is something I was hoping you might help me with," Jayne said. "There is a chess connection."

"Is it related to your new freelance career?"

She nodded. In line with MI6 rules, Jayne had never actually told him she had worked in the past for the service, although he had always seemed to assume that was her employer. But she had mentioned at their last meeting that she was now working for herself as an international security adviser.

"I have a question," Jayne said. "But first, can I ask for a promise that what we will discuss will go no further and you'll mention it to nobody else—I need complete discretion and confidentiality."

"You have my word, yes."

Jayne had had a lengthy discussion with Vic about whether to approach Geldard and whether he could be trusted. In the absence of another viable option, at least in the short term, he had eventually agreed.

She glanced around, checking for any sign of coverage. There was nobody within earshot. Indeed, the nearest person, an old man walking his dog, was more than fifty yards away.

"How well do you know a candidate for the FIDE presidency by the name of Kira Suslova?" she asked.

Geldard exhaled audibly and swept his hand through a straggly gray mop of hair. "I've come across her several times. She asked me a couple of times to play her."

Jayne almost did a double take. "She asked *you* for a game of chess?"

Geldard nodded. "I was at the Central Chess Club in Moscow for a match. She spoke to me afterward. Then she asked me again a year later when we were both watching a world championship match, also at the Central Chess Club."

"Did you ever play her?"

"No. I would have, but it wasn't possible. Both our schedules were difficult, and there wasn't enough time. She was quite persuasive. I wondered what her motives were. Whether she was trying to recruit me or something. I know she was former KGB."

Jayne felt slightly stunned. "Are you supportive of her candidacy for the FIDE role?"

"That's a good question. I have strong reservations. She's a difficult person, like many chess players. She knows her chess. She was a very good player. But she also knows her politics, and she's probably as good at that as she was at chess. We all know what the Russians are like. And also, I don't feel that I know her well enough to make a proper judgment, frankly."

They resumed walking. "She's more than just a politician," Jayne said. "And more than just a chess diplomat. Are you aware of that?"

Geldard hesitated. "I know she's close to the president, yes. We used to call her the chess queen on the tournament circuit—she behaved a bit like she ran the place."

Jayne lowered her voice. "Nick, she's one of Putin's right-hand people. She's former KGB, like Putin, but she behaves like she's still working for them. And she's causing the UK and the United States a lot of difficulty. I can't give you all the details, but we're told she's intending to use her FIDE presidency, if she secures it, primarily for non-chess objectives. I'm talking Russian influencing operations. We need to get access to her, which ordinarily is virtually impossible."

They took another few steps before Geldard replied. "And you think that chess, and her candidacy for the FIDE job, might somehow provide that access?"

Jayne shrugged. "I'm trying to explore all options. You're the English delegate to FIDE, so I thought you might bump into her at times. I gather she's very eager to secure this presidency. So much so that she's doing rather a lot of lobbying work to ensure she gets the required number of votes."

"She is certainly lobbying, yes—very actively. There are one hundred and eighty-nine chess federations worldwide. She needs their votes, and I'm told she's therefore doing a lot of flying."

"Is it just lobbying—or is it more than that?" Jayne asked.

Geldard's head turned sharply. "You can probably imagine how she's operating—she's Russian. Almost certainly she'll be buying her votes where she sees an opportunity. Cash will be changing hands, believe me."

"Has she lobbied you?" Jayne asked.

"She has asked for a meeting later this year. We have not fixed a date or a place yet. But I did mention to her that we could perhaps meet at my villa in Lausanne. That would make sense."

"Lausanne?"

"I have a villa there overlooking Lake Geneva. And that's where the FIDE headquarters are. So it seemed to make sense to meet her there."

"Ah, I didn't know you had a property there. Lovely location." In the past, Jayne had spent several holidays in Geneva and the area surrounding it, including Lausanne.

"It is beautiful. My parents owned it, so I inherited it. They didn't advertise the fact they had property there. They were quite discreet."

"I remember them that way, yes."

Now the combination of Suslova's invitation to Geldard to play her at chess, coupled with the disclosure about the villa, had set Jayne's mind whirring.

"Can I ask what type of property is it in Lausanne?"

Geldard glanced at her. "It's a lovely old villa on Avenue du Léman, on the waterfront. Very private and secure. It dates back to the early 1900s and originally belonged to a wine merchant from Lausanne, but it had deteriorated. My parents restored it. It was my father's retirement project. You'll remember he was in house building."

"Of course I remember. And how far is this villa from the FIDE headquarters?"

"A ten-minute drive. I love going there. In fact, I'm due to go there the week after next because FIDE is having a special conference of representatives there. Normally, we have a full congress every two years, but there's a lot of issues currently on the table on which decisions need to be taken urgently, so we've been called together for this interim meeting over two and a half days."

"What's on the agenda?" Jayne asked.

"Oh, a variety of things. One is corruption in the game and how to deal with it—there have been problems in Southeast Asia. Another is the location of the next Chess Olympiad, which might or might not be in Russia. Drug testing's also on the agenda. There's a big surprise social event planned for the Tuesday evening too, apparently."

Jayne nodded. "Do you have photos of your Lausanne house?"

Geldard gave her a curious look but took out his phone, tapped on the screen, and held it in front of Jayne. "There. That's the house."

Jayne scrutinized the photograph. It was an aerial view that showed an extensive stone villa with a circular turreted tower at one side and a terra-cotta tiled roof, set in land-scaped grounds that sloped down to the lake. In the garden was a giant chess set.

"Looks magnificent."

"It's my retreat."

"I like your taste in garden chess sets—very appropriate," Jayne said. She leaned over and used her finger and thumb to enlarge the photograph on the phone screen. "The set looks identical to that in your house here in London."

"They are identical. They prove very popular when I hold garden parties." Geldard flicked through several more photographs of the property from various angles, as well as interior ones that showed an immaculately kept and furnished house. There were a couple of photos of the gardens, including a boat shed and landing jetty on the lake.

"It's quite useful for me now given the proximity to FIDE," Geldard said. "I'm there on business from time to time, quite apart from holidays. It's the main reason I stood for the FIDE delegate's role—it gives me a good excuse to travel there more often."

They walked on a little farther. A mother with two toddlers came in the other direction, looking harassed and hot.

To their left behind the trees, a train hummed past on the line that ran into Clapham Junction.

"I have two questions," Jayne said.

"Which are?"

"First, would you be willing to bring forward your meeting at the Lausanne villa with Suslova, assuming she's available? I mean sometime very soon, if possible. For example, if you're both going to be at the conference, could you do it then?"

Geldard gave a half laugh. "No idea. She's always busy, I believe, and she doesn't seem the sort of person who'll move her diary around to suit me. I'm guessing that others have more pressing demands on her time, like Putin, for instance."

"You have a good point about her diary, which brings me to my second question. So hypothetically, just to try and get her attention, would you be willing to dangle a carrot—let's say, sell your villa to her?"

This time, Geldard let out a slightly strangled squawk. "*Sell* it to her? You're absolutely joking. No."

Jayne smiled at him. "I don't mean actually sell it. I mean, let her think you're going to sell it. Put it up for sale. Get her interested and show her around. That's all you have to do. If she's trying to get the president's job at FIDE, then maybe she'll need a property in town, anyway."

Geldard's eyes widened. "She already has a property in Switzerland, up in the mountains near Grindelwald. It overlooks the Eiger and the Jungfrau. I know she owns a huge chalet there—it's more like a fortress, I heard. She goes skiing there in winter."

"How far is it from Grindelwald to Lausanne?"

Geldard shrugged. "It's probably two and a half hours by car, usually. At least a hundred and eighty kilometers."

"Listen. Kira Suslova has a huge weakness for property, if you didn't know. She has mansions and villas all over Europe. I'm willing to gamble that if a property like yours comes up for sale, ten minutes from the FIDE building, then she will at least want to take a look. I mean, how often do such properties come onto the market?"

"Never."

"There you are, then," Jayne said. "What would the house be worth?"

"A lot. Maybe twenty million euros."

"I think she'd jump at an exclusive property like that. She'd love it. Especially if she's the frontrunner for the president's role and the property suggestion comes from FIDE.

Do you think you could get them to plant the idea with her?"

"I don't know. I also don't feel comfortable showing her around my villa when I have no intention of actually selling it."

"You wouldn't have to do it," Jayne said. "We would have a real estate agent put it on the market. It would be done properly and would need to look like a genuine sale opportunity. You would simply take it off the market once we were done. That happens all the time. People change their minds." She paused for a couple of seconds. "We'd make it worth your while—there would be a large payment if you agreed, for very little work on your part."

Geldard rubbed his chin and continued to walk. "How much?"

"We'd have to work out a mutually acceptable fee."

"And which real estate agent would you use?" Geldard asked. "Who would do that?"

"An upmarket operator. Preferably one with a track record in selling to Russians, of whom I believe a significant number own property in Switzerland. There must be some who know her already if she owns a Grindelwald house."

"And who would show her around the house?"

"Me." Jayne folded her arms. "In fact, we would probably have a few agents there to help her look around."

Geldard stopped and faced Jayne. "A few agents? I assume you don't mean property agents. What exactly do you intend to do to Suslova once she's in the house?"

"Ask her a few questions. Tell her a few things."

"I can imagine what type of questions you might ask. And you really think she is going to answer them?" Geldard asked.

"We have ways of persuading her."

Geldard shook his head vigorously. "Look, I try to see the world beyond the chessboard. I know there's a bigger picture to consider. And I know that having yet another Russian heading FIDE has implications, given her background. But I'm not prepared to get involved in some sort of huge subterfuge on my property that could easily turn nasty and ruin my reputation in the chess world. I might want to run for the FIDE presidency myself one day—I'm not ruling it out. And I don't want to cross swords with people from some of the darker corners of the planet, let's say, who I might want to canvas for votes if that happens. There are a surprising number of Russia supporters out there."

He paused. "So my answer is no. I'm not going to help, Jayne. You'll have to find someone else. Can't you use another property?"

"Come on, Nick. You know it's going to be extremely bloody difficult for me to secure another property like that in Lausanne. There's a lot at stake here. I really need your help —it would mean a lot. We would pay you very well indeed for the inconvenience."

"I said no. I'm not interested. I don't need your money."

CHAPTER TWENTY-TWO

Monday, October 3, 2016
London

Jayne climbed somewhat wearily up the stairs to her second-floor apartment on the corner of Portsoken Street and Minories, carrying a take-out cup of latte from the Starbucks on the ground floor of the building.

She let herself into her apartment, unlocked the door that led to her balcony, and sat there sipping her drink while enjoying the vista south toward the Tower of London and Tower Bridge. It had been the view that convinced her to buy the place eleven years earlier.

Just as she drained the cup, her phone rang. It was a call on her secure comms app from Mark Nicklin-Donovan. Because of the Fradkov connection, she had kept him updated on her movements and events via brief secure messages. But she had not spoken to him since leaving for Russia.

"Jayne, I've got some news from MI5," he began. "Something you ought to know."

"What's that?"

"They've had analysis results back from the labs on the various items found in Pyotr Fradkov's house after the killing. Included in that were a few hairs on the chair opposite the sofa where he died. The DNA tests are showing they were black hairs, quite different from his, and are Russian-Slavic in origin, I'm told."

"There's a surprise," Jayne said.

"Yes. And here's another. They came from a woman."

"A woman?"

"Could our Kira Suslova have done the deed herself?" Nicklin-Donovan asked. "Is that in character?"

"Normally I'd expect her to send a GRU hit team, not do the job herself. But a GRU hit team wouldn't play Fradkov at chess. Can't they get an identification?"

"There are no DNA records for her. There's a discussion going on about how they might go about obtaining one, but nothing yet. Pity there was no CCTV from the house."

"Suslova was having an affair with the guy," Jayne said. "So that would explain how she got access to the house. Have they checked flight records into the UK?"

"Of course. No record of Suslova entering the country under her real name."

She briefed Nicklin-Donovan on the conversation she'd had earlier that day with Nick Geldard and outlined her plan to try to get access to Suslova in Lausanne.

"Problem is, Nick isn't buying into it," she concluded. "He says he might want to stand for FIDE president himself one day and doesn't want to trash his reputation."

"Keep working on him."

They ended the call and agreed to keep in touch.

Having survived on snacks and sandwiches for the past

several days, Jayne decided to cook herself a proper meal for a change. She made her way down to a nearby mini-super-market and collected chicken, rice, vegetables, a few sauces, and a bottle of her favorite Cloudy Bay New Zealand sauvignon blanc for later.

Jayne put her current favorite album, Adele's 25, on the hi-fi and began to prep the chicken. She popped it into the oven just as the sonorous tones of "When We Were Young" began to play. As she peeled the carrots, her phone rang.

Jayne glanced at the screen. It was Carrie.

Although Carrie often called her when they were at home together in Portland, it was the first time she had ever done so while overseas. She knew Jayne was often busy when away on work trips and usually sent WhatsApp messages if she needed to ask something or check in with her.

Jayne knew Carrie and Joe were still in Amsterdam.

She turned the music down, slowly pressed the green button, and placed the phone to her ear.

"Hi, Carrie. How's Amsterdam?"

The first thing she heard was the sobbing.

Then came Carrie's voice, high-pitched, tense, and panicky.

"Jayne, help. It's dad," she wailed.

A chill ran through Jayne.

"What's happening?"

"He went out to buy some snacks and I called him to ask him to buy some other stuff too. He was walking in the street when I spoke to him. Then I heard him yell out. Then there was what sounded like a fight and men shouting—not in English, and I think not Dutch either. I heard Dad shout at them to let go of him, to leave him alone. Then the phone went dead."

Jayne felt the scalp prickle on top of her head.

Shit, shit, shit.

"How long ago was this?"

"A few minutes. I called you right away. I don't know what to do."

Then Carrie broke down in a flood of tears.

Bloody Russians.

It had to be them. This was straight out of their playbook. They'd failed to take her down before she left Russia, so they'd gone for her family instead.

She should have foreseen this.

Damn it.

"Listen, Carrie. Stay calm. We'll fix this. Have you told anyone else yet? Have you called the hotel desk, or the police?"

"No. Nobody."

"Do you know where your dad was? Which shop he was going to?" Jayne asked. "And how many men do you think there were—how many voices?"

"He was near here, down the street. We shopped there a few times. A mini-supermarket. I don't know how many men, but there was more than one voice."

"And there's been no sign of your dad since?" Jayne asked.

"No. He hasn't come back," Carrie said. "And he hasn't called me."

"Did he have a room key with him?"

"No. I was going to let him back in."

"Just listen and do what I tell you," Jayne said. "First, you need to call the emergency number for police, 112, and tell them exactly what's happened and where you are and where your dad was going. Then—"

"Wait, Jayne," Carrie said. "There's someone at the door. They're knocking. It's not Dad—he always knocks three times and calls out, so I know it's him."

Shit.

"Carrie, do not open that door."

Jayne knew this was serious. Whoever had attacked and possibly kidnapped Joe was likely coming for his daughter too. A classic SVR or GRU operation. She had been here before.

Would they have kidnapped him?

Quite possibly—likely, even.

"Stay in your hotel room," Jayne rapped out, trying to keep her voice as calm as she could but knowing she was failing to do so. "Lock the door from the inside right now, fasten the chain, and don't answer it."

"Okay."

Jayne heard footsteps, then a click and a rattle as Carrie did as instructed. But then she heard the unmistakable sound of more knocking, forceful and persistent, and a muffled voice.

"I've done it," Carrie said. "But they're still knocking and asking me to open."

"Look through the peephole in the door and see who it is."

There was a pause. "It's a man in a dark jacket. I don't think he's a hotel worker."

"Ignore him. Get away from the door. Go into the bathroom, lock the door, and call the police from there. Now."

There was a short pause and the sound of a door slamming shut.

"I'm in the bathroom."

"Good," Jayne said. "When you've spoken to the police, call the hotel reception desk, explain what's happened, and ask them to escort the police to the room when they arrive. Do nothing until you're completely sure it's the police and hotel staff. So when they get there, ask them for ID and look through the peephole to check it properly. If you're not completely sure, don't open the door. Got it?"

"Yes." Now Carrie's voice sounded fractured and trembling.

"I think the person outside will go once he realizes you're not opening the door. Listen, I'm in London right now. When you speak to the police, give them my number. Then call me straight back and let me know what's happening. Okay?"

"Yes, okay." Carrie burst into tears again. "I'll call 112 now."

"Take some deep breaths before you call and stay calm. Your dad needs you calm so you can help as best you can. I'll speak to you soon."

"I will." Carrie ended the call.

Jayne knew she needed to move quickly. It was quite believable that whoever had attacked Joe might well try again to get Carrie—they'd done that before once. Like last time, they would likely aim to spirit them back to Russia, where they'd use them as some kind of bargaining chip.

They probably wanted Maria Fradkova back. Or would they want her, Jayne, instead? Or both.

That wasn't going to happen.

She needed to call Vic, who was still in Kyiv, working out of the CIA station alongside Ed Grewall. He had good contacts at the Dutch AIVD, the General Intelligence and Security Service.

And Vic would also need to get the US embassy and CIA station in the Netherlands involved immediately, not just to help locate Joe but also to look after Carrie and ensure she wasn't also targeted again.

Jayne jabbed at her phone screen, turned on her secure comms app, and called Vic's number.

PART THREE

CHAPTER TWENTY-THREE

Monday, October 3, 2016
London

It was dark outside by the time Jayne, seated at the dining table of her London apartment, convened with Vic, Ed Grewall, and Marchenko at the Kyiv CIA station via a secure video conference call. The CIA needed to coordinate with the Ukrainians, given the implications for and potential threat to Maria Fradkova as well as Joe.

By then, Jayne at least knew that Carrie was safe.

She also knew for certain that Joe had been abducted, not just attacked. CCTV footage obtained by police from a camera in the street outside the hotel showed the abduction taking place and Joe being bundled into a white Volkswagen panel van.

Carrie had called again to tell her that police and hotel staff had come to her room and she had been taken to a police station in Amsterdam. From there, the Dutch national crime squad commissioner running the investigation into Joe's disappearance had taken personal charge of her. Carrie reassured Jayne that she was being looked after and the woman was giving as much information as she could.

The commissioner had booked Carrie on a flight back to Portland in the morning. One of the US embassy officers based in The Hague would escort her to Amsterdam Schiphol Airport. Then on arrival, Joe's sister, Amy Wilde, who Jayne had called, would meet her and look after her and Peter until Joe returned.

Thankfully, Carrie sounded a lot calmer than earlier, but she was still emotional.

When they had finished speaking, Carrie handed the phone over to the commissioner, who further reassured Jayne that everything was in hand in terms of Carrie's safety.

But the commissioner had nothing positive to report about Joe. A nationwide alert had gone out to all regional and national police units and to border control officers, but so far there had been no sign of Joe or the people who had taken him.

The alert had inevitably triggered media interest, but the commissioner said she had ensured that the brief details given to journalists downplayed the incident and characterized Joe's disappearance as probably perpetrated by a drug gang, not by Russian intelligence officers. Such drug-related offenses were not uncommon in the Netherlands, and resultant TV coverage was thankfully muted and brief.

Checks on the white van's license plate, which was visible on the CCTV footage, showed it was stolen. The van was found a few kilometers outside Amsterdam, abandoned in a country lane. The assumption was that Joe had been moved to another vehicle.

The kidnappers' faces were partially obscured on the CCTV by a combination of baseball caps and wraparound dark glasses. A lamppost and a shop sign near the camera also partially blocked the view. No identification was possible.

"I'm glad Carrie's okay, but what about Joe—what do we do next?" Vic asked after Jayne had briefed them on the commissioner's update and on her calls with Carrie.

Jayne stared at her screen. Vic was sitting with elbows propped on a table, his face illuminated in a somewhat ghostly fashion by a desk lamp. Next to him sat Grewall, his lips pressed in a thin line.

Marchenko, who Jayne could see was unwrapping a new pack of Marlboros, looked equally subdued.

"The Kremlin's behind this," Jayne said. "I predict we'll hear from them soon, probably with a demand for Maria Fradkova in exchange for Joe's return. Given they confiscated Maria's passport, my guess is they intended to give her another going-over at Lefortovo at some point."

She glanced at Marchenko. "Is Maria safe, Valentin?"

Marchenko nodded as he lit a Marlboro. "She's in a safe house and under guard. She's fine. Her children will visit later, also under guard."

"Good," Jayne said. "Our next job is to get to Suslova herself. According to Shevchenko, she is likely the handler for the two Kremlin assets in the West—we need to find out who they are."

Vic nodded. "We need to get to her. But how?"

"I'm thinking potentially blackmail," Jayne said. "Her attempts to bribe her way to the International Chess Federation presidency have to be the starting point. But perhaps we can add to that. If we can gather the ammunition, I'd be happy confronting her face-to-face."

Jayne outlined the plan she envisaged, using Nick Geldard's property in Lausanne as bait to draw Suslova in.

"Suslova also invited Nick to play her at chess a couple of times," Jayne said. "He thinks she might have been trying to recruit him. Perhaps we could get Nick to offer her a game? She might jump at the chance—view his property near the FIDE offices, try to bribe him over the presidency, and play him at chess."

"Sounds like a possibility," Vic said.

"There is one slight problem, though," Jayne said. "Nick is refusing to let us use his house. He says he doesn't want to get a bad name among the many Russian-supporting chess federations elsewhere in the world. He thinks he might run for the FIDE presidency one day."

There was silence on the call.

Jayne cleared her throat. "I'll see if I can fix that. When he hears about what's happened to Joe, he might change his mind."

"There might be another problem," Vic said. "Suslova must be on red alert for this type of operation against her."

"Sure," Jayne said. "But I think Nick is sufficiently distanced from us not to arouse suspicion. Suslova's had several chess-related dealings with him before. She's expecting to speak to him again about FIDE, and I doubt she would easily uncover my links to Nick. We've hardly been in contact the last few years. Anyway, we don't have any other options right now."

She hunched over her laptop screen and eyed Marchenko. "Valentin, have you made any progress pinpointing how Suslova has bought all her property?"

Marchenko leaned forward. "I've found out which bank she's been using to handle the property deals—Moskva Bank. They have offices all over Europe, as you probably know, as well as in the US. We have tried a few times in the past to hack into their systems, but they're watertight."

Jayne frowned. "What about all the other enablers involved in these transactions? There must be lawyers, property experts, surveyors, and so on. Can you get into any of the law firms' systems? They're generally less secure than the banks, in my experience, and yet they'll likely have details of all the bank accounts involved in these deals."

A crooked grin crossed Marchenko's face. "Great minds think alike. I have also discovered her law firm—Minorsky and Partners. And like the bank, they have offices in many European capitals. A property and corporate specialist, known for their aggressive tactics in hostile takeover bid situations. They are very good at lying about and undermining their opponents, and very sharp at using the media to manipulate investor and press opinion. And not well liked. But they are not so sharp in their IT security department."

"So they're hackable?" Jayne asked.

Marchenko's grin broadened. "That is one way of putting it. There's a friend of mine, Grigori Azarov, who runs an underground unit called Cyber Penetrators. He operates out of a basement on the western side of Kyiv. There are few Russian companies whose systems he's not been into—not that any of them will know about it."

"Cyber Penetrators?" Jayne asked.

Marchenko nodded. "Until recently, it was only the Five Eyes who were hacking into Russia's key systems, and Ukraine was being pummeled by Russian state-backed hackers."

Jayne knew that the Five Eyes group of intelligence services, comprising the US, UK, Canada, Australia, and New Zealand, had been active in the way Marchenko described.

"But that's changing?" she asked.

"The boot is indeed now on the other foot," Marchenko said. "Our defenses have been massively improved, so it's harder for Moscow to get to our systems, and we're finding a lot of new ways to hack into theirs. We have our own hackers now, including Cyber Penetrators."

Marchenko outlined how, to some extent, the tables had

been turned on the Russians over the previous year or so by a
new wave of Ukraine-based hackers. Most were covertly
funded and trained behind the scenes by a variety of
international intelligence and cyberwarfare specialists,
including the United States' National Security Agency—the
NSA—as well as Britain's Government Communications
Headquarters, commonly known as GCHQ, and Israel's Unit
8200. Cyber Penetrators was privately owned but was given
financial backing by the Ukrainian government, Marchenko
explained.

"They're giving the Russians a taste of their own medi-
cine," Marchenko said.

"So, can your guy Grigori get us what we need?" Jayne
asked. "Suslova's bank account details and sources of her
funding, her list of property purchases, who she's paid money
to in the chess world. All that kind of thing?"

"He's confident," Marchenko said. "We'll find out soon.
He'll be on the case tomorrow evening, once all the key staff
at Minorsky and Partners have gone home—he'll be into and
out of their system like a thief in the night. They won't feel a
thing. If you can get a flight over here, you can come and help
Vic and me supervise it."

Jayne quickly calculated her priorities. The US embassy in
The Hague and Dutch police were taking good care of Carrie
and had arranged her safe flight home. Meanwhile, the police
and Dutch intelligence services were investigating Joe's disappearance. So there seemed little she could contribute in the
Netherlands for the time being. There was equally little
mileage in staying in London—apart from one task she
needed to complete.

"I'll get a plane in the morning," Jayne said. "After I've
revisited Nick."

CHAPTER TWENTY-FOUR

Monday, October 3, 2016
   Amsterdam

The inside of Joe's mouth tasted horribly metallic, and he felt like he was going to be sick. The side of his head was throbbing from where he had been hit, and he was having difficulty breathing because of the duct tape that was wound around his head and formed a seal over his mouth.

His hands and feet were lashed to the back and legs of a heavy wooden chair with thick plastic cable ties, so he couldn't move. He felt thirsty and hungry, and from the sensation on the side of his head and face, he could tell there was quite a lot of dried blood. There were also several bloodstains on his pale blue sweatshirt.

Bastards.

He ran his tongue gently around the inside of his mouth. There was a large cut on the inside of his cheek that was still oozing blood every time he moved his jaw.

He looked around. This wasn't a house. The light from a

single central lightbulb told him it was some kind of work-shop. There was a workbench to his right, with saws, pliers, screwdrivers, and other tools hanging on the wall. A reel of black duct tape and a pair of scissors was also on the bench.

To his left was a single mattress on the floor, pushed up against heavy metal shelving units. There were two sets of handcuffs attached to the shelving, one on either side of the mattress.

From outside came the distant but distinctive roar of jet engines. It sounded to Joe like a large aircraft at a fairly low altitude, or perhaps taking off.

What the hell happened?

Gradually, it came back to him.

The man tapping him on the shoulder as he walked, his phone clamped to his ear as he talked to Carrie.

Joe had turned to see a bald man wearing a dark jacket and shirt, and then there came an almighty blow from behind to the side of his head, which had caused him to collapse to the ground.

He had tried to kick the guy, but was feeling dizzy and didn't make contact. He vaguely recalled the man and another one grabbing him, one beneath the arms, the other by his ankles. They had thrown him through the side door of a van, where he had landed on a metal floor. One of them had jabbed something sharp into the side of his neck.

After that, he couldn't remember any more. He must have blacked out.

Even through the fog of confusion, Joe knew that this was almost certainly linked to the operation that Jayne had been running in Russia. He had made his own enemies in Russia in the past, for sure, but the timing here was just too coin-cidental.

Despite being on vacation with Carrie, he had continued to be vigilant and to continually check for any sign of surveillance. It wasn't just an old habit born of his time in the CIA and as a war crimes investigator inside the Department of Justice's Office of Special Investigations. He was only too aware of how the Russian intelligence and security machine operated.

However, he had allowed himself to become briefly distracted while walking to buy snacks and drinks. Carrie had called to ask him to get a few additional items, he had lost focus on his surroundings, and he was now paying the price.

The last time, it had been Carrie, her brother Peter, and Joe's sister Amy, who had been the victims of a Russian kidnapping. Now it was his turn.

He hoped to God that it was only him and that Carrie was safe. He had always instructed his children to call Jayne if anything happened to him and likewise, to call him if anything ever happened to Jayne. Hopefully, she had done that.

But how anyone was going to find him, he had no idea. He didn't know what had happened to his phone, wallet, and passport, but he knew he couldn't feel them in his pocket. No surprise there. His watch was also gone.

Whoever had taken him was professional. There had been no sign of surveillance in the days before, but someone must have been watching him.

Joe tried to focus on the building he was in. There was a concrete floor and a pair of steel sliding vehicle doors away to his left. Parked against the far wall was a black Ford Transit van, presumably the one used to bring him here. He couldn't see the license plates from his current position. Next to the vehicle doors was a small pedestrian door.

On the opposite wall to his left, two orange canoes were lying on a rack, and there was a small sailing boat on a trailer, its mast folded down.

From outside somewhere came the distinctive sound of

outboard engines.

This was some kind of boathouse, he guessed. That would make sense. This was presumably still Amsterdam, with its network of canals.

There was a click as the pedestrian door opened and a man walked in.

As he drew near, Joe realized it was the same bald man who had approached him outside the hotel. He looked like a fit military type, stocky and muscular.

He stood in front of Joe and placed his hands on his hips.

"You will be here for a while," the man said in heavily accented English. "Until we get what we want from your girlfriend. So you had better hope she cooperates."

Definitely Russian.

"Are you thirsty?" the man asked.

Joe nodded.

The man walked to him, grabbed the end of the duct tape around his head, and yanked it off forcefully and painfully. He grabbed a bottle of water from the workbench, removed the top, and applied it to Joe's lips. "Drink. And don't even think about shouting out. There's nobody around to hear you."

Joe gulped down the water, gasping for breath between swallows.

While he was drinking, Joe caught a glimpse of the man's digital watch on his hairy wrist. The time was 8:46 p.m. That was more than five hours after he had left the College Hotel. Had he been unconscious all that time?

When Joe had drunk the entire bottle, the man put it back on the bench and stood in front of him again.

"So. Do you know where your girlfriend is?" the man asked.

Joe stared at the man. "Where are we?"

"You don't need to know that."

Joe could feel anger building inside him. "What do you

want?"

"Like I said. I want to know where Jayne is."

"She's away, working," Joe said. "I have no idea where. I don't discuss that kind of thing with her—it's her business. I've been here on vacation."

Again came the rumble of a jet aircraft somewhere in the far distance. He figured they must be somewhere within range of Schiphol, Amsterdam's main airport, southwest of the city.

"Don't give me bullshit," the man said. "You know exactly where she is. Tell me. And the second thing I want to know is, tell me where's the woman she brought out of Russia, Maria Fradkova."

Joe shook his head. "I know nothing about anyone by that name."

The last thing he was going to do was tell this guy anything about either of the women if he could help it.

The man took a step forward and slapped Joe hard across the side of his face with the flat of his hand, causing a fresh flow of blood from the cut inside his cheek. He could feel and taste it in his mouth.

"All right. If that's how you want to play it. You need to think about your daughter, Carrie. In fact, one of my colleagues is paying her a visit right now. We know which room she's in at the College Hotel."

Joe felt the bottom drop out of his stomach. "My daughter has nothing to do with this. Leave her alone."

"We are going to ensure she does have something to do with this." The man stared at him. "Now. Are you going to tell me where Jayne is?"

Joe hesitated.

His instinct told him that if these people were going to seize Carrie, they would have done it at the same time as they grabbed him, not several hours later.

Joe shook his head. "No."

The man then bent down and, with a short backswing, delivered a sharp left-handed upward punch straight into Joe's liver, right below the right rib cage. The pain was sharp and instantaneous, and sent a shock wave through his brain. Then he punched him again. This time, it felt like he had been stunned by a cattle prod.

Joe gasped for breath and slumped in his chair, white lights dancing in his eyes, his abdomen feeling as though a sword had been run straight through it.

"Life will be difficult for you until you talk," the man said. "Until that happens, your pain levels will rise. Think about that."

He grabbed the duct tape and scissors from the bench, wound a length around Joe's head again, resealing his mouth, and trimmed it off with the scissors.

"I'll be back soon for another chat," the man said. "That will give you time to think."

He walked out of the building.

* * *

Monday, October 3, 2016
London

Nick Geldard slowly shook his head. "I'm very sorry to hear about this situation with Joe, but if I get involved in a sting operation against a FIDE presidential candidate, I'm finished in the game. I'm history."

"Nick—" Jayne began.

But Geldard threw out his hands, palms upward, and leaned back in his armchair. "I have no option, Jayne. I can't help you."

Jayne bit her lip and held back from the angry response she felt like giving. She glanced at her watch. It was almost half past ten at night, and she had just explained what had happened to Joe.

She had felt bad knocking on Geldard's door at such a late hour, but had decided a personal approach had a far better chance of working than a phone call. Thankfully, he had not gone to bed early. Even better, he had poured them both a glass of shiraz.

She put her wine down, stood up, and walked across Geldard's living room, past the antique ivory chess set that had irritated her on her previous visit, and went to the window. The moon was rising behind a tall birch tree.

This was going to take all her powers of persuasion, she could see that.

Her mind went back to when they had both been teenagers in Nottingham.

"You remember that time back home when you were worried about that British Championship final in 1977?" She turned around and looked at Geldard. "We were both sixteen, I think. You said you didn't think you could win it, but I told you there was nothing to worry about, to take one move at a time, and to let the outcome take care of itself."

Geldard nodded. "And a week later I did win it—walked off with nine hundred pounds. It seemed like a lot of money back then."

"Exactly. You beat some thirty-year-old. And now I'm telling you, there's nothing to worry about here now. Trust me. Let the outcome take care of itself."

Geldard placed both hands behind his head and stared at Jayne. "You're just saying that because it's your man who's at risk. You're thinking about him, not me. I've got myself to worry about—nobody else is going to do it for me."

Jayne shook her head. "You're wrong about that on several

levels. It's partly about Joe, yes, but much more than that. I really shouldn't tell you this, but I feel you need to know why I'm asking for your help. The basic facts are, we're talking about a Russian operation that could do a lot of untold damage to our country and other countries. And Suslova is heavily involved in it. We'd like to put a spanner in the works of that, and you can help us."

"Really?" Geldard said, raising his eyebrows. He looked slightly stunned.

"And I *am* thinking about you," Jayne continued.

"What do you mean?" Geldard asked.

"It's because if we can take down Suslova for what she's doing, FIDE is going to need another candidate for the presidency. And that candidate could be you."

Jayne did not know if it would actually play out that way, but she thought it was worth putting the idea into Geldard's head.

"Me?" Geldard's eyebrows shot up. He took a long sip of his shiraz. "You think so?"

"Is there another obvious candidate?"

A trace of a smile crossed Geldard's face, but he said nothing.

"So," Jayne said as she sat down again and picked up her wineglass. "Are you in?"

Geldard shrugged. He reached over toward the ivory chess set that stood on a table between him and Jayne and slowly knocked over the black king in a symbolic gesture of mock surrender.

"You were always better at winning arguments than me, even if your Sicilian Defense wasn't usually up to scratch," Geldard said. "But we're going to need a damn good opening gambit against that bitch. She takes no prisoners, either on the board or off it."

"Don't worry. We'll have one."

CHAPTER TWENTY-FIVE

Tuesday, October 4, 2016
Kyiv

The office building on Nahirna Street looked run-down and abandoned from the outside when Jayne arrived with Vic and Marchenko. Weeds were growing from its gutters and between the cracks in the deserted parking lot outside the front door. Several of the windows in the four-story building were boarded up, and others had broken glass.

Marchenko, puffing a Marlboro, led the way to a rear door, attached to which was a high-tech security system that belied the decrepit nature of the rest of the building. It was opened almost immediately by a security guard carrying a pistol in a holster at his hip. Behind him stood another guard with a camera.

After Marchenko had shown his ID and Jayne and Vic had been photographed and had shown their passports, a short climb up a concrete staircase to the second floor brought them to a secure unit, protected by more armed guards. It had a double-door entry system equipped with fingerprint recognition technology.

This was the Kyiv office of Cyber Penetrators, a short walk from Marchenko's own office on the top floor of the building occupied by the SZR farther along the same street.

A small man with a shaved bald head and thick black glasses strode down the corridor toward them and greeted them in heavily accented English. He was introduced by Marchenko as Grigori Azarov, the mastermind behind a secretive hacking operation that had already wrought significant damage on Russia.

Azarov guided them through the security doors and into a long, open-plan office. It was equipped with three long rows of desks, all of which were occupied by young, casually dressed men and women, focusing hard on large computer screens in front of them. In a small kitchen next to the office was a large coffee machine for the staff. Clearly, the place ran on caffeine.

"The SZR has paid for most of this," Marchenko said, waving his hand toward the banks of monitors. "It's been a great investment."

Azarov led them into a private office at the rear of the room, marked with his name on the door.

"I will personally carry out this piece of work," Azarov said. "For something of this sensitivity, I do not want any of my team involved. Take a seat."

He indicated toward seats that were placed on either side of his own, which was positioned in front of three large monitor screens and a keyboard. He also had a laptop open on his desk. Jayne and Vic sat to Azarov's left, Marchenko to his right.

"We've spent the morning beating off a bunch of hackers in Moscow who were trying to take down our country's power grid," Azarov said. "It would have blacked out all of Kyiv. So let's see if we can send some traffic the other way. Now, Minorsky and Partners. I'm not going to tell you exactly how I got into their system—that's a valuable trade secret. But in layman's language, I've already set up a backdoor access into it—I used an email Trojan. One of their secretaries opened it. That's given me root access. No problem—wouldn't have been so straightforward with the banks. Their systems are mostly tighter."

"Will they know you've been in there?" Jayne asked.

"No. We'll be invisible. It won't be logged," Azarov said. He toggled from an internet browser to a different app that Jayne didn't recognize. Then he spent the next few minutes tapping his way through three different security screens.

"We're in," Azarov said eventually. He turned to Jayne. "What do you need?"

She explained. And then she and the others sat and drank coffee while Azarov searched the darkest corners of Minorsky and Partners' servers.

The whole time, Jayne had difficulty keeping her mind off Joe and the situation she knew he must be in. If Russia's GRU or maybe freelance operatives were involved, it would almost certainly be painful. No doubt there would be a demand soon, delivered via some back channel. Now she was relying on Azarov to obtain the ammunition needed to get him back.

Eventually, Azarov located a client list that detailed which of the law firm's partners were ultimately responsible for which clients.

Having pinpointed the two partners who appeared to work on behalf of Kira Suslova—both based in the law firm's Zürich office—Azarov then drilled into their accounts. He quickly located the folders within which documentation relating to her property deals were held. There were several dozen subfolders, one for each of the properties she had acquired over a period of fourteen years. They began in 2002,

Jayne noted, not long after Putin had come to power in Russia.

"Get me details of her property in Grindelwald, Switzerland," Jayne said. "Then I'd like the financial details for all of them. We need to know precisely where the money for these deals is coming from, what the total is, which bank accounts it's drawn off, and if the cash has been moved around. If it has, we'll need the paper trail of other accounts and what they show."

Azarov navigated his way through all the property deals listed on the system, occasionally copying documents and pasting them onto a portable hard drive. He also typed in summary details of all the property acquisitions into a spreadsheet, with a running cumulative total of the values showing at the bottom and a list of the bank accounts down the side.

Finally, Azarov leaned back in his chair and tapped the desk with both hands. "Right. She's frequently moving funds out of this account, which she's labeled with a nickname, the *Shakhmaty Schet*," he said, pointing at a box on his spreadsheet. "The chess account. It's held offshore in Moskva Bank's branch in Cyprus."

He turned to Jayne, who recalled Maria Fradkova's reference to her late husband advising Suslova to use the "chess account."

"You mean you've got the details of the account? Number and everything? Passwords?"

Azarov nodded. "It's all here in the legal documents. The law firm has the log-in details because Suslova is the only signatory on the account. They have a power of attorney to operate the account in case anything ever happens to her—there's a document that spells out what they must do if she dies. They have to move all the money to some other Kremlin account. There's no other backup, it seems. So she clearly trusts her lawyers." He gave a sarcastic laugh.

"How much has come out of that account?" Jayne asked.

Azarov hunched over the monitor screen again. "Nearly a billion dollars over the past five years."

"Bloody hell. Where's she moving the money to?" she asked.

"I was also wondering that. Let me see if I can find out."

Jayne nodded, glanced at Vic and Marchenko, and agreed they would grab a latte while Azarov continued working.

Twenty minutes later, they returned, Jayne carrying a cup for Azarov, which she placed on the desk next to him. "Any luck?"

Azarov picked up the cup and took a sip. "Thanks. I just got into the Cyprus account, the chess account. The balance in it right now is still over two billion, despite the money flowing out. Two billion and seventy-nine million dollars, to be precise."

Jayne looked at him, wondering if she had heard correctly. "*Two billion?*"

"Yes."

Jayne exhaled. "Are you sure you're not going to be detected?" She glanced at Vic, who was pursing his lips. It could screw up the entire operation if Suslova realized someone had been into the account.

Azarov shook his head. "Again, I'm not going into detail, but definitely not. I wouldn't have done it otherwise."

"All right. So where's she been transferring the money to?"

Azarov toggled to a spreadsheet where he had pasted some numbers and pointed to one of the columns. "The largest amounts—totaling more than five hundred million—are going into this numbered Swiss account." Azarov placed an index finger on another box on his spreadsheet. "I'm assuming that's a private account. She's then purchasing all the properties with money from there. You asked about the Grindelwald chalet—that cost her nineteen million Swiss francs. She bought it, and most of the others, in the name of Knight Rook International. It's a company that was set up in the British Virgin Islands by Minorsky and Partners' office in Panama."

"Knight Rook—another chess reference," Vic said.

Azarov nodded. "Oddly, the big transfers from Moskva Bank into the Swiss account are being dressed up as loans. All of them are at ridiculously low interest rates, half a percent, and they're all unsecured. There's no schedule for repayments and no evidence of any repayments. She's used that same process with all the properties. Two yachts have been bought the same way. Sleight-of-hand accounting—there's no way these are loans."

"You mean she's just taking the money but trying to avoid it looking like she's doing so?" Jayne asked.

"Something like that," Azarov said.

"And there are smaller payments too?" Vic asked.

"There are many smaller transfers into various accounts in several countries," Azarov said, running a finger down the spreadsheet.

"That'll likely be the bribery money to various chess federations," Jayne said. "Thank you, Grigori. You've done a great job there. It's very helpful information."

She glanced at Vic, who raised an eyebrow.

"Surely she must be doing all this with Putin's blessing," Vic said. "Moskva Bank is basically his private cashier."

Azarov shrugged. "It's not possible to know whether she's got his blessing. She's the sole signatory on the chess account. But the low-interest loans seem very odd."

"What if she's pickpocketing Putin?" Jayne asked. "She's no oligarch. No big oil business or telecoms company to fund her lifestyle. Her money must come from the Kremlin. So her lifestyle is subject to the whim of Putin. And if she upsets him?"

Vic leaned back in his chair. "Maybe Putin's screwing her and the money is payback?"

"That's what Shevchenko told me," Jayne said. "Putin and Suslova are close—even rumored to be lovers. And if so, he wouldn't want that fact made public. He'd be very pissed off with Suslova if that happened—and so would his wife. Sufficiently pissed off to withdraw her funding and torpedo her lifestyle. Maybe even lock her up in a labor camp."

There was a brief silence. Nobody needed telling what the leverage possibilities would be if it were true that Putin and Suslova were in a relationship of some kind.

"Trouble is, we don't have proof of the reason she's getting this cash, or of any relationship between Suslova and Putin, do we?" Marchenko said.

"Not yet," Jayne said. "But there has to be a reason—so let's bloody well go and get it."

* * *

Tuesday, October 4, 2016
Kyiv

It was precisely as Jayne had expected—the demand for Maria Fradkova in exchange for Joe's release came that afternoon.

A printed, unsigned letter was delivered by commercial courier to the US embassy in London, addressed to Jayne Robinson and Vic Walter.

Given that both were still in Kyiv, the letter was picked up by Arthur Veltman, still in London, whose face was now filling the large monitor screen in front of Jayne, Vic, and Ed Grewall.

"I will read this letter to you," Veltman said, his voice a

little strained. "I suggest you brace yourself. It's not good news."

"Go ahead," Jayne said. "I wasn't expecting anything positive from this."

Veltman cleared his throat and began to read.

"The Russian government requires the return of Maria Fradkova to Russia. Her departure was illegal and happened despite the confiscation of her passport. She is the subject of ongoing investigations within Russia and is a suspected spy, like her late husband. We require you to exchange Maria Fradkova for US citizen Joseph Johnson, being held in Kaliningrad as part of investigations into previous espionage operations against the Russian Federation. The exchange should take place at the Queen Louise Bridge over the Neman River, at Sovetsk, on the Kaliningrad-Lithuania border. Send your response to the email address below."

Jayne felt a shockwave run through her.

Kaliningrad?

Veltman looked up. "That's the whole of the letter. There's a Gmail address at the bottom of the page."

"The bloody Russians have got him to Kaliningrad?" Jayne asked. "How the hell?"

She had been to Kaliningrad before. It was a wedge of Russian territory stuck between two NATO member countries, Poland and Lithuania, and faced out onto the Baltic Sea. It was an exclave that was more than 350 kilometers west of the rest of Russia. To get there by land required a journey across Lithuania and Latvia—another member of NATO—or through Belarus, a close ally of Russia.

Kaliningrad, part of Germany until World War II, was captured by the Soviet Union in 1945 and remained under its control following the postwar settlement at Potsdam. Jayne knew the Kremlin viewed it as a highly strategic piece of territory on the fringe of Western Europe.

"The bastards must have flown him there from Amsterdam," Vic said. "The damn Dutch airport security and customs must have been asleep."

"Bloody useless," Jayne said.

"Obviously some private jet," Grewall said. "Maybe they sneaked him through the diplomatic channel?"

Jayne cursed again. It was incredible, but then again, she shouldn't be surprised. It was far from the first time something like this had happened.

Damn it.

This was tearing her in two.

As Joe's partner, her heart was telling her to send Maria back to Moscow for whatever fate awaited her and to get Joe back at all costs. Her head was shouting at her not to give in to blackmail and that through determination and focus, they could get Joe back through other means.

She realized everyone was looking at her.

"Well, we can't give up Maria," Jayne said. "So we need another way to extract Joe. I say we press ahead with our operation against Suslova, and make sure it works. That'll give us the leverage we need."

"The issue is if Joe's situation is being run at a higher level than Suslova, of course," Vic said. "Then it might be out of her hands."

There was a long silence. There was no answer to that one.

"We'll just have to hope that's not the case," Jayne said. She stood. "I'm going to call Nick Geldard. We need to get that house on the market right now."

CHAPTER TWENTY-SIX

Thursday, October 6, 2016
 Lausanne, Switzerland

The FIDE managing director and deputy chairman, Evgeny Dobkin, poked his head around the office that Kira Suslova was temporarily using at the chess organization's headquarters within the modernistic Maison du Sport International building.

"Hello, Kira. Can I have a quick word?" he said.

Suslova nodded. "Of course."

She spoke regularly to Dobkin, who was also a Russian, as she knew she needed to keep him onside during her run for the FIDE presidency. Dobkin had been a top-ranking grandmaster himself in his prime two decades ago and, in her opinion, was now doing a good job in Lausanne in a very demanding role at FIDE.

Dobkin walked in, closed the door behind him, and sat on a chair in front of Suslova's desk. The office, like the rest of the building, was fitted with gray granite floors and trendy orange-and-gray furniture. The MSI complex housed several international sporting and leisure organizations, including World Rowing and the International Boxing Association.

"Is this about next week's conference?" Suslova asked. The management team was focused on preparations for the forthcoming two-day meeting, which involved most of the 189 FIDE delegates. Suslova viewed the meeting as a major opportunity to lobby for support in her campaign for the presidency. Indeed, she had been working hard on a private entertainment event where that lobbying could be escalated.

"Kira, we spoke a few months ago about property here in Lausanne," Dobkin said in his low bass voice. "You said you may be interested if something appropriate came onto the market."

"Possibly, yes."

"I have heard from a real estate contact that a lakeside villa is likely to be available for purchase," Dobkin said. "I thought I'd let you know."

Suslova sat up in her chair. She had put feelers out herself via an agent who specialized in Russian buyers, but so far he had come up with nothing.

"What is it?"

"It's large—top end of the market. A stone villa, extensive grounds, with a boathouse on the lake." Dobkin waved a hand at the window toward Lake Geneva, a short distance to the south across a tennis and soccer sports complex. "It's even got a giant chess set in the garden."

"Where is it, and how far from here?"

She listened as Dobkin described the location. The ten-minute drive from FIDE headquarters seemed to be perfect. Lausanne was a beautiful place.

"Do you have any idea what the price is?" Suslova asked.

"Probably about twenty million euros. And there's one

other thing—it's currently owned by someone you might know."

"Who?" Suslova asked.

"Nick Geldard," Dobkin said.

"Nick Geldard?" Suslova echoed, momentarily taken aback. "He's selling? I know of his house. I requested a meeting with him some time ago, and he mentioned we could meet there."

"So you haven't yet been to the house?"

"Not yet."

"Shall I tell the agent that you might be interested? I don't have to name you if you prefer."

Suslova paused. "Who is the agent? Are they trustworthy?"

"We've dealt with her several times on property sales and rentals. She's the managing director of Cailler International Realty, Lina Cailler. Very professional. Discreet. Top class. We've had no issues with her."

Although Dobkin had now piqued her interest, she felt a spike of caution run through her.

She had come across Geldard a few times before at chess events, and in a different life, she might even have wanted to get to know him well. He was an attractive man who she had somehow felt a strong pull toward. She had even in the past suggested they get together for an informal game of chess at some point, but nothing had materialized, which she regretted. In her long experience, the intimacy of a game of chess could sometimes lead to intimacy of a different kind. It was a useful ploy at times.

She also needed to lobby Geldard regarding her candidacy for the FIDE president's role. Perhaps there was a way of killing two birds with one stone here.

But she didn't particularly want Geldard to know she was interested in his house just yet. She might not even like it.

And she certainly didn't want to tour around it with him there. If she really liked it, then it might be different. She might want the personal contact then and to turn on the charm if there was a deal to be done.

"Tell the agent I'm potentially interested," Suslova said. "And tell her I could view the property in the next few days. But tell her I would only want the selling agent present, at least for the initial viewing. I would not want Geldard to be there."

"I will pass on the message. I've got to go—I'm late for a meeting. But I just wanted to tell you that piece of news."

Dobkin rose and walked out of the office.

Suslova stared out the window. Beyond the tennis club, the waters of Lake Geneva glinted in the sunshine. It made a pleasant change from the view from her Kremlin office across Red Square.

Her thoughts flicked to the other situation that had been uppermost in her mind recently, the need to get Maria Fradkova back to Moscow. The operation to kidnap Joe Johnson and apply leverage to Jayne Robinson and her colleagues had gone to plan. Andrey Peskov currently had Johnson safely locked up in a workshop in Kaliningrad. But so far there had been no communication from Vic Walter or Robinson in response to her demands for an exchange.

It was interesting that this property opportunity in Lausanne had come at the same time as the Fradkova operation was underway.

Was there any possibility at all of a connection between the two?

As someone who always approached any situation with a skeptical mindset, Suslova tried to think it through.

Was the Geldard property some kind of trap?

Probably not. She smelled nothing untoward. Dobkin knew the agent, and she, Suslova, knew Geldard.

But it would pay to proceed with caution.

She would need Peskov with her as a security backup, regardless. Peskov could arrange for his colleague, Feodor Matrosov, also a Vagnar Group associate, to take charge of Joe Johnson while he was away from Kaliningrad.

She picked up the phone and called Peskov's number, using her encrypted service.

"Andrey, I need you in Lausanne as quickly as possible. There's something going on."

"Sure," Peskov replied. "What's the issue?"

"I'll brief you when you're here."

"I'll call the Mustang pilot now," Peskov said. "I can get there later today."

As usual for her trips to Lausanne, Suslova was using her spare aircraft, a lightweight Cessna Citation Mustang, because Lausanne Airport's runway was too short for her favorite Citation Excel. She also had a fast helicopter on standby at Lausanne Airport, an AgustaWestland AW109, which she used to shuttle from the airport to her chalet home up in the Swiss Alps, at Grindelwald, about a hundred kilometers to the east.

Suslova knew Peskov was also using a Mustang, which he had borrowed from the Kremlin's fleet at Chkalovsky, the military air base northeast of Moscow. He and Matrosov had used the twin-engine jet for the operation to kidnap and transport Joe Johnson from Amsterdam to Kaliningrad.

"Good," said Suslova. "I'll need you to be fully armed."

CHAPTER TWENTY-SEVEN

Friday, October 7, 2016
    Lausanne

Anyone looking on would have likely been deeply sympathetic as the TCS roadside assistance mechanic battled to fix the Volkswagen Polo. Occasionally, he went to the rear of his large yellow truck to fetch a different tool. But he appeared to be having no luck.

Inside the truck, Jayne Robinson was perched on a stool with Vic Walter to her right, together with Ed Grewall. They had traveled from Kyiv, where Marchenko had remained at the SZR, while also being ready to work with Azarov at Cyber Penetrators in case any further hacking was required.

The Bern CIA chief of station, Alvin Coleman, a six-foot African-American with a graying crop of wiry hair and designer stubble, was also in the truck, having arranged the surveillance operation. It was parked a couple of hundred meters from the house belonging to Nick Geldard, who sat to Jayne's left.

The team, all wearing headphones with microphones, watched intently as a Bern CIA station technical officer, seated in front of four monitor screens and a laptop, fiddled with his sound levels.

Jayne had only recently finished a call with Carrie, who thankfully was now safely back with her aunt Amy in Portland. Although she remained intensely worried about her father, she at least sounded relieved to be back on home soil.

Jayne glanced up at the top left monitor screen. It showed Lina Cailler, the managing director of Cailler International Realty, who had been employed by Geldard two days earlier to sell his house. However, she knew nothing of the operation going on behind the scenes or the surveillance equipment in the house.

Cailler, whose well-coiffured blonde hair and understated designer dress spoke of high commissions and extravagant bonuses, had wasted no time in making use of her long-standing contacts at FIDE. She was now standing in the main living room of Geldard's property, awaiting Kira Suslova.

The Russian had insisted on viewing the property in the company of Cailler only, who had been instructed not to allow anyone else in.

Jayne and Vic had no choice but to agree to the request, which had been received by Cailler the previous afternoon.

However, they had a detailed plan to seize Suslova midway through the viewing, ideally while she was touring the gardens. It was assumed she would bring at least one bodyguard with her, and plans were also in place to deal with them if so.

Four armed officers from the CIA station in Bern, two of whom were former US Navy SEALs, were waiting farther down the street in a Honda SUV with blacked-out windows. The plan was for them to covertly enter the property once the viewing was underway, disarm any bodyguards, secure

Suslova, and then bring in Jayne, Vic, and Grewall to carry out the planned interrogation. Geldard had an explanation and apology prepared for Cailler.

The surveillance equipment, including microphones and hidden cameras, had been swiftly installed the previous evening by another tech team from the CIA station, with the cooperation of Geldard. Thankfully, the kit so far appeared to work as intended.

Coleman's CIA station in Bern, on the top floor of the heavily fortified six-story United States embassy building in Sulgeneckstrasse, was one of the best equipped in Europe and one of the Agency's most important operational centers. The main public reason for this was the large number of international organizations based in the country, but Jayne knew very well there were private reasons, too. Chief among these was the CIA's need to make use of Switzerland's highly confidential banking practices to provide cover for its array of international operations.

Given the stakes, Coleman had reluctantly agreed to the operation on his Swiss patch. In theory, an unwritten protocol between intelligence services said that he should clear any such operation with the head of the Swiss Federal Intelligence Service. But all of them knew the FIS would decline the consent, and so, following a short discussion, they pressed ahead anyway. They had all been in this position before. The Swiss were notoriously difficult to deal with.

A separate CIA surveillance team, detailed to monitor Suslova's movements, reported that she was in the FIDE offices. She had flown by helicopter that morning from her chalet high in the Alps in Grindelwald to Lausanne Airport and had then been whisked to the office by a chauffeur. They were ready to follow her at a discreet distance once she set off to view Geldard's property.

The tinkle of Cailler's phone, picked up by the hidden

microphones, came through the speakers on either side of the bank of monitors.

Jayne looked up at the monitor just as Cailler answered the call.

"Hello, Ms. Suslova."

Cailler then listened for several seconds before replying.

"That's a pity, Ms. Suslova. I understand you are busy. You would benefit from viewing the property in person, but let's see what we can do. I will set up the Skype video call and then call you back."

Geldard turned around to look at Jayne, who felt her stomach hit the floor.

Out of the corner of her eye, Jayne could see Grewall had his eyebrows raised.

Shit.

Cailler could be seen finishing the call. She then immediately tapped her phone screen again. A few seconds later, Geldard's phone rang.

The volume was turned up on Geldard's device, and Jayne could hear what Cailler was saying to him. So could everyone else in the van.

"Ms. Suslova has decided not to go ahead with the personal visit we had planned," Cailler told Geldard. "Instead, she would like me to give her a video tour of the property, using Skype."

There was nothing she could do. So she just nodded and gave Geldard the thumbs-up.

"Yes, go ahead, please," Geldard told Cailler. "It's not ideal, but we will have to live with it."

"Bloody hell," Jayne muttered when Geldard finished the short call. She looked around the van. Everyone looked a little stunned.

"She obviously got cold feet," Geldard said. "Maybe she's not really interested."

Jayne shook her head. "Has she smelled a rat? Has someone tipped her off? Or has she just decided to be cautious?"

She glanced at Vic, who shrugged.

"Probably just caution. At least she still wants to view the property," Vic said. "Even if it is by video call. We're not necessarily out of the game just yet—are we?"

"Bloody well better not be," Jayne muttered, although she felt they might well be just that.

It was their only chance of getting close to Suslova.

There was no plan B.

All Jayne could think about was Joe locked up somewhere in Kaliningrad—out of reach and doubtless guarded by some grizzly Russian Neanderthal. This operation had to work.

She exhaled in an effort to release the tension she was now feeling. "Let's listen to the video call and see what's said. The mikes will pick up most of it."

* * *

Friday, October 7, 2016
Lausanne

There was no time for the techs to tap into Lina Cailler's Skype account, so they had to make do with the audio feed and occasional glimpses of Cailler's phone screen as she made her way around Geldard's property. She gave Suslova a running commentary as she went, being relentlessly upbeat in typical real estate agent's style.

An early view of the Skype screen via the hidden cameras showed Suslova wearing an elegant black dress that matched her shoulder-length hair. She was sitting at a desk, presumably at the FIDE headquarters building.

"Is the property actually available now?" Suslova asked. The audio feed was clear enough for a note of cynicism to be quite obvious in her voice.

"It is," Cailler said. "The owner is not enthusiastic about selling, but he has decided to do so because the property is too large. He is planning to downsize."

Cailler moved into the living room and could be seen on the video feed monitor slowly doing a complete turn so Suslova could view all elements of the room.

"This is the main reception room in the house," Cailler said. "As you can see, it is perfect as a focal point for entertaining and has folding doors that open out onto the terrace, and—"

"No need to give me the bullshit. Just show me the main features."

There was a short pause.

"Of course," Cailler said politely, ignoring Suslova's rudeness.

For the next half hour, Cailler conducted a careful tour of the property, both inside and outside. The tour included the boathouse at the bottom of the garden, where the tech team had placed one camera and microphone. Jayne noticed how Cailler reduced her sales talk to a bare minimum after Suslova's earlier comments.

Suslova asked the questions that any potential purchaser of a luxury property would ask, including details of security systems, local taxes, gardening services, and maintenance issues and costs. She seemed interested and engaged in her questions but offered no opinions about what she was seeing.

The surveillance team in the TCS van listened carefully, looking for some clue what Suslova's thinking was. But she was giving virtually nothing away.

Jayne watched on the monitor as, finally, Cailler walked to

the terrace, where the tech team had installed two cameras and microphones.

"So, I appreciate it's difficult when you're only viewing the property on Skype," Cailler said. "But what are your thoughts on the house?"

"I like it," Suslova said. "It is in a good location for my needs, both in terms of work at the chess federation and for entertaining. But we would need some negotiation. There is quite a lot of work required to get the house to the specification that I would desire—it will take investment. Security would need to be drastically increased."

"What do you mean, 'some negotiation'?" Cailler asked.

"We would need to discuss it. Mr. Geldard is the owner, and I would like to meet him. I know him already, so I don't want to negotiate with you. I am now happy for you to tell him my identity. And you can pass on a further message from me too. As well as discussing the property, I would like to play him in a game of chess—we both play the game at a high level. He will remember that I have suggested this before. A game would be a good basis for a negotiation over the property. Let's see what he says."

Jayne glanced at Geldard, who raised an eyebrow but then caught her eye and gave a slight nod, indicating he was happy with the suggestion.

"I'm glad to hear you like the property and would like to negotiate further," Cailler said. "I would need to speak to Mr. Geldard to see how he would like to proceed. I didn't realize you know him already. So I presume that next time you would be happy to come to the property to discuss all this further?"

Suslova shook her head. "Not yet. I would need him to come to my home in Grindelwald for the negotiation and for the chess game. In any case, we also have other chess-related matters I would like to chat with him about. He will know what I mean."

"But if I might just suggest, I do feel that before you negotiate, it might be wise to view the property in person because—"

"I said no," Suslova interrupted. "He needs to come to my house."

"All right," said Cailler. "I will speak to him and suggest that."

"Let me know. Otherwise, we have no deal." Suslova abruptly ended the call, leaving Cailler holding her phone, a blank expression on her face.

Jayne felt a shock wave run through her.

This operation was going rapidly south.

"Bitch," she muttered to herself. It took little imagination to know what kind of challenge it might be for her to get into Suslova's own property, let alone interrogate her there, or what levels of security she was likely to have in place given her position at the Kremlin.

Vic was shaking his head. He looked up and caught Jayne's eye.

"This is all going to shit," he said.

Jayne turned to her left and looked at Geldard, who grimaced.

"It depends on you, Nick," she said. "Are you up for it?"

Geldard placed his hands behind his head and pressed his lips together. "What exactly am I getting into here? I mean, I'll give it a go if you think it's safe to do so, but I want a full briefing. As it stands, I'm not sure."

He looked inquiringly at Jayne.

To her right, Jayne heard Vic swear under his breath.

CHAPTER TWENTY-EIGHT

Friday, October 7, 2016
Lausanne

Nick Geldard went up rapidly in Jayne's estimation. He not only insisted on playing a part in the operation to put Kira Suslova in a position where she could be compromised by the CIA team, but helped come up with ideas about how they might achieve it.

"It's like playing chess in real life," Geldard said. "One false move and you're screwed. Maybe not immediately, but eventually."

Jayne nodded. She had often thought precisely the same thing herself about her long career in espionage for MI6 and then as a freelance operative.

During a chat with Lina Cailler, during which Geldard pretended he knew nothing about her conversation with Suslova, he agreed to go to Grindelwald for negotiations and a game of chess. He rightly wanted Cailler to report directly back to Suslova that he was looking forward to meeting her.

"Give her my email address and phone number, and ask her to get in touch directly," Geldard said.

However, the issue now was not so much agreeing on a time and date to get Geldard into Suslova's property but finding a way in for Jayne and Grewall.

Coleman moved with impressive speed to get the operation underway. His starting point was a covert surveillance program on Suslova's property in Grindelwald, without alerting either Suslova or the Swiss authorities, given what he was doing was illegal.

Grindelwald, a seventy-five-kilometer drive southeast of Bern, was a large, quaint village, almost a small town, perched over a thousand meters up in the Alps. It was almost entirely focused on tourism, with skiers descending on it in winter and hikers and climbers in summer.

Running a full-scale surveillance program would not be easy. It was, in fact, Geldard who, employing his knowledge of Switzerland, suggested that the team position themselves as a group of hikers who were visiting Grindelwald for a few days. "You'll fit in perfectly," he said.

It turned out to be a sound idea. Someone at the Bern CIA station used a local property rentals website to book a four-bedroom wood-framed chalet house on Spillstattstrasse with an underground car garage, around a kilometer from Suslova's chalet.

By early evening, the team was installed in the house, complete with hiking boots, backpacks, and trekking poles. At Jayne and Vic's insistence, Geldard had remained alone at his property in Lausanne, just in case Suslova checked on his whereabouts. He could drive to Grindelwald via Berne in around two and a half hours when required.

One of the three drones that Coleman's team had brought was immediately dispatched from the broad first-floor balcony that ran around the outside of the house on Spillstattstrasse. It was soon transmitting pictures from high above Suslova's property.

To Jayne's relief, flying drones seemed to be a popular pastime among tourists in Grindelwald, given that the magnificent mountain scenery provided instant gratification for drone photographers. The presence of other devices in the skies offered good cover for the CIA's machine.

The pictures that came back to Coleman's laptop from the drone immediately revealed the scale of the issue facing the team. Jayne, Vic, and Grewall gathered around Coleman to view them in real time.

Suslova's chalet was about a kilometer to the west of the village center, in an area where the properties were more widely spread on larger plots. Her chalet was on a particularly big plot, more than 150 meters from the nearest neighbor. Few of the other houses had fences to mark their perimeters, but Suslova's was surrounded by a high black steel security fence with matching electric gates.

The chalet also had an expansive flat area of short grass at the rear of the house, where a black twin-engine AgustaWestland AW109 helicopter stood, its engines switched off.

There was a security hut just inside the front gates, manned by two guards, and a red-and-white boom which they raised when vehicles needed to enter or leave. Other security guards patrolled the property.

From the gates, a driveway led approximately eighty meters to the house, which was a lavish affair in typical Swiss style, built from wood, with large overhanging eaves, several balconies, and a low-pitched red-tiled roof. There was a separate annex to one side of the house with two outbuildings.

There was an underground parking garage beneath the lawn at the side of the house, with a ramp leading down from the parking lot at the end of the driveway.

A Swiss flag flew from a pole next to the house, which

Jayne decided was a nice touch, given the nationality of the owner. A Russian flag likely wouldn't have gone down well in this area of the Alps.

The view looking south from the front of the property was jaw-dropping. Across the valley was the almost vertical north face of the Eiger, a mountain of rock and ice almost four thousand meters high that dominated the area. Behind it were the equally impressive Mönch and the Jungfrau.

Apart from the drone, a more conventional human surveillance team had been drafted in by Coleman from his CIA station. The team, similar to those used by the Agency elsewhere, comprised two men and two women. They were all retired intelligence officers from Switzerland and Germany who were now freelance operatives. Coleman had used all of them regularly before and rated them highly.

At a lengthy briefing, the surveillance team was detailed to keep a close watch on Suslova's property and look for patterns of arrivals and departures, especially staff members and local delivery drivers. The thinking was to seek out weak points that could be exploited—for example, failures by the gatemen to check credentials on arrival.

The four of them devised a strategy that involved posing as locals and making frequent changes of clothing, hats, and glasses, as well as deploying a variety of bicycles, motorbikes, and cars to conceal their identities. The plan was for them to start work first thing in the morning.

But not long after the briefing had concluded, Jayne's phone rang. It was Geldard, calling on the encrypted secure comms app that the CIA's tech team had installed on his phone.

"Jayne. There's something you need to know," Geldard said. "I've just had an email from Suslova. First, she wants to negotiate about the villa."

"That's good."

"Also, you remember I said there was a surprise social event after the FIDE conference in Lausanne concludes next Tuesday?"

"I do remember, yes," Jayne said.

"I've just discovered what it is. Suslova's email included an invitation to a big party she's holding at her Grindelwald chalet that evening. All the FIDE delegates are invited."

Jayne, who was lounging in an armchair in the living room of the rented chalet, sat up straight. "A party?"

"It's going to be a huge event. She's running a fleet of luxury minibuses up to Grindelwald from FIDE headquarters to take everyone there. Some are also traveling by helicopter. She's also paid for overnight accommodation for everyone at hotels in the village, including me. Guests can be taken to the hotels first to freshen up, if they want to, or be ferried directly to the party, in which case the minibus drivers will take their bags to the hotels. I think this is the real start of her lobbying campaign for president. But she wants me there early so we can discuss the Lausanne villa before the party begins."

Jayne's mind immediately began to turn over the possibilities. A party of that scale would require significant resources and organization, involving catering, bar and waiting staff, as well as drivers and security people. This could provide the opportunity they needed to get in.

"Have you accepted?"

"Not yet, but I will," Geldard said. "Everyone will be going. And there's more."

"What?" Jayne asked.

"She wants me to play her a game of fast chess as the centerpiece fun event of the evening. The idea is that everyone will watch, she says."

"Really? What do you think about that?"

Fast chess was a variety of the game that Jayne had

enjoyed, particularly in her teens. It allowed far less time per player than the classical form of the game, meaning moves had to be made extremely quickly.

"It's going to be difficult to decline without looking like a spoilsport," Geldard said. "I guess it will be a good laugh for those attending—people will be drinking and running bets on the winner."

This was sounding better and better to Jayne. The image of Suslova and Geldard slugging it out over a board at the center of a large group of drunken FIDE chess officials went through her mind.

A perfect distraction.

"It would be a good idea to accept," Jayne said. "Such a game would keep your profile high among those who matter at FIDE. You'll need to avoid getting drunk yourself, though."

"I think I can manage that," Geldard said. He paused. "What do you have in mind?"

"This could be an opportunity," Jayne said. "Can you forward the party email to me, please? I'd like to see it."

"Sure."

Certainly, the scenario Geldard had described seemed to her like good cover for a potential operation.

But there also seemed little doubt that someone like Suslova would realize that. Were they being tempted into a potential minefield?

CHAPTER TWENTY-NINE

Saturday, October 8, 2016
Grindelwald

News of the FIDE party at Suslova's chalet opened up a number of potential options to get into the building, all of which were put under the microscope for stress testing by the CIA team at the rented chalet, helped by a battery of colleagues at Langley via a series of video conference calls.

"The favorites have to be substituting some of the minibus or car drivers going in and out, impersonating FIDE delegates, or substituting catering staff," Jayne said as the team gathered for a discussion around the dining table.

Vic nodded. "You're the one best qualified to talk chess and impersonate a FIDE official," he said, pointing a stubby index finger at Jayne. "The only problem is finding one in their fifties who looks like you—you're too slim, Jayne. And then persuading or coercing them to let you take their place at the party."

Jayne held back the grin she was tempted to make at the

flattery. He was probably right about her being best qualified, though. The others would certainly struggle to hold down an in-depth conversation about chess with a FIDE official.

"Well, let's get profiles and mugshots of the delegates and see if anyone fits the bill," she said, turning to Coleman. "Is someone on your team able to do that?"

Coleman inclined his head. "Sure. Most of these people have profile pages on their own countries' chess federation websites."

"We'll also need to find out which companies Suslova's using to organize the party," Vic said. "I'm thinking of catering, bar, waiting, transport, and security services. We then need to get wiretaps on their phones and get into their emails. I'll talk to Alex Goode."

Jayne knew Alex Goode. An old contact of Vic's, he had recently been promoted to director of the National Security Agency's signals intelligence directorate. This put him in charge of the agency's entire global operations for the collection of data, from phone hacks to emails to computer networks, and even penetration of radar and weapons systems. The promotion also elevated Goode onto the NSA's senior leadership team, based at the agency's headquarters in Fort Meade, Maryland. He was one of the most knowledgeable, quick-minded people in the business.

While Vic talked to Goode on a secure video link, Coleman was on the phone with someone at the CIA station in Bern. It was typical of the CIA teams Jayne had worked with that they would move so quickly.

However, the first major lead, the identification of the company providing the minibuses to transport the FIDE delegates, came from one of the retired female intelligence officers on the Grindelwald surveillance team.

She was walking past the gates to Suslova's house, wearing a backpack and ostensibly heading off on a hiking trip, when she spotted a large black Mercedes minibus enter the site. It had a discreet gold logo on the side—Gebrüder Schmidt Executive Transport.

The surveillance officer didn't hang around, but the drone camera confirmed that the minibus, which had blacked-out windows, remained on site for twenty minutes, then left again.

It took little effort to establish that Gebrüder Schmidt Executive Transport was based in Bern and serviced a variety of corporate clients in Switzerland, chiefly in the banking sector. Vic immediately fed the information to Goode.

Four hours later, Goode reported back that the NSA's Tailored Access Operations team had hacked into and had control of Gebrüder Schmidt's company router. This enabled them to get into the office manager's PC, which they achieved by deploying a bogus Google web page to install a piece of software. They then swiftly discovered emails and attachments concerning bookings for minibuses that had been sent to a man who was the house manager at Suslova's property in Grindelwald.

From there, it had been an easy process to install identical software on the house manager's PC. This time they deployed a more old-fashioned method—malware buried in an attachment to an email that they sent from the Gebrüder Schmidt account. The house manager had opened the attachment almost instantly, presumably having recognized the sender's name and therefore having no cause for suspicion.

"What about the router at Suslova's house?" Jayne asked immediately as Goode explained the development over a secure video conference call from the TAO's offices within the highly secure Remote Operations Center at Fort Meade.

"We've just got access to that," Goode said, his sandy hair swept across his bald head in an attempt to hide it.

"Does Suslova have a laptop or a phone connected to it?" Jayne asked. "Can you get into them, if so?"

"Both. A laptop and a phone. We're trying to get into them, but they both have extra layers of security, unsurprisingly. We're working on them."

The Gebrüder Schmidt manager's PC showed that Suslova's house manager had ordered a fleet of twenty ten-seater executive minibuses. They were to pick up the FIDE delegates from Lausanne on Tuesday afternoon, transport them to Grindelwald for the party, then return them from their hotels to Lausanne on Wednesday.

As the NSA team continued to trawl at speed through the emails and files on the house manager's PC, more information emerged.

First came details of the three hotels at which the FIDE delegates had been booked in Grindelwald. Then, an hour later, and even more usefully, came hotel room numbers and names for each of the delegates, together with scans of their passports and the minibus drivers' passports.

Finally, the NSA sourced a detailed floor plan of Suslova's house from the Municipality of Grindelwald, dating from when planning consent was given for the building twelve years earlier. It showed a huge four-story property with an extensive underground parking garage and a double basement. The property included an oval ballroom on the ground floor, together with a gym and indoor swimming pool in the second basement.

One issue for Jayne was that the party invitation email, which Geldard had forwarded to her, said that all guests would be thoroughly searched as part of security arrangements. That came as no surprise, but it meant there was no chance of taking a weapon in.

Jayne spent a few minutes setting up her sports watch, which operated using three different global navigation satellites, to send an SOS alert to Vic's and Coleman's phones if she got into difficulties and pressed a button on the device. If she could not make a phone call or send a message, that was the next best option. Grewall, who would also pose as a FIDE delegate, did likewise.

She and Grewall also had a long and heated discussion with Vic and Coleman about precisely what Vic should do if he received such an alert.

Eventually, they all agreed on a course of action.

After that was done, Vic called the team together in the chalet living room and briefed them on the new information and the plans discussed with Jayne and Grewall.

"I've got a draft plan that I'd like to run through with you all," Vic said. "It'll need refining, but I think it's a starting point. Tell me what you think. We've got until Tuesday to get this right—let's make it count."

There was silence in the room as Vic described the operation he had in mind.

When he had finished, Jayne sat back in her chair. It was a somewhat daring plan, but it sounded credible to her.

She caught Grewall's eye. He gave her a firm nod, clearly thinking the same way as her.

Now all they had to do was execute it.

There seemed no margin for error.

CHAPTER THIRTY

Tuesday, October 11, 2016
Grindelwald

The luxury Mercedes Sprinter minibus, custom-built for Gebrüder Schmidt Executive Transport like all those in the company's fleet, wound its way steadily upward along the twisty valley road heading east toward Grindelwald.

The driver, Ernest Honegger, rounded another sharp bend, accelerated, and climbed once more. The towering peaks of the Alps soared above him on either side of the valley.

Behind Honegger, in leather business class–style seats and sipping champagne from the minibar, were three delegates from the International Chess Federation, FIDE, preassigned to his vehicle.

He had collected them from the organization's headquarters in Lausanne a couple of hours earlier and was now just twenty minutes from Grindelwald.

Honegger's vehicle was the only one of the fleet of twenty minibuses that wasn't full. His passengers had been the last ones to leave Lausanne. His small group, two middle-aged men and a woman, all seemed in a very jovial mood.

Warholm, Pavic, and Johanssen were their names, according to the email he had received from the head office. Honegger was to drop them at their hotel, wait until they had placed their bags in their rooms and freshened up, and then transport them to a nearby chalet for a party.

Honegger, a gray-haired father of three, had chatted a little to one of them in English, a language he spoke almost as fluently as his native Swiss-German. He discovered they had been at a chess conference and were now ready to relax at the party that evening.

At the top of a rise in the highway, Honegger came to a halt at a set of temporary traffic lights that were on red, despite there being no sign of any workmen or any other obvious reason for the lights to be there.

Eventually, the lights changed to green. Honegger slotted the stick shift into gear and pressed down on the gas pedal. But the engine immediately cut out.

Honegger swore to himself. He was certain he hadn't stalled it. He reached for the ignition key and turned it in an attempt to restart the motor.

Nothing happened.

He tried again, and then again. But still, there was no response. The starter motor wasn't even turning the engine over.

Honegger glanced in his mirror. Coming up the hill behind him was a truck, marked in the distinctive yellow-and-red livery of TCS, the Swiss roadside assistance and break-down service.

Gebrüder Schmidt had a corporate account with TCS.

Indeed, there was a membership card in the glove compartment. Honegger had needed their help on a couple of occasions in the distant past. He was a top-class driver, but he didn't claim to be a great mechanic, especially now that modern engines were so heavily reliant on microchips and sensors.

Honegger had to decide quickly what to do; otherwise, the breakdown truck would be past him and gone. He grabbed the membership card from the glove compartment, opened his driver's door, climbed out, and stood next to the traffic light. As the TCS truck approached, he waved at it. The truck slowed to a halt behind the minibus. The driver wound down his window and leaned out, so Honegger walked around to speak to him.

"What's the problem?" the uniformed TCS driver asked in German, but with an accent that Honegger struggled to place. "Got trouble?"

"Engine won't start," Honegger said. "It cut out just a minute ago. I can't get it restarted."

The TCS driver glanced at his watch. "I'm not in a rush. Do you want me to take a quick look?"

Honegger nodded and showed the card. "My company has corporate membership with TCS, so I would appreciate it. Yes, please."

The TCS mechanic got out, walked around to the minibus, and tried to start it himself. There was no response, so he reached down, pulled the lever to open the hood, then walked around and stuck his head into the engine compartment.

While he did that, a taxi coming in the opposite direction also pulled to a halt next to the minibus. There were no passengers on board.

The taxi driver wound down his window. "What's the problem here?"

Honegger shrugged. "We're trying to find out."

"Those Sprinters, always picking up electrical faults," the taxi driver said. "My brother-in-law has one. Costs him a fortune. Typical Mercedes."

The TCS mechanic resurfaced. "I'm uncertain what's wrong," he said. "Probably your starter motor. I think you'll need to get to a Mercedes dealer. It's nothing I can fix out here."

Honegger cursed. "I've got three passengers here who I need to get to Grindelwald. This is really annoying."

The taxi driver leaned an arm out of his window. "I can take them if you like."

Honegger hesitated. Perhaps this might be the best option. The last thing he wanted were three irate passengers on his hands, just twenty minutes away from their destination but with no means of getting there.

"Okay, thanks," Honegger said. "How much?"

"Let's say thirty francs. Cash."

Honegger nodded, took out his wallet, and handed over the money. He could claim it back on expenses. He then got into the minibus and explained apologetically to his three FIDE passengers that their journey needed to be completed by taxi.

A few minutes later, the taxi disappeared back toward Grindelwald, the three delegates on board.

Honegger watched it go. Just as he was about to turn and thank the TCS mechanic for his efforts and ask if he might give him a lift into Grindelwald, the man grabbed him from behind. His heavily muscled forearm locked tight around Honegger's throat.

Honegger tried to protest, but such was the pressure on his throat, and the sudden shock, that he could only squawk.

The next thing he knew, something sharp had pricked him in the side of the neck.

He tried to struggle, but the man was far too strong. Swiftly, his vision became blurry.

The last thing he saw was a blonde woman emerging from the back of the TCS truck, along with another man.

Then he blacked out.

CHAPTER THIRTY-ONE

Tuesday, October 11, 2016
   Grindelwald

Jayne brushed aside a few stray strands of hair from her shoulder-length curly blonde wig and adjusted her black prescription-free glasses. She then leaned forward and peered through the windshield of the Gebrüder Schmidt Executive Transport minibus. The driver, a member of the CIA team based in Bern, maneuvered his way past a group of tourists outside Grindelwald's railway station and then accelerated up the hill.

The minibus they were in was the same one that had been halted at a set of temporary traffic lights twenty minutes outside Grindelwald. The staged breakdown had actually been caused by Goode's team in Fort Meade, who had covertly taken control of the remote vehicle immobilization system installed on the Gebrüder Schmidt office computer. All vehicles in their fleet had similar remote security immobilizers installed, allowing the office staff to switch off their engines using a mobile 4G data connection if the vehicle was stolen.

The three FIDE delegates assigned to the final minibus had also similarly been selected by hacking the office computer.

Once the delegates had been taken on to Grindelwald in their taxi, the minibus engine had been restarted after the immobilizer had been turned off again, also remotely. Jayne and Grewall then switched vehicles from the TCS truck, in which they had been traveling, to the minibus.

The same TCS truck was now safely locked away, out of sight in the underground garage at the CIA's rented safe house, where Vic and Coleman were ensconced.

In her pocket, Jayne had a printed copy of an official invitation to the FIDE party being held that evening at Kira Suslova's chalet. The invitation, in the name of the FIDE delegate for New Zealand, Aimee Warholm, had been retrieved by Alex Goode's Tailored Access Operations team from the computer belonging to the chalet manager, who had emailed personalized copies to all attendees.

Jayne glanced at Ed Grewall, sitting in the seat opposite. Like her, he had significantly changed his appearance. He had been subjected to a severe haircut with a set of clippers, reducing his graying locks to a short stubble, and had shaved off his stubbly beard.

Grewall also had an invitation to the party, in his case in the name of the Croatian delegate, Fedor Pavic.

Both Jayne and Grewall also carried printed copies of passports belonging to Warholm and Pavic. They had been obtained from scans that had been emailed to Suslova's chalet manager to enable her to identify the delegates as they arrived.

The disguises, implemented with the help of a specialist from the Bern CIA station, meant that Jayne and Grewall now bore a striking resemblance to the photographs of the delegates they were impersonating.

The substitution had been carefully calculated. Notes on both Warholm and Pavic that had been procured from the FIDE computer system, again by the Tailored Access Operations team, showed both delegates had been appointed by their home chess federations very recently. Neither had yet met any officials from FIDE headquarters, which gave Jayne the confidence she needed to press ahead with the substitution.

The real Warholm and Pavic, together with another colleague, had not only suffered an unfortunate breakdown as their minibus neared Grindelwald but had then succumbed to a serious bout of vomiting after drinking from bottles of mineral water and eating peanuts offered by the taxi driver who was taking them on to their hotel. All three were now confined to their beds, while the taxi driver, actually another member of the Bern CIA team, was acting as part of the backup team that would exfiltrate Jayne and Grewall from the party, if required.

On the seat next to Jayne was a printed copy of the detailed floor plan of Suslova's property, which she and Grewall had both memorized.

"You'll need to time your arrival to coincide with other minibuses bringing guests from the hotels," Jayne instructed the driver. "We want the security guards to feel pressured so they rush and minimize the checks."

"Good suggestion," the driver said. He glanced in his rearview mirror. "Actually, there's two more buses behind us right now." He jerked his thumb toward the rear of the minibus. "I'll go first and let them form a line behind."

"That's good," Jayne said. "Do that."

Her thoughts turned to Nick Geldard, who was already inside Suslova's chalet. He had complied with the request to arrive early for a private discussion about the potential purchase of his villa in Lausanne. Jayne had been quite anxious about it, fearing that Suslova might have discovered there was an operation running against her and Geldard was involved. But there seemed no alternative. For him to decline would likely have invited suspicion.

Geldard was fitted with a tiny microphone and transmitter inside the lining of his shirt collar behind the brass stiffener. Jayne could hear the output from the device through the micro earpiece she had tucked inside her right ear, although she found that it occasionally faded out, probably due to a weak 4G signal to her device.

Geldard's feed was also being transmitted to Vic and Coleman in the safe house, where everything was being recorded, and to Grewall.

Jayne had heard Geldard arriving at the chalet, going through identity checks, and then being greeted and escorted in by the house manager, who asked him if he would like a glass of champagne.

So far there had been no sign of Suslova greeting him, but Jayne guessed that would happen soon.

The risk was that if Suslova gave him an interrogation, Geldard might not prove up to it. But there was nothing Jayne could do about that. She just had to hope for the best.

There was a huge amount at stake here.

CHAPTER THIRTY-TWO

Tuesday, October 11, 2016
  Grindelwald

The ivory chess set was standing on a square table in the center of an oval ballroom. Chairs for spectators had been placed two rows deep around the edge of the room and colored nightclub-style strobe lights flickered across the walls and floor.

Nick Geldard's first thought was that it was over the top. His second was to wonder why Kira Suslova was going to all this trouble. He glanced at her, and perhaps his face gave away his thoughts.

"I thought it would be a bit of fun for the guests," Suslova said in her heavily accented English. "We'll make it a fifteen-minute game per player, so it doesn't go on too long and nobody gets bored. You know, two old has-beens, having a joust over the chessboard for half an hour. People will think it's a good laugh. It'll be a talking point for the evening. It doesn't matter who wins. My people will clear away the chairs and board afterward, then this becomes the dance floor. What do you think?"

At the far door, a heavily muscled man with a bald head and wearing a black suit stood facing them. Every so often, he turned and scanned the corridor behind him.

Geldard sipped the glass of champagne that his host had handed him. "Hmm. I'm not sure people will want to see us playing chess. We've had our day. But fine, I'll do it. No problem. It's an entertainment."

Suslova straightened her diamond necklace, which reached down to her cleavage. Her flimsy black dress left little to the imagination, but surprisingly for someone in her fifties, she looked very good in it, Geldard thought. It might be more difficult than he thought to concentrate on the chess match. Maybe that was the intention.

"But while we're waiting for the rest of the guests to arrive, let's go to my office for a few minutes, shall we?" Suslova said. "I'd like to have a quick discussion about your property in Lausanne."

Geldard nodded. "Sure, I'm happy to discuss it. It's a pity you weren't able to view it in person."

"Hopefully, I can do so soon. It's a lovely property. The video tour was more than adequate. I saw what I needed to see. Come this way."

Suslova turned and led the way past the man at the door. Geldard followed, and the man walked behind as they left the ballroom. There were already sixty or so guests in the reception rooms, Geldard noticed, most of them chatting in small groups of three or four.

They walked along a short corridor and past a set of open double doors. There she turned up a broad flight of stairs covered with a deep pile red carpet.

On the landing, Suslova turned into another corridor and then entered a well-equipped office with an oak desk. She indicated to Geldard to sit in a padded chair in front of the desk and spoke quietly to the bodyguard, who waited outside. She then shut the door, walked to a chair behind the desk, and sat down, closing the lid of a laptop that stood on the surface in front of her.

On the walls were photographs of various Moscow landmarks, including the Kremlin and another building that Geldard recognized immediately, the Central Chess Club.

"So," Suslova said. "Your villa in Lausanne. You definitely would like to sell it?"

Geldard knew he had to go along with this charade. "I need a pied-à-terre in Lausanne, but I don't need a property of that scale. I'm downsizing."

Suslova placed her hands flat on the desk and leaned forward. "I would like to buy it—I need a place in Lausanne. And I'm hoping that we can come to an arrangement. There are many ongoing issues at the moment, many of them interlinked, in which we both have an interest. You follow me?"

"Not entirely," Geldard said, slightly confused. "What do you mean?"

Suslova fixed him with a pair of ice-blue eyes. "You would like to sell a property, and I am prepared to make you a very good offer. You will also be aware that I have decided to stand for the presidency of FIDE. I would hope that our interests in the chess world are well aligned. I am focused on encouraging the development of the game in many poorer regions, not least Africa, Southeast Asia, and parts of the Middle East, as well as ensuring its health in Europe and the Americas."

More like aiming to use chess as a political tool for your boss in places like Syria, the Philippines, Kenya, Tanzania, and South Africa, Geldard thought.

"So what are you asking?" Geldard said.

"I would like to request your support for my candidacy,"

Suslova said. "I believe it would be mutually beneficial. You know how strongly I feel that when chess is healthy in England, it is healthy internationally."

She raised an eyebrow at Geldard, who pursed his lips but said nothing.

Such bullshit.

"At the same time, as a gesture of my good faith toward you, I am willing to table an offer of fifty million euros for your villa in Lausanne," Suslova said. "I trust that reflects a solid premium to the current market value."

Geldard involuntarily jerked upward in his chair, slightly spilling his champagne over his trousers as he did so.

"Fifty million?" he said, a note of incredulity in his voice. That was thirty million more than the valuation he'd been given.

"Yes," Suslova said in a level tone. "Fifty." She leaned forward over the table, folded her arms, and looked Geldard directly in the eyes. "I'm keen on the property, given my ambitions for the presidency. What do you say?"

"It's a very generous offer. Don't worry, I'm minded to accept it, but I don't want to do so formally tonight. I'll need to think about it."

Suslova raised an eyebrow. "Really? There won't be any other buyers willing to offer two and a half times the asking price. It's a way of giving you what you want, plus some extra, and also helping to facilitate my campaign, which will properly get underway this evening."

Geldard inclined his head. "Yes, I know what you're offering and expecting. I'm interested. But as I said, I'll think about it all over the next day or so, then let's have another conversation."

"All right," Suslova said, pursing her lips. "But there can't be too much to think about."

As she spoke, the door opened and in came the bald,

black-suited bodyguard who had followed them from the ball-room. He didn't say a word but just closed the door, then stood facing them, his arms folded, legs apart.

"I have just one or two other questions," Suslova said. "There is one thing bothering me a little."

"What's that?" Geldard said.

Suslova cupped her chin in her right hand, her elbow propped on the desk. "The timing of your decision to put your house on the market. Why now?"

Shit.

Geldard shrugged. "I've been thinking about downsizing for a little while. I just wanted to get things moving with a sale before the winter started."

"I see. And was it entirely your idea?"

He nodded. "Of course. It's my house."

Where the hell was she going with these questions?

"I mean, I heard about the property from Evgeny Dobkin at FIDE," Suslova said. "But I'm wondering, how, exactly, did FIDE get to know about the property being on the market? Because I note that it's not on the real estate agent's website, nor are there any marketing boards outside the house."

"I assume that the real estate agent was doing her job and contacted FIDE," Geldard said. "It's a very exclusive property. I didn't really want everyone to know I was selling, and the agent agreed that the subtle approach was best. Marketing boards would cheapen it. We were thinking of adding it to the website, but hadn't agreed on that yet."

"Of course, of course," Suslova said, her voice low.

She paused and eyed Geldard from beneath her black eyebrows. "Well, have a think about what I said. I hope you enjoy the party—and our chess match."

CHAPTER THIRTY-THREE

Tuesday, October 11, 2016
  Grindelwald

The minibus rolled through the gate and came to a halt in front of the red-and-white boom next to the security hut at the entrance to Suslova's chalet. Jayne watched as a guard in a dark suit and tie emerged from the hut and walked briskly to the driver's window, which was already open.

The driver passed the guard the two printed invitations for Aimee Warholm and Fedor Pavic.

"Open the passenger door," the guard said.

The driver jumped out and opened the rear sliding door. The guard peered in.

Jayne smiled at him. "Good evening," she said, making her best attempt at a faint New Zealand accent.

The guard nodded, then lifted his phone and tapped the screen a few times. Jayne caught a glimpse of the scanned copy of Warholm's passport on the display. The guard compared her to the photograph on his device, glancing from one to the other a couple of times to make certain. He frowned a little but eventually inclined his head from side to side, as if to say it just about passed, and handed back the invitation. Then he did the same with Grewall.

"Okay," the guard said. "Continue up the drive, then follow the sign down the ramp into the underground garage at the first basement level. There is a drop-off point where you'll be searched by the security team. Then someone will show you to the elevator that will take you to the ground-floor reception area. The minibus will then need to leave the premises. It will return to collect you after the party."

"Thank you," Jayne said.

A few minutes later, having navigated the security check, they emerged from the elevator into a high-ceilinged hallway. The sounds of chinking champagne glasses, laughter, and the hum of conversation were everywhere.

A woman in a well-cut navy suit greeted them and introduced herself as the house manager. "Welcome to Grindelwald," she said, after they had given their names. She indicated toward a waitress standing nearby. "Please enjoy a glass of champagne, mingle with the other guests, and help yourself to canapés." She ticked off Warholm and Pavic on the printed guest list she had pinned to a clipboard.

The woman eyed Jayne. "New Zealand. You're a long way from home. Have you been a FIDE delegate for long?"

"Not long," Jayne said. "Only a few weeks, actually. It's all new for me. I'm looking forward to being involved and finding out more."

The woman nodded, and Jayne thanked her, as did Grewall.

She was clearly busy and didn't pursue their conversation or question them further, which Jayne took as a good sign. It suggested that they weren't on some special watch list or anything like that.

They both took a glass and moved across the hall and through a set of double doors into a large reception room. There were already upwards of a hundred guests there, by Jayne's estimation. She continued to listen to the feed from Geldard's hidden microphone, which was still breaking up occasionally.

It became clear that Geldard was now having a one-to-one conversation with Suslova about the sale of his villa.

"Fifty million?"

"Yes. Fifty. I'm keen on the property, given my ambitions for the presidency. What do you say?"

"It's a very generous offer. Don't worry, I'm minded to accept it, but I don't want to do so formally tonight. I'll need to think about it."

At that point, the signal was lost again, and the feed cut out. Jayne cursed to herself.

However, it didn't matter much. Suslova had just provided A-grade and incontestable evidence that she was offering huge bribes in return for support in her drive to become FIDE president.

As planned, Jayne and Grewall made their way to the far side of the room, next to a door that they knew from the floor plan gave access to a rear staircase to the upper floors of the building.

Several minutes later, Jayne spotted Geldard appear through a set of double doors on the other side of the room. She did not want to get anywhere near to him tonight for fear of arousing suspicions.

There was no sign of Suslova. Perhaps she was still in her office—which was top on the list of rooms Jayne wanted to access when the opportunity arose.

For the next twenty minutes, Jayne and Grewall pretended to engage each other in intense conversation, the object being to avoid having to talk to others. That wasn't too difficult. Many chess players were notoriously introverted and uncomfortable in social situations.

The numbers present continued to grow as more guests arrived. Most of the delegates were talking quietly in small groups rather than working the room, although Jayne guessed that would likely change in direct proportion to the volume of alcohol consumed as the night went on.

Suddenly, there came the sound of a small bell being rung. The room went silent, and then Suslova emerged through the same double doors that Geldard had entered by.

At the same time, Jayne noticed two other men quietly enter the room by the main entrance from the hallway. Both were heavily built in dark suits, one bald, one with short-cropped black hair. Presumably, they were Suslova's bodyguards.

Suslova held both her hands up to silence the applause and, when the room was once again quiet, spoke in English to thank everyone for making the long journey from Lausanne. She went on to say that she would address the gathering later about her intended run at the presidency, but to get the entertainment underway, she would first take part in a game of fast chess with Nick Geldard. Everyone was welcome to get another drink and come and watch.

"I realize that not everyone will relish the prospect of two old chess dinosaurs going head-to-head with each other," Suslova said, indicating toward Geldard, who was standing near her. "But it's a bit of fun, and I am certain our game will provide a talking point for the remainder of the evening. Hopefully, it will be entertaining. So please, follow me into the ballroom, and we will get proceedings underway."

Suslova turned and made her way out of the room through the double doors behind her, closely followed by Geldard. The rest of the gathering slowly headed after her.

This was Jayne's opportunity. She glanced around. One of

the two bodyguards had followed Suslova; the other was still in place, but had his back turned.

"Let's go," Jayne murmured to Grewall. Still with an eye on the room to ensure they were not being watched, she half opened the door behind her and slipped through. Grewall followed, silently closing the door behind him.

Visualizing the floor plan of the chalet in her mind, Jayne headed up the rear staircase to the next level, where she knew Suslova had her office. The landing was small and there was just one door, which she knew from the floor plan led into another corridor.

Jayne eased the door open a fraction and applied her right eye to the crack. There appeared to be nobody in the corridor, presumably because they were all downstairs in the ballroom for the chess match.

She glanced back at Grewall, who nodded to her to go ahead.

Jayne opened the door and slipped through. The office, she knew, was the fourth door on the left, opposite the main central staircase that rose from the reception area.

The corridor floor was carpeted, making it possible to walk on without making a sound. Jayne nevertheless trod as softly as she could until she reached the office.

She pulled down on the handle, fully expecting it to be locked.

But it clicked open.

Without hesitating, Jayne walked in and flicked on the light switch.

This was risky as hell.

But they had no option.

The best they could do was move as swiftly as possible and hope that the fast chess game downstairs would distract everyone for as long as possible. Jayne knew it was going to last around half an hour, maximum.

Through her earpiece, Jayne could hear Geldard and Suslova confirming to each other that they were ready and starting their game. After that, neither of them spoke. Jayne could hear chatter, clinking glasses, and faint music in the background through the earpiece, but little else.

"We need her laptop," Jayne said as Grewall closed the door behind him. There was no sign of any device on the desk. Jayne pointed toward the far end of the room. "I'll search the cupboards starting that end, you start this end."

They began going through the long row of full-height cupboards that ran along one wall of the office. There were books, files, and a variety of office equipment, such as staplers, spare pens, and notebooks in the first three that Jayne opened. But no laptop.

From behind her, Grewall suddenly muttered. "Got it. In this cupboard."

She turned to find him holding an Apple MacBook Pro.

"Good work," she said.

Jayne swiftly calculated what they should do next. There were really only two options. The first was to leave and take the laptop with them, hoping that the information they needed to identify the two Kremlin assets in the West was contained somewhere within it. That was possible, but uncertain. Maybe even unlikely.

The second was to remain where they were and try to upload the laptop's contents immediately to Langley, and then seek the face-to-face confrontation they needed with Suslova, hopefully with even more ammunition in the locker.

If they took the first option, then Jayne's opportunity to confront Suslova in order to bring about Joe's release and get information about the Russian spies would vanish, likely never to return. If the laptop also didn't yield the necessary information, then they were almost back to square one.

There seemed no debate to be had, in Jayne's mind.

There was, of course, a risk that a confrontation with Suslova here on her own property could go horribly wrong. But she would cross that bridge if she got to it—it was part and parcel of the job.

Jayne calculated that with everyone occupied downstairs, they could get away with carrying out the upload from here, undiscovered. Then she and Grewall could move back downstairs and engineer a discussion with Suslova a little more on their own terms, not hers, as the party continued.

"Put the MacBook on the desk?" Jayne said. "Don't start it up yet."

Grewall placed the laptop on the desk and waited while Jayne tugged at the back of her blonde wig, pulling it away from her scalp. She removed a small high-speed USB drive from its hiding place beneath the latex base that held the curly wig in place, along with a short cable. She connected the drive to one of the sockets on the laptop.

Then Jayne flipped open the lid, and the machine hummed into life. Within a couple of seconds, the startup screen appeared and the familiar Apple chime sounded.

But then the screen went blue, and a message appeared.

Booting.

A progress bar appeared at the top, which soon moved from left to right across the screen to indicate the laptop had booted up using the doctored operating system on Jayne's drive rather than the native one on the machine.

Then another progress bar appeared beneath it.

Copying files.

Jayne watched as the second progress bar began to move.

Estimated time remaining: 4 minutes.

The app was designed to identify and copy any user files and emails at high speed, ignoring unwanted system files and apps. Four minutes was very little time. There clearly wasn't much data on the machine. She glanced at her watch.

The drive, which drew its power from the laptop's USB socket, was fitted with a micro 4G card that connected automatically to a server at Langley. It then transmitted and uploaded any data plundered from the target computer.

Jayne could feel the butterflies fluttering around in her stomach.

It was the waiting, and not knowing.

All she could hear was the faint humming of the laptop.

She tapped her fingers on the desk, willing the hardware to spill its secrets faster so they could get out of there.

Jayne again glanced down at the laptop screen to check the progress of her data download.

Estimated time remaining: 2 minutes.

As she looked up again, there came a sharp double knock at the door.

Jayne jerked her head up as if electrified.

Shit.

Grewall spun around.

Jayne reacted immediately.

The upload would have to be aborted.

That could mean losing the data.

But there was no choice.

Jayne yanked the cable from the USB socket and simultaneously pressed the machine's off button. She slammed the laptop lid shut.

There was no time to fiddle around replacing the drive and cable beneath her wig. So she shoved them in the only hiding place she could see—a small gap between two books on the shelf behind her. There was also no time to hide the laptop.

"Hold the handle up," she hissed. "Don't let them in. Put your foot against the door."

Grewall moved fast. He took two rapid strides toward the door and reached out to grab the handle.

But he got no farther.

There was a click, a bang, and the door flew back with tremendous force.

It smashed straight into Grewall's left shoulder and sent him spiraling backward onto the floor.

In the doorway stood the bald man in a black suit that Jayne had seen downstairs in the reception room.

He was pointing a handgun straight at her. Behind him was another man.

"Don't move," he said calmly. "Put your hands up. Now!"

Jayne slowly raised her hands high above her head.

CHAPTER THIRTY-FOUR

Tuesday, October 11, 2016
Kaliningrad

"Sit up," the man ordered in his now familiar attempt at English, as he unlocked the handcuffs that bound Joe to the metal shelving units at the head of his mattress.

Joe struggled to raise himself upright, wincing as he did so. He had sores on his backside from being forced to lie in the same position for hour after hour, day after day. They were now causing continuous pain. He hoped they weren't becoming infected.

He was also suffering sharp spikes of agony around the base of his rib cage, where he had been repeatedly punched. He suspected that his liver had been badly bruised, if not worse, and at least one rib was fractured.

Taken altogether, he had struggled to get much sleep and felt as though his head had turned to concrete.

But through all of that, all he could think about was whether Carrie was undergoing a similar ordeal. He tried to convince himself she wasn't; otherwise, his captors would have told him and goaded him. But the thought still made him feel sick.

The man cut the plastic cable ties that bound his ankles. "Stand," he ordered.

The bald, military-looking man who had tried to interrogate him over the first two or three days had vanished. His sidekick had taken over ever since. Also Russian, he had a similar military physique, with a full head of short, dark hair. Joe was certain he had heard the bald man call him Feodor at one point.

Joe did as he was told. He didn't want another punch to the ribs.

Feodor handcuffed him once again, this time holding his wrists together.

"Walk to the van," Feodor ordered, pointing toward the black Transit parked against the far wall. He shoved Joe in the small of the back, making him stumble a little.

When they reached the van, Feodor unlocked the twin rear doors. Now Joe could see the license plate. It had "39 RUS" in the segment to the right of the main number. So it was Russian.

Then he spotted the Ford logo and the dealership's name in small capitals below the number.

FORD CENTER KALININGRAD.

Joe swore to himself.

That confirmed it.

It was the ninth day since he had been kidnapped in Amsterdam. He knew that because he had counted carefully.

He believed for much of that time that, contrary to his initial impression, he wasn't actually in Amsterdam. He had heard scraps of distant conversation from outside the building he was in, and he was sure they were in Russian. It certainly wasn't Dutch.

It could have been his kidnappers talking, who definitely were Russian, but Joe didn't think so. One of the voices had been female, and he hadn't seen a woman the entire time he'd been there.

Yes, they were near water, and he frequently heard the sound of outboard boat engines. But he had increasingly suspected the water was not that of Amsterdam's canals.

There were also the aircraft sounds. He had heard jet engines, but they were few in number and spaced irregularly. Schiphol would be much busier.

But Kaliningrad?

Holy shit.

They must have flown him here.

"Where are we going?" Joe asked.

"You will find out," Feodor muttered.

There was a thin rubber mat on the metal floor of the Transit. Feodor pointed to it. "Lie on that."

Joe just looked at him. "You bastard."

Before Feodor could respond, either verbally or physically, Joe did as he was told, groaning from the pain in his ribs as he heaved himself into the van, using his handcuffed hands for leverage.

Feodor then grabbed four pieces of rope from a bag and lashed both of Joe's legs and his hands, still cuffed together, to the vertical struts of the van's rear compartment, which was separated from the driver's cab by a solid steel bulkhead.

The van door slammed shut and Joe was in the dark. There were no windows.

Then he heard the grating sound of the workshop door sliding open. The engine started soon after, and the van moved off.

Where they were going, Joe had no idea.

* * *

Tuesday, October 11, 2016
  Grindelwald

The bald gunman's eyes flicked between Jayne and Grewall, who was on the floor.

"Who are you?" the guard asked. "What are you doing in here?"

There was a pause.

"We're delegates from the International Chess Federation," Jayne said. "We are here for the social event, the party, as guests of Ms. Suslova. I am Aimee Warholm, from New Zealand. This is Fedor Pavic, from Croatia."

She figured the longer she could keep him talking, the less likely he was to notice the laptop.

"Chess? Don't bullshit me," he snapped. "Everyone from chess is downstairs. This is a private office."

Jayne stared at him. "We're just exploring the house, that's all. It's a lovely building. We have properties like this in the mountains in New Zealand, where I come from, so I was just interested in the layout."

The man's lip curled upward in a clear expression of disbelief. "*Bljad.* Sonofabitch. What the hell is this? How did you get in here?"

"We came up the stairs. How do you think we got here?" Jayne asked. "We were told to make ourselves at home." She figured it was the kind of thing an innocent New Zealander might say.

The man shook his head and looked down at Grewall. "Get up, you," he ordered. "Both of you, up against the wall, hands up, facing toward me. And keep them up where I can see them." He pointed the pistol, a Makarov, straight at them.

Jayne had her hands raised high. As she moved slowly to the wall, she inched them close together until they were touching. Then, using her right index finger, she pressed the top left button of her watch, on her left wrist, until it gave a faint beep.

"What was that?" the guard snapped. He turned his attention from Grewall, who was now on his feet, to Jayne.

"Nothing," Jayne said.

"I heard a beep."

"I think it was my alarm," Jayne said.

The gunman looked up at her watch, then moved around the room, allowing space for his colleague to enter. He too had a Makarov in his hand, raised in firing position.

Jayne flattened herself against the wall and kept her hands high, facing the gunmen as instructed. Grewall did likewise a couple of meters farther along the same wall.

It was then that the first gunman noticed the MacBook on the desk, its lid closed. Jayne gave thanks that she had just managed to hide the drive and turn the computer off before the man burst in.

"What are you doing with this laptop?" the first gunman said, his voice gathering in intensity. He flipped open the lid, glanced at the screen, then, seeing it was switched off, closed it again. "Are you stealing it? It should be in the cupboard."

"Of course not," Jayne said.

The sound feed from Jayne's earpiece suddenly cut out. She guessed that Vic and the team in the safe house had terminated it after the SOS signal from her watch.

"Look, there's some major misunderstanding here," Jayne said. "Can we just rejoin the party, please? We only wanted to look around Ms. Suslova's house while we were here. We're not doing any harm. Honestly, you've made a mistake."

The bald guard ignored her, a dismissive expression on his face. "Fasten their hands," he snapped.

The second man walked to Grewall first, took two plastic cable ties from his jacket pocket, and used one of them to lash his hands together in front of him. He then repeated the procedure with Jayne.

Jayne cringed as he reached into her pockets, one at a time, and removed her phone and the printed copies of Aimee Warholm's party invitation and passport scan. She had left all her other personal identification at the safe house.

"What are you doing?" she asked forcefully. "This is outrageous. Leave me alone. That's my phone you've taken."

"No purse? No wallet? Credit cards?" the man asked, continuing to ignore her.

Jayne shook her head. "Of course not. I didn't need to bring them to the party."

The man moved to Grewall, from whom he also took a phone.

"Get these two to the basement room," the bald guard said.

The next thing Jayne knew, the barrel of a gun was jammed painfully into her right kidney.

She decided the best option here was to short-circuit this whole charade. There was no point in wasting more time. Joe was still imprisoned somewhere, as far as she knew, and there were still two high-level Russian spies operational. She needed to speak to Suslova now.

"Come on," Jayne said. "This is awful. Wait until Ms. Suslova hears about this. Can I speak to her now, please? Call her in here. She'll be outraged, you do—"

"Shut up, unless you want to get shot," the second guard interrupted. "Walk. Out the door, turn right. Go to the elevator."

Jayne hesitated momentarily, but given the gun, she decided to comply. She walked slowly to the door and along the corridor to the elevator door, the guard's gun still stuck in her lower back.

He pressed the elevator call button, and the door opened immediately.

Then the man spotted the tiny earpiece in Jayne's ear.

"What's this?" he demanded. He plucked out the earpiece with the thumb and index finger of his left hand, while keeping the gun pushed into her back. "Is this a monitor? A listening device or something? Are you a spy?"

Jayne shook her head. "It's my hearing aid."

The man exhaled loudly. "Bullshit."

"Get in the elevator," the guard ordered. "Stand against the wall."

He pushed her into the car and then waited until the bald guard ushered Grewall in before pressing the lower basement button, which Jayne noted was the level below the drop-off point where the minibus had left them. The doors closed, and they descended.

Jayne exchanged glances with Grewall. He momentarily rolled his eyes, indicating there was little they could do for now.

Once at the lower basement level, they were both marched down a bare corridor. They stopped outside the first door on the right, which the bald gunman opened. He pushed Grewall inside.

"Guard him in there," the bald gunman instructed his colleague.

The second gunman left Jayne and entered the room. Jayne glimpsed a white-painted room equipped only with a table and four chairs.

"Do I go in here too?" Jayne asked.

The bald gunman shook his head as the door slammed shut behind Grewall and the guard.

The bald guard grabbed Jayne, pushed his Makarov into her back, and propelled her farther down the corridor to a similar room. He took a chair, placed it at the far end of the room, and instructed Jayne to sit on it.

"Don't even think about trying anything stupid," he said. "Or else I'll beat you to a pulp."

The guard then secured Jayne's ankles to the chair legs using plastic cable ties, leaving her completely immobilized.

Then he stood, legs apart, his Makarov pointed directly at Jayne's head. "You will sit here until you have told us exactly why you are here, how you got in, what you are doing, and who you work for. And don't tell me again that you are FIDE delegates."

Jayne looked up at him.

This was going to be all or nothing.

She just hoped that Geldard wouldn't also be caught. She also had to hope that it would be some time before the external drive she had hidden in Suslova's bookshelf was found and that at least some files from the laptop had been uploaded to Langley.

"For the second time, I need to speak to Kira Suslova," Jayne said, as forcefully as she could. "We have very important things to discuss. Call her—now."

* * *

Tuesday, October 11, 2016
  Grindelwald

Vic Walter sat on the edge of the table in the safe house, his arms folded tight across his chest. Every few seconds, he glanced down at his smartphone on the surface next to him.

It had been about two minutes since he had received the alert from the tech team at Langley to tell him that an upload from Jayne Robinson's external drive had begun to feed through to the CIA's server. It had given an estimated upload time of four minutes.

"I hope this works," Vic said, looking across at Alvin Coleman on the other side of the table. "It doesn't really—"

But he broke off as there came a loud beep from his phone. He grabbed the device and read the alert that had popped up on his lock screen.

Data upload aborted.

"Damn it," Vic muttered. He glanced up at Coleman. "The upload from Jayne just aborted."

He tapped on the app, hoping there might be more detail about why. But there was nothing.

A minute later, there was another beep, another alert.

SOS received from Jayne Robinson. Tap here to view location.

"Oh shit. This is bad news," Vic said. "Jayne's just fired off an SOS. They must have been blown."

Coleman grimaced. A second later, his phone also beeped. He scrutinized the screen. "I've got it too."

This was the type of scenario Vic hated. Using a top-class independent operative like Jayne to do his dirty work gave him deniability and, more importantly, gave President Ferguson deniability if the shit hit the fan. But when things went wrong, it also left him short of official options to resolve matters.

Coleman leaned forward in his chair. "What do you think?"

Vic hesitated. "We have no choice. We'll have to give Marchenko and Azarov the green light. That's what we agreed." He glanced uncertainly at Coleman. "I don't like doing this, but I'm not seeing any alternatives."

Coleman gave a short nod. "Let's do it. We have to."

Vic screwed up his face. "I hope I'm not signing Jayne's death warrant. It feels a bit like lobbing a grenade into the situation and hoping the blast wave goes in the right direction."

Coleman shrugged. "What's the alternative? Call the local police? When we're running an illegal operation on Swiss soil? When we're breaking into and entering a private property—even if it is owned by one of Putin's acolytes?"

Vic shook his head but said nothing.

"It's the only ammunition we've got," Coleman said.

Vic closed his eyes momentarily. He hated doing this job sometimes. It felt like playing Russian roulette, he thought to himself, then realized the irony of his own thoughts.

He was using one deniable operator to get another—Jayne —out of trouble. But Coleman was right. It was the only safeguard they had.

He nodded and began to tap out a prearranged secure message to Marchenko on his phone screen.

Tell Azarov to drain the swamp—NOW.

CHAPTER THIRTY-FIVE

Tuesday, October 11, 2016
Grindelwald

The sound of the rapid-fire clicking of stilettos along the concrete corridor was unmistakable. Jayne knew Kira Suslova was on her way, even before the door had opened.

This was it, then.

A few seconds later, the door burst open, and in strode a slim woman with dark hair, not dissimilar in color and length to Jayne's own, and of similar age. She was wearing a suggestive black dress and a diamond necklace and carrying a Saint Laurent clutch bag.

Suslova stood there for a couple of seconds, taking in the sight of Jayne bound to a chair at one end of the room.

"*Bozhe*, God. What do we have here?" Suslova said in her thick accent. She dropped her clutch onto the table and then strode straight over to Jayne, grabbed her blonde wig, and pulled sharply.

The wig came off in Suslova's hands, revealing Jayne's natural black hair, flecked with gray.

"Couldn't the CIA's disguise department do better than that, Ms. Robinson?" Suslova said.

Jayne remained silent. There seemed little point in speaking right now. Clearly, Suslova was going to enjoy herself for a while, and Jayne didn't want to add fuel to the flames by reacting.

"So it wasn't enough for your partner, your boyfriend, whatever you want to call him, to fall into our hands," Suslova continued. "You decided you would hand yourself to us on a plate as well and double our bargaining power. That was incredibly thoughtful of you."

Suslova threw the wig across the room onto the floor. "Good of you to give me a few options. I can offer Washington two Western spies in exchange for the wife of one Russian spy, who appears intent on doing as much damage as she can to her Motherland. I speak, of course, about Maria Fradkova. She is in Ukraine, I understand, and I am sure that your friends in Kyiv can facilitate her return home to Moscow."

Jayne knew she had to respond to that.

She gave a sardonic laugh. "So that you can put her in Lefortovo and torture her to death?" Jayne said, eyeballing Suslova. "Forget it. Russia is the last place she is going."

Suslova took a couple of steps and stood in front of Jayne, looking down at her, arms folded, legs apart. Her three-inch black stilettos gave her even more of a height advantage.

Typical intimidation attempt.

"It wasn't a request," Suslova said. "It was an instruction. Maria Fradkova will be returned to Russia."

"No, she won't," Jayne said, her voice level.

The Russian narrowed her eyes, anger written across her face. "If we do not get her back, your friend Mr. Johnson will find himself at the bottom of the Neman River. And you will likely be joining him. Together in life, together in death."

The Neman was the river that formed the border between Kaliningrad and Lithuania before finally flowing into the Baltic Sea. Jayne had been on the Lithuanian side of the river while working on an MI6 operation several years earlier, and she knew Joe had also worked in that area in the past.

Jayne had expected this kind of threat. An image of Joe tied up in some concrete basement, maybe in a not dissimilar situation to herself, flashed across her mind.

"You're making a serious mistake," Jayne said. "You might think that the tidal wave of Putin's money washing around inside your bank account is going to be the making of you. But you're very wrong. It's actually going to be the breaking of you."

"*Mudak*. You shithead," Suslova spat. "The only ones breaking will be you and your friend."

"Let me ask you a question," Jayne said. "How do you think the chess world will react if it's made public that you are trying to buy your way to the FIDE presidency? That you are offering bribes for votes left, right, and center?"

"Bullshit," Suslova said. "Completely untrue. There's no proof of that."

"But there is. That's why you're holding this event tonight, isn't it? It's part of a campaign that's built on graft, bribery, and corruption. Everyone here will be given something. You're offering money and property to the rich delegates, mostly through payments to shell companies registered in obscure offshore locations. You're promising waived FIDE subscriptions, cash to fund grand chess tournaments. And so on, and so on. And all because your boss wants to use chess as a political battering ram to gain influence all over the world."

"Allegations," Suslova snarled. "You can't give me a single

example or a single piece of solid evidence. I suggest you focus on getting Maria Fradkova back onto Russian soil."

Jayne did her best to put on a sarcastic smile. "We know about the over-inflated prices you offer for FIDE delegates' properties, the cash transfers."

She had an urge to name Geldard and the fifty million euros offered for his twenty million villa but knew it would immediately land him in deep trouble.

Suslova's face didn't flicker, so Jayne continued.

"It's not going to look good for you, and not good for FIDE either, when all these details are made public."

"If you've been given false information by some source with an axe to grind, I would treat it with extreme caution," Suslova said. "You don't know what you're getting into."

Jayne shook her head. "We have evidence, believe me."

The snarl disappeared from Suslova's face. She rocked back on her heels and said nothing for several seconds. Jayne could almost see the cogs whirring inside her mind.

Jayne pressed ahead. "How many properties do you now own around the world, Suslova? And how many of those were obtained through massively overpriced deals with FIDE voting delegates? I doubt that your Putin is going to enjoy a tidal wave of condemnation when what you're doing is plastered all over the news. It reflects badly on him at home. It adds more fuel to the fire for his critics inside Russia, the ones who can do him the most damage. And we all know what he does when he becomes annoyed at his employees' miscalculations and mistakes. Prepare for a one-way ticket to a labor camp, Ms. Suslova, and the loss of all your wealth."

Suslova raised her hand, whipped her palm hard across Jayne's left cheek, then spat into her face. Jayne could feel a large blob of spit trickling down her chin. Her cheek was stinging, and she tasted blood on her tongue.

"Liar," Suslova said. She turned to the bald gunman, who

had continued to keep his weapon pointing toward Jayne. "Andrey, get this *suka*, this bitch, out of here and onto the helicopter. And take her friend with her. We'll take them to the airport and fly them to Kaliningrad. They can go into the river alongside her boyfriend."

Andrey. Jayne registered the name.

He stepped forward toward Jayne.

"Wait," Jayne said. "We're not quite done yet. There are a few more things I need to discuss."

"Such as?" Suslova asked.

Despite the pain Jayne was now feeling, she was thinking clearly enough to know she needed to get rid of Suslova's guard. She didn't want a witness to what she was about to say.

"I want to do it privately—not with your guard present. Send him upstairs for a few minutes. This is sensitive."

Suslova stared at Jayne. "No. You're going to Kaliningrad."

Jayne had expected that. "Seriously, you'll regret it if you don't let me have a private discussion with you."

Somewhat to Jayne's surprise, Suslova paused, then turned to Andrey and inclined her head toward the door.

"Are you certain?" he asked.

"Just get on with it," Suslova snapped. "Go upstairs and wait there. I'll call you when I'm ready. But let me borrow that Makarov. You have a spare?"

Andrey nodded, handed over his pistol, and went out the door, closing it behind him.

"Well?" Suslova asked.

Jayne lowered her voice to a murmur. "Is this room bugged?" she asked. "Microphones? Cameras?"

Suslova shook her head. "No, it is not." She checked the Makarov. Jayne could see the safety lever was off. Then Suslova strode back to the door, opened it, and looked out into the corridor. Presumably, she didn't trust Andrey. Then she closed the door again.

While she was doing that, Jayne looked carefully around. There was no sign of hidden devices. There were no telltale tiny pinpoints of LED light, no reflections from glass lenses in the ceiling or walls.

"Talk," Suslova snapped.

"I'll start by asking about where all your money is coming from to do these property deals, to bribe these FIDE delegates, to pay off so many people?"

"What I do with my money is my business, as is where it comes from," Suslova said.

"Except it's not your money. It sits in your so-called *Shakhmaty Schet*. Your chess account. It's held offshore in Moskva Bank's branch in Cyprus. And the money in it is provided by Vladimir Putin."

Jayne thought that Suslova was going to implode. Her face went a shade of crimson. So Jayne decided to add another bit of detail, just to ensure Suslova got the point.

"There was just over two billion dollars in that *account* the last time I checked," Jayne said.

"The last time you checked?" Suslova snarled, a note of incredulity in her voice.

"Yes," Jayne said, deliberately slowing her words. "When was the last time you checked? Can you check now, on your phone?"

Suslova exhaled vigorously, now visibly rattled. "Why would I want to do that?"

Jayne just raised an eyebrow in response and gave a faint smile.

Suslova stared at her, then walked over to the table and took her phone from her clutch bag.

The Russian tapped a few times on the screen, then applied her thumb to the screen, presumably to sign into her Moskva Bank account.

Jayne watched her closely. She drew breath, then her

pupils dilated. Finally, her cheeks went from purple to white as the blood drained from her face.

Suslova slowly looked up from her phone. "*Mudilo*. You motherfucker," she murmured, her voice barely audible. "You're making a big mistake."

* * *

Tuesday, October 11, 2016
Grindelwald

After agreeing to an honorable draw in his game with Suslova, despite being quite confident he had a winning position, Geldard tried to relax with a glass of wine and worked the room, chatting with some of the other FIDE delegates who he knew.

He had offered the draw, not wanting to humiliate Suslova at her own party, and she had immediately accepted. She seemed a little rusty and had made a couple of blunders that he hadn't expected, allowing him to build a good position quite quickly.

Afterward, she had shaken hands with him to loud and somewhat drunken applause from the crowd that had gathered to watch.

Suslova's house manager had then approached her and the pair of them held a whispered conversation. At that point, Suslova left the room, and so far hadn't returned.

Now Geldard was wondering what was happening behind the scenes. He had no way of checking what Jayne was doing, but he knew that she and Ed Grewall had arrived as planned, because he had seen them at the far side of the room before the chess game had commenced. After that, they disappeared.

Twenty minutes later, the two men he had seen at the beginning of the evening, who looked like bodyguards with their dark suits and white shirts, returned to the ballroom together.

Geldard kept an eye on them as they held an animated conversation.

He just hoped that Jayne had not run into difficulties.

CHAPTER THIRTY-SIX

Tuesday, October 11, 2016
   Grindelwald

Jayne deliberately kept a poker face, fighting the sudden urge to laugh out loud, despite her situation and the pain she was feeling. In part, this urge stemmed from a sense of relief that Azarov's confidence in his ability to drain Suslova's bank account had been justified.

"I'm guessing you'll want all the money back," Jayne said.

Suslova's face resembled a white marble statue.

"So this is what the CIA now resorts to," Suslova said eventually. "Street theft. Gutter operations. Desperate times."

That's rich coming from a Kremlin chief, to say the least.

"I could kill you now," Suslova said, her voice level.

"You could," Jayne said. "Just like you killed your lover Pyotr Fradkov over a game of chess. Forensics found your hairs on the chair."

Suslova's face twitched a little. She didn't reply.

The line about forensics was a gamble, given the lack of a DNA match for the hair. But the reaction told Jayne all she needed to know.

"You kill me, you sign your own death warrant," Jayne continued. "Because I can assure you that not only will you never get President Putin's money back, but all the information I've got is neatly packaged up with his address on it, ready to go. I have a very good team ready to deliver it within minutes if anything happens to me."

Suslova said nothing.

"So, I assume you want to avoid that," Jayne continued. "But first, there are a few things you'll need to do for me."

Suslova's eyes narrowed again. She resumed her earlier stance, legs apart, apparently regaining some of her composure, but still didn't speak.

"First is the immediate return of Joe Johnson, unharmed," Jayne said. "The same goes for myself and Mr. Grewall—we need to leave here unharmed. And then you need to call off the attack dogs who are chasing Maria Fradkova."

Suslova remained silent.

"But there are other things too," Jayne continued. "I am not an international chess player or a FIDE delegate. But I used to play a lot, and I do like to see the game played and run in a fair way. So, you will abandon any thoughts of coercing, bribing, or otherwise skewing your way to the FIDE presidency. In fact, I want you to step down as a candidate."

Suslova immediately shook her head. "That is nonnegotiable. President Putin is insisting I secure the presidency. If I fail, he would probably put me in a prison cell."

Jayne pressed her lips.

Maybe Suslova was right. She might have to let her continue with the campaign, much as it grated.

"Obviously, I don't want you to fall foul of your president."

Suslova's eyebrows shot up. "Thanks for your concern."

"Well, I wouldn't want to see you lose your job in Moscow," Jayne said, a marked note of sarcasm in her voice.

There was some confusion on Suslova's face, so Jayne cleared it up for her.

"I'll tell you why." Jayne eyeballed Suslova. "Let's just recap so far. You killed Pyotr Fradkov, and you ordered Anastasia Shevchenko killed, and—"

"Shevchenko was careless," Suslova interrupted. "She was a traitor—like Fradkov."

Jayne paused.

Careless?

Had Shevchenko somehow made a mistake with the SRAC device or her surveillance detection methods before the meeting? She had a sudden urge to ask. But there was no point. What was done was done.

"My point is, I need a fresh asset inside the Kremlin, a replacement for Shevchenko," Jayne went on. "And *you* are that replacement. You work for us now—not just for Putin."

Suslova took a step back, visibly stunned. "No. Never. I'm not doing that."

Jayne shrugged. "If you'd rather not take up my offer, or if anything happens to me, all the documentation showing the properties—and the yachts—you've bought for your own use, via your own offshore companies, with the president's money, will go to his office. Putin will also be interested in how you have funneled money from the Moskva account into your own personal Swiss bank account—all dressed up as loans at minuscule interest rates. And none of which have been repaid."

She knew she'd provided enough detail to make Suslova certain there was no bluff involved.

Suslova swore.

"Before we go any further," Jayne said, "you can remove these cable ties from my wrists and legs. They're painful."

Suslova grimaced but went to a cupboard in the corner, opened it, and took out a penknife. She held it in her left hand to slice through the ties that bound Jayne, while keeping the Makarov pointed at Jayne with her right.

"Thank you," Jayne said. She shook her wrists and wiggled her ankles. Immediately, she could feel her feet tingle as the circulation came back. "And can you stop pointing that gun at me?"

"Surely you can't believe I'm going to work for you. What do you really want?" Suslova asked, ignoring the request but moving two steps back. "And what do I get in return? I want my money back immediately."

Jayne stood slowly and flexed her legs. Her ankles were extremely stiff and sore. "What do I want, apart from the items I've already mentioned? Well, now we come to the important stuff. I happen to know that the Kremlin has two major assets in the West—high-level ones. They're code-named ILYA and ALYOSHA. Before the funds are restored to your *Shakhmaty Schet* account, I need to know who those assets are. I also need full details and updates on Operations Imperiya and Peshka. You can look upon this as your first bit of work for me. In return, you get your money."

Suslova's eyes widened. "How . . . ? Don't tell me. Shevchenko? That traitorous bitch? Screw you."

Jayne ignored the outburst. "I know that Imperiya is the plan to invade Ukraine. And I know that Peshka is the operation to run ILYA and ALYOSHA. But who are they?"

Suslova walked toward the door, her stilettos clicking loudly on the hard floor.

"Very well," Jayne said. "I'll look forward to hearing of your fate at Lefortovo."

Suslova cursed, then turned around and walked back again.

"I can't tell you who any assets are," Suslova said. "If I did, it would mean a death sentence for me—and then you'd have no asset in Moscow. You'd be sabotaging your own plan."

"Well, if you don't tell me, you'll be facing a death sentence anyway once those documents reach President Putin. And we will also let him know that you—Putin's mistress—were also having a secret affair with Pyotr Fradkov. That's true, isn't it? You were screwing both of them?"

Suslova shook her head but looked up to the left.

A tell.

"And I'll also inform Putin that you confided top-secret Kremlin information to Fradkov," Jayne continued. "Pillow talk. And that you subsequently had him murdered in an attempt to stop him leaking it. But by then, it was too late—the horse was out of the stable door, and we have uncovered all this information as a result of what you started. Putin will enjoy the story."

"*Bozhe*," Suslova said. She glanced up at the ceiling. For the first time, she looked vulnerable.

Checkmate, Jayne thought to herself.

"I can't tell you about the assets myself," Suslova said. "They would know for sure it's come from me if you go directly from me to the assets. There are safeguards and traps in place of the kind you can't imagine. If Operation Peshka leaks, Putin's counterintelligence people, Gennady Sidorenko, will be all over it. You'll need to do your own investigation—and leave a trail that proves you've done your own investigation."

"What kind of traps?"

"I can't tell you. Find other sources—and leave a trail. There must be no fingerprints of mine on this. I've got to be a hundred percent clean—otherwise, I'll be dead in weeks. Then I'll be no use to you at all. Think it through."

Shit.

Jayne could see Suslova's logic, sort of.

Of course, there would be a massive counterintelligence witch hunt in Moscow if Operation Peshka was compromised. Putin would want a scapegoat, a head on a platter.

"So who can tell me, then?" Jayne asked, trying hard not to show her frustration. "Which other sources?"

Suslova looked down at the floor. "There's only one person who knows their identities, apart from me. The handler."

Jayne's heart jumped. "So you're not the handler of ILYA and ALYOSHA? Who is?"

Now Jayne sensed that Suslova's anxiety levels were rising. She exhaled.

"You're not getting this information from me."

"Obviously not," Jayne said.

"Try the president of the German chess federation, Wolfgang Paulsen," Suslova murmured eventually, her voice only just audible. "He's the handler. Always has been."

"Bloody hell," Jayne said. She felt as though a shot of rocket fuel had gone through her veins.

Paulsen—the guy who had beaten Nick Geldard in two candidates tournament semifinals during the 1990s.

"The guy who's head of chess in Germany is the handler?" Jayne asked. "Is he upstairs at the party?"

"No. He is the FIDE delegate for Germany, as well as the president, but he couldn't make it here."

"How long has Paulsen done this?" Jayne asked.

"Since 1988."

"Since *1988*? Operation Peshka has been running since 1988? You're joking?" But she could tell that Suslova was not. "How?"

"Simple. As you know, Paulsen earned a law degree and trained as a lawyer, and he continued to play chess internationally alongside that. But all the time he also worked part-time for the Stasi."

Jayne's eyes widened. The Stasi, or the Ministry for State Security, to give its full title, was the much-feared security and intelligence service of East Germany from 1950 until the reunification of Germany in 1990, when it was disbanded.

"How did that start?" Jayne asked.

"I got to know Paulsen when I was working in East Germany for the KGB," Suslova said. "And so did President Putin."

Now the pieces of the jigsaw clicked together in Jayne's mind.

"Were you his handler in East Berlin?" Jayne asked. "You recruited him?"

Suslova inclined her head. "I can take the credit for that recruitment."

Of course. The chess queen.

Jayne paused and scrutinized Suslova.

Could she believe a word she was being told?

She was fairly certain the Russian was telling the truth about Wolfgang Paulsen, but less certain about the rationale for not giving the identities of ILYA and ALYOSHA herself.

However, she went along with it.

If she could secure Suslova as a CIA agent in Moscow, while simultaneously uncovering two long-running Russian assets in the West, maybe it was worth playing the game.

But her gut feeling was that it would not be that straightforward.

"All right, if you think it will ensure your security, we'll do it your way," Jayne said. "We'll find a way to get this information out of Paulsen. But if you warn him, I'm going to send all that detail straight to Putin. You'll be dead. And if we don't get what we need from Paulsen, the same thing will likely happen."

Suslova shrugged. "You make it sound like I have no choice."

"You don't. And I'm not going to hand back the money until we've got what I want."

Suslova blew her cheeks out. "How do I know you mean what you say?"

"It's how I operate," Jayne said. "And how should we approach Paulsen to get this information? Does he keep any records? And how does he communicate with the assets—and with you?"

Suslova pursed her lips. "It's all completely compartmented. I know very little about how he operates or communicates with them. I only see the information that comes from the assets and the instructions that go to them. He uses old-school methods, not digital. Dead drops and signals—I don't know where or what they are. Then he and I meet occasionally, infrequently, and we have a channel to communicate digitally. I'm not going to tell you what you don't need to know."

"Does Russian countersurveillance watch Paulsen?" Jayne asked. She was concerned that she could be walking into an ambush.

"No."

"Now give me Paulsen's details. Where does he live?" Jayne asked. "We can find out anyway, so you might as well just tell me."

"Berlin. Next to Lake Wannsee. He's a lawyer, a joint partner in his own firm, called Paulsen and Liebermann. They specialize in advising about corporate matters. It's a low-profile but lucrative business."

"I also need to set up a secure way to communicate with you," Jayne said.

Suslova grimaced and opened her mouth as if she was going to object, but then nodded. "Set up a comms channel, then, and protocols for connecting with you. It will need to be watertight. Until then, use a burner phone I have, but only if it's extremely urgent, and put nothing sensitive on it."

She recited a Russian cell phone number, which Jayne committed to memory.

"If we uncover Paulsen, the Kremlin will ask you how we found out about him," Jayne said. "What are you going to say? And how are you going to explain how you let me walk out of here, and how Joe Johnson is allowed to walk out of Kaliningrad?"

"Thanks to you, I have a scapegoat to take the hit—a dead one," Suslova said. "I will blame everything on Shevchenko. They will not be able to prove otherwise—and they had concerns about her before, so they'll believe it. I will say that she informed you about Paulsen just before she was shot dead—a killing that was coordinated by me, not by the incompetent fools in the FSB. It is quite credible that she could have found out about Paulsen—but never about the identities of ILYA and ALYOSHA."

Jayne eyed Suslova. This was a dog-eat-dog world, and this woman was a pro, much as it stuck in her throat to admit it. She had ice running through her veins, which was likely why she had risen to be one of Putin's *siloviki*, his inner circle.

"Very well," Jayne said.

Suslova gave a curt nod. "And as for explaining how you walked out of here, and how Mr. Johnson walks out of Kaliningrad, well, nobody at the Kremlin knows you've been here, or knows about Johnson. You came here as FIDE delegates. It will stay that way. My guards only say what I tell them. They are utterly loyal, I make sure of that."

The Russian walked to the door and opened it. She then turned to Jayne. "Get out of here now, and take Grewall with you. I'll get him from the other room. And if I don't get my money back, you know what will happen."

Jayne nodded. "If I get taken down, so do you. Remember that."

She paused next to Suslova as she walked out. "I want to see Joe Johnson safely out of Kaliningrad—immediately."

PART FOUR

CHAPTER THIRTY-SEVEN

Wednesday, October 12, 2016
Berlin

The surveillance team assembled to tail Wolfgang Paulsen was already waiting at the CIA station at Berlin's Pariser Platz by the time Jayne, accompanied by Vic and Grewall, had arrived from Bern.

It had taken some time for Vic to debrief Jayne following her return late the previous night from the heavily fortified chalet in Grindelwald.

But to Jayne's relief, once Vic was finally satisfied with her account and she had convinced him she had not somehow fallen for some enormous deception sowed by Suslova, he swung rapidly into action. Helping him was the CIA's relatively new Berlin head of station, Pieter Bone.

Vic spent much of the journey from Switzerland frantically working his phone and messaging app, communicating with Bone and others in the Berlin station to put the pieces in place for a round-the-clock surveillance exercise. He also passed on to London the tacit admission by Suslova that she was responsible for Pyotr Fradkov's death.

Meanwhile, the tech team at Langley had reported back that the upload from Suslova's laptop in Grindelwald had failed completely. When Jayne had prematurely stopped the upload, it caused all the files to become corrupted. It had proved impossible to restore them.

Now the entire team was seated in a secure meeting room in the Berlin station, on the top floor of the enormous US embassy building. Jayne could see the sculpture of a chariot and four horses atop the Brandenburg Gate out of the window as she sipped a black coffee, trying to stave off the tiredness that was threatening to envelop her.

Vic sat to her right at the head of the table, running the meeting, while to her left were Bone and Grewall. On the other side of the table sat a key member of the Berlin operations team, Mary Gassey, together with the surveillance team. Jayne had worked with them all a couple of years previously on an operation that had also involved Joe.

The surveillance unit comprised five people, including a team leader, Klaus Ortner. Of the others, three were retired former operatives with the German BND foreign intelligence service and were now in their sixties. This trio, who now worked for the CIA as freelancers, comprised Otto Bernstein and Maria Bernstein, who were a married couple, and a single woman named Gertrud Hoffman. The final member of the team was a woman in her thirties named Renate Hogedorn, who had recently left the BND.

Because of their mainly senior age profile, the team had long ago been nicknamed *die Rentners,* the German word for pensioners.

Jayne had been deeply impressed with their professionalism on the previous operation, and nothing had changed. They quickly got to grips with the brief.

Meanwhile, Bone and Gassey passed around copies of a short file on Paulsen, the contents of which had been compiled by the Berlin team overnight. There had been no previous reason for the Agency to hold a file on him, Gassey said, although it was obvious to Jayne that Paulsen had somehow just slipped through the net.

Jayne scanned through the file, which was only four pages long. Paulsen was aged fifty-eight and lived alone after his wife divorced him a couple of years ago. He had two grown-up children who lived elsewhere.

Three photographs of Paulsen showed a tall man, probably six feet two at least, with a wiry frame and a narrow face. His hair looked somewhat unkempt, but given his otherwise smart appearance, with a dark suit, white shirt, and tie, Jayne wondered if he deliberately cultivated it that way.

The file corroborated the detail about Paulsen's career that Suslova had given Jayne. He was indeed a partner in a Berlin law firm, Paulsen and Liebermann, which he had jointly set up fifteen years earlier. Before that, he had worked for a large national law firm that was the product of several mergers of smaller firms, some from the former East Germany, some from West Germany.

Paulsen had originally come from East Germany but had been allowed to travel frequently to West Berlin to play chess, the file said, as well as sometimes for work reasons.

Jayne looked up. "That must have been rare, for an East German chess player to get permission to travel to play in West Germany."

Gassey, who had overseen the production of the file, nodded. "I'm sure that's true."

Jayne finished reading the file, which brought Paulsen's background up to the present day. He now frequently traveled to the United States and the United Kingdom on business, as well as to France and other countries, mainly in

Continental Europe. His current clients appeared to be chiefly German companies with overseas operations.

Paulsen's chess, initially sponsored by the former East German government, had consumed much of his time during his twenties and early thirties, apparently at the expense of his law career, which had been unremarkable during that period, with few promotions. That had changed in his mid to late thirties after he was made a partner in his firm. He subsequently departed with a colleague to found their own business, taking several clients with them.

"Paulsen's work and his top chess ranking and status seem to have provided him with a perfect cover story if he's handling assets in the West," Jayne said. She looked over the table at Gassey.

Gassey nodded. "He spends a lot of time in New York, London, and Paris. Also Madrid and Rome. We're working on a list of people he meets."

Paulsen had been elected as president of the Deutscher Schachbund (DSB), the German Chess Federation, in 2009 and was reelected four years later. Prior to that, he had held several other offices with the DSB and remained the federation's FIDE delegate.

He was still an active chess player when time permitted, with a FIDE world ranking of 234 and a rating of 2593. That was well down from his peak in the 1990s when he had been ranked number two in the world for a short period with a peak rating of 2698, and compared to the current world champion, the number one ranked player, with a rating of 2859. But for someone of his age who now played only part-time, it was outstanding.

"Let's put this guy under the microscope," Vic said. "We need surveillance on him at work and at home. We'll get the NSA to tap into his phones and email."

It also struck Jayne that if Paulsen had been operating as a handler for Western assets and had worked for the Stasi, there may be a Stasi file on him somewhere, or maybe a CIA file. Most of the old Stasi files had been recovered after the reunification of East and West Germany in 1990, she remembered. She discussed it with Vic, who agreed that she should explore ways to access the files.

The Rentners team swiftly compiled a rotation that ensured Paulsen would have coverage everywhere he went. Otto and Maria would keep their eyes on him during his working day at his law firm, while Gertrud and Renate would take over at home.

The meeting room was swiftly turned into an operations center. Desks and chairs were brought in by the techs, who also installed cables that allowed them all to plug in laptops and connect to the CIA's secure network. The door was allocated its own passkey, with fingerprint recognition so that only those on the restricted list could enter the room.

The Rentners set up desks for themselves at one end of the room, while Jayne, Vic, and Gassey established themselves at the other. Bone decided to remain in his station chief's office and simply dip in and out as required, as he had two other ongoing operations in Berlin to supervise. The large conference table remained in the center of the room to be used for updates and briefing meetings.

The surveillance operation began with a session with the CIA's disguise officer, who had produced a package of props that would enable each of them to significantly change their appearance within a few seconds. The items included different glasses, reversible jackets, hats, and special orthotics that, when inserted into a shoe, could create an authentic-looking limp.

Meanwhile, Vic disappeared to the office that Bone had allocated to him to put in another call to Alex Goode at the NSA with his latest set of requests.

It left Jayne with a few minutes to try to take a step back and evaluate where they were with the investigation.

She knew that the information gained from Suslova had been a big step forward. Whether her recruitment paid off in the long term, and whether Suslova became an asset she could reliably use, time would tell.

Recruiting someone through blackmail and coercion was far from Jayne's favorite method. She preferred gentle persuasion, coupled with an element of ideological impetus on the part of the target, and maybe a long-term cash inducement. In her long experience, the motivation was far higher in such circumstances, as of course was the resultant quality of information received.

But it was now up to Jayne to manage the situation as best she could. After all, the recruitment of Anastasia Shevchenko had come under not dissimilar circumstances, and that had worked well until her horrific death, although in her case, the cash had been far more of a factor.

In Suslova's case, offering more money was not going to work, as she had so much of it already. Jayne just had to hope that the converse—the fear of losing her existing power, freedom, and wealth—would prove a powerful persuader. It had to be a very real concern with someone like Vladimir Putin as a boss.

The key concern that was bothering Jayne even more than the activities of Wolfgang Paulsen was the safe return of Joe from Kaliningrad.

So far, there had still been no word from him. So Jayne had to assume he was still incarcerated somewhere within the Russian exclave on the Baltic.

* * *

Wednesday, October 12, 2016

Sovetsk, Kaliningrad

The bruises from the previous day's journey on the floor of
the Transit van were starting to come out. Joe had red and
purple blotches down his legs, arms, and torso from where he
had been repeatedly bounced around.

The bindings tying his wrists had been secure enough to
stop him from freeing himself but loose enough to allow him
to be tossed about. The road surface had been bumpy, and he
had a stiff neck from holding his head up to prevent it from
being smashed onto the van floor.

Now he was locked in another small room with no
windows and dirty, chipped walls.

He knew he was once again near to water because he
could hear the occasional outboard boat engine. There was
also the hum of traffic, so Joe also guessed he was in an urban
area. But here there was no noise from aircraft engines.

Where the hell was he? It was impossible to tell exactly,
but he had to assume he was still somewhere within Kaliningrad. He had no sense of having crossed a border
checkpoint.

The same guard, Feodor, was present. He periodically
appeared to either dump a plate of food on the table or to
exchange the toilet bucket in the corner for a clean one.
There was always a second guard standing in the corridor
outside, pointing a Makarov directly at him while Feodor did
whatever was necessary.

There was no shower or sink in this room either, but Joe
had gone past the point where he was bothered by his own
body odor. There was nothing he could do about it.

An hour after Joe had finished the bowl of borscht and
bread he had been given for lunch, he was lying on the bed.
There came a rattle of keys in the door lock, and in came the

bald guard, Andrey, who had seized him in the first place in Amsterdam. He was back again.

"Get up," Andrey ordered. "Put your shoes on. Then come."

Joe did as he was told. As soon as he stepped outside the door, Feodor jammed the barrel of his Makarov in his back, causing another spike of pain, and followed him along a bare concrete corridor and down a flight of stairs.

When they reached a heavy exterior door, Andrey turned. "You will walk between us until we get to where we are going. Do not try anything, or else my colleague here will put a bullet between your eyes. Understood?"

Joe nodded.

Andrey opened the door and led him outside. After such a long period in the gloom, the sunlight almost blinded Joe. But he quickly realized they had emerged from a warehouse onto a busy tree-lined street, next to a tobacconist.

Where the hell was he?

He followed Andrey, who had now put his gun in a holster beneath his jacket, past a row of terraced houses and an alley. On the opposite side of the street was an ugly five-story apartment building, with women hanging out washing on several of the balconies.

Were they going to push him down the alley and shoot him?

They rounded the corner and Joe caught sight of a broad river to his left, beyond a stretch of grass. A road bridge spanned the river, decorated with an arch built from stone, with twin turrets.

Ahead of them was a checkpoint surrounded by security fencing with two white huts. Uniformed guards were checking a truck that was stopped outside one of the huts in a lane marked for incoming traffic. A parallel lane, with a large stop sign next to it, was designated for outbound traffic.

"This is the Queen Louise Bridge," Andrey said.

Immediately, Joe realized where he had been taken. This was the city of Sovetsk and the Neman River, which formed the border between Kaliningrad and Lithuania. He had worked on the Lithuania side several years ago while hunting a Nazi war criminal.

"Sovetsk?" Joe asked, looking quizzically at Andrey, who nodded.

"So, what now?" Joe asked.

"Go." Andrey pointed at the checkpoint. "Leave Kaliningrad."

Andrey reached into his pocket and removed a passport, wallet, a watch, and a small Faraday pouch, from which he removed Joe's phone. He held them out.

With a surge of relief, Joe realized he was being freed. He reached out and took his belongings.

"Now?" Joe asked.

Andrey nodded. "Go."

Joe had an urge to ask why they had decided to release him, and why they had held him in the first place. But instead, he turned and walked toward the Russian customs checkpoint. All that mattered was getting away.

Twenty minutes later, he strode out of the Lithuanian checkpoint on the far side of the bridge. He had received a few stares from the customs and immigration officers, but they'd let him through. In contrast to the bustling city of Sovetsk, behind him on the Russian side, here there were little more than a few houses, cheap hotels, a couple of cell phone shops, dilapidated warehouses, and flat arable fields.

From the checkpoint, Joe walked until he came to a modern motel named Agirija, which had a bar and restaurant. After many days of incarceration without a shower, all he wanted to do was check in, sink into a hot bath, and drink a beer.

But he needed to first call Jayne to let her know he was safe and to find out how Carrie was, which was his biggest concern.

His phone had been switched off by his captors, so he now turned it on. There was still plenty of charge left in it, although he had to assume it had been hacked and the contents downloaded. Thankfully, there was not a lot of sensitive information on it, as he viewed that as a security risk while traveling.

There was a whole stream of text and voice messages on his device, which he ignored for now.

Joe wasn't going to risk using his own phone to call Jayne until it had been given a thorough security check. So he went into a cell phone shop opposite the hotel and bought the cheapest device they stocked together with a Lithuanian prepaid SIM card.

He then sat on a bench in the outdoor bar area of the hotel, ordered a coffee, and used the phone to call Jayne.

"Thank God," she said as soon as she answered. "Joe, are you okay?" He could hear the relief in her voice.

"A few bruised ribs. Just tell me Carrie's all right," Joe said. "That's all I want to know."

"She is," Jayne said. "She's gone safely back to Portland. Amy's looking after her. She's fine, Joe."

"Thank God for that," he said. He took a swig of coffee. "I'm feeling better already. Now just tell me what the hell is going on."

He listened with some incredulity as Jayne gave him a brief outline of events in Switzerland and some of the information obtained.

"I'll give you all the detail when I see you," Jayne concluded. "Including exactly how we got you released."

By now, Joe's brain was feeling a little more switched on as the coffee took effect. He could tell from the tone of Jayne's voice that she was making good progress, even if she wasn't giving him all of the more sensitive information.

"So this guy Paulsen wasn't just a chess grandmaster, but he worked for the Stasi?" he said, suddenly feeling more interested.

"It seems so. But we need more on him. Got any ideas?"

"He must have reinvented himself then after reunification," Joe said. "Probably lucky to avoid prosecution. And if that's the case, it would be worth trying to get hold of his old Stasi file. He must have one. There could be some useful information in there if he's originally from East Germany."

"I discussed that with Vic earlier. But how do we get access to the files?"

Joe hesitated. Part of him just wanted to fly home to Portland to be with Carrie and Peter. But if Amy was taking care of them and Carrie was now secure, he was less worried. He would give Carrie a call immediately after finishing up with Jayne and double-check.

Furthermore, after his experience over the past several days, he was feeling extremely angry.

If he could contribute to Jayne's investigation, then maybe he should do that.

"I've got contacts inside the German Stasi Records Agency," Joe said. "They administer the old files. I know them from several of my previous investigations into German war criminals."

He paused. "How about if I fly to Berlin? I just need to get myself to Vilnius Airport. I might be able to help."

He had no idea how he could get to the airport that served the Lithuanian capital, but he was sure he would find a way.

"We've got our hands full trying to track down Paulsen's present movements," Jayne said. "So some assistance delving into his past would be very helpful. I'll tell you precisely why when I see you."

"Right, I'll do it, then," Joe said. It was obvious he might be able to make a contribution.

There was a pause on the line. "Are you sure you're up to it, Joe, given what happened?"

"I'm up for it," Joe said. "Let's get the bastards."

CHAPTER THIRTY-EIGHT

Wednesday, October 12, 2016
Berlin

The line of white Mercedes taxis standing outside the entrance to Terminal A of Berlin's Schönefeld Airport all looked identical. There were at least twenty of them.

Kira Suslova pulled her headscarf forward and scrutinized the cars as she walked beneath the enormous blue canopy that covered the area between the drop-off zone and the terminal entrance. She was grateful for the shelter because rain had been hammering down from a leaden sky since her Cessna Citation Mustang had landed half an hour earlier.

The scene made her think of her first visit to the former East Germany thirty years earlier, in September 1986, when she had landed at this same airport on a flight from Moscow. She was preparing to start her first tour of duty as a KGB officer in what was then a satellite state of the Soviet Union. A few months later she met Vladimir Putin.

During that Cold War era, Schönefeld, eighteen kilometers to the south of Berlin, was the main airport serving the former East Berlin, while Tegel Airport, north of the city, served West Berlin. After German reunification, Schönefeld was relegated to a minor role.

Now a massive building project was underway a few hundred meters to the south of Schönefeld to build Berlin Brandenburg Airport, the new main airport for the city, into which Schönefeld would be integrated on completion. Tegel would then be closed. Suslova could see the construction cranes towering above the Brandenburg site.

She walked on until she spotted the taxi she was looking for, marked by a piece of red card in the front window.

She opened the front passenger door, climbed in, and closed it behind her. In the driver's seat was a tall, gaunt man with straggly gray locks.

"Hello, Wolfgang," she said. "It's been a while."

Wolfgang Paulsen nodded, pressed down on the accelerator, steered neatly out of his parking place, and headed out of the airport.

"It certainly has," he said, yawning.

They hadn't met in person for over a year, a longer gap than usual, although they kept in touch by other means too.

"You're lucky to find me here," Paulsen said. "I only got back from New York this morning. The jet lag's killing me. Now, can you tell me exactly what is going on?"

Suslova had not originally intended to divert to Berlin en route back to Moscow from Switzerland. But once her FIDE guests had all finally left her chalet, she had sunk into a chair and sat there deep into the night, thinking.

She had never felt as outmaneuvered as she had following the disastrous encounter with Jayne Robinson. Not even the masters of internal politics at the Kremlin had achieved that.

The theft of $2 billion from a Moskva Bank account she

had viewed as torpedo-proof had left her feeling as though she had just been in a car crash.

How had they done it?

And the threat, and risks, of having her long-term affair with President Putin exposed had stunned her almost as much.

But the more she thought it through, the more determined she had become.

She wasn't going to take this humiliation.

Furthermore, she would escape the situation.

Yes, she had capitulated to Robinson, given all that had been thrown at her. She had handed over Paulsen's name, feeling at the time that she had little choice. Almost instantly, she regretted doing so.

Now was the time to fight back. The release of Joe Johnson would hopefully help convince Robinson that she was going to deliver on her side of the bargain. It would buy time—enough time to ensure Robinson didn't get ILYA and ALYOSHA's identities.

If that meant losing $2 billion, so be it—she had accepted that. She would have to work out how to cover it up, if necessary.

But overall, she figured that the long-term value of those two assets to the Motherland—and to her—was far, far more than two billion.

Maybe she could find a way out of this nightmare by trading some other intelligence with the CIA in exchange for the return of the money.

Whatever.

There was always a solution to a problem. She'd never backed down from a challenge.

But whatever the ultimate solution ended up being, she knew what step one had to involve—she had to get Paulsen onside. Apart from that, she needed to involve as few people from Moscow as possible and keep this away from the president's ears.

"We have a problem," Suslova said. "There's an operation underway to uncover ILYA and ALYOSHA. A British woman, an intelligence operative who works for the CIA, has found out that you're the handler."

Paulsen glanced sideways and shifted in his seat, his face frozen. "*What*? How did they find out?"

"From an SVR counterintelligence director, Anastasia Shevchenko," Suslova lied. "I discovered she was spying for the Americans. I had her shot dead. There was no other option. But it seems not before she had passed this information to the British woman."

Paulsen tipped his head back against the headrest. "*Scheisse*. Shit. After all this time. But they don't know who ILYA and ALYOSHA are?"

"No."

"Who's the Brit?" Paulsen asked.

"Jayne Robinson. She worked at MI6 for a long time. Now a freelance operative."

"So how the hell did Shevchenko find out I was doing the handling? And how did you find out Robinson was running this operation?"

"I don't know how Shevchenko found out. She was counterintelligence, so maybe something crossed her desk. I can't exactly ask her now. And I found out about Robinson from an asset I have in Western intelligence, I can't say who."

There was no way Suslova was going to tell Paulsen anything about the ambush she had suffered at Robinson's hands at her Swiss chalet or the connection to her FIDE presidency campaign. And she certainly wasn't going to admit she had felt forced to divulge Paulsen's identity in order to claw back $2 billion that had been heisted from one of her accounts. She was going to keep this on a need-to-know basis.

"Anyway, the important thing is, step one, we need to dispose of this Robinson before she can do any more damage," Suslova said. "You can't let her get anywhere close to you, or to ILYA or ALYOSHA."

"So, what's your suggestion?"

Suslova paused as Paulsen swung his fake taxi onto Autobahn 113, the highway that headed north from Schönefeld toward Berlin. The autobahn partly followed the route marked by the former Berlin Wall during the Cold War era. There was no danger of their conversation being monitored here, and no sign of a tail behind them.

"We could deploy my guys, Andrey Peskov and Feodor Matrosov," Suslova said. "They'll both be here soon."

The last time she had met Paulsen, Peskov had been with her and they had all had a long discussion and dinner together. He had not met Matrosov.

The two Vagnar Group men had earlier overseen the release of Joe Johnson. They were now flying that evening to Berlin from Kaliningrad, which was five hundred kilometers to the east.

Paulsen glanced sideways at her. "How serious is this threat?" he asked.

"It's serious. And we may not have much time. Your personal security may be at risk."

"Well, wouldn't it be best to get Moscow involved then? Should we bring in the heavy hitters—Sidorenko, or Igor Ivanov? They can ship in a Spetsnaz unit."

Suslova shook her head. "Far too messy, far too high profile. We need to keep this below the radar. You know what would happen if the Kremlin and SVR counterintelligence get to hear about this unnecessarily. They'd put you under a microscope for weeks, months, trying to work out how this leaked. You'd face interrogation after interrogation. I'd have the same. It would be unbearable. Much better we deal with it quietly—Andrey and Feodor will do the necessary. They're the best. They're Vagnar Group, discreet and professional."

She knew he'd hate the idea of a hugely intrusive counter-surveillance investigation.

Paulsen pursed his lips as he took the off-ramp from the autobahn. "All right."

When Suslova had first met Paulsen in the 1980s, he rented a decrepit two-bedroom apartment in East Berlin. He had upgraded since.

She had been to Paulsen's house a few years ago. He now lived in a huge mansion, dating back to 1888, on the edge of trendy Lake Wannsee, southwest of Berlin, with its yachts and marinas. She guessed it was now worth at least ten million euros. It had been bought partly with the rewards from his legal career, partly, she assumed, with the money channeled to him from Moscow for his invaluable services, and partly from his global chess winnings.

Paulsen had proudly given her a detailed tour of the house, which during the 1930s and 1940s had been occupied by a senior Nazi Party official, an *Oberführer*, or senior colonel, in Hitler's leadership team.

Indeed, the owner had been among the elite group of Nazi Party officials who had attended the Wannsee Confer-ence at a much larger, grander villa across the other side of the lake, at 56-58 Am Grossen Wannsee street, in January 1942. The conference was held to brief party leaders and government officials on the Final Solution—the plan to exter-minate Europe's Jewish population.

As the war progressed, the Nazi owner of Paulsen's house had added a couple of special features that would help him flee if the worst happened and he needed to run. Paulsen had shown Suslova the additions, which she had noted with great interest.

Suslova glanced at Paulsen. "Are you able to get out of your house for a few days until we resolve this?" she asked.

"I have another place, yes," Paulsen said.

"Where?"

"You don't need to know where. I don't tell anyone if I can help it."

"And I'm assuming there's nothing in your house that could compromise you?"

"Nothing," Paulsen said. "Tell Andrey to get this done quickly and cleanly. The sooner we get back to normal the better. I'll take you back to the airport now. You can brief him. I don't want to be involved unless I have to."

"All right," Suslova said. "And obviously, make no attempt to contact ILYA or ALYOSHA while this is ongoing."

Paulsen steered around the roundabout and down the on-ramp to the southbound roadway, heading back toward Schönefeld Airport.

"If you're able to be out of your house, perhaps you'd allow Andrey to use it, if required," Suslova said.

"*Andrey* to use it?" Paulsen turned and looked at her as he accelerated. "Use it how?"

She gave a wolfish smile. "Thinking logically, I suspect your property will be a honeypot that will attract the CIA's bees—like Robinson and company."

"It had better not get damaged."

"I will pay for any repairs needed. But trust me, Andrey is a good beekeeper. He never gets stung."

CHAPTER THIRTY-NINE

Thursday, October 13, 2016
Berlin

Video surveillance cameras mounted in the four cars being used by the Rentners, as well as regular verbal updates via the tiny comms devices they were equipped with, gave Jayne and Vic a good picture of what was happening out in the field as the surveillance exercise against Paulsen got underway.

Jayne sat at her desk, overlooking the Brandenburg Gate, and scrutinized two monitor screens the techs had installed.

Two research analysts delegated to the team had done some useful background work overnight, including pinpointing Paulsen's house, a huge villa overlooking Lake Wannsee.

The day began well, with Otto and Maria in two separate cars tailing Paulsen as he left the house in a silver BMW and drove twenty-five kilometers to his office on the third floor of a glass-fronted building in Oranienburger Strasse. It was only a couple of kilometers from the US embassy and almost opposite the Oranienburger Tor tram stop.

There Paulsen remained until one o'clock when Otto called in to report that he had popped out for an hour's lunch break with a male colleague at an Italian restaurant.

It was at that point that Jayne received a message from Joe saying he had booked a flight from Vilnius to Berlin's Tegel Airport that evening. She replied to say that barring a major unforeseen complication in the surveillance operation, she would be there to meet him.

At six o'clock, Paulsen emerged from his office and collected his car. He then began his journey home through Berlin's rush hour traffic. Otto and Maria again tailed him, joined this time in a third car by Gertrud. They took turns to get close and then hang back, allowing one of the others to take their place.

Jayne sat glued to her monitors, watching the camera footage and listening through her headset to sporadic comments from the surveillance team. Next to Jayne, Vic was also listening in.

It wasn't proving as easy a task in the heavier evening traffic as it had been that morning. On several occasions, the traffic lights worked against the team, leaving them much farther back than they would have liked and losing eye contact with their target. Twice, they were a little fortunate to regain contact.

Paulsen used a rat run route to try to get around the worst of the traffic. He took what looked like a well-practiced stair-step maneuver through the Mitte district and into Charlottenburg-Wilmersdorf.

"This is making it difficult," Jayne said. "We're going to need more cars tomorrow, so we can have some ahead of him as well as behind."

She turned to Bone, who nodded. "I'll get another two teams involved."

"Do you think he's realized he's being tailed?" Jayne asked.

"I don't think so," Vic said. "But he certainly knows Berlin's back streets."

However, after another ten minutes, there was a set of red lights too many, and the surveillance team lost Paulsen altogether in the area near Berlin's International Congress Center.

"He's gone," Gertrud reported over the comms network. "I'm sorry, I've lost him. I couldn't get too close; otherwise, I'd give myself away. Then I got boxed in by trucks."

"Not to worry," Vic said. "We've got Renate in a car just down the street from his house. She can check him in when he arrives home."

But by mid-evening, it became obvious that Paulsen was not heading home. Renate had a good view of his driveway entrance, and he had not appeared.

Over the following three hours, Renate did three separate drives past his property. Although some of the house lights came on, Renate's view was that they were likely on security timers, as she had not seen Paulsen return. There were also a handful of outside lamps to illuminate the driveway and front door that came on automatically when darkness fell.

"We'll try again tomorrow," Vic said. "He's single, so he's probably got a woman somewhere. Or he's drinking in a bar."

Jayne rocked back in her chair and folded her arms. "Or he's been warned," she said.

Vic looked across sharply at her. "How likely is that, do you think?"

Jayne shrugged. "I told Suslova that if she warned him and that meant we couldn't get what we wanted, she wouldn't get her money back and we'd do her a lot of other damage.

Simple as that. But it's impossible to predict how she's reacting."

Vic folded his arms. "Maybe she's more of a patriot than we think, and she's decided to be the fall guy, warn him, protect him and the two big assets, and to take the consequences."

"Well, her first instinct was that she wasn't going to lose two billion dollars," Jayne said. "That's why she gave up Paulsen. She struck me as a proud person who's not easily going to surrender the trappings of power. Has she had a rethink? Who knows?"

Jayne glanced at her watch. It was time to head to the airport to meet Joe.

She stood and put on her jacket. "Let's see if Paulsen returns home later tonight, then. And I'll see if Joe's got any thoughts on this—Berlin's his territory. Then we can regroup in the morning."

* * *

Thursday, October 13, 2016
Berlin

A drip of sweat ran down Jayne's nose and onto her upper lip. She felt it dribble down and flicked her tongue upward to lick it away.

Was it her sweat, or Joe's? She didn't really care.

His face was so close above hers that she couldn't properly focus on it.

"That's why I'm glad they let you out of that hellhole," Jayne said. She reached around his heavily bruised torso and pulled him down further, then moaned a little as he ground against her. "But I think we're done, at last."

"I think we are done," he said, finally rolling away onto his back on the bed next to her. He winced as he did so. "That hurt, but it was a nice kind of hurt."

She smiled. "Mission accomplished, then."

Once Joe had ascertained that his rib cage was only badly bruised and that no ribs had been fractured, he had insisted on making love.

"It's restorative," he said.

They lay there in silence for several minutes. The only sound in their room was their breathing, which gradually became quieter.

Bone had arranged for them to stay at a CIA safe house near Berlin's Botanic Garden. It was a large detached two-story property set well back from the street in Limonen-strasse, a quiet cobbled residential avenue. Jayne had used the white-painted house once before on a previous investigation. She and Joe had a double bedroom upstairs, while Vic was using another room on the opposite side of the house.

Jayne had already given Joe the full background on the information coerced from Suslova and how that had been achieved.

"So you think this Paulsen has run, do you?" Joe asked.

"It seems that way. He's not returned home, and he did make what could have been a disguised attempt to throw off our surveillance team. He succeeded, anyway, whether it was down to us losing him or him getting away. We'll find out soon enough, if he doesn't come back tonight at all. Or doesn't turn up at his office in the morning."

"Maybe he's just got a girlfriend elsewhere in town?" Joe asked.

"That's possible," Jayne said. "He is divorced, after all. The team is working hard right now to find out if that's so. My gut feeling is he's run, though."

Joe reached out, grabbed the beer that he'd left on the

bedside table, which caused him to wince again, and took a swig. "Either way, I think it might be worth me making some inquiries tomorrow. If Paulsen was working for the Stasi as an agent, then they would, without doubt, have had a file on him."

"Is it worth pursuing, you think?"

Joe shrugged. "Don't know. If there is a file, it might shed some light on how he got involved with the Russians. Let's face it, we're not going to get our hands on his SVR or FSB file, assuming there is one. But the old Stasi file might be a starting point. Like my old OSI boss Mickey Ralph used to say, 'Never die wondering, my friend.'"

"How are you going to get access to them?" Jayne asked. "I thought it was difficult."

"It is. But there were a few investigations I did at the OSI involving former Stasi officers who had been Nazis during World War II. I got to know the chief archivist at the Stasi Records Agency, Jurgen Giesen. He's still there—now he's been promoted to federal commissioner and runs the place. They hold all the files that survived."

After being fired by the CIA in 1988, Joe joined the Office of Special Investigations, set up within the Justice Department to trace Nazi war criminals in the US. Then in 2006, a year after the death from cancer of his wife, Kathy, he moved to Portland and set up his own private investigation business.

"Thanks for the help," Jayne said. "We'll take all we can get."

"Of course," Joe said. "But what's your plan for Paulsen if he has just run?"

Jayne leaned over and slowly ran her index finger down Joe's belly, avoiding the worst bruises as she went. "Good question. If his house is standing empty, then maybe while you're delving into the archives, Ed and I should go and take a closer look at it."

CHAPTER FORTY

Friday, October 14, 2016
Berlin

The high-definition video footage from the CIA's drone clearly showed the appeal of the house belonging to Wolfgang Paulsen. The property, on Am Sandwerder street on the eastern side of Lake Wannsee, was in one of the most upmarket areas of Berlin.

Jayne watched on her monitor screen in the CIA station as the drone, equipped with a military-grade infrared thermal camera, flew around the site. The house sat near the top of a long, broad plot that ran about two hundred meters from the street down a significant slope to the lake shore.

At the bottom end of the garden, there was a boat shed and jetty, where a gray inflatable dinghy was moored among the trees.

The house, with a slate roof, had a terrace at the rear, facing out over the lake below, and neatly manicured gardens.

It looked as though it contained at least six or seven bedrooms, judging by the number of upstairs windows.

"Paulsen's doing well," Jayne said. She turned to Mary Gassey. "Still no sign of him at his office, I assume?"

Gassey shook her head. "No sign of him anywhere."

It was now midmorning, and it was becoming obvious that Paulsen wasn't simply staying at a girlfriend's overnight and that his evasion of the surveillance team the previous evening hadn't been simply accidental.

Meanwhile, Joe had already left for the head office of the Stasi Records Agency, the building formerly occupied by the Ministry for State Security, two kilometers east of the Brandenburg Gate. The CIA's tech team had checked his phone and given it security clearance. Surprisingly, no surveillance software was installed during his imprisonment in Kaliningrad.

Jayne looked back at the monitor screen. The drone, operated by one of Pieter Bone's team from a van a kilometer away, was now hovering high over the front of the house, near the street. There were no vehicles parked in the driveway or the turning circle outside the door, and the only visitor that morning had been the postman. The infrared camera on the drone indicated that the heating system in the property was probably turned off, as there was little heat leakage showing from the windows.

"What are you thinking, Jayne?" Vic asked.

"I'm thinking if Paulsen has gone AWOL, and if his house is empty, then it would be a mistake not to have a look around."

Vic paused, appearing to weigh up the suggestion.

"I can go in with Ed," Jayne said.

Grewall, sitting next to Vic, nodded. "Happy to do that."

Vic leaned back in his chair, his hands placed behind his head. He gave Jayne a somewhat skeptical look. "Do you really think, if he's working for the Kremlin, Paulsen would have left evidence lying around that links him to his assets?"

"Unlikely," Jayne said. "But I've learned that people sometimes do the most stupid, unprofessional things. And it therefore pays to leave no stone unturned."

Vic nodded. "All right. But wait until it's dark."

Jayne turned to Pieter Bone, who was standing next to them. He was frowning.

"There is the slight issue of legality," Bone said. "I'll ask the tech team head, Paul Muller, to come and advise you on how best to avoid ending up in a Bundespolizei cell tonight. I'm sure Vic wouldn't thank us if that happened."

While they were waiting, Jayne ran through a few other items on her checklist.

"Can we have access to your weapons locker?" Jayne asked Bone. "I'll need a Walther PPK and extra magazines if you've got one. With .32 ammo, please. If there's no Walther, a Beretta will do."

"We have a Walther," Bone said. He turned to Grewall. "And you?"

"Beretta?" Grewall asked.

The team also agreed to use the Rentners as a surveillance detection team for the evening. Their role would be to act the part of local residents and look out for potentially hostile approaches, including the Bundespolizei.

Another item that Jayne wanted was a floor plan of the property, but despite the efforts of Bone's team, they had not been able to locate one. The building apparently dated back to the late nineteenth century and there had been various extensions, but none were recent. Therefore, there were no planning applications available online.

They were going to have to enter the property somewhat in the dark, metaphorically as well as literally.

When Muller, a CIA veteran, arrived in the ops room, the first item on the agenda was entry to the site.

Muller decided the best option would be for a lookalike security van decorated with fake magnetic vinyl logos to transport Jayne and Grewall to the house. The drone coverage showed several such private security vans visiting properties along Am Sandwerder street—not surprising given the ostentatious wealth on display.

"And what about the burglar alarm system?" Jayne asked Muller. "I'm assuming there'll be underfloor sensors, infrared beams, that kind of thing. We'll need to disable all of them."

The drone footage had, predictably, revealed alarm units mounted on the exterior walls.

Muller winked at her. "One of my guys will fix that, don't worry. He's better than any burglar at disarming security systems. We've seen from the drone footage what manufacturer the system comes from. He thinks he may be able to hack into it if we can get Paulsen's email address. He's working on that."

Jayne knew a little about how such systems could be either decommissioned or switched off, either remotely or while in the property, without the owner's authorization.

"Can he show me and Ed?" Jayne asked.

"Sure."

Muller and Bone led them along a corridor to a room stuffed full of computers, electronic boxes, monitors, cabling, and other gadgets.

There, Muller introduced them to Chris, a tech officer, whom he asked to explain the process.

Chris looked up, a slightly arrogant grin on his face. "I've done it, Paul. Just got in. All I need now is the green light from you, and I'll turn the system off."

Chris pointed to his monitor screen, which was entirely

filled with lines of computer code in black, blue, and green type.

"This system that he's got installed at the house has certain vulnerabilities which have not been patched, or corrected," Chris said. "It uses Wi-Fi and radio frequency ID technology so users can enter the property without a key. There are thousands of these units installed all over Europe. Very popular."

"So, what are the vulnerabilities?" Jayne asked.

"Well, if you know what you're doing, they can be exploited. I needed the owner's email address, which I got from his company website. Then I was able to query the API, that's the security application's programming interface, and get the IMEI number for the actual alarm unit. That's the identity number, or serial number. Once I'd got the IMEI number and the email, I was able to make an unauthorized request that allows me to turn the whole system on or off."

"Bloody hell," Jayne said.

Chris pointed to the top line of code on his screen, which began with the word POST. "We call it a POST request, which in layman's language is used to send data to the server to make a change."

Jayne bent down to study the lines of code in more detail, but they meant nothing to her.

Chris pointed to a line of code farther down the screen that began with the word "arm." Next to it was the number "1."

"If I change that to a zero instead of a one, that will turn the system off," Chris said. "I'm leaving it on for now. I'll only switch it off when you guys tell me to, when you're ready to enter the house."

Grewall folded his arms. "Are you telling me all security systems have this vulnerability?"

Chris shook his head. "No. They're all different. But usually, there's some way of getting in."

This sounded promising to Jayne. "What about actually getting into the property? How do you suggest we do that?"

Chris's grin became broader, and he pointed at his monitor screen again. "This is not just the alarm system, it's also the locking system. It's keyless entry. Uses a keypad with a five-digit code as the lock. He probably thinks he's being smart and installing the latest advanced locking system. But look at this."

He applied his finger to the monitor screen and traced down the lines of code until he came to one that read "lock." Next to it was the number "1."

"See that one? As soon as I change that one to a zero, bingo. You're in."

"What do you mean, I'm in?"

"Just push the handle down and open."

Grewall clasped his chin. "Are you sure that's going to work?"

Chris nodded. "That's how this system operates. It's bombproof—provided nobody hacks into the code that controls it. I'll reinstate it after you're done. It won't be easy for them to work out what we've done, although they'll likely get there, eventually."

Jayne stood up straight. "And the front vehicle gate? Don't tell me. That's hooked up to the same system as well."

Now Chris's grin was even broader. "You got it. All part of the same remote system. Paulsen controls it all from an app on his phone. Looks like great security on paper. Not so good in practice."

"Any sign of underfloor sensors, infrared beams, or anything on that system?" Jayne asked.

Chris shook his head. "Nothing like that on here."

"Will he get any kind of alert when you make the

changes?" Jayne asked. She was concerned that there might be some kind of push notification or text message sent to Paulsen's phone if the gate or door was opened by an unauthorized person.

Chris pointed to a line of code farther down the screen. "It is currently set to send out an alert if that happens. But I can change that temporarily so it doesn't. There'll be no alerts. I'll switch that back again afterward, too."

Jayne made a mental note to herself never to be sucked in by marketing hype for this type of supposedly impregnable system for her own property.

"I hope this all works as intended," Jayne said. "We're aiming to go into the house tonight, probably after midnight when neighbors are asleep and there's less likelihood of police patrols."

"I'll stay here as long as you need me," Chris said. "You'll just need to let me know when you need to enter, and then when you leave, so I can lock up again."

Bone folded his arms. "Thanks, Chris. I'll give you the alert when we need you."

CHAPTER FORTY-ONE

Friday, October 14, 2016
Berlin

"I'd have thought you'd have run out of old Nazis to chase. Aren't they all dead yet?" a heavily accented, growly voice spoke from behind Joe.

Joe turned in his seat in the reception area of the eight-story Stasi Records Agency building just as a hand slapped him on the back.

Jurgen Giesen was somewhat fleshier and more jowly and his neatly trimmed hair significantly grayer than when they had last met. But his deadpan humor remained unchanged.

"They can't run much anymore," Joe said. "They're too old. So I've moved on to tougher targets."

Giesen inclined his head. "Don't let them off the hook, though. You'd better come for a coffee and explain what you need."

Giesen had worked for a decade and a half at the archive building on Karl Liebknecht Strasse. It was the same forbidding building, 170 meters long, from which the Ministry for State Security had operated during the Communist era, albeit now modernized.

Joe knew Giesen's story well. Originally a dissident journalist in the old East Germany, he was several times imprisoned and tortured by Ministry for State Security officers for his outspoken views. He then developed an obsession with bringing the perpetrators of the terrorization, torture, and killing of thousands of dissidents during the Communist era to justice.

After reunification and the dismantling of the Stasi, that mission had taken him to the head archivist's job at Karl Liebknecht Strasse, which was when Joe had got to know him. Then, two years ago, Giesen had been promoted again to the top job, the Federal Commissioner for the Stasi Records.

It put him in charge of the old Stasi files on 5.6 million former East German citizens—roughly a third of the total population prior to 1990. Stasi officers had begun shredding the files to cover their tracks after the fall of the Communist government in late 1989 but were stopped within weeks by groups of angry citizens. The files were then preserved for further investigation and future reference, both by citizens and by law enforcement and legal officials.

Giesen led the way at some pace through a set of steel-and-glass doors, up a staircase, and along a white-painted corridor. Each door was marked with a printed label giving a room number and function.

Halfway along the corridor, Giesen stopped and threw Joe a questioning look. "Are you all right? You're limping and grimacing."

"Ah, yes," Joe said. "I came off worse in an encounter with a couple of Russians. Long story. I'll tell you sometime. But I'll be okay."

Giesen nodded. "I'll walk slower. Sorry."

He paused and took two coffees from a machine in a corridor, handing one to Joe.

"Hard to believe this was a chamber of horrors before 1990," Giesen said. "Now it's modern and sterile, like any other office building. A bit boring, really."

He opened the door at the far end of the corridor and led Joe into a room that stretched as far as he could see, filled with gray steel shelves, all packed with red, brown, green, and blue card folders, box files, index cards, and brown cartons.

In a section in the middle were rows of tables and chairs, some of them occupied by people who were reading papers from files.

Giesen walked past them and into a private room. "Take a seat," he said as he closed the door. "Explain what you need."

Joe did so, giving the background information about Wolfgang Paulsen that he had got from Jayne.

"I need Paulsen's personal files from the 1980s," Joe said. "The exact reasons why I can't tell you, but we think he may be involved in something serious that has links back to that time."

Joe briefly outlined the information on Paulsen that was contained in the short file that the CIA had put together, which Jayne had given him. "That is a starting point, but we need more," Joe said. "I'm interested in what he was doing at that time, but even more in who he was associating with."

Giesen went to the door, beckoned an assistant, and rattled out a series of instructions. She nodded and disappeared again.

The coffee tasted good. Joe sat back in his chair and sipped it slowly. "This city is so different from the 1980s when I was in Berlin. You could smell the neglect and fear in those days."

Joe had majored in history at Boston University, gradu-

ating in 1980. He had then done a four-year PhD in the
economics of the Third Reich at the Freie Universität Berlin,
finishing in 1984. During his time in Berlin, he had become
fluent in German and Russian.

After that, he joined the CIA, including a stint in
Pakistan and Afghanistan, where he worked alongside Vic
and met Jayne, who was there working for MI6.

"It is very different," Giesen said. "But there are still many
people in this city, in this country, who did things they need
to be brought to account for. That said, I've not had this guy
Paulsen crossing my radar previously, and I have to tell you,
anyone of significance usually has come to my attention at
some point." He shrugged.

"Well, I'm here because, in my experience, it's best to
check every blind alley."

Giesen gave a thin smile. "As someone who is still over-
seeing the piecing together of files ripped apart twenty-six
years ago by the Stasi, I'd tend to agree. It's sometimes
surprising what you find in the darkest corners."

Joe knew what Giesen was talking about. He'd seen the
countless bags of scraps of paper that had been salvaged from
the attempts to shred all the old Stasi files. Most of them
hadn't gone through actual shredding machines, as the Stasi
didn't have enough that worked. Rather, the majority had
simply been ripped by hand, which meant they were often
salvageable, with effort. They were gradually being pieced
together like jigsaw puzzles, then scanned into the digital
archive. It would take many more years yet before Giesen's
team completed the task.

The two men reminisced for another half an hour, then
there came a knock at the door. In came Giesen's assistant.

"I'm sorry, sir," she said. "There's no sign of any files under
Wolfgang Paulsen's name. Nothing. I've checked everywhere.
There's nothing in the archive."

Joe felt his stomach sink.

"Are you certain?" Joe asked. "This guy was a contender for the world chess championship at one point and top of the East German rankings. He was well known, and he traveled frequently to West Berlin during the Communist era. Surely there must be something on him. He must have been on the security services' radar."

The girl threw up her hands. "I'm very sorry. I've searched every way I can think of. There's nothing there."

Joe glanced at Giesen, who gave a slight shrug and checked his watch. "We can have another look tomorrow— we'll need to close up here soon." He paused and stroked his chin. "It is possible, of course, that his file is among those that were ripped up by the Stasi. In that case, it's probably sitting among the sixteen thousand brown bags full of fragments we've still got on the shelves upstairs. It's just bad luck."

This was more than irritating.

"Is there possibly any other explanation for why it's not there?" Joe asked.

Giesen considered the question. "I guess someone could have stolen it. It would be far from the first time that's happened. Or it's also conceivable that there never was a file on him in the first place if someone senior ordered there not to be."

"So, is there any way of finding out for certain whether it's been stolen? Or why it's not there?" Joe asked.

Giesen shook his head. "I've been there before, many times. Usually, it's impossible to find out."

CHAPTER FORTY-TWO

Saturday, October 15, 2016
Berlin

The boathouse on the western side of Lake Wannsee was silent. All that Andrey Peskov could hear was the lapping of tiny waves against the bow of the Zodiac black rubber inflatable boat in which he and Feodor Matrosov were sitting.

The two men were clad in black Spetsnaz Mabuta combat jackets and trousers and ski masks that covered everything apart from their eyes and mouths. They were almost invisible in the darkness.

Peskov, who was sitting behind the steering wheel on the boat's starboard side, stared through the open boathouse door across the inky waters beyond. His gaze was focused on a house a kilometer away on the other side of the lake.

It was now twelve thirty, and it was the second night that they had spent in the boathouse, which belonged to an empty property on Am Gross Wannsee street. The boathouse door had been left open, probably because there were no boats in it and therefore nothing to steal. Peskov and Matrosov had decided to make use of it.

It was only a few hundred meters from the massive villa at 56-58 Am Gross Wannsee that Suslova said was used by the Nazis in 1942 for the infamous Wannsee Conference. The conference had put into place the plans for the Holocaust—the extermination of six million European Jews.

Peskov shifted in his seat. The boat was designed to seat four people at a push, but only two in any comfort. It was functional at best, and Peskov was feeling somewhat jaded after struggling to sleep during the day. But Suslova had given them a financial inducement they couldn't refuse and told them it was almost inevitable their targets would show up.

Once they did, all they had to do was dispose of them.

Peskov picked up the set of chunky Fraser M25 high-powered binoculars from the double seat next to him and clamped them to his eyes. Designed for the US military, they were equipped with an I2 night-vision attachment on the front and had been obtained through his black market connections.

Also on the seat were two GSh-18 9mm semiautomatic pistols and two SR-3M Vikhr compact assault rifles, chosen because of their small size but also because they had a detachable suppressor and took 9x39mm subsonic cartridges, making them extremely quiet.

Peskov slowly swept the binoculars up from the boathouse at the bottom of the sloping garden to the house at the top. He paused several times to scrutinize the darker areas of the gardens in particular detail—the bushes and trees, the corners, and the tall brick walls that ran down either side of the garden and separated the property from its neighbors.

"See anything?" asked Matrosov, who was sitting diagonally opposite Peskov on the port side of the boat.

"Nothing obvious," Peskov replied, also in a low murmur.

There was a little intermittent light from the moon, but even when it was hidden by clouds, which was most of the time, the I2 attachment gave him good visibility, even in the dark shadows.

Peskov had twenty-twenty vision, and he was confident that if there was an anomaly across there, he would spot it. If Jayne Robinson and her colleagues entered the house—and Suslova was confident they would try—there would almost certainly be some clue that they had done so. That was assuming, of course, that they managed to negotiate the alarm system, which Suslova had told him was highly sophisticated.

At that point, he and Matrosov would move.

He knew precisely what their angle of attack would be, and it certainly wasn't what Robinson would be expecting, of that he was sure.

* * *

Saturday, October 15, 2016
  Berlin

The dark gray Volkswagen Caddy van, with a discreet black-and-white corporate *Sicherheitssysteme* logo on the side, looked no different from the company's other vehicles that could be seen operating in Berlin and its suburbs. Indeed, Jayne had spotted one patrolling Am Sandwerder street just twenty minutes earlier.

But this van was not under the control of *Sicherheitssysteme* —which translated as Security Systems.

Jayne and Grewall sat in the rear, behind the sliding door,

wearing gray-and-white uniforms that were identical to the company's standard-issue garments.

Otto, from the Rentners team, who was at the wheel, steered the van slowly along Am Sandwerder.

Jayne peered past Otto and out through the windshield from her seat in the back. The clock on the dashboard read 12:35 a.m.

An old lady, her back hunched and her gait hesitant, was ahead of them, taking her dog for a late-night walk along the right side of the street. Jayne watched her. That was Maria, Otto's wife, and the dog, a bitch called Sugar, did actually belong to her, which was presumably why she was behaving so obediently.

When the van passed Maria and drew within fifty meters of Wolfgang Paulsen's house, Otto turned his head. "Street's all clear. I'm going in."

He flicked a button on his secure radio, mounted on the dashboard. "The dog's finished his walk. There are no other dogs around who want to play with him. I'm taking him in for supper," he said. "Is the canary still quiet?"

The canary was a reference to the drone. Otto wanted to be certain that nothing untoward was showing up on the video stream from the device, which continued to hover over the house. Bone had given a virtual guarantee that at the operating height he had selected, the drone's night-vision camera would pick up any human movement within a hundred meters of the house.

"Canary's very quiet—there's nobody indoors for him to sing to," came Chris's voice from the speaker. That indicated that there was nothing untoward showing up from the drone footage on the video screen in the operations room and the alarm system in the house remained switched on, suggesting there was nobody at home.

"I'll get the dog food ready—doing it right now," Chris said.

As the van drew near to the house on the right, Jayne could see the black solid steel security gate sliding slowly back. This looked promising. Despite her lingering doubts, Chris's software hack was working so far.

She picked up the pair of thin rubber gloves that lay on the seat next to her and put them on. Grewall did likewise. The last thing they wanted was to leave fingerprints.

Otto drove through the gate and up a cobbled driveway to a turning circle, which had a small pool and statue in the shape of a queen chess piece in the center. There, he braked to a halt near the front door.

Jayne looked at Grewall, who appeared as inscrutable as ever. It was always difficult to tell what he was thinking or how he was feeling.

"Shall we go?" Jayne asked. Out of habit, she patted her Walther PPK, which she had stuffed into her belt. It had a full magazine holding seven of her preferred .32 caliber ACP cartridges, which had more stopping power than the .22s she sometimes used. In her pocket, she had two spare magazines.

Grewall nodded and opened the door. They both slipped out onto the driveway.

Without wasting time, they both walked to the heavy front door. Jayne pushed down the handle, and sure enough, it clicked open.

She stepped across the threshold onto a black-and-white checkered tile floor, just like a chessboard, with Grewall following behind.

Of course, Paulsen would have to have a chess-themed floor in the entrance hall, Jayne thought to herself.

There was no squawking alarm, no flashing lights or siren sounding.

Jayne let out a breath, turned, and gave a thumbs-up to

Otto, who returned the signal and then slowly drove around the remainder of the turning circle and back down the drive toward the gate.

Jayne closed the door, then stood still. It was almost completely dark. All she could make out was the black-and-white pattern of the floor tiles. There was no way they were going to navigate around the house without some kind of illumination, no matter how minimal.

"Flashlight?" she murmured to Grewall.

"Dim setting. Finger over the lens," he replied.

She took a micro flashlight from her pocket and clicked it to the first setting, her finger masking the light. A faint glow gave just enough illumination to show that they were standing near a central staircase that rose to the landing above.

Grewall took out a similar flashlight and turned it on.

On the ground floor, behind the staircase, the broad hallway stretched on toward the rear of the house. To her right, an ornate chess set stood on a large, heavy-looking wooden table.

Jayne felt comfortable that the faint light would not prove a security risk. It would not be visible from outside, she was certain.

"Let's look for the office," Jayne said. There was no time to waste.

She opened the door on the right, nearest to her, which had a small brass plaque on it marked KELLAR UND BOOTSHAUS—cellar and boathouse.

Behind the door was a set of wooden stairs heading down to a cellar. The boathouse exit sounded interesting, but she certainly wasn't going down there now to investigate it, so she closed the door again.

Grewall opened a door on the other side of the hall but immediately withdrew again, shaking his head.

The next door Jayne tried opened to a lavishly decorated bathroom, and the one after that, through a set of double doors, to a grand wood-paneled dining room with a long table and chairs.

Next to the dining room was another door. Jayne opened it to find a library, with shelves stacked floor to ceiling with books and a few comfortable armchairs. She closed the door again and moved down the hall.

Grewall was also having no luck.

The hallway, it emerged, ran right through to the rear of the house, where there was a set of double patio doors. There were no keys in the locked door. Corridors ran off the hallway to the right and the left.

An enormous living room, with doors at each end onto the hallway and the right-hand corridor, ran across part of the rear of the house. A quick inspection showed that the living room had floor-to-ceiling glass doors with heavy curtains that were closed. Jayne wasn't going to risk opening them, but she assumed the room looked directly out over the lake.

After several minutes of further investigation, they reached the end of the corridor to the right of the hallway. By now, Jayne's eyes were adjusted better to the gloom.

First, she opened the door to the right at the end of the corridor. Behind it was a staircase, which Jayne assumed was a secondary set of stairs, perhaps to give another route down from the floor above in case of fire, or simply for convenience. She wasn't going up now, so she closed the door again.

Next, Jayne opened the door on the left side of the corridor. It was immediately obvious that this was probably the private office they were looking for. A monitor screen stood on an oak desk, but there was no computer. There were two filing cabinets and several shelves that housed storage boxes.

Jayne noticed the blind that covered the lake-facing window was not quite down. She flicked her flashlight off, walked over, and pulled the blind fully down to the windowsill.

"No computer," Grewall said.

Jayne shrugged. "Was hoping, but not expecting."

"Shall we go through all these filing cabinets and boxes?"

Jayne nodded. She knew that in a house this size, hunting for anything was always going to be like looking for a needle in a haystack. But they had to try, and this was the obvious starting point.

"You do the boxes, I'll do the cabinets," Jayne said. "Let's get on with it—else we'll be here until dawn."

She flicked her flashlight back on.

CHAPTER FORTY-THREE

Saturday, October 15, 2016
   Berlin

Peskov forced himself to focus hard, despite the tiredness
that he could feel seeping through his brain. It was a habit he
had practiced often while on operations with the Spetsnaz
GRU and had now become ingrained.

As he had done the previous night, he carefully and
systematically swept the M25 binoculars from window to
window on the facade of the house far across the other side
of the lake, starting with the left side on the ground floor.

When he had checked every window, he widened the field
of view of his binoculars to get a picture of the entire house.
Then he narrowed it again, went back to the first window,
and restarted the process.

In Peskov's experience, it was extremely difficult for
someone who was inside a strange house at night, when it was
pitch dark, not to give some slight hint to an external
observer that they were there. They would always require

some kind of illumination at some stage. The difficulty was to spot it when it appeared.

The two men had the option, of course, to head across the lake in the boat and carry out surveillance from much closer. But that would carry its own dangers. Peskov preferred to take such a risk only when he judged it was necessary.

He mentally blocked out the sound of the lapping waves and the slight rustling of Matrosov's tunic and concentrated on the task in hand.

It was just as he was looking at the house overall, having widened his field of view for the umpteenth time, that he thought he glimpsed something in the center of the house on the ground floor.

Swiftly, he zoomed in on that part of the building, where it appeared there were full-height windows leading onto the terrace.

Was it a momentary reflection of moonlight on the window—because the moon was occasionally appearing through small breaks in the cloud? Or was it something inside shining out, a sliver of light through a curtain or blind? It was difficult to say.

Peskov lingered his focus on the windows for a good minute or more, but there was nothing further evident.

Had he imagined it?

Peskov decided to restart his scan of the building, constantly telling himself to concentrate. He swept the binoculars to the left of the building and focused on the first ground-floor window.

As he did so, he caught another very faint hint of light from that window.

It only lasted for a second or so, and it was no more than a fragment of brightness. Then it disappeared again.

This time, there was no mistake.

Peskov knew what he had seen.

Like bees to a honeypot.

"I think there's someone in there," Peskov said, his voice low and barely audible. "Quick flash of faint light."

Next to him, Matrosov jerked up on the boat seat.

"You certain?" he asked. There was a note of skepticism in his voice.

Peskov continued to focus on the left-hand ground-floor window. "I'm certain. It's gone now. Maybe they either turned it off or closed the blind or curtain or something. But it was definitely there."

He removed the binoculars from his eyes and turned to Matrosov. "Let's go. Must be Robinson. Nobody else would be in there at this time of night, unless Paulsen's got burglars by some huge coincidence."

Matrosov untied the boat from its mooring, then Peskov reached forward and turned the Zodiac's ignition key. The ultra-silent electric outboard motor that was attached to the stern of the boat behind him began to hum almost imperceptibly.

Peskov grabbed the steering wheel in front of him and pushed the throttle lever forward, and the boat moved toward the door of the boathouse.

He knew that the Zodiac, with its black hull, black engine and fittings, and with both occupants dressed head to foot in black, would be scarcely visible as he steered it at only walking pace across the lake. He didn't want to risk creating a wash behind the boat.

When Peskov got to within two hundred meters offshore, he steered away to starboard, then finally swung the boat back to port in order to approach the wooden jetty and boat shed at the end of Paulsen's garden from an angle. That meant there was no direct line of sight from the house to his approach, as the boat was shielded by the trees at the bottom of the garden.

He throttled the boat back even further and allowed it to drift in behind another, larger gray inflatable boat that was moored against the jetty. It had a Yamaha outboard motor attached to the stern.

Finally, Peskov's inflatable bumped up against the black car tires that had been placed to prevent damage to boats or to the jetty's wooden structure.

As soon as it did so, Matrosov lashed the boat to a mooring bollard with a rope. The two men then each grabbed a GSh-18 pistol and a SR-3M assault rifle and climbed up onto the jetty.

Peskov, holding his pistol and with the SR-3M slung around his neck, then paused to check out the boat shed. As Suslova had told him, it was more a shelter than a shed, with a doorless opening for boats and a doorless pedestrian entrance.

He led the way along the jetty and into the shed through the pedestrian entrance.

The shed stank of diesel and creosote, and Peskov cursed as a spider's web got tangled across his face. There was almost no light in there, but he could just about make out the outline of a door at the back of the shed, as Suslova had described.

The two men got up close to it, at which point Peskov pulled out a small narrow-beam flashlight and a small plastic folder from his pocket and handed the light to Matrosov.

"Shine this on the lock," Peskov said. "Keep it shielded."

Matrosov did as instructed, while Peskov removed his lock picking tools from the folder, comprising a small tension wrench and rake set. Picking locks was taught to all Spetsnaz operatives as routine. It was viewed as a mission-critical skill.

He went to work on the lock that secured the heavy wooden door. It took him more than ten minutes to pick it—nothing new there—swearing softly to himself as he battled with the rake to get the lock pins to align so he could turn the wrench and open the door.

Eventually, however, it swung open.

He beckoned Matrosov through the door and closed it behind him.

"Turn the light up," Peskov said.

Matrosov did so, and it became clear that the two men were in a tunnel that was only wide enough for one person but which had decent headroom and was properly built with wooden planks lining the walls and a cement floor. There were lamps on the ceiling at regular intervals and a light switch nearby, but Peskov decided not to take the risk of turning it on.

On a hook next to the door hung two keys, one of which was clearly for the door. The other was a short, stubby key with a Yamaha logo across it—presumably for the other boat's ignition. Peskov gave a wry smile. He could have done with the door key outside, not in here. Never mind, he thought—he could use it to lock up on the way out.

The tunnel, which had widely spaced steps on the floor, climbed upward into the darkness and appeared to curve away to the right. It certainly wasn't straight. This was just as Suslova had described it. It was a tunnel originally built during the Second World War by the property's Nazi owner to provide him with an escape route to his boat, if needed. These days, it simply provided shelter for anyone needing to reach the boathouse in bad weather.

"Next stop, the basement," Peskov said. "Let's go."

CHAPTER FORTY-FOUR

Saturday, October 15, 2016
Berlin

Jayne and Grewall worked fast. They flipped through the files
and papers in the boxes and cabinets in Paulsen's study, but it
rapidly became obvious that virtually all the contents were
related to his law firm.

There were briefing documents about clients, draft
contracts with annotations in spidery handwriting, shareholder agreements, nondisclosure agreements, directors'
service agreements, and employment contracts.

Jayne would have been astonished if there was anything
that had any relation to Paulsen's supposed role as a handler
for the Kremlin, and certainly anything that might be linked
to ILYA and ALYOSHA.

However, she had somehow hoped there might be something that gave them a further lead.

But as she worked her way through another folder that
contained personal household documents, including gas and

electricity bills and local tax accounts, she became less optimistic.

Jayne glanced up at Grewall, who was busy flipping through a ring binder.

"Got anything?" she murmured.

Grewall shook his head. "Just chess documents—records of old games, mainly."

He closed the file and put it back on the shelf.

Jayne grabbed another box file from the shelf, marked "Schach," or chess, and opened the lid.

It didn't contain documents, but rather items relating to Paulsen's career in the game. There was an old analog chess clock, a few chess pieces with stickers on them, showing they were the ones used during some of his biggest tournament victories, and a watch with hands in the shape of chess bishops. There was also an engraved glass paperweight commemorating Paulsen's victory in the German chess championship of 2001.

Nothing seemed particularly interesting.

She picked up a thin leather wallet at the bottom of the box and opened it.

Inside were two old chess club membership cards, both dated 1988. One was for the Schach-Club Kreuzberg, which Jayne, as a keen follower of the game, knew was one of the biggest chess clubs in West Berlin. Indeed, she knew Kreuzberg well from her visits to the city. During the Cold War, it had been one of the city's poorest areas, but it had since been gentrified and had a thriving arts scene.

The other card was for the Schachverein Berolina Mitte club, which she had also heard of and was well known. The address on the card showed it was in the Prenzlauer Berg district of Berlin, an area that had been part of East Berlin during the Cold War. Both cards bore the same passport-size photograph of Paulsen—then a youthful-looking man in a white shirt and tie.

Jayne looked at the cards. It was interesting that he had been a member of clubs on either side of the Berlin Wall, she thought. But presumably, as a resident of East Berlin, he was given special travel permissions by the East German authorities to play in the West. They obviously trusted him.

She replaced the cards in the box.

There was nothing of further use in that particular box, so Jayne put it back on the shelf and grabbed the next one, which was full of papers.

She had flipped through about half of the papers, all legal documents, when from behind her, through the slightly open door of the office, she thought she heard a faint squeak.

Jayne jumped and turned. Grewall, who was also leafing through papers, looked up at her and raised an inquiring eyebrow. Clearly, he had not heard it.

She turned her flashlight off, put a finger to her lips, and cupped her ear to indicate she wanted to listen.

Grewall took the hint and immediately turned his own light off.

There was silence for several seconds.

But then came, unmistakably, a second faint squeak.

It sounded as though it might be a floorboard. Or was it a door hinge?

Jayne wasn't sure, but she padded to the door and peered around the edge of it, standing completely still and trying to breathe as shallowly as possible.

There was nothing to be seen down the corridor other than impenetrable blackness.

But then came a slightly louder creak from somewhere distant, followed by a higher-pitched noise that to Jayne's mind could not be anything other than a footstep, causing a wooden floorboard or stairstep to squeak.

But although distant, the noise was coming from somewhere within the building, back in the direction of the central hallway from where they had come.

How the hell?

There had been no alert or message from the operations center. Given the presence of the drone above with its all-seeing camera, Jayne definitely expected to have received something if a person had approached and entered the building. This was more than a little odd.

Jayne withdrew silently into the study. She just caught the outline of Grewall's face in the darkness and leaned in close, placing a hand on his shoulder to get her bearings.

"Someone's inside. We need to get out," she murmured into Grewall's ear.

Now Jayne's mind was working overtime.

Whoever it was—whether it was some kind of security employed by Paulsen, German police, a burglar who by some huge coincidence just happened to be here at the same time, or, possibly the worst scenario, a Russian protection force who had got wind of their covert visit and were trying to ensure Paulsen's secrets remained secret—she knew they couldn't afford to get caught or even be seen.

As she rapidly went through the list of possibilities in her mind, she knew none could be ruled out.

It was highly unlikely to be Paulsen himself. He would surely have driven through the gate and entered normally, she reasoned.

"Where do you think they are?" Grewall said, his voice so low Jayne could barely hear it.

"Near the hallway, I think."

"We could get out the window?" Grewall said.

Jayne paused to consider the idea. That might be the best option. "Okay."

She edged her way by feel toward the window, going on

her memory of what furniture stood where to avoid it in the darkness. She wasn't going to switch the flashlight back on.

After what seemed like an age, she felt the window blind ahead of her with her hand, then moved her hand behind it until she located the window handle.

Jayne tried to pull the handle up, but it refused to budge. So she tried again, and again, before she realized.

"Shit. It's locked," she whispered to Grewall. "No key."

"Up that back staircase?" Grewall suggested.

"Good thinking," Jayne said.

Still feeling her way in the dark, she edged toward the door, bumping into Grewall as she did so, then got her bearings and found the door handle.

As they moved out into the corridor, there suddenly came the sound of footsteps moving swiftly from the direction of the hallway.

Jayne guessed they had been heard and whoever was there was now coming.

She glimpsed the shiny brass door handle to the rear staircase that she had seen earlier, grabbed it, and opened the door.

As she passed through, followed by Grewall, a deep male voice rang out in heavily accented English from somewhere down the corridor outside.

"Come out. Show yourself. Put your hands above your head."

The corridor light clicked on just a fraction of a second before Jayne shut the door behind her.

Immediately there came a burst of suppressed semiautomatic gunfire that, despite being relatively subdued, echoed through the house. It ripped holes through the door behind them, and sent splinters splattering everywhere.

Bloody hell.

Jayne flicked on the light switch next to the door frame.

"Get up the stairs, quick," she snapped as she launched herself up the wooden staircase, taking it two steps at a time.

She clattered up to the landing, Grewall's heavier footsteps thundering behind her as more rounds hammered through the door.

Now Jayne did not know where she was going, but rather than go up the next flight of stairs above, she opened the first door ahead of her and emerged into a lavishly furnished master bedroom. She flicked on the light switch to her right. There was an open door to an ensuite bathroom to her left and another door ahead on the far side of the room.

Grewall slammed the bedroom door shut behind him.

"Keep going," he said.

He had removed his Beretta from his belt and now racked the slide and flicked off the safety. Jayne did likewise with her Walther, holding it in firing position as she continued through the far bedroom door.

She emerged into a corridor that mirrored the one downstairs. Again, Grewall shut the door behind them.

Although the corridor lights were off, there was illumination in the landing at the far end that appeared to be coming up from the stairwell and the hallway below it.

"Let's see if we can get down the main stairs and out the front door," Jayne said, recalling the layout of the entrance hallway. "The bastards are coming behind us, not from in front."

"You hope."

Jayne ran along the corridor, which was carpeted, unlike the tiled one downstairs. She then flattened herself against the wall when she neared the landing, which formed a square that completely surrounded the stairwell leading down and up.

She inched herself along the wall, not wanting to expose

herself until she was certain nobody was waiting on the stairs, ready to take her out.

But from behind there came the sound of a slamming door and running footsteps, and the squeak of the door handle from the master bedroom.

"Move!" muttered Grewall from behind Jayne.

There was no option.

Jayne ran for the stairs. As she reached the top, there was another brief burst of gunfire behind her and she heard Grewall swear violently.

A few rounds smashed into the far wall of the landing ahead of her, creating holes in the plasterwork, and she knew instantly they must have only just missed, given the tight angle.

Jayne hurtled down the stairs, again taking them two at a time, hoping she didn't twist an ankle or trip as she did so.

If she could just get to the front door and out, they would have a chance.

When she reached the bottom of the stairs, Jayne leaped onto the checkered tile floor and instinctively looked around to check there was nobody farther back in the hallway behind the stairs.

Just as she turned, a man dressed entirely in black appeared in the hallway from the corridor on the right.

He immediately raised a pistol with a silencer on the barrel.

Jayne reacted instantaneously.

She threw herself sideways onto the floor behind the heavy table that carried the big chess set she'd seen before, just as a round whistled past her.

Now she was lying up against the door she'd opened earlier that led down into the cellar and to the boathouse exit. She wondered momentarily whether the gunmen had come into the house that way. It seemed likely.

There was another burst of gunfire, and several rounds kissed the floor tiles near her left hand, sending chips of marble flying. A round thudded into the table in front of her, shoving it a little toward her, although it was too solid to penetrate.

Jayne propped herself up on her elbows and eyed the gap between the table and the wall. Could she move the table a little and get a shot through the gap? It was a tight space, but maybe it was doable.

She glanced sideways at Grewall, who had rightly stopped at the bottom of the stairs. He couldn't break cover, given the gunman's position farther back in the hallway.

It was at that point that Jayne noticed there was blood dripping from Grewall's left arm—not a great deal, but enough.

Shit, he'd been clipped by a round in the corridor upstairs.

She caught his eye, but his face remained inscrutable. He wasn't reacting, wasn't showing pain. She knew the adrenaline was likely masking it, at least for the time being.

But then, from above, Jayne heard the muffled sound of footsteps running along the carpeted upstairs corridor toward the staircase.

She realized they were completely trapped.

With one gunman coming for them from above and another cornering them below, there was no way they could make it to the front door without being riddled.

Even if they stayed still, they were goners.

They'd been set up, somehow.

And it had to be Suslova who'd done it.

CHAPTER FORTY-FIVE

Saturday, October 15, 2016
  Berlin

Peskov sprinted down the corridor toward the landing and
the top of the staircase, his SR-3M Vikhr assault rifle in his
hand.

He knew that the shots he had fired down the corridor at
the two people he was chasing, one of whom was presumably
Jayne Robinson, had come close.

He wasn't going to let them get away now.

As he neared the landing, he heard more shots from
somewhere downstairs, and the whine of a ricochet.

Good.

That was presumably Matrosov taking them down as they
descended the stairs.

Instinctively, Peskov slowed as he reached the point
where the corridor wall ended to his left and where he was
going to emerge onto the landing. He needed to be sure he
could go down the stairs safely.

Then came another two shots in rapid succession from below, followed by a heavy thud.

Had Matrosov just taken one of them down?

Then Peskov noticed drops of blood on the floor, leading from the spot where he was standing, across the landing, and down the stairs. He *had* hit one of them, then. It must have been the man at the rear.

He poked his head slightly around the corner, but immediately there came multiple gunshots, and the wall just behind him erupted in an explosion of plasterwork.

Dermo.

He hadn't even seen who fired the shots. Where the hell had they come from?

Then came another volley of gunfire from downstairs that also smashed into the plasterwork near him.

A couple of seconds later he heard a faint squeak and the sound of a door closing.

Then silence.

Peskov knew in his gut that whoever was down there had just exited the hallway—and it likely wasn't Matrosov. This no longer felt good.

He again put his head around the corner. This time there was no incoming gunfire, so he made his way across the landing and began to descend the stairs, pausing on the top step to check below again.

There was still no sign of anyone.

He continued down, his weapon held ready.

The drops of blood led down the stairs. At the bottom there were a few more.

Then Peskov noticed a couple of slightly bloody footsteps, almost certainly a man's, on the tiled floor—leading from the base of the stairs through the door that led to the cellar.

Peskov stepped onto the hall floor, and it was at that point that he looked left toward the back of the hall.

Matrosov was lying motionless on the hall floor, blood running from his head and torso.

"*Svoloch*. Bastard," Peskov muttered. He could feel a rising tide of fury growing inside him.

His first instinct had been to run to Matrosov and see if there was any chance of saving him. But just one glance told him there was nothing he could do.

How could that have happened?

But Peskov knew what he was going to do next.

He would ensure there was payback—he was going to make sure his friend and colleague hadn't died for nothing.

Peskov strode to the cellar door, flattened himself against the wall to the right of it, his gun in firing position, and threw it open. There was no reaction from within.

Slowly, he eased his head around the door frame.

The light was on. That told its own story. He had switched it off and closed the door when he and Matrosov had exited the cellar into the hallway after coming through the long tunnel from the boat shed.

He'd pick off those bastards in the tunnel. They'd only had a short head start.

Peskov clattered down the stairs into the cellar.

* * *

Saturday, October 15, 2016
Berlin

The tunnel led downhill, curving first to the left, then to the right. Jayne ran as quickly as she could, thankful that the surface was well maintained and lit, with Grewall a couple of paces behind.

The handful of shots she had fired at the guy in the hallway in the black tunic had been a gamble, as she was aiming with only one eye from around the side of the chess table. But she had heard him fall heavily, and one look had told her all she needed to know. She had then put two more rounds into him.

There had been no alternative. It was him or her.

A second or two later, Grewall, despite his injured arm, had opened fire on the gunman upstairs as he emerged from the corridor, forcing him to take cover again.

After that, the only realistic option was the cellar door next to her. The front door was a no-go, as they would have been sitting ducks for the gunman at the top of the stairs if he reemerged. And they didn't have keys for the rear patio door.

Jayne felt that if there was an exit to the boathouse, as the plaque on the cellar door indicated, it was worth a try. She motioned at the door to Grewall, who nodded in agreement.

Grewall provided cover from the guy at the top of the stairs by firing more rounds while Jayne opened the cellar door.

They had both then run for it, shutting the door behind them.

Jayne could hear Grewall panting as they continued down the tunnel. They rounded another curve and ahead of them there was a closed door.

She ran up to it, grabbed the handle, and turned it. To her relief, the door swung open.

"Keys up there," Grewall said, pointing up at a hook behind the door. "We can lock the door behind us. There's one for a boat engine too."

Jayne nodded. That was well spotted.

She grabbed the door key and then, almost as a second thought, took the Yamaha ignition key, too.

She glanced at Grewall's arm. The round had torn his jacket and nicked his arm, which continued to bleed.

"It's okay," Grewall said. "Just caught me. Could have been much worse."

"Lucky," Jayne said. She turned and they went through the door, which she then locked behind them. She had no doubt that the gunman would be able to blast his way through the lock if needed, but it would buy them a little extra time.

Now she found herself standing in a boathouse that contained no boats.

To her left was a pedestrian exit, which she ran out of. The moon had reappeared, and in its light she could see she was standing on a wooden jetty alongside a mooring point where there were two inflatable dinghies, one small, one large.

The large boat, at the front, was gray and had a Yamaha engine, to which the key she was holding clearly belonged.

The other boat was smaller, with just four seats, but looked more modern and had an electric engine. She guessed that was the craft used by the gunmen.

Jayne crouched down and felt the electric engine with her hand to confirm her thoughts. It was indeed quite warm.

She swiftly calculated the options. They couldn't swim for it, as they'd be shot like fish in a barrel. Access to the neighboring properties might be a possibility, but Jayne had no idea whether there was actually a way through or not.

Then she had a quick thought and turned to Grewall.

"I've an idea," she said.

"What?"

She told him, her voice staccato-like as she stumbled over her words in her haste.

CHAPTER FORTY-SIX

Saturday, October 15, 2016
Berlin

Peskov ran up to the wooden door, grabbed the handle, and turned it. It rattled in his hand, but nothing happened. He turned again and shook it. It just wasn't budging.

Then he glanced up at the hook where he had earlier seen the door key and boat key and realized what had happened. Both were missing.

"*Bljad,*" he swore. Sonofabitch.

From outside, he could hear the chug-a-chug-a-chug of an outboard engine and he knew what was going on. There wasn't much time.

There was only one solution. He raised his assault rifle, pointed it at the lock, and fired. Splinters of door and door-frame flew.

But the door was made of heavy hardwood, and the lock was stronger than he expected. He grabbed the handle, which now had a piece missing at one side, and tried to open the door again. But it still wouldn't budge.

Peskov again raised the rifle and let fly with another burst of bullets, now concentrating on the latch.

This time, the door burst open.

Once Peskov was certain there was nobody outside waiting to ambush him, he emerged from the door.

Nobody there.

And the sound of the outboard motor was receding.

He ran out of the boathouse and onto the jetty.

In the moonlight, he made out the white wash in the water and the gray inflatable that had been moored next to his own boat. It was slowly heading away from shore.

Peskov raised his gun and fired two short bursts at the boat. But from this distance, his chances of success were less than optimal.

He jumped down into his own boat. He figured he could quickly overtake the other, given its slow speed—then he could make sure the job was done properly.

He checked for any damage to the boat, then swiftly pulled the mooring rope off the bollard, sat down, and turned the ignition key. The engine hummed into life.

Peskov nestled his rifle against his right side and pushed the throttle forward. The boat moved off and Peskov steered out toward the other boat. This time, he didn't worry about leaving a wake behind.

A few seconds later, all hell broke loose.

There was a firecracker explosion of noise as someone opened fire at him with a semiautomatic from the clump of bushes on the shore a few meters to his left.

Peskov jumped as if he'd been electrocuted.

Rounds ripped through the port side of the boat, punching large holes in the rubber hull.

This was a complete ambush.

Instinctively, Peskov tried to flatten himself on the bottom of the boat to make himself a smaller target and give him some protection. At the same time, he grabbed his assault rifle from his side.

He raised it and blazed a burst of rounds in the direction of the muzzle flashes he'd seen in the bushes.

But then another burst came back at him, from a different, lower position.

Before he could adjust his aim to return fire, he felt a round slam into his right shoulder joint, causing a huge spike of pain to shoot through his arm. Involuntarily, he dropped his gun back down to his side.

Peskov grunted in agony and he again lay flat.

There was a pause in the firing, and he tried one more time to pick up the gun.

But the incoming gunfire resumed a second or two later, and yet another round struck him, this time in the upper right arm. Then another bullet hit him in the right thigh.

Peskov let out an involuntary scream.

Dermo.

He looked down to find blood spurting out of his arm and shoulder, where he could see there was a sizable hole. His right arm was now completely unusable—it just hung uselessly and extremely painfully at his side—and he struggled to move his right leg.

Peskov tried to push himself up using his left leg and arm but lost his balance. He lurched sideways onto the inflatable tube on the starboard side of his boat, which had collapsed after being punctured by the gunfire.

The boat's engine had stopped and the vessel, now seriously destabilized, tipped to starboard under Peskov's weight. He fell headfirst into the water.

It was at that point that he blacked out.

* * *

Saturday, October 15, 2016
   Berlin

When she saw the gunman fall into the water and heard the splash, Jayne jumped up and emerged from behind the bush where she had flattened herself on the ground.

Still holding her Walther in her right hand, she took out the flashlight from her pocket, turned it on, and directed it toward the man's boat. She knew she had hit it several times, and it was badly damaged. The engine had cut out, and it was stationary.

There was no sign of the gunman in the water. She was certain, from his movements and the grunt and squeal, that she had hit him at least a couple of times but had no clue what his injuries might be.

Jayne then turned and flashed the light several times at the boat out on the water, signaling to Grewall, who was at the helm.

Grewall turned the boat around and headed back toward her, now moving at a quicker pace.

She then pointed the flashlight back at the gunman's boat. There was still no sign of him in the water, and the boat was now largely deflated.

Shit.

The intention had been to incapacitate, not kill, but it was very difficult by moonlight. Jayne's gut feeling was that with her second burst, she'd hit him around the shoulder and the leg, but she couldn't be certain.

Faced with a man armed with a semiautomatic rifle, she had just done the best she could.

One thing was for sure: Jayne knew she'd taken the guy

completely by surprise—a classic ambush, right in line with the plan they had devised on the spot.

She had anticipated his return fire at the place he'd seen her muzzle flashes, changed her position in the darkness to counteract that, and then hit him again. Her magazine change had been quick, and her decision to opt for the heavier .32-caliber cartridges had paid off.

Grewall had also played his part perfectly, ensuring the gray inflatable had acted as bait to draw the man's focus—he hadn't gone too quickly, nor too slowly, which would have invited suspicion.

A surge of relief flooded through her, but she knew they were not done yet.

They needed to get out of there quickly.

She did not know whether the two gunmen had backup nearby or whether neighbors had heard the gunfire and called the police. Either outcome seemed likely and would be disastrous.

Jayne hurried back over the grassy bank to the jetty, while Grewall guided the boat back to its mooring point, tied it up, and jumped out.

He clapped Jayne on the shoulder. "Great job," he murmured. "What happened to him?"

"I hit him and he fell in. Hasn't resurfaced."

Grewall looked out over the water. "There's nothing we can do. We need to get out of here."

"That's my thinking. Back out the way we came?" She pointed toward the boat shed and its hidden tunnel.

Grewall nodded. "That's the simplest."

Jayne pointed at Grewall's injured arm. Blood was still dripping from it and soaking into his jacket. "How is it?"

"It'll be okay," he said. "Need to get it cleaned up and bandaged."

Jayne nodded, turned, and headed toward the shed.

She felt frustrated. They had drawn a complete blank in the short time they'd had in the house, and the ensuing gunfight had now created new problems.

The entire operation had gone completely sideways, as well as being a waste of effort.

She had to hope Joe had achieved a better outcome at the Stasi archives.

Suslova had double-crossed them. Jayne hoped she had a damn good set of excuses ready for Putin—because if Jayne had anything to do with it, she was history.

CHAPTER FORTY-SEVEN

Saturday, October 15, 2016
  Berlin

A funeral cortege was passing near the American embassy on Pariser Platz when Jayne and Joe arrived. A line of black Mercedes and BMWs was moving at a walking pace. It felt quite appropriate somehow.

Jayne had only managed three hours of sleep at the safe house in Limonenstrasse before being woken by her alarm, which she'd set for eight o'clock.

It had taken some effort to blank out the mental replays of the night's events that were whirring around in her head and to finally doze off. It was the usual story after an operation.

Unavoidable as it had been, it was the image of the Russian gunman toppling off his boat and disappearing into a black, inky grave that had been the biggest and most difficult to dislodge.

Now, as the team gathered around the conference table in

the CIA station's operations room, the mood was equally funereal. Someone came in with a fresh pot of coffee, placed it on the table, and tried to crack a joke, but nobody responded.

Jayne poured a cup for Grewall, who was sitting next to her, a heavy bandage on his arm, one for Joe, and one for herself, which she drank quickly. She then poured herself a second.

Her head felt as though it was pressurized and rigid. Every movement seemed to take forever, as if it were happening in slow motion, even lifting the coffee cup to her mouth.

A TV screen on the wall was showing a news report live from Lake Wannsee. The report from Das Erste, one of the biggest public broadcasters, showed footage of the wreckage of the Zodiac that Jayne had shot up. In the background, a diving team was searching the lake bottom. The reporter said that the body of an unknown man, carrying no identification but who had several gunshot wounds, had been recovered from the lake, and a search was continuing for more evidence.

The incident had followed a gun battle and an apparent burglary at the house on Am Sandwerder street in the middle of the night, the reporter said.

Another man, holding a gun, had been found dead inside the house, the reporter continued, quoting police sources.

It was assumed that the various parties involved entered the house via a two-hundred-meter tunnel that led to the boathouse on the lake, the reporter added. But the police remained confused, because the burglar alarms and electronic keyless entry systems in the house appeared to be functioning and were intact. The owner had not been present, and efforts were underway to trace him.

Meanwhile, it had become clear that the failure of the CIA's infrared drone to spot Suslova's men entering the house, and thus give Jayne and Grewall advance warning, was purely down to the fact that it was only covering a hundred-meter radius around the property, not the boathouse, which was much farther away.

Eventually, Vic came in and took a seat at the head of the table.

On the video monitor on the wall, Valentin Marchenko's image appeared. Vic had invited him to join the meeting remotely.

"First, well done, Jayne and Ed, on the operation," Vic began. "But that bitch Suslova is never getting her two billion bucks back, the way I'm feeling right now. What the hell? She's the one who should be at the bottom of the lake."

He looked around the team, an angry expression on his face.

Jayne had to agree. The appearance of two of Suslova's Spetsnaz apes at the house indicated either she had rethought the agreement she had been coerced into or the whole thing had been a setup from the start.

It raised many questions. If she'd had a rethink, had Suslova decided that in the interests of self-preservation she would have to take the enormous hit to her bank account, thus avoiding a confrontation with Putin for the time being? Or had she thought of a way to explain herself to Putin? Or was there some other covert Kremlin operation now ongoing behind the scenes?

There was much to think about. Should they now press the button and destroy Suslova by sending details of her financial maneuverings to Putin? Or, conversely, should they hold off and explore whether they could still turn her into a viable asset inside the Kremlin? Surely she couldn't just get away with losing two billion of the president's cash? This would not be straightforward.

Next to Jayne, Joe was sipping his coffee.

"We're running out of time," Vic said. "Tomorrow President Ferguson and Prime Minister Parker are meeting with Erich Merck and the French president, Martinez, to discuss policy toward Russia. It's now agreed that the intelligence heads will be there too—Veltman and me, plus all the others. We need this all put to bed before then so we can brief Ferguson ahead of that meeting. If we're going to get the Germans and the French on board with combating the Russian threat to Ukraine, we need a result. We need to know who the traitors are."

The sound of Marchenko clearing his throat came over the speaker, and everyone turned to the monitor screen.

"I'd agree with all of that, Vic," Marchenko said. "My country needs a united Europe behind us—we're under attack. Putin needs to see that his attempts to divide and conquer and weaken his enemies won't work. But right now, I'm not seeing that unity. There's no room for traitors—they must be found. Once you know more, I'll meet with President Doroshenko to brief him. I'm also seeing Maria Fradkova on Tuesday. It would be nice if I can tell both of them we've made some progress."

Vic nodded. "It certainly would."

He turned to Jayne. "So what next? We can't go back to Paulsen's house and resume the search. Nothing turned up during the time you were in there, anyway. So we're no nearer to finding out who ILYA and ALYOSHA are, are we?"

Jayne shook her head. "We'll have to turn the screw on Paulsen some other way."

"How?" Vic asked, leaning forward. "We don't even know where he is."

That was true enough. Jayne didn't reply. She had no answer right now.

Vic turned to Joe. "What about the Stasi archives, Joe? Can you update us?"

Joe had already briefed Jayne at the safe house on his

abortive visit the previous day to the Stasi Records Agency, which had done nothing to lift her mood. He now gave similar details to the others.

Vic listened in silence, stroking his chin.

"So the upshot is, they just don't have a file on Paulsen there," Joe concluded. "Someone's likely stolen it—or destroyed it. Maybe they have information on him somewhere else in the archives, but finding it is going to be like looking for a needle in a massive haystack. And that's even if it's intact—quite a lot of the old Stasi files were ripped into pieces. They're still in bags waiting to be restored. It could take years."

Jayne leaned back in her chair and stared at the ceiling.

It was at that point that a lightbulb flashed somewhere inside her mind.

She had been feeling despondent all morning, partly because of the previous night's events, and partly because of the lack of general progress.

But now, as Joe finished speaking, she had a flashback to the office in Paulsen's house.

She turned to Joe. "Did you just say there could be information on Paulsen elsewhere in the archives?"

Joe nodded. "Could be, somewhere. It's just finding it. Everything was double-entered. If a piece of information was relevant to more than one person, or more than one organization, it would be entered into both files."

"Right," Jayne said. "I've just had a thought. What about Paulsen's chess clubs? I saw old membership cards in a box in his study for two clubs, dating back to 1988—one in East Berlin, the Schachverein Berolina Mitta club, and one in West Berlin, the Schach-Club Kreuzberg. I kind of thought it was interesting he had memberships on both sides of the Berlin Wall but thought no more of it. If he was a Stasi member, would they have possibly used him to recruit in

West Berlin and therefore given him the travel permits to cross the border? If you can't find the Paulsen file, maybe there's something of interest in the files on the chess clubs?"

Joe stared at her. "Good thinking," he said. "We can give that a try, for sure."

Jayne leaned forward. Now her mind was buzzing. "In West Berlin, Paulsen would have had access to people from the American sector, the British sector, and the French sector. If he was recruiting for the Stasi or for the Russians, he was in a perfect position to do so with a perfect cover —chess."

She suddenly knew it made sense. Following World War II, Berlin had been divided into different sectors, all under the control of different member countries of the Western Allies who, together, had defeated Germany. Paulsen could have easily met with many senior people in influential positions from any of those countries.

Vic looked at Joe. "Sounds like a good suggestion. Can you get down there again?"

"Sure," Joe said. He drained his coffee and stood.

"I'll come with you," Jayne said. "I need to refocus on something else after last night."

CHAPTER FORTY-EIGHT

Saturday, October 15, 2016
  Berlin

"You again?" Jurgen Giesen said, a twinkle in his eye as he walked up to Joe and Jayne in the reception area. "Do you think I'm a magician? That I can somehow just conjure up that file you wanted?"

Jayne glanced at Joe, who was shaking his head, a slight grin on his face. "I've written it off," Joe said. "But there are a couple of others I'd like to try to find."

Joe explained fairly succinctly to the Federal Commissioner for the Stasi Records what they were looking for. "Chess clubs this time, not individual people. The Kreuzberg and Berolina Mitta clubs."

Giesen led them to a private meeting room that Joe said was the same one he had used the previous day.

About half an hour and two more coffees later, an archives assistant brought them two chunky orange cardboard document folders, one labeled "Schachverein Berolina Mitta," the other "Schach-Club Kreuzberg."

Both had been heavily used in their time. They were dog-eared, with tears in the covers, and were stuffed full of type-written yellowing documents, some of which had annotations in ballpoint pen in the margins. There were creased photographs, maps, handwritten diagrams, transcripts of telephone calls that had been tapped, and other assorted detritus.

"I'll leave you here to go through these," Giesen said. "There's a management meeting I need to attend. I'll be back in an hour." He disappeared out the door.

Joe passed Jayne the Kreuzberg file and took the Berolina Mitta file for himself. "Let's get to work," he said.

They began to carefully go through the documents. Most of the material within had been obtained from a single source, Joe informed her, pointing to an identification number at the top of many of the documents that was common to several of them.

There were also code letters to indicate which type of informant had supplied them. The most common of the five different types was labeled IM, which Joe said stood for Inof-fizieller Mitarbeiter, or unofficial collaborator, which was by far the most widespread type of source in the old East Germany. They were not on the Stasi's official payroll, but rather would have received benefits or privileges in return for information.

"The IM was probably some club member or helper," Joe said.

A few were labeled with the IMS codeword. That stood for an informant who was assigned to report on people or activities in workplaces or areas that were important to state security, Joe informed her.

Jayne was fluent in German, and so was able to easily read the documentation. Most of it seemed uninteresting and included day-to-day descriptions of the activities of club members and who was friendly with whom. There were photographs of players and games in progress, and also records of the moves in each game that the players kept as the contest progressed. There were even lists of what food and drink the chess players consumed while attending their regular Thursday night club meetings.

Their lives appeared to be fairly humdrum.

After about an hour, Jayne was roughly halfway through her pile of documents. Joe had made similar progress with his.

So far, none of the documents mentioned Wolfgang Paulsen.

She leaned back in her chair and yawned. By now, exhaustion was getting the better of her.

Jayne went to fetch a fresh coffee for them both. When she returned, she removed a handful of black-and-white photographs from the top of the pile next to her. All of them depicted scenes from one of the Kreuzberg club's Thursday night meetings on various dates in 1987 and 1988. The pictures showed players, nearly all of them men, sitting on either side of dozens of wooden chess tables that were arranged in long rows in a large room with iron supporting pillars running from floor to ceiling at intervals and arched windows at the far end. The games were in various stages of completion, and all the tables also had old-fashioned analog chess clocks in place.

Jayne scrutinized each of the photographs. All were labeled on the back with the words "Schach-Club Kreuzberg," the date, and the names of the people pictured. But the names meant nothing to Jayne, and there were no accompanying notes to indicate why they had been photographed.

The fifth photo she picked up also showed a game in progress in the same room.

As soon as she saw the image, Jayne shot straight up in her seat, a jolt of adrenaline running through her system.

The photograph showed two men sitting opposite each other at a chessboard. The game was partly completed.

The player sitting on the left, nearest the camera, was Wolfgang Paulsen. There was no mistaking his thin face, and although the hair looked darker and more lustrous than in his recent pictures, it fit with the ones she had seen at Nick Geldard's house of their matches during the 1990s.

Paulsen was smiling and looking directly at his opponent, who looked vaguely familiar, but Jayne couldn't put a name to the face, so she turned the picture over. There was a date on the back, Thursday, November 3, 1988, and the names of the players.

This time, she froze.

Of course.

"What is it?" Joe asked.

Jayne just pointed at the photograph. "It's a picture of Paulsen at the chess club in 1988. Guess who he's playing against?"

"Who?"

"You're not going to believe this." Jayne put the photo back down on the table and pushed it across to Joe. "It's the German chancellor."

Joe leaned across to look at the image. "Who? Helmut Kohl, you mean?"

Jayne shook her head. Kohl had been the long-serving West German chancellor from 1982 to 1998, including during the period of German reunification as the Cold War ended. "Not Kohl, I mean the—"

"What, the current chancellor, you mean?" Joe interrupted. "Merck?"

Jayne nodded. "Erich Merck."

Joe stared at her, then down at the photo. He picked it up and studied it. "Holy shit. It can't be, can it?"

Jayne shrugged. "Well, it is him."

"Could he have recruited Merck there? Surely not?"

Jayne shrugged. "It fits with what Shevchenko and Suslova told me."

She picked up the remaining two photographs. The next one also showed Merck and Paulsen, this time fully engrossed in a game. It was taken a week later, on Thursday, November 10, at the same place. Neither man was looking at the camera.

"They obviously spent quite a bit of time together at the club," Jayne said.

The final photograph also showed Paulsen, but this time playing chess against another man with neatly cut dark hair and a smart jacket. Again, Jayne felt that she vaguely recognized him, but no name came to mind.

She turned the photograph over. The date was Thursday, November 24.

Jayne sucked in a deep breath. "Bloody unbelievable," she said. "Another photo from that November. Paulsen's with Jean Revel in this one, also playing chess."

Joe's eyes widened. "The French military intelligence chief?"

"That's the one. Head of the DRM. He's the right-hand man to the French president, especially when it comes to advising on matters concerning Russia. He's a four-star general."

Jayne paused and ran her hand through her hair.

Yet again, Shevchenko's words before she was shot dead in Moscow ran through her mind.

Putin apparently has at least two very high-level assets in the West who are helping him prepare the ground for an invasion of Ukraine—they are code-named ILYA and ALYOSHA.

Everything was now clear.

"These two have to be ILYA and ALYOSHA," Jayne said. "Two very high-level assets in the West. That's what Shevchenko told me. I can see now—Suslova's handling Paulsen, and Paulsen is handling Merck and Revel."

Joe looked skeptical. "I don't know."

"Listen," she said. "Based on what Suslova told me and what I'm now seeing in this file, my gut feeling is that Paulsen was running a recruitment operation out of that Kreuzberg chess club for the Stasi and the KGB. What jobs were those two doing at the time that could have made them attractive?"

Joe took his phone from his pocket. "Let's have a look at their CVs."

He tapped on his screen a few times. "Here we are. Merck trained as a lawyer after university, then in the 1980s and 1990s worked for energy companies as a chief legal counsel— he was on the supervisory board of some. His last job as a legal counsel was for the company that eventually built the Eurostream One gas pipeline from Russia to Germany."

Joe stopped and looked up at Jayne.

"Bloody hell," Jayne said. "I can see where this is going."

"Yes," Joe said. "Merck then moved from Eurostream One into politics and was elected to the German parliament, the Bundestag. The rest is history. Chancellor in 2005. The CV also says that Merck relaxes in his spare time by playing chess."

Jayne leaned back in her chair. "So the Russians spotted him, recruited him, groomed him, and put him as their man into Eurostream One, then the Bundestag, and then into the chancellor's job. And he's always been a huge backer of Germany buying Russian gas and oil—he's been supporting the Eurostream Two project to build another gas pipeline running parallel to the first. He's also been a driving force behind Russian oil companies taking stakes in several

German refineries—which, of course, process Russian oil. Unbelievable."

"You got it," Joe said. "I lived in West Berlin during the 1980s. There were a lot of highly capable, ambitious, intelligent people based there during the Cold War—with little for them to do in their spare time because of all the restrictions. An invitation to come and play chess probably seemed appealing. And it looks like Paulsen hit the jackpot, given Merck's incredible career path since then."

"What about Revel?" Jayne asked.

Joe jabbed at his phone screen a few more times. "Revel is a career spy. He was in Berlin for the DGSE, French foreign intelligence, from 1987 until 1993. Obviously, the Russians got their teeth into him then. Then he moved to military intelligence, the DRM, where he's been ever since. Now he's the chief adviser to the French president on Russian matters. You couldn't make this up. No wonder the French are so cozy with Moscow—and why they too are so strongly in favor of buying more Russian gas through Eurostream One and Two."

Jayne waved a hand at the photographs. "This is no coincidence, is it?"

Joe nodded. "It makes me wonder who else Paulsen recruited." He picked up one of the photographs. "But there's one slight issue. The photos, good as they are, aren't proof those two have been spying for Russia and that Paulsen has been their handler. It could be quite innocent— just chess. In the absence of the Stasi file for Paulsen, that's not going to be easy to get. And I'm assuming there won't be files on Merck and Revel confirming their status as Russian assets—otherwise, they'd have been caught long ago."

Jayne nodded and said nothing. He was completely correct. And the odds were that such proof was going to be extremely difficult to obtain.

There came a knock at the door and Giesen stuck his head into the room.

"Any progress?" he asked, looking alternately at Joe and Jayne.

"We have, actually," Joe said. He hesitated. "You'll need to give me your word you'll keep what I'm about to say completely confidential."

Giesen nodded, stepped into the room, and shut the door. He leaned over and shook hands with Joe. "I always keep inquiries confidential. I give you my word—my handshake."

Joe nodded. "Good. I have a question. And I'm guessing the answer to this is no, but do you have files for Erich Merck?"

Giesen's eyebrows rose. "We do, but they're clean, if that's what you're wondering. When Merck ran for president, and even when he was elected to the Bundestag, they were put under the microscope to make sure there was nothing untoward in them. Why?"

"Okay, then do you have a file for Jean Revel, head of France's military intelligence service, the DRM?" Joe asked, ignoring the question.

"That rings no bells at all, but I can check," Giesen said.

Jayne exchanged glances with Joe. This was no surprise.

She turned back to Giesen. "I'm wondering if there's any other way you might track down what happened to that missing file for Paulsen? I have a feeling it is going to be quite crucial."

Giesen pursed his lips. "I don't see how we're going to find out. The likelihood is that if it's missing, it's been shredded and is in pieces, moldering somewhere in a bag. You'll never find it. Other files disappear—occasionally they are stolen. Keeping control of them is like trying to herd cats, though we do our best."

This was irritating. "If the archive had made digital copies of the files, then it wouldn't be an issue if you lost a physical one," she said.

"We have digital copies of some," Giesen said. "But there are so many, we haven't been able to digitize all of them. Anyway, if the person it relates to is alive, we don't make the digital copies available."

There was a loud squeak as Joe pushed his chair back and sat up. "Wait," he said. "Digital copies. What about the Rosenholz files—the Stasi microfilms that the CIA got hold of?"

There was a short silence.

"We do have the Rosenholz files," Giesen said, a little embarrassed. "Good point. We can look in there if you like."

Jayne caught Joe's eye and raised an inquiring eyebrow. She had heard of the Rosenholz files but was trying to recall the detail.

"In 1990, when the Stasi folded on German reunification, a KGB officer covertly sold the Agency many Stasi files on microfilm," Joe said. "The files belonged to the HVA, the Stasi's foreign intelligence service. Priceless. The CIA copied them all onto their computer systems and onto CD-ROMs and eventually returned them—after checking them carefully to see if any of their people were Stasi agents."

"The Rosenholz microfilms did include copies of several paper files that had been shredded," Giesen said.

Jayne again found herself glad that Joe was around. This was his area of expertise.

"There's another question," Joe said. "If the named files for Erich Merck and Jean Revel are clean, might there be something separate under their code names?"

Giesen did a double take. "You're trying to tell me you think Erich Merck had a Stasi code name?"

"Possibly. And Revel. And they might be KGB code names, not Stasi."

"*KGB?*" Giesen's voice rose in astonishment.

Joe nodded.

Giesen paused. "Well, the Stasi had complex filing systems to protect the identities of its high-value sources. And it worked hand in glove with the KGB, of course. But I think what you're saying is highly unlikely."

He explained that apart from the named files, the Stasi held index cards on all of its assets. There were so-called F16 cards, containing an asset's real name, registration number, and other details, and F22 cards, containing only their code name, the registration number, and the name of the agent who recruited or handled that asset. The cards also listed which files existed on that person. An identity would only be fully confirmed if both cards were viewed together.

"There is no F16 card for Erich Merck in the Stasi files," Giesen said. "I can guarantee you that. Nothing to indicate he was a Stasi asset, or a KGB asset, for that matter. If there was, we'd know—it was checked when he ran for chancellor. Revel I have no idea about."

"Can you try the code names, anyway?" Jayne asked. "See if there are F22 cards under ILYA or ALYOSHA." Jayne asked. She spelled out the names, so there could be no mistake.

Giesen shrugged. "I can look—but if there's no F16, there won't be an F22."

"But you can look, can't you?" Joe asked.

"I have a feeling I'm playing with fire here. This is the chancellor we're talking about. And a four-star French general. But I will check. And I'll check the Rosenholz files for Paulsen too. Give me a bit of time."

He went out the door, closing it behind him.

Joe stood. "I'll get us another coffee—I need a break before we continue with this."

* * *

Saturday, October 15, 2016
   Berlin

Twenty minutes and one very welcome coffee later, it was
time to resume. Joe picked up the remaining documents in
the Berolina Mitte chess club file, while Jayne did likewise
with the Kreuzberg ones. She knew this was the crunch point
of their investigation.

There was no doubt in Jayne's mind that the KGB and the
Stasi must have worked in tandem to run Paulsen during the
period at the end of the Cold War—they were partner
services, after all. Although it seemed Paulsen had been
recruited and run primarily by Suslova, the Kremlin would
have needed the Stasi to also be involved by, for example,
providing travel passes and safe passage to West Berlin. They
would have kept a very close watch on him. Therefore, there
was a good chance that Stasi cards existed for Merck and
Revel and that they might contain the KGB codenames.

She finished sifting through her file, but there was
nothing else of significance. As she closed it, she noticed Joe
was staring at a photograph. "What have you got?"

Joe pushed the photograph across to her. "Who's that
woman?"

The black-and-white photograph showed Paulsen standing
in a room in front of several rows of chess tables, a few of
which were occupied by games in progress. Next to him was a
slim, beautiful woman with shoulder-length black hair, whose
hand was draped around his shoulder. Neither were looking at
the camera.

Jayne felt her scalp tighten.

"Kira Suslova," she said. "No doubt."

She turned it over. The label on the back confirmed that it was indeed Suslova and Paulsen. It stated that the photograph, dated Thursday, April 21, 1988, had been taken at the Berolina Mitte chess club's headquarters. It also gave the address: Wichertstrasse 9 in East Berlin. Jayne checked it on her phone. It was only a kilometer behind where the old Berlin Wall had been.

"This is useful," Jayne said. "They were obviously very close. I wonder if this was prior to or after recruitment, and whether they were also having an affair?"

"They do look physically close here," Joe said.

The door opened and Giesen returned, carrying a file folder. He sat down and removed three items from it, placing them on the table.

"There you go," Giesen said. "Two yellow F22 transaction cards, which I believe you might find of interest—there are no corresponding F16 cards to them, interestingly enough. Both are marked as KGB assets, not Stasi. There's also one copy I've just taken from the Rosenholz microfilms of an F22 and an F16 for Paulsen."

Jayne picked them up.

The rectangular yellow F22 cards, similar in size to a postcard, were preprinted with spaces for name, code name, code number, handler, and other information to be either hand-written or typewritten in or stamped.

On the first, the code name section had the word "ILYA" typed into it and above it was a registration number, XV5218/88. Below that was stamped the letters KGB. The handler section was marked "Paulsen XIII509/87."

The second card was similar. It had "ALYOSHA" in the code name box and registration XV6311/88. It also had the KGB stamp and "Paulsen XIII509/87" marked in the handler section.

She glanced at the printout of the Rosenholz microfilmed

cards. The copy was black and white and low quality, but was readable. These cards clearly related to Paulsen, as he was named on the F16 card. On the F22 card, his code name was marked as "VOLKER." Well, that was new information. And his registration number was marked as "XIII509/87," which corresponded with the handler numbers on the ILYA and ALYOSHA cards.

Jayne looked up at Giesen. "Thank you. This is fantastic information. And there's definitely no Stasi F16 card for Merck or Revel?"

"No."

"So we still have nothing that definitively ties the ILYA and ALYOSHA codenames to Merck and Revel?" Jayne asked.

This time, Giesen completely opened the folder, at which point Jayne noticed something else in there. He removed two photographs, which he handed to Jayne.

"I've saved the best until last," Giesen said.

She looked at them. One was a headshot of Merck, the other of Revel. Both had been taken from a distance with a zoom lens.

"Check the back of the photos," Giesen said. "They were in the ILYA and ALYOSHA files. No names, just code numbers."

Jayne turned them over. On the reverse of each was a handwritten code number.

The photograph of Merck had the registration number XV6311/88 on the back, but no name, while the one of Revel had the number XV5218/88, also with no name.

Jayne read the numbers carefully, then compared them with the yellow F22 cards that were lying on the table.

She felt her stomach twist inside. Then she saw what she needed and read it a second time to make sure.

"So Merck is ALYOSHA, and Revel is ILYA?" Jayne asked, not quite able to believe what she was reading.

Giesen nodded. "Nobody would have thought to cross-check these photographs, or the F22s, with the separate named Stasi files for Merck when he was running for political office. The named files wouldn't have those code numbers, or the code names. There's no electronic cross-checking system available for these old Stasi files, so nothing would have been flagged, like you'd get with a modern computerized system. Until you came in here with the name of Merck's chess clubs and the codenames, enabling us to find the photographs, we wouldn't have known."

"Bloody hell," Jayne said.

"Indeed," Giesen replied.

"We've got them," Joe said, a slow grin crossing his face.

Jayne exhaled and looked at Giesen. "Don't say a word to anyone about this—we'll deal with it. You haven't seen us in here."

Giesen nodded. "I understand. If what you say is true, they all deserve what's coming to them."

Jayne stood up, looked at Joe, and punched the air. "Merck—the queen's pawn. Who'd have believed it?"

CHAPTER FORTY-NINE

Saturday, October 15, 2016
  Berlin

Vic sat in the operations room at the CIA station with his arms folded, his face stonelike, as Jayne summed up hers and Joe's visit to the Stasi archives.

She placed copies of the photographs, the F22 and F16 cards, and the other documents on the table. Before leaving the archive, Jayne had got Giesen to carefully scan and print all of them so she had digital and physical copies.

"This is just incredible," Vic said. His voice cracked, giving away his emotions. "It's unprecedented. A European head of state in the Russians' pocket—and for all this time. Merck's been chancellor since 2005. It explains a lot about how Germany's behaved."

"Personally, I think Ferguson should confront Merck with this at the heads of state meeting tomorrow," Jayne said. "We can't let this go on any further."

Vic nodded. "I agree. The biggest scandal here is that,

thanks to Merck, Germany's the biggest buyer of gas and oil from Russia. And France is not that far behind. They buy thirty billion euros worth of gas and oil a year between them from Putin—thirty damn billion. And what's he doing with all that cash? He's arming his military ready to invade Ukraine—Operation Imperiya. Buying tanks, fighter jets, helicopters, rocket launchers. You name it."

Jayne leaned forward. "But it's worse than that, Vic. Putin's taking the heroin dealer's approach—he's got Germany, France, Italy, and the others addicted to his gas and oil. Then it's going to be impossible for them to wean themselves off it for the foreseeable future."

"She's right, Vic," Joe said. "Merck's doing Putin's dirty work for him—he's the dealer on the street corner, while Putin runs the cartel from the Kremlin. And now that they're addicted, if Germany and the others stop buying Russian gas and try to get it elsewhere instead, the price of world gas is going to skyrocket so high there'll be uproar, chaos, social upheaval everywhere. That's what Putin is banking on—he thinks he can invade Ukraine and the whole of Europe will just let him do it out of fear of the huge economic and social consequences if he shuts their gas off."

There was a pause.

"Spot-on," Jayne said. She always admired Joe's ability to get to the heart of an issue.

Vic leaned back in his chair. "Ideally, I'd like Merck's banking, phone, and email records. There's bound to be more evidence there somewhere—Moscow must be paying him a fortune. I'll get the NSA on to it tonight. But they won't be able to get all that for tomorrow's summit meeting."

He pursed his lips, visibly thinking through his options.

"Screw it," Vic said. "We've got enough material here. And there's no time to waste. I'm going to talk to Ferguson now."

He pointed at Jayne. "I'll get him to include you alongside

me and the other intelligence heads at tomorrow's meeting. In the meantime, you need to talk to Nicklin-Donovan and get him to brief Parker."

Jayne nodded. "Sure."

"Then we'll ambush that bastard Merck, and also Revel," Vic said. "I'm not going to get the BND or the German police involved beforehand—that can come afterward. Then they can find Paulsen and clear up the mess."

"Agreed," Jayne said.

She hesitated. "One other thing. What are we going to do about Suslova? I know you said you felt she should be at the bottom of the lake, and we probably all feel the same, but—"

"Yes, well, I've been thinking about that," Vic said. "That's the problem with our business. The people who are most useful to us are sometimes the nastiest, most untrustworthy, the scummiest ones. Those you'd sometimes rather see dead. I mean, we could terminate Suslova easily enough by ensuring all our info gets into Putin's hands. He'd do the job for us, I suspect. But—"

Jayne interrupted. "But then we've lost a potential asset."

"Correct. Unfortunately, you're right—Suslova may be more use to us alive than dead right now, if we play this right." He shrugged. "Who knows? Time will tell."

"So let's keep her two billion for now, then," Jayne said. "And let's hold fire with sending the stuff to Putin—we can then try to play her and see what we can get out of her. She might now be desperate enough to play along with us after the failure of her little ploy at Lake Wannsee."

Vic inclined his head in agreement. "There's something else we need to remember."

"What?"

"Suslova initially did get on our hook and gave us key information that's going to destroy Moscow's biggest assets in Western Europe for decades. So besides the two billion dollar financial leverage we have over her, we could also threaten to inform Mr. Putin with the true story about how Merck was betrayed by Suslova."

Jayne gave a faint smile. "Putin would go ballistic if he found out, given his long-standing relationship with Suslova."

Vic nodded. "So I think we need to dance with the devil, threaten her, and see what happens. Do you have dancing shoes, Jayne?"

CHAPTER FIFTY

Sunday, October 16, 2016
Berlin

Jayne followed the rest of them into German chancellor Erich Merck's seventh-floor office. Ahead of her were Vic, President Ferguson, Arthur Veltman, British prime minister Daniel Parker, the MI6 chief Richard Durman and deputy chief Mark Nicklin-Donovan.

The first thing she noticed was the group of giant decorative chess pieces that stood beneath the window. There were eight of the thigh-high pieces, not a complete set, and they weren't laid out on a board. But they were rather symbolic of the story that Jayne had pieced together.

Merck had played political chess with the rest of the world's leaders for more than a decade, with Kira Suslova in the background dictating the moves. Now, with luck, he was about to be checkmated.

Jayne had to suppress a smile as she walked past the chess pieces to the meeting table where Merck and Norbert

Wessel, the head of Germany's foreign intelligence service, the BND, were already waiting with the French president, Pierre Martinez, and Jean Revel, head of the French military intelligence service, the DRM.

Ferguson had been stunned the previous evening when Vic, Jayne, and Veltman—who had come straight from the airport—had arrived to brief him at his hotel, the famous Hotel Adlon on Unter den Linden, near the US embassy.

But he had quickly focused his mind, understood the brief, and now had copies of all the damning Stasi files and photographs tucked inside his document folder.

Parker, Durman, and Nicklin-Donovan, who had flown into Berlin the previous day, had also been brought up to date by Jayne during the evening and had been equally shocked.

Merck, who was at the head of the table, indicated that Ferguson and Parker should sit to his left, Martinez to his right. Veltman and Vic sat next to Martinez, with Wessel and Revel on their right. Durman, Nicklin-Donovan and Jayne sat opposite, next to Parker.

The meeting was now one of the most high-powered that Jayne had ever attended.

She glanced around Merck's office. The enormous post-modern Federal Chancellery building, in which it stood, had only been opened in 2001 and had a futuristic look. Through the floor-to-ceiling bulletproof windows, Jayne looked out across the grassy green expanse of the Platz der Republik to the imposing domed Reichstag building, home of the Bundestag parliament, and the Brandenburg Gate beyond.

On the wall behind Merck's desk on the other side of the room hung an enormous painting of Konrad Adenauer, the first chancellor of West Germany after World War II. Next to it were a black, yellow, and red German flag and a blue European Union flag. Jayne had to wonder what Adenauer would have made of his successor's behavior.

Merck was surely in his final few hours in this building.

Merck's personal assistant poured coffee for all the attendees, then left the room.

"Welcome all of you, including the intelligence community," Merck began in his fluent, though heavily accented, English. "We have much to discuss ahead of tomorrow's NATO summit. As we know, the big topic for discussion there will be whether heavier sanctions should be imposed on Russia given their occupation of the Crimea. I would like us to be united on this at NATO, and I believe you all know my view."

Nobody needed to be told Merck's view. He had expressed it often enough. His argument was that tougher sanctions would result in Putin hitting back by interrupting gas and oil supplies to Europe in the middle of winter. That would cause grievous difficulties to ordinary people in Germany and everywhere else.

Ferguson leaned forward, clasping his hands in front of him and eyeballing Merck.

"I have a question, Chancellor," Ferguson began. "What precisely is the motivation behind your suggestion that we should not toughen sanctions on Russia following their highly provocative and illegal invasion of Crimea—part of a sovereign Ukraine?"

"I have told you before, this is—"

"I must ask," Ferguson interrupted. "Is it anything to do with this?" He opened the document folder, removed two photographs of Merck and Wolfgang Paulsen at the Schach-Club Kreuzberg, and placed them on the table in front of the German chancellor. "That's you, isn't it, Chancellor?"

Jayne, who was watching Merck closely, saw a momentary flicker in his eyes as he looked at the photographs. Was it fear?

"That's a long time ago," Merck said, his brow creased. "What the hell is this about?"

"Yes, a time when you were young, and impressionable, and willing to take risks," Ferguson said as he ran a hand through his manicured gray hair. His voice was level and unemotional. "Risks that saw you form a friendship, a partnership, with someone you shouldn't have—Wolfgang Paulsen, a man strongly allied with the Stasi and the KGB. Paulsen, a top chess player and a highly capable young lawyer like you, saw you as a source of valuable information about the energy companies you worked for and as someone who could help Russia fulfill its agenda. It was the start of a long partnership, wasn't it?"

Merck's expression froze and he paused a beat before answering. "What *are* you suggesting, Mr. President?" he asked.

Wessel, sitting opposite Jayne, frowned. "With respect, Mr. President, this sounds nonsensical. We have a lot to discuss. Let's get on with the business at hand."

"But it's not nonsensical, I assure you," Ferguson continued in the same level tone. "Since 1988, as you rose up the legal and corporate ladders, and then into political life, you have become an asset of increasing value to Moscow— indeed, they could probably hardly believe their luck when you not only were elected to the Bundestag but were then further promoted to chancellor. They hit the jackpot. And all the way along, you've used your position to ensure that Germany helps Russia the best way it can. Most obviously, you're buying enormous quantities of Russian gas—tens of billions of euros of the stuff. First, just after you took office as chancellor in 2005, you signed a deal to build a huge pipeline beneath the Baltic Sea to import gas into Germany from Russia—Eurostream One. And you're now about to push through consents for a sister pipeline—Eurostream Two. You've engineered it for Russian oil companies to buy big stakes in German refineries. And guess what? The multibillion euro proceeds are being used to fund a planned full invasion of Ukraine—Operation Imperiya, as the Kremlin calls it."

Jayne could not help but be impressed with the very forensic way that Ferguson was handling this, given that the briefing he had received had been short.

Merck's face had now gone white, but he shook his head vigorously. "Are you going quite mad, Stephen?"

"On the contrary, Chancellor," Parker chipped in. "The mad one appears to be you, for having done what you've done these past several years."

Jayne glanced at President Martinez, who was watching and listening, his mouth hanging slightly open. Revel, further along the table, had his arms folded, his jaw clamped tight.

Ferguson opened the folder in front of him again and removed a copy of the yellow Stasi F22 index card for Merck and placed it in front of him.

"I am sure your colleagues in the Bundestag will be interested in this," Ferguson said. "It's the proof that you had a Stasi and KGB code number and code name—ALYOSHA. Your handler, Wolfgang Paulsen, was code named VOLKER."

Merck leaned back in his chair. "I don't know who gave you this rubbish, but I can tell you there is no truth in it at all. This card does not relate to me."

Ferguson reached into his folder again and this time removed the headshot photo of Merck, with the telltale registration number on the back.

He placed it on the table, pointed to the image, then turned to Jayne. "Can you please explain to the chancellor the significance of this?" Ferguson asked.

Jayne nodded, hiding her surprise that the president

wanted her to take over the narrative. "Of course, Mr. President."

She indicated toward the photograph on the table.

"This is you, isn't it, Chancellor?" Jayne asked.

Merck gave a short nod. He had no choice but to confirm that it was him.

Jayne stood, stepped around the table and picked up the photograph, which she turned over. She then pointed to the registration number, XV6311/88.

"You see that number?" Jayne asked. "It's a Stasi registration number for the person in the photo, which is you. And it correlates to the registration number on this F22 index card for the asset codenamed ALYOSHA. Which is also you, isn't it? You'll note the KGB marking, denoting that the asset, you, was handled by the KGB."

Merck visibly swallowed.

Jayne paused for a moment, then continued. "You probably know that the Russian operation to recruit and handle you and others has a very apt code name—Operation Peshka. Quite appropriate that you have a few pawns over there." She pointed toward the giant chess pieces beneath the window. "You'll also doubtless know that the operation has been masterminded by a woman you're well aware of, Kira Suslova, also a highly capable chess player. She's known by some as the chess queen. I suppose that makes you the queen's pawn, doesn't it?"

Jayne was sure she heard Parker mutter "checkmate" under his breath as she returned to her seat.

There was also no doubt that more evidence would have been helpful. The NSA had begun working on it overnight, but it would take a little more time. However, what they had already was damning enough.

Martinez folded his arms and rested them on the table. He looked directly at Ferguson and finally spoke. "What do you propose we do with this information, Mr. President? To me, it looks fairly conclusive and fairly damning."

Ferguson nodded. "It is. But I have some more bad news for you, President Martinez. Unfortunately, the story does not end at the chancellor's door here in Berlin."

He paused and glanced around the others. "I have to tell you, there is another traitor in this room."

Now it was Martinez's face that froze.

Around the table Jayne saw the other attendees looking at each other, expressions of astonishment on their faces.

"What do you mean?" Martinez asked, an unusual note of uncertainty in his normally confident, forthright voice.

Ferguson leaned forward and looked directly at Martinez. "I'm sorry to report that the problem extends much further —to your administration in Paris."

"Mine?"

Ferguson pointed at Revel. "President Martinez, I need to tell you that your director of military intelligence, Jean Revel, is also an asset of the Kremlin and has been since 1988. That is why he constantly advises you to ally yourself with Moscow, to buy more Russian gas, and to decline sanctions against Russia. He was on the KGB's payroll in 1988, and he still is a Russian agent."

Martinez glanced down the table at Revel, then back at Ferguson. "What is this? I have had first-class advice from my director for many years. He has outstanding knowledge of Russia and the motivations of its leadership, and I can assure you France's stance, and my stance, is founded on extremely well-researched information and intelligence, which has come from him and his service. You're making an outrageous allegation. What proof do you have?"

Revel tapped the table with his fingers. "There will be no proof. I can confirm that what my president says is absolutely correct. I have no links at all to Moscow, and I am certainly not a Russian spy. To suggest that is insulting and highly damaging, and I deny it absolutely."

Ferguson sighed and reached once more into his document folder. He went through a virtual repeat of the performance he had given for Merck, producing similar documents in the same order, with an almost identical commentary.

He again called upon Jayne to provide the required detail on the significance of the headshot photograph and the corroborating registration number.

Martinez and Revel sat and listened in silence.

When Jayne had finished her second explanation, Ferguson sat back and folded his arms. "So, what are you going to do now?" he asked, looking first at Merck, then at Revel and Martinez. "The proof is unequivocal."

"The proof is trash," Merck said. "And also—"

"If you prefer, we can make all of this public and advise your parliament to do due diligence on your bank accounts, your phone records, and other electronic communications, and your digital footprint, Chancellor," Ferguson said.

"You bastard," Merck said. "You're bluffing."

Ferguson slowly shook his head. "No bluff involved."

There was silence in the room for several seconds.

"I will tell you what I want you to do," Ferguson said. "Unfortunately, neither I nor the United States government have any jurisdiction in Germany. But I feel that I have right on my side, and I am certain I have public opinion on my side."

Ferguson shifted in his seat and eyeballed Merck. "You will go to the NATO meeting on Monday and when you make your speech, you will admit that you were wrong and that stronger sanctions should indeed be placed on Russia. The list of individuals and companies who are subject to asset freezes and travel restrictions should be extended, and you should argue for greater restrictive measures on European companies to stop them investing in Crimea. You will also spell out that the Eurostream Two gas pipeline from Russia to Germany will never be completed. You will stop it. And you will cancel the Russian oil companies' stakes in German refineries."

Ferguson paused and leaned forward. "Then, in front of all the other leaders at NATO, you will announce your resignation as chancellor of Germany. You will step down, and you will never again hold public office. If you do not do this, I will announce it for you, and I will make all of these documents public. I imagine that what you have done will leak at some point anyway, but whether it does or not, you will confess to your electorate and subject yourself to the German judicial system. I doubt that the German courts will look too kindly on such a gross instance of espionage and treason. It will be in your interests to come clean and confess your sins to your German public immediately. It will look a lot worse if these things come out via some exclusive story in Bild or one of the other tabloids—which can easily be arranged. Am I correct?"

Merck narrowed his eyes, but said nothing. Jayne could see beads of sweat rolling down his forehead.

"Then finally," Ferguson continued, "you will take the many millions of euros you have received from the Kremlin and you will distribute the money to charities in Germany and elsewhere that are coping with the flood of refugees coming out of the Crimea and Eastern Ukraine following Russia's intervention."

Parker leaned forward. "I concur with everything the president has just said. You need to do as instructed, Chancellor."

Ferguson took a sip of coffee, then turned to Martinez and Revel. "I would advise you, Monsieur President, to make a similarly robust speech at the NATO meeting, arguing along similar lines to Herr Merck. Your director of military intelligence will resign immediately—or perhaps you would prefer to fire him. I suspect you will want to follow due process of law against him. I know that acts of espionage are not viewed sympathetically in France, especially over such a long time. You have had the wool pulled over your eyes systematically, and you would be forgiven for taking a quite colorful revenge on Monsieur Revel. It may not reflect well on you when this surfaces in public, so I suggest you get your excuses ready. The French public may not take a generous view of such a gross misjudgment of character on your part."

Jayne heard Martinez swear heavily under his breath. He threw Revel a look that needed no translation: the director of military intelligence was about to suffer an extremely painful *coup de grâce.*

Martinez stood and faced Revel. "Get up, get out," he said in French, in a low tone. "We will return to the embassy, where you will be dealt with."

Revel slowly rose to his feet, his face ashen, and followed his president out the door.

Merck just sat there, punch-drunk, looking as if he'd just taken a beating in the boxing ring.

"There is one other thing we require from the chancellor," Vic said, looking at Ferguson. "That is the issue of Wolfgang Paulsen, the linchpin in this operation. He appears to have gone into hiding and, given our very limited resources in Germany, we haven't been able to determine where he is. However, Germany's law enforcement agencies will have no such restrictions—we need the Bundespolizei to track him down and have him brought to justice for his major part in this act of espionage against Germany, France and the rest of Europe. We just need the chancellor to give the order. We need to act quickly before he's exfiltrated out of Germany by the Russians—assuming it hasn't happened already."

Ferguson nodded at Merck. "You heard the man. It would

be advisable to get it done immediately before Paulsen flees the country. If he escapes, we'll hold you responsible, and we'll ensure everybody knows about it."

Merck was now looking utterly defeated. He was surely facing a long spell in a federal prison.

The chancellor held up his hands and glanced down the table at Wessel. He spoke in a faltering voice. "Can you deal with the police? Just brief them for now that we have evidence that Paulsen is involved in espionage. Have him brought in for questioning. We can fill in the gaps afterward. I just need time to think through how I manage this—I admit that mistakes have been made." He lowered his head and stared at the floor.

"I'll handle it," Wessel said. He also looked dumbfounded at what had just taken place.

Jayne knew, and doubtless Wessel himself realized, that his career had also just hit the buffers. For an intelligence chief not to realize that his boss, the chancellor, was a Russian spy without doubt made his position untenable. Fair or not, he would have to resign immediately after Merck had done so.

Merck stood slowly, as did Wessel a moment later. Without a word, the German chancellor walked toward the door of his own office, Wessel close behind.

Ferguson stood and spoke as Merck walked. "I want to see action on all the points I mentioned. Or else we will take matters into our own hands, and you won't like the outcome."

Without turning around, Merck nodded. Then he and Wessel exited the room.

Ferguson sat back down, drained his coffee, and eyed Jayne.

"I would like to thank you, Jayne," Ferguson said. "The work you have done in uncovering one of the most outrageous pieces of long-running espionage, of enormous treachery, in my lifetime has been outstanding."

"I completely concur with all of that," Parker said.

The president nodded and turned back to Jayne. " You put yourself at great personal risk to achieve this outcome, and for that I am deeply grateful—yet again."

"Thank you, sir," Jayne said. "I'm grateful to you too for the support you've given me, and to Vic, for his backing and support, behind the scenes for the work I've been doing. I certainly couldn't have done it without him. We should also remember who actually uncovered these documents at the Stasi Records Agency."

The president gave a half smile. "Ah, yes. Give that person my regards, please. I know he's only playing a contributory role in some of your operations lately, but he always adds good value."

"I will, sir," Jayne said.

"Now Mr. Parker and I need to fly to Warsaw, don't we? Shall we get going?"

The president picked up his papers, stood, as did Parker, and moved toward the door. Then Nicklin-Donovan, Jayne, and Vic followed the two men out of the office that Merck had occupied for the previous eleven years.

CHAPTER FIFTY-ONE

Monday, October 17, 2016
Berlin

The television on the wall of the Picoteo tapas bar, just off Gitschiner Strasse in Kreuzberg, was tuned to a news program on Das Erste. Many in the bar had stopped eating to listen, and with good reason. The entire bulletin so far had been devoted to the dramatic and unconventional resignation of the German chancellor, Erich Merck, during a speech to the NATO heads of state summit meeting in Warsaw.

Jayne sipped a Coca-Cola as she listened, while Joe, next to her, cradled a beer. Opposite them, Nick Geldard also had a beer.

"My God, he's done it," Jayne said. She had been slightly skeptical that Merck would actually go through with what had been demanded of him, although she knew that, in reality, he had little choice. He had been completely backed into a corner.

"I have let my country and myself down," Merck said

during his address. "I have not acted in the best interests of the German or the European people by promoting heavy investment in Russian gas and oil over the past decade and a half. We will need as a country to discuss how we balance our supplies better in the future. I would like to go further and condemn the occupation by Russia of the Crimea—which is part of a sovereign Ukraine—and its aggression in Eastern Ukraine."

Jayne put her drink down. "So he's not admitting publicly to espionage and treachery, then," she said. "Or to being on the Kremlin's payroll while he made those decisions to become Russia's biggest gas and oil customer. If he doesn't do that in the next day or so, and repay that money to charity, we'll make it public for him."

"He'll be in prison for a long time either way," Joe said.

The Das Erste news anchor mentioned, almost as a footnote, that the head of the French military intelligence service, Jean Revel, had also resigned. He cited as his main reason the poor advice given to the French president, Pierre Martinez, to increase his country's purchases of Russian gas. "It is unclear whether the two resignations are linked," the anchor concluded, before moving on to interview several Russia experts.

The waiter appeared at their table to take the order and realized they were all glued to the television.

"I knew Merck was bad," the waiter said, brandishing his notepad. "Never liked him. He's obviously in bed with Putin. I'm glad he's quit."

Jayne gave Joe a look. "See, even he knows," she said, nodding toward the waiter. "Merck might as well come clean now."

They ordered a series of tapas dishes to share between them, and the waiter disappeared.

Jayne sipped her drink and eyed Geldard. "Have you

heard anything more from Suslova about your Lausanne house?" she asked. Although there had been no sign that Suslova had linked her to Geldard, she couldn't rule it out and was wondering what was happening.

"Well, strangely enough, I had a message today from the agent, Lina Cailler," Geldard said. "Suslova's told Cailler she's reconsidered and is no longer interested in the house."

Because she doesn't have the money.

"Did she really?" Jayne said. Although she'd been forced to give Geldard some background information, there was no way she was going to confide in him about the raid on Suslova's bank account. "Well, that's a relief. It's one less headache."

"It was a relief," Geldard said. "I'm thinking that maybe I should leave it on sale for another two or three weeks, for appearance's sake, and then quietly take it off the market."

"Good thinking," Jayne said. "Yes, do exactly that."

"And what's happening with Suslova and the FIDE presidency?" Geldard asked. "Will she step back?"

Jayne paused, recalling the conversation about Geldard potentially taking her place. "Unfortunately, I don't think that will happen, at least for the time being."

"Why not?" Geldard asked. He waved a hand at the television. "I'd have thought that with all this, you have enough material to discredit her."

"Yes, but it's not that simple," Jayne said. She shifted uncomfortably in her seat. She was going to have to tell Geldard some of the truth. "Between you and me, we need Suslova to remain in Putin's good books for the time being at least—and FIDE is crucial to that. I had hoped that we would find a way to remove her from FIDE, but it's not down to me. I can't give you the exact details about why this is happening. You'll just have to trust me. There are things going on that I can't possibly brief you about, and I'm trusting you to remain silent about anything that you know already."

A look of disappointment crossed Geldard's face. His hopes had obviously been raised.

"I'm sorry, Nick," Jayne said. "It's for the greater good, believe me. I'm sure you'd do a better job than her, but . . ."

Geldard nodded. "I understand. Just one of those compromises you have to make in your line of work, I guess."

There was a certain note of cynicism in his voice, and Jayne could understand why, because it was true. It was yet another big compromise, and she felt deeply uncomfortable about it and unable to defend what was happening. In truth, leaving Suslova in pole position to take the FIDE presidency left more than a very bad taste in her mouth. But there seemed little option right now.

However, there was other work ahead yet to be done, which was the reason Jayne had asked Geldard to fly to Berlin from Lausanne the previous night, and which she'd already discussed with him.

Paulsen needed to be caught and brought to justice. He had been the linchpin in one of Europe's biggest espionage scandals since the Cold War. And Geldard was going to help find him.

Although German police had not gone public regarding their hunt for Paulsen, the CIA station knew that there had indeed been a widespread search for him. But so far, they had failed to track him down. He had not returned to his home or office.

Jayne was starting to assume that he might already have been exfiltrated out of Germany and taken to Moscow. The presence of two hit men at his house would suggest that as likely. If so, Suslova had to be behind it. Either way, surely Paulsen must know that Merck and Revel had been blown.

But until it was actually proven that he had gone, the

search needed to continue, and Jayne had no idea whether the German police could be trusted to do a thorough job.

Acting on gut instinct, Jayne had checked the Schach-Club Kreuzberg chess website the previous evening and discovered that they had a session on Monday night. While realizing it was a shot in the dark, and not knowing whether the police had already spoken to people at the club, she had decided to pay a visit. Someone might know where Paulsen was. After all, he was a long-standing club member.

The tapas bar was a stone's throw through a small park and across the street from the chess club, which was accommodated in the House of Sports, a three-story brick building visible through the trees.

When they had finished the meal, they waited for the clock to tick around to six o'clock, when the club session was due to begin. Then Jayne paid the tab, and they strolled through the park and between some apartment buildings to the club.

Jayne pushed down on the Walther PPK that she was carrying in the inside pocket of her jacket and zipped it up. She didn't want anyone at the chess club spotting that. In her other inside pocket, she had copies of the Stasi archives documents that proved Paulsen's complicity with Merck and with Moscow.

The chess club was on the second floor of the House of Sports, which, it emerged, was home to several sports and games clubs. There was an outdoor children's playground as part of the complex.

When Jayne, Joe, and Geldard walked in, they found three long rows of chess tables that stretched almost the full length of the meeting room. All of them were occupied with players, mainly youngsters, concentrating fiercely as they did battle.

An elderly man approached and introduced himself as the

club secretary. Jayne let Geldard do the talking, as they had planned.

He explained he was a British grandmaster and had played at the club in 1988 and was interested in seeing it again.

The secretary's eyes lit up as he recognized Geldard's name. Jayne guessed it wasn't every day that a foreign grandmaster walked in off the street.

The secretary immediately began to explain that the building had been refurbished since Geldard was there last, providing new meeting rooms for the chess club, which was founded in 1949 as the Cold War began. He said that the club had moved to the nineteenth-century building in 1987, just before Geldard's visit.

Another older man appeared through the door and walked up to them. The secretary introduced him as the club president.

"I played two candidates tournaments semifinals in the 1990s against one of your members," Geldard said casually to the two club officials.

"Wolfgang?" the secretary asked.

Geldard nodded.

"The matches were in Moscow, right?"

"Unfortunately, he got the better of me on both occasions," Geldard said. "He was very talented. Is he still around and playing? I'd love to meet with him again."

Jayne felt herself tense up a little as she waited for the response. She glanced at Joe, who looked equally anxious.

"He is very much around," the president said. "He's often in here. Still our highest-ranked player, despite getting older now."

"I thought we could call in and hopefully see him," Geldard said. "We actually went to his house at Lake Wannsee, but there was nobody at home, which is why we came here. Do you have any idea where he might be?"

The secretary shook his head. "I'm sorry. I've not seen him here tonight, and I can't say whether he's coming in."

"That's a shame," Geldard said. "Do you have a phone number, by any chance?"

The president nodded. "I think one of our committee members has a number. Just wait here. I'll go and ask." Jayne watched as he walked out the door and into a neighboring room.

Jayne's instincts had been correct. The German police had obviously not visited the chess club as part of their search for Paulsen; otherwise, the officials here would not be reacting the way they were. That seemed more than a little sloppy, she couldn't help thinking. She wondered precisely what instructions had been given to the police by Merck and how seriously they were taking the search.

A few minutes later, the president returned and handed Geldard a piece of paper with a number on it. "Here you go. Our committee man said he thinks Wolfgang might be at his apartment if he's not at home. If you call him, you'll find out."

Jayne's alert system immediately flashed red.

"His apartment?" Geldard asked. "I didn't know he had another property in Berlin."

The president nodded. "It's near to here. Five or six minutes' walk. He bought it off the committee member I just spoke to, actually—one of his friends. He uses it sometimes after club sessions if they have a drink afterward and he doesn't want to drive home."

Geldard nodded. Jayne could see he was trying not to react. So was she, and out of the corner of her eye she could see Joe also pretending to be disinterested.

"Hmm. I guess we could just give the apartment a try if it's close by," Geldard said. "Do you know the address?"

The president gave an address on Fraenkelufer street. "It's a penthouse apartment. It overlooks the Landwehr Canal and the Admiral Bridge that crosses it. Lovely location. Give that a try. I'm sure he'll be pleased to see you and chat about old times."

Geldard nodded. "Thank you so much. I'm grateful."

"Glad to be of help, especially for a British grandmaster."

They said their farewells and walked out of the complex and down the street toward the canal.

If Paulsen was there, which Jayne somehow doubted, then they'd have to be careful. What sort of state of mind would he be in, given Merck's resignation, which he must surely be aware of? If he realized the chancellor had been blown, he must assume that he too most likely had been uncovered.

The building housing Paulsen's apartment was a modern six-story affair that looked as if it had been built recently to replace one of the much older buildings that stood alongside it. It stood in a prime position right next to the historic cobbled Admiral Bridge and was well designed with balconies overlooking the canal on every floor.

"If he's in there by chance, I'll pretend to be your wife," Jayne said to Geldard. "Just say we're here for a few days and you thought it would be good to catch up after so long. When we get inside, we can get down to the proper business. I'll do the talking then."

"Do you want me to stay outside?" Joe asked. "Then I'll be around in case you need me and I can communicate with Vic if required."

Jayne nodded. "Good idea. Three would be a crowd, I think."

The building's front entrance had a security lock operated by a PIN. Jayne didn't want to push the external buzzer for Paulsen's apartment, which was located with all the others on a panel outside the entrance. Doing so might simply cause him to run via another exit. It was better to get to the front door of his actual apartment, inside the building.

So she and Geldard waited until an elderly lady entered, using her PIN, and then tailgated in just behind her while the door was still open. They then made their way up in the elevator to the top floor.

The entrance to Paulsen's apartment was on the landing. Geldard pushed the doorbell, stood back, and waited.

A few seconds later, the door half opened and there stood a tall, thin man with silver hair.

Geldard stepped forward with a smile. "Wolfgang? I'm Nick Geldard. You remember me? I'm sorry to call unannounced."

Paulsen didn't smile in return. His forehead was creased and his eyes flitted anxiously between Geldard and Jayne. He scratched the top of his head.

"Nick Geldard. Ah yes. Of course I remember you," Paulsen said. "But this is something of a surprise. What are you doing here now?" He glanced behind him momentarily, then looked back at Geldard, a frown on his face.

"We're in Berlin for a few days and I just thought it would be nice to catch up again after such a long time," Geldard said. "I should have contacted you before, but didn't plan ahead very well. I do apologize."

"How did you find me here?" There was an interrogative note to Paulsen's question.

"The chess club sent me, actually," Geldard said. "We called in there looking for you, and they directed me here."

Paulsen hesitated, scrutinizing first Geldard, then Jayne, who could almost see the cogs in his brain whirring.

"This is my wife," Geldard said, indicating toward Jayne. "I don't want to invite myself in, but do you have time for a quick coffee? It would be good to chat about old times, and the games we had."

Paulsen glanced at his watch, then looked at the floor. Jayne tensed as she waited for a response.

"I don't have much time, unfortunately," Paulsen said, a clear note of reluctance in his voice. "I need to leave in half an hour. But we could have a quick coffee."

He held the door open and Geldard walked in, followed by Jayne.

The apartment was decorated in a minimalist style, with the obligatory chess set in pride of place in the living room.

Paulsen, who was as wiry as in the photographs Jayne had seen, shook Geldard's hand, then Jayne's.

"I'm surprised the chess club sent you here," Paulsen said to Geldard. "Very few people know I've got this place. But it's good to see you, after such a long time, especially as we haven't kept in touch." He looked inquiringly at Geldard, as if to ask why he was there.

The television in the living room was tuned to a news bulletin, and Jayne noticed that Paulsen also had a laptop open on the coffee table at a Reuters story about the resignation of Erich Merck as chancellor.

"I see the chancellor's resigned," Jayne said. "That's a real shock, isn't it?"

"It was a shock indeed," Paulsen said. He indicated to the sofa. "Take a seat. I'll make some coffee."

While Paulsen was fetching the drinks, Jayne sat on the sofa, took out her phone, and rapidly tapped out a secure message to both Vic and Pieter Bone in the Berlin CIA station.

With Paulsen at his apartment near chess club. Get police here asap. I will get as much info as I can out of him. Joe waiting outside if needed.

She sent a second message with the address and slipped her phone back into her pocket. She knew that Bone, and others at the US embassy, had good contacts within the Bundespolizei. They should be able to quickly pull the right strings, particularly as a police search for Paulsen was already underway.

It was then that Jayne noticed two large suitcases standing behind an armchair. Maybe they were just in time. She quietly unzipped her inside jacket pocket, just in case she needed the Walther, although her instinct said that it was unlikely Paulsen was going to start a gunfight.

When Paulsen returned with the coffees, she decided they had no time to beat around the bush. She needed to get to the point.

"Was Merck's resignation really a shock to you?" she asked as she sipped her drink.

Paulsen sat still and looked at her. "What do you mean? Of course. Nobody expected that to happen."

"And did you not expect the resignation of Jean Revel as France's head of military intelligence either?" Jayne asked.

There was a short silence.

Paulsen slowly put his coffee cup down on the table and stared at Jayne. "Who are you?" he said in a low voice. He glanced at Geldard. "What the hell is going on here?"

"I'd have thought that given you have been handling both Merck and Revel on Russia's behalf for the past twenty years, you would be long gone by now," Jayne said. "But lucky me. You're here."

She pointed toward the suitcases. "You won't need those. You'll not be going anywhere other than a federal court."

"I asked, who are you?" Paulsen said, his voice rising.

"I work for Western intelligence," Jayne said. "Nick is a friend. He has nothing to do with this."

"Western intelligence? Your accent—you're a Brit. MI6, then?"

"I'm working for the CIA," Jayne said.

Paulsen rolled his eyes. "Jayne Robinson. I know who you are, actually."

"No doubt Kira Suslova told you," Jayne said. "And CIA or MI6, it doesn't make any difference. We're all equally horrified at what you've been doing. You realize you're helping Russia to finance a planned invasion of Ukraine? If that happens, before you know it, Poland will be next, and there'll be Russian tanks on the border with Germany—sixty kilometers from here."

She paused and leaned forward. "Why have you done this? You were a top chess player. You're a leading lawyer. Why ruin your reputation? Have you lost your sanity?"

Paulsen's eyes flicked between Jayne and Geldard. She could tell he knew there was no way of arguing his innocence. There was a hint of surrender written across his face.

"So, my old chess rival decides to finally get his revenge for those candidates tournament semifinal defeats," Paulsen said. "He wants to put me behind bars. So he informs on me to the CIA."

"Not at all," Geldard said. "I only just found out what you've been doing. I just want to help Jayne and her colleagues put a stop to all of this. Nobody wants war in Europe. So, just tell us why you've done it."

Paulsen sighed. "When you came to Berlin in 1988 and we played at the chess club here in Kreuzberg, I was an East German citizen during the Cold War. I was living in a dilapidated two-room apartment in East Berlin. No heating, no hot water, a toilet shared with other apartments. I had no money and no prospect of earning any money under the Communist regime. The future was bleak, despite my chess ability. Then I was approached one day at my club in East Berlin, Berolina Mitte, by someone, a chess player who—"

The words of Suslova came instantly to mind. *I can take the credit for that recruitment ...*

"Kira Suslova," Jayne interrupted.

A slight nod from Paulsen.

"I was approached by a chess player who offered me what I didn't have," Paulsen continued. "Money. A ticket to visit the West whenever I wanted to. A different and better life. It was a case of 'if you can't beat them, join them,' and there was no beating the Stasi or the KGB. So I did join them. I became a Stasi informer, then a handler. And I was instructed on what to do—to join the Schach-Club Kreuzberg and use that as a base to recruit in West Berlin. A lot of highly placed foreigners, as well as Germans, were in the city at that time. Many of them enjoyed chess at various levels. They were easy pickings. I was playing more and more in the West, international competitions."

Geldard nodded. "Even a couple of candidates finals."

"But I lost in both finals so never had a go at the world title," Paulsen said. "Nevertheless, I was a big name. People found that attractive if they were into chess."

"And among them were Erich Merck and Jean Revel," Jayne said, her tone as dry as she could make it.

Paulsen inclined his head. "I knew Merck was going to make it big one day. I didn't quite know how big, though."

It seemed to Jayne that Paulsen was quite enjoying telling his story, but it suddenly occurred to her that there was a piece of the jigsaw missing.

"So, who actually clinched the deals with these people— with Merck, Revel, and whoever else?" Jayne asked. "Was it you?"

Paulsen gave a faint smile. "Not me. I just lined them up."

"So who, then?"

"Suslova. She clinched the arrangements. She was extremely good at that, at pulling off the deals, so to speak."

It was the tone of voice he used and the expression on his face.

A lightbulb went off in Jayne's head.

"You mean, she seduced them?" Jayne asked.

Paulsen nodded. "Usually while playing chess. I'd get them interested in playing chess against a beautiful woman—and she was extremely attractive, very sensual, when she wanted to be. Of course, they were all keen. Suslova used to come across the border under various aliases and play a game against them. We'd put them in seductive surroundings, low lighting, ply them with a drink or two. Then part of the way through the game, they'd find her foot rubbing up against their leg or something, and then they were putty in her hands. Job done."

Jayne shook her head in disbelief. "Was that what happened to Merck and Revel?"

"Precisely. Once they were on the hook, they never got off it. Every so often she'd come to Berlin, just to refresh things between them. They might play a game of chess first, or maybe not bother with that. With Revel she used to go to Paris, after he returned there."

"Bloody hell," Jayne muttered.

This was dynamite.

"None of that is in the Stasi files," Jayne said.

"Did you expect it to be?" Paulsen asked.

"And this continued after Merck became chancellor?"

"Of course. Less frequently, but often enough. Every couple of months. It still happens occasionally."

The idea of Germany's chancellor having a long-running affair with Putin's right-hand woman was something that she had never considered.

From outside came the distant wail of sirens. They were drawing nearer.

Paulsen lifted his head and listened. Then he glanced at Jayne and Geldard.

"I'm just going to make another drink before my apparent arrest," Paulsen said. "Would you like one?"

Jayne shook her head. "No, thanks."

Geldard also declined.

Paulsen stood and walked across the living room, carrying his coffee cup. He then went through a door to the left, toward the front of the apartment.

The sirens outside were getting louder.

Jayne knew instinctively they were coming as a result of her message to Vic and Bone.

But alarm bells were now ringing inside her head—what was Paulsen doing? He had accepted his end with too much grace.

The sirens, now deafening, suddenly stopped, and there came a screech of brakes from outside, followed by a series of shouts and yells.

Acting on instinct, she jumped to her feet and ran to the door that Paulsen had vanished through. As she went, she pulled her Walther from her jacket pocket, flicked off the safety, and in one movement, racked the slide.

Holding the gun in her right hand, she took in the scene at one glance.

In front of her was a kitchen that ran across the front of the apartment. On the far side was a full-height glass sliding door that was open. It led out onto a terra-cotta tiled balcony that faced the street, six floors below.

There, beyond a steel-and-glass table and chairs and parasol, Paulsen had one leg up on the safety railing that ran across the front of the balcony.

No. He can't.

"Stop!" Jayne yelled as she ran to the sliding door. "No!"

She could see she would not get to Paulsen in time.

Even if she could, she doubted she'd be able to overpower him.

Down in the street, she could hear several people shouting.

Jayne raised her gun, aimed at Paulsen's trailing leg just as he began to lever himself up and over the railing, and pulled the trigger, then pulled it again.

The two rounds smashed into the back of Paulsen's thigh, throwing him completely off balance as he pushed his body upward and causing him to let go of the railing and throw his arms behind him.

Paulsen yelped in pain and tumbled backward onto the balcony. His body, with arms flailing, thudded onto the red tiles. The back of his head struck the base of the metal table with an audible crack.

There he lay still.

CHAPTER FIFTY-TWO

Tuesday, October 18, 2016
  Berlin

"Any update on Paulsen?" President Ferguson asked as Jayne took her seat at the conference table in the US embassy.

"He'll live," Jayne said as she sat down and poured herself a coffee from the pot on the table. "They took the rounds out of his leg, repaired it, and stitched up the back of his head. He took a while to regain consciousness, but seems to be doing okay."

Vic, sitting next to her, nodded. "He'll need to be fully conscious when they put him in court. The public prosecutor general is preparing a long list of espionage charges to throw at him."

"Sounds like you did a great job to stop him throwing himself off," Ferguson said.

"Better than the German police were doing, that's for certain," Vic said.

"And what of Merck and plans to prosecute him?" Ferguson asked, a grim expression on his face. "I'm still struggling to believe it, frankly. He's been the face of Western Europe for more than a decade, my number one counterpart apart from Parker, and the man I thought I could rely on and trust."

"Meanwhile, he was having an affair with Putin's right-hand woman," Vic said. "You couldn't make it up. From what I gather, the prosecutor is struggling to work out how to react. It's an unprecedented situation. Likewise with the justice minister, who was close to Merck. But two things are certain: the trial will be fascinating, and they will send him to prison."

Ferguson nodded his satisfaction, then leaned back, hands behind his head. "I think that Pyotr Fradkov, if he's looking down on you and Vic and Ed Grewall and the rest of your team, will think that you've done your best to make up in some way for his death in London. And if it makes Putin think twice about invading Ukraine and prevents the US from facing a possible war in Europe, it will be worth it. But I am skeptical about whether it will stop Putin."

"I agree, it might be too late," Vic said. "Germany is up to its neck in Russian gas—thanks to Merck. I don't easily see Germany just turning off the taps. They need to heat their homes, fuel their factories, and cook their dinners."

Ferguson grimaced. "Unfortunately, you're right. It will be a tough call for whoever takes over as chancellor. Daniel Parker and I will, of course, do our best to persuade them to start finding other energy sources as quickly as possible—including the Middle East, Australia, and our gas from the US."

Jayne glanced out the window. There were the usual crowds of tourists buzzing around the Brandenburg Gate.

She leaned forward. "Mr. President, you might also want a quick update on what will happen to our highly placed asset, or possibly a non-asset, in the Kremlin, Kira Suslova. Having given us the lead that cracked this investigation open, she did a U-turn and sent in a couple of hit men to try to take down Ed Grewall and me. However, we still have the slight tactical advantage of holding two billion dollars removed from her bank account, which almost certainly belongs to Putin, not to her."

A faint smile slowly spread across Ferguson's face. "'Slight' is one word you could use. I could think of others. But first, I'd just like to say that I'm not hearing anything about siphoning cash from Suslova's bank account. It never happened as far as I'm concerned."

"Me neither, Mr. President," Vic said. "Me neither."

"I somehow doubt she's going to confess to Putin that she's mislaid the money," Ferguson said. "Privately, you've got my approval to try to leverage that in the future, assuming that Putin doesn't throw her in Lefortovo in the meantime."

"That's a big assumption," Vic said. "Surely he must know she's screwed up."

Jayne shrugged. "I don't know about that. The credit could quite easily be given to Joe Johnson—a known historical investigator—for his work in uncovering the Stasi files that held the information that proved key to unmasking Merck. It could have had nothing to do with Suslova."

"I like that," the president said, sitting up straight in his chair. "Let's give Joe the entire credit for the Stasi archives investigation, then. How about if we get *The Washington Post* to run a background feature on how he alone cracked open the mystery of why Germany was so obsessed with buying Russia's gas, of why they were so smitten with Putin?"

Vic nodded. "That's a good idea, Mr. President. It's worth

a try. Moscow might believe it, given Joe's track record against them. And as long as we have that two billion, and providing Suslova can't afford to completely write it off, we have very strong leverage."

Jayne took a sip of her coffee. "We do, after all, need a replacement A-grade asset of some kind inside Moscow for Shevchenko."

"Likewise with Pyotr Fradkov," Vic said. "Speaking of whom, I can inform you all that his widow, Maria, and their children are being relocated to the United Kingdom under new identities. She would like to be close to where her husband passed away. We've agreed to it with Mark Nicklin-Donovan. They will be safe there."

Ferguson inclined his head. "I'm pleased to hear that."

The president looked at his watch. "I need to wrap up here. I'm flying back to DC in a couple of hours. Just to sum up, it seems to me you have a task ahead of you to see if you can maximize this opportunity with Suslova—if it works, it could be very valuable. But I'll leave it to you intelligence experts to work out exactly how you do that and when. I'm only interested in results. And so far, you're certainly delivering those. Keep it up."

"I doubt Moscow is going to let up on us, or on Western Europe, sir," Vic said. "You know they have this long-running Operation Pandora against us. It's only a matter of time before the next phase of that emerges, I suspect. We'll need every advantage we can get if we're going to combat them."

"Agreed," Ferguson said. "You've got my approval to do what's needed."

That was what Jayne wanted to hear. A carte blanche from the US president to operate as they saw fit, and a vote of confidence thrown in too. It certainly made hers and Vic's life easier.

Ferguson stood and shook hands with Vic and Jayne, then made his way out.

After he had gone, Vic grinned across the table at Jayne. "We'd better go and tell Joe he's about to become a media star. Let's just hope that Putin believes what he reads in the *Post*."

CHAPTER FIFTY-THREE

Tuesday, October 18, 2016
Moscow

"Well, Kira. How did this happen? Perhaps you can tell us," Putin said, his blue eyes boring like a pair of lasers into Suslova. "*Dermo*. Our two main assets are not just blown, but torpedoed, destroyed in a very public way. The Kremlin has been humiliated. It is the biggest embarrassment of its kind for this country since Gorbachev allowed the Berlin Wall to come down—and a disaster for us."

There were five sets of eyes focused on her from around the meeting table in Putin's personal office at the Kremlin, like vultures staring down at a dying wolf.

Suslova decided she had no choice but to try to brazen this out. There was no way she was going to admit error. Otherwise, this bunch of predators would have her in a basement torture room at Lefortovo in no time.

"We, or rather Merck and Revel, have fallen victim to an unfortunate combination of events," Suslova said. "First, a traitor to the Motherland, Anastasia Shevchenko, handed some information to an operative working for the CIA, Jayne Robinson. I had Shevchenko terminated during the meeting, as you're aware, sir, but it seems she had by then passed on a lead to Robinson, who subsequently escaped Russia, taking Maria Fradkova with her. The FSB could not catch them, despite it taking all night and well into the next day for her to reach the border. That was the critical development."

Suslova threw a pointed glance at Nikolai Sheymov, director of the Federal Security Service. It had indeed been quite unbelievable how the FSB could have failed to reel in Robinson and Fradkova before they crossed into Ukraine.

Putin also glared at Sheymov, who shifted uneasily in his seat.

"Do not worry," Sheymov said. "I am dealing appropriately with my head of counterintelligence who ran that operation, Colonel Leonid Pugachov."

Typical that Sheymov should blame his underlings by name so publicly.

Putin then turned back to Suslova. "What is the latest with Fradkova? Has she been found?"

Suslova shook her head. "She has been spirited away by the CIA or the SZR. No trace of her after she crossed the border into Ukraine."

Putin pressed his thin lips together. "The FSB's failings have not gone unnoticed, I can assure you," the president said. "But I am sure that Shevchenko didn't know who our assets in Germany were. There is absolutely no way she could have known. That information was so tightly compartmented it was airtight."

"That is probably true," Suslova said. "But logic tells me that Shevchenko must have known who the handler was, Wolfgang Paulsen. She also knew, somehow, what the code names of our assets were."

"How did she know?" Putin demanded.

The eyes bored into her again. Apart from Putin and Sheymov, there was the counterintelligence rat Gennady Sidorenko and the obese SVR director Maksim Kruglov, as well as Igor Ivanov, the Black Bishop of the Kremlin and the president's close adviser.

"I have no idea, sir," Suslova said. "We can't ask her. But that information, which she must have passed to Robinson, was enough to give them a starting point. It's no coincidence that this all happened immediately after Robinson and Shevchenko met here in Moscow. I understand the CIA used a war crimes investigator who has caused issues for Russia in the past, Joe Johnson. My understanding—"

"That bastard," Ivanov interrupted. The president's special adviser's forehead was so furrowed that his eyebrows had joined in the center.

"Yes, him," Suslova said. "My understanding from a source inside the BND is that he unearthed several old Stasi files at the archive in Berlin using the code names and the handler's chess clubs and somehow managed to draw links between them. He put two and two together and came up with four. It's not the first time."

There was a long silence around the table.

The only sound was the tapping of Putin's index finger on the table. It was a recent habit that the president had developed, and Suslova found it increasingly irritating as well as unnerving.

Suslova noticed Putin's gaze swivel around to Gennady Sidorenko, chief of DX, the specialist small SVR counterintelligence team that was seconded for part of the time to Putin's office.

Bljad.

Sonofabitch. Surely Putin wasn't going to ask Sidorenko to start an internal investigation into this.

"Gennady," the president said. "I would like you to take a close look at the circumstances behind ALYOSHA's exposure in particular, but also ILYA too. How did it happen—what did Shevchenko know and pass on before she died? Maybe the reasons are as Kira has described, or maybe there is more to it. Either way, I would like to know. Report back to me by Saturday."

Shit.

"Yes sir," Sidorenko said. His blue eyes seemed to stick out like organ stops. He patted his stomach, which stuck out even farther than his eyes, with both hands. "I will take pleasure in getting to the bottom of this, sir, don't worry."

"Good," Suslova said. "If I can help, please just ask."

Sidorenko looked sideways at her. "Don't worry, I will do exactly that."

Putin propped his chin in his right hand, elbow resting on the table, and eyed Suslova again. "And the FIDE presidency. How is the campaign going?"

"It's on track, sir," Suslova said. "The lobbying program is progressing. Most chess federations I've met are on board, and those that are not, I'm applying whatever level of persuasion is required to get them there, financial or otherwise."

"I hope this fiasco in Berlin isn't going to affect the German federation's stance," Putin said.

"There's no reason why it should. We will lose the federation president, Paulsen, of course, but I have already put generous arrangements in place to support the wider game in Germany. I hope that will prove sufficient to persuade Paulsen's successor to vote in my favor."

"I hope so too," Putin said, his tone ice-cold. "For your sake. I have provided you with an extremely generous level of funding to ensure the FIDE presidency is secured."

"You have, sir. I'm grateful for that."

Suslova knew she would have to think very hard about

how to resolve the missing two billion. There was no doubt the CIA had played a good hand—that bitch Robinson was not to be underestimated. She obviously couldn't mention it to Putin or indeed anyone else in the Kremlin without slitting her own throat. It was something she would need to fix herself—and fairly quickly.

She would somehow have to persuade the CIA to give the money back. But they would without doubt want a high-value trade in return—unless, that is, she could think of a way to force the issue.

Suslova was now regretting sending in Peskov and Matrosov to terminate Robinson at Paulsen's house on Lake Wannsee. It was still unclear what had gone wrong there, and she might never find out. But it had done no good, and had cost her two top-class operatives. That would now be another headache, to find replacements, but she did have a couple of people in mind who would fit the bill. There was no shortage of former Spetsnaz or Vagnar Group men available.

Suslova sat back in her chair.

Suddenly, at fifty-nine, and after thirty-five years working for the Motherland, she was feeling the pressure.

Was the umbilical cord that tethered her to the Motherland about to be cut? Was the president going to wield the knife?

It was impossible to say. But Suslova knew she needed to work fast and effectively to salvage her situation.

EPILOGUE

Saturday, October 22, 2016
Portland, Maine

The front-page headline in *The Washington Post* summed it up.

"How Ex-Nazi Hunter Nailed German Leader—Putin's Crony," it read.

The story was being scrutinized by an old man nursing his coffee in Becky's Diner.

Jayne watched from the neighboring table as the man read the text, then turned to an inside page, where the story continued. He put the coffee down, folded the paper in half, propped it up against his ketchup bottle, and carried on reading as he started to munch a slice of toast.

There was a photograph of Joe holding two chunky files in front of the Stasi Records Agency building in Berlin. Next to it were headshots of Erich Merck and French intelligence chief Jean Revel.

Becky's Diner, an all-day two-story eatery on Portland's waterfront, had been one of Joe's longstanding favorite places for a breakfast treat ever since the place had opened in the early nineties. It was always full of dockworkers, fishermen, locals, and tourists.

Since moving across the Atlantic to join him, Jayne had come to look forward to their occasional visits to the diner on Hobson's Wharf with his children, Carrie and Peter.

Jayne turned her attention away from the old man and back to the waitress, who was standing next to her. She didn't bother looking at the menu but just reeled off her choice.

"Eggs Florentine with sautéed spinach and grilled tomatoes," she said. "And a blueberry pancake, please." She was the last of the family to order,

"The usual, then?" the waitress said with a grin as she scribbled it onto her notepad.

"That's it," Jayne said. "Well done. You don't need that notebook."

"Coffee refill?" the waitress asked with a smile, picking up the steel flask that she had placed on the table.

Jayne drained the remains of her first coffee from a white mug with "Becky's" emblazoned on the side and held it out for more.

When the waitress had gone, Jayne sank back into the red padded bench seat.

She was still feeling completely jet-lagged after their long flight back from Berlin to Portland the previous day, via New Jersey's Newark Airport. The bottomless coffee was making only a marginal impact on her level of exhaustion, despite nearly ten hours of sleep.

Becky, the cheerful brunette who owned the diner, walked past wearing a blue sweater with a large Stars and Stripes knitted into the front. She nodded at Joe and Jayne. "Good to see you guys again," she said.

To Jayne's left on the red seat, lounging up against the window, Carrie sipped an orange juice. She now looked somewhat less emotional than when she had greeted them at the airport, along with her brother Peter and her aunt Amy.

Carrie, Peter, and their father had hugged in a tight circle in the arrivals hall as if they would never let go of each other.

"So, Dad," Carrie said. "You can tell us now how you got them."

"Got what?" Joe said.

"Those bruises. I saw them, all down your side when you pulled your shirt up this morning. Purple and green. Horrible things. What happened?"

"You don't want to know," Joe said, his lips pressed together. "All I'll say is, it was the Russians who took me from Amsterdam. But it didn't do them any good, because neither of them will give anyone a bruise ever again."

"What, they're dead?" Carrie asked.

Joe nodded.

There was a pause.

"You're not telling me you killed them, are you?" Carrie asked, a note of incredulity in her voice.

"No, I'm not, because I didn't," Joe said, truthfully. "Now, no more questions about that. Let's enjoy our breakfast."

Jayne was thankful that Carrie took her father's hint and didn't ask her if she had played a part in the demise of the two Russians. She was still getting vivid flashbacks of the second one falling into Lake Wannsee. He had eventually been identified by German police as Andrey Peskov, a member of the private military unit the Vagnar Group, while the other was Feodor Matrosov, also a Vagnar employee.

It had taken little deduction for Jayne and Joe to work out that the two men killed at Paulsen's home were the same pair who had kidnapped Joe, and that Peskov was the "Andrey" who'd grabbed her and Grewall in Suslova's house.

"Anyway, it seems that you're famous, Dad," said Peter, who was sitting next to his father on the opposite side of the table. He nodded toward the old man at the neighboring table, having also noticed what he was reading.

Joe put his fingers to his lips. So far, neither the old man nor anyone else in Becky's seemed to have realized that the man in the news was sitting nearby.

The plan, inspired by President Ferguson and delivered by Jayne, Vic, and the Berlin embassy's communications adviser, seemed to be working perfectly so far.

The Washington Post's Berlin bureau chief had written the story, based on an initial background briefing from Vic and then an on-the-record interview with Joe. It described in some detail how Joe had pieced together fragments of detail sourced from various Stasi files and index cards to finally identify two Kremlin moles at the apex of Western European politics and their handler, a leading figure in German chess and lawyer, Wolfgang Paulsen.

There was no mention of Kira Suslova, Jayne Robinson, the deaths in Berlin of two Vagnar Group assassins, or the gruesome killing in Moscow of CIA agent Anastasia Shevchenko. Neither did it mention any link to the murder in London the previous month of Pyotr Fradkov.

In fact, Fradkov's demise seemed like half a lifetime ago to Jayne. A lot of water had passed down the Moskva River since then.

A text message that Jayne had received that morning from a Russian burner phone had lifted her spirits.

I believe I am cleared here. Internal investigation found nothing. You had better ensure this remains the case.

The message was unsigned. But the number was the one that Jayne had memorized in Suslova's basement.

Now she just had to hope that *The Washington Post* story was taken at face value by the Kremlin and any potential remaining heat was removed from Suslova.

Jayne's gut feeling was that the $2 billion still sitting in a

CIA offshore account would prove an extremely valuable blackmail tool, as would their knowledge of her lovers, and that they had saved her from a horrific ordeal in prison—or worse. It should mean that useful intelligence could be extracted at some point further down the line from the chess queen.

There was no way of knowing what those circumstances might be, or whether it would happen at all.

But for now, the job was done.

Joe caught Jayne's eye while Carrie and Peter got into a separate conversation about a band they were due to see the following night in Portland.

"How are you feeling?" he asked.

"I feel like we've achieved something significant, and NATO is cranking up sanctions against Russia," Jayne said. "But I'm less sure what the impact is going to be. We've removed two serious traitors and their handler, but the fact is, Germany is hooked on Russian gas."

Joe nodded. "If you want my view, I think Russia will try to march into Ukraine before Germany does anything about that. I seriously hope I'm wrong, but let's see. Anyway, you've more than done your bit to stop it—a fantastic achievement, Jayne, even if I took all the credit for it."

He grinned broadly and waved his hand toward the man at the next table, who was still reading the interview feature. A separate story on the front page reported that the German chancellor had now been charged with treason and espionage and was in police custody awaiting trial.

"Nothing changes in this business," Jayne said. "The real workers get none of the recognition."

"I'll make it up to you once we get home," Joe said. He winked and rubbed his foot slowly up and down Jayne's calf beneath the table. "That will be the real exclusive story of today—one that the *Post* missed out on."

Jayne suddenly forgot her tiredness as a shot of chemicals ran through her. She glanced sideways at Carrie and Peter, but they were still engrossed in their own conversation.

"That's a deal," she said.

* * *

PRE-ORDER THE NEXT BOOK:
Book 5 in the **Jayne Robinson** series

The Dam Keeper

If you enjoyed ***The Queen's Pawn***, you may like to pre-order the next book I am writing. It will be Book 5 in this **Jayne Robinson** series, entitled ***The Dam Keeper***. It is scheduled to be published in mid-2023, depending on progress. It is available to pre-order in Kindle format on Amazon—unfortunately, Amazon does not allow pre-orders for paperbacks. If you make a pre-order, the book will be automatically delivered to your reading device as soon as it is published. You will only be charged on delivery.

To pre-order ***The Dam Keeper,*** just type "Andrew Turpin The Dam Keeper" in the search box at the top of the Amazon page and you'll find it.

I should mention here that if you like **paperbacks**, you can buy copies of all of my books at my website shop. I can deliver to anywhere in the US and UK, although not currently other countries. That may change in the future. You will find generous discounts if you are buying multiple books or series bundles, which makes them significantly cheaper than using Amazon. Go to:

https://www.andrewturpin.com/shop/

To give you a flavor of **The Dam Keeper**, here's the blurb:

Two CIA officers die during an undercover operation on a Ukrainian dam. Intelligence operative Jayne Robinson is tasked with unearthing the reason for the hit. And the United States faces a horrifying new threat.

The dead CIA officers were part of a team trying to gather intelligence on how best to defend Ukraine's dams against a possible Russian strike to destroy them, and flood its cities and towns.

But the killings happen as Russia appears increasingly intent on a military invasion of Ukraine—so what is the Kremlin so anxious to hide?

The United States president, who is desperate to avoid being dragged into a war with Russia in Europe, urgently needs to know.

Robinson gets involved in a high-stakes game of international poker with a top-level asset she now has inside the Russian president's inner circle.

Can the asset—recruited under coercion—be trusted? Can Robinson get what she needs? Or will her operation, already on a knife-edge, go badly wrong?

The Dam Keeper, book number five in the internationally top-selling Jayne Robinson series, is another gripping spy thriller with dramatic twists that will keep readers up deep into the night.

* * *

ANDREW'S READERS GROUP

If you enjoyed this book, I would like to keep in touch. This is not always easy, as I usually only publish a couple of books a year and there are many authors and books out there. So the best way is for you to be on my Readers Group email list. I can then send you updates on the next book, plus occasional special offers. There's no spam and you can unsubscribe at any time.

If you would like to join my Readers Group and receive the email updates, I will send you, **FREE**, the ebook version of another thriller, *The Afghan*, which forms a prequel to both the **Jayne Robinson** series and my **Joe Johnson** series and normally sells at $4.99/£3.99 (paperback $11.99/£9.99).

The Afghan is set in 1988 when Jayne was with Britain's Secret Intelligence Service and Joe Johnson was with the CIA —both of them based in Pakistan and Afghanistan. Most of the action takes place in Afghanistan, then occupied by the Soviet Union, and in Washington, DC. Some of the characters and story lines that emerge in my other books have their roots in this period. I think you will enjoy it!

The Afghan can be downloaded **FREE** from the following link:

https://bookhip.com/RJGFPAW

The **Jayne Robinson** thriller series so far comprises the following:

1. The Kremlin's Vote
2. The Dark Shah
3. The Confessor
4. The Queen's Pawn
5. The Dam Keeper (due to be published mid-2023)

If you have enjoyed the Robinson series, you will probably also like the **Joe Johnson series**, if you haven't read them yet. In order, they are as follows:

Prequel: *The Afghan*
1. *The Last Nazi*
2. *The Old Bridge*
3. *Bandit Country*
4. *Stalin's Final Sting*
5. *The Nazi's Son*
6. *The Black Sea*

To find my books on Amazon just type "Andrew Turpin" in the search box at the top of the Amazon page — you can't miss them!

* * *

IF YOU ENJOYED THIS BOOK PLEASE WRITE A REVIEW

As an independently published author, through my own imprint The Write Direction Publishing, I find that honest reviews of my books are the most powerful way for me to bring them to the attention of other potential readers.

As you'll appreciate, unlike the big international publishers, I can't take out full-page advertisements in the newspapers.

So I am committed to producing books of the best quality I can in order to attract a loyal group of readers who are happy to recommend my work to others.

Therefore, if you enjoyed reading this novel, then I would very much appreciate it if you would spend five minutes and leave a review—which can be as short as you like—preferably on the page or website where you bought it.

You can find the book on the Amazon website by typing "Andrew Turpin The Queen's Pawn" in the search box.

Once you have clicked on the page, scroll down to "Customer Reviews," then click on "Leave a Review."

Reviews are also a great encouragement to me to write more!

Many thanks.

THANKS AND ACKNOWLEDGEMENTS

I would like to thank everyone who reads my books. You are the reason I began to write in the first place, and I hope I can provide you with entertainment and interest for a long time into the future.

Every time I get an encouraging email from a reader, or a positive comment on my Facebook page, or a nice review on Amazon, it spurs me on to press ahead with my research and writing for the next book. So keep them coming!

Specifically with regard to *The Queen's Pawn*, there are several people who have helped me during the long process of research, writing, and editing.

In particular, I have two editors who consistently provide helpful advice, food for thought, great ideas, and constructive criticism, and between them have enabled me to considerably improve the initial draft. Katrina Diaz Arnold, owner of Refine Editing, again gave me a lot of valuable feedback at the structural and line levels, and Jon Ford, as ever, helped me to maintain the authenticity of the story in many areas through his great eye for detail. I would like to thank both of them—the responsibility for any remaining mistakes lies solely with me.

As always, my brother, Adrian Turpin, was a very helpful reader of my early drafts and highlighted areas where I need to improve. I also had very valuable input from my small but dedicated Advance Readers Group team, who went through the final version prior to proofreading and also highlighted a number of issues that required changes and improvements—a big thank-you to them all.

I would also like to thank the team at Damonza for what I think is a great cover design.

AUTHOR'S NOTE

In my younger days, when free time was not the luxury it often seems now, I used to enjoy playing chess for school teams and during rainy lunch breaks. As a child of the Sixties and Seventies, alongside my interests in cricket, soccer, and music, I found myself following in a minor way the clashes between international grandmasters such as Bobby Fischer, Boris Spassky, Anatoly Karpov, and Viktor Korchnoi.

The game of chess, with its adversarial head-to-head nature, has often seemed like a metaphor for the conflict between East and West, between the Soviet Union and then Russia on one hand, and the United States and its allies on the other.

It is not simply a game played in isolation from the global geopolitics that go on between the superpowers. Indeed, the antagonism seen between rival players has reflected quite closely the jousting seen in the political arena.

The Soviet chess grandmaster Boris Spassky perhaps summed it up in 1972 after his famous Cold War era "Match of the Century" for the World Chess Championship with the American star Bobby Fischer.

"This is about everything but chess," Spassky said.

He eventually lost to Fischer, an eccentric genius who had a tendency toward somewhat erratic and controversial behavior and whose petty demands of the organizers of the 1972 match became greater and greater.

For Spassky and Fischer, read Soviet presidents Leonid Brezhnev or Mikhail Gorbachev, and US presidents Richard Nixon, Jimmy Carter, or Ronald Reagan. Chess was a proxy for politics. Winning represented more than just victory in a chess match.

Needless to say, the conflicts between players across the

board have extended to the governance of chess, too. The Russian Chess Federation's trustee board is chaired by Dmitry Peskov, who is Putin's press spokesman and is the Kremlin's deputy chief of staff. The board is stuffed with other leading political figures and allies of the president, such as the defense minister Sergei Shoigu, and billionaire oligarch Gennady Timchenko, one of Putin's oldest and most loyal allies.

And half a century after the Spassky-Fischer match, it was the drama surrounding the latest election of the president of the game's overall governing body, the International Chess Federation, known as FIDE, that caught my eye.

The FIDE election in 2018 came about because Russian oligarch Kiran Ilyumzhinov, the president since 1995, was forced out of office. This was due to US sanctions imposed on him because of his support for and assistance to the dictatorial regime of the Syrian president Bashar al-Assad, an ally of Russia.

The lengths that Russia went to in order to gain victory for Arkady Dvorkovich, its replacement candidate in the 2018 election, were remarkable. Having held the presidency of FIDE since 1995, Russia wasn't prepared to surrender it easily.

Dvorkovich, previously the deputy prime minister of Russia, was elected amid widespread allegations of bribery of many of the 189 national chess federations who vote for the FIDE chairman. Large amounts of cash allegedly changed hands. There were offers to boost national chess federation funds, other financial incentives such as support for chess tournaments, and further down the scale, free tickets to soccer World Cup games, and so on. Much of the activity was coordinated through Russian embassies in many countries.

Such methods are a perfect illustration of how Russia has aggressively set out to use sport and games in a strategic way for political ends. Think of the many doping scandals that have enveloped the Russian athletics and gymnastics teams, for example.

One key objective has been to try and demonstrate the superiority of the Russian system. But another has been to use FIDE to influence and recruit highly placed individuals in order to further Russia's strategic objectives globally.

It struck me that all this would form an excellent backdrop for one of Jayne Robinson's investigations, especially as she had a strong interest in and capability at chess when younger. For decades, key figures in Russian chess have been agents of Russian intelligence—the KGB and its successor agency the SVR. So who might they have recruited among Western countries? And what damage might those individuals have done since?

This, of course, has coincided with the Russian invasion of Ukraine, which began in 2014 with its annexation of the Crimea and infiltration of the eastern Ukrainian provinces of Donetsk and Luhansk, where it provided military assistance to separatist forces.

In early 2022, as I was plotting this book, Russia launched a full-scale invasion of Ukraine. A key element of Russian president Vladimir Putin's strategy has been to try to head off international opposition to the invasion from European countries by blackmailing them with threats to cut off the huge volumes of Russian gas that they import.

This gas is delivered to Europe through a number of long distance pipelines, including the Nord Stream 1 pipeline under the Baltic Sea from Russia into Germany, which began operations in 2011. Putin has threatened to cut off Germany and its other customers if they countered the invasion. Until then, Germany and other European countries had supported the construction of the pipelines and spent billions of dollars on gas from Russia. Indeed, a new Nord Stream 2 pipeline, adding much more gas import capacity from Russia to Germany, had almost been completed when the invasion took place.

One of my other interests is energy—as a financial journalist I used to cover the gas, power, and oil sectors, and then I worked in corporate communications for three large energy companies. I began to wonder, how exactly did Germany and its European neighbors become so dependent on gas from such a dangerous, unpredictable state as Russia? Why did they sign up to such long term deals with Moscow? Surely they must have seen the risks?

That was the question that became the starting point for *The Queen's Pawn*.

In real life, the former German chancellor Gerhard Schröder, who was in office from 1998 to 2005, was an instrumental figure in the construction of the Nord Stream 1 pipeline. He signed off the deal to build it just before leaving the chancellor's office.

As *Washington Post* journalist Rick Noack reported in 2018, "In 2005, Russian President Vladimir Putin's friend Schröder hastily signed the deal just as he was departing the office from which he had been voted out days earlier. Within weeks, he started to oversee the project implementation himself, leading the Nord Stream AG's shareholder committee."

I should point out that in answer to the question of why did Germany sign such a deal with Putin, from this stage on, the rest of my plot and the characters within it are purely fictional. Any resemblance to real life events and people is entirely coincidental. On the occasions where I have described real life places and organizations, I have done so in an entirely fictional manner. This includes the depiction of the Russian president, whose character and actions as portrayed in this book stem from my imagination.

In particular, there is no suggestion that there is actually a

German chancellor named Engel Mankel who was corrupted by a chess-playing Russian agent in order for Russia to sell more gas to Germany. That is despite the questions being asked about why the German government became so close to and dependent on Russia's gas supply operation over recent decades.

Prior to the 2022 invasion of Ukraine, Germany sourced about fifty-five percent of its gas and a third of its oil from Russia. Some leaders in Germany clearly thought this a good idea, despite numerous warnings from the United States and others about the dangers of becoming too close to Russia.

Similarly, my depiction of Jean Revel, head of the French military intelligence unit, the DRM, is entirely fictional. However, it is true to say that before the invasion, France bought around a fifth of its natural gas requirements from Russia. The French government had clearly been advised, and had decided, that this would not create problems in future.

To the best of my knowledge, no German grandmaster used those two well-known chess clubs in Berlin, Schach-Club Kreuzberg and Schachverein Berolina Mitte, as a base to recruit agents for the Soviet Union or Russia in the West during the Cold War or afterward. My apologies to both clubs for using them in such a dramatic manner in my story.

Also the German Chess Federation, the Deutscher Schachbund, has never been led by an agent of Russia, and former Stasi agent, such as my fictional president Wolfgang Paulsen, to the best of my knowledge.

Chess enthusiasts will comb the records of past matches in vain for the names Paulsen and Nick Longland, as neither exist in real life.

I have slightly twisted the chronology of FIDE's head-quarters location in Lausanne to suit my plot. In 2016, when the book is set, FIDE was actually based in Athens. The organization decided only in 2018 to return to Lausanne, and that relocation to the Maison du Sport International complex was completed in 2019. FIDE had previously been based in Lausanne from 1995 to 2004.

For details of further reading relating to the plot of **_The Queen's Pawn_**, see the next section, which covers some of the sources I used during my research prior to and during the writing of this book.

All the best,
    Andrew

RESEARCH AND BIBLIOGRAPHY

Given the Russian invasion of Ukraine, which occurred just after I had begun researching this book, my background reading and online trawling took on a whole new level of interest. I decided to find an angle on this story for my protagonist Jayne Robinson to investigate—and there was no shortage of options.

What follows here is necessarily a truncated list of the hundreds of sources I used while researching this book. Hopefully the list forms a kind of highlights package on which you can draw if you are minded to do further reading on the subject of modern Russia and how it has been shaped to Vladimir Putin's will—as well as the importance of chess within the country.

One of the initial sparks for my plot came from reading a book with the irresistible title *The KGB Plays Chess*, written by a former KGB officer and a Russian journalist with contributions from two chess grandmasters. It describes how the Soviet secret police controlled the game and the players within it and used some of them as political tools on the world stage.

The two grandmasters involved in the book, Boris Gulko and Viktor Kortschnoi, both ended up defecting to the West, Gulko to the United States and Kortschnoi to Switzerland. They both suffered intimidation, restrictions, and targeting by the KGB.

By contrast, the KGB favored another Russian grandmaster and world champion, Anatoly Karpov, who toed the Kremlin line far more and was a KGB agent with the codename Raoul as well as a favorite of Soviet leader Leonid Brezhnev.

Particularly enlightening are the accounts of how the

KGB, on Brezhnev's instructions, ensured that Karpov emerged victorious in a world championship match against Kortschnoi in the Philippines in 1978.

Later, yet another Russian genius grandmaster and world champion who opposed the regime, Garry Kasparov, also ended up fleeing abroad. He moved first to the United States and then to Croatia, where he has gained citizenship.

But the biggest underlying message of the book is the extent to which the KGB, directed by the Kremlin, saw chess as part of its strategy in its conflict with the West.

Following the breakup of the Soviet Union, little has changed. Russia's successor foreign intelligence agencies to the KGB, principally the SVR and the GRU, still operate along similar lines, as seen in the immense effort to retain the Russian presidency of the International Chess Federation, FIDE, in 2018.

You can find *The KGB Plays Chess* here: https://www.amazon.com/dp/B0044XV6ZC

Another fascinating insight into how the Russian security machine focuses on chess to help achieve much broader objectives comes in Garry Kasparov's book, *Winter is Coming*. The book describes the threat to the West and to the Russian people stemming from President Putin's dictatorship over the past couple of decades. *Winter is Coming* can be found here: https://www.amazon.com/dp/B010KMZTTY

For a more general view of how the old KGB has been effectively resurrected under Putin, slamming the door on any hopes of greater democracy in Russia, look no further than *Putin's People* by former Financial Times Moscow correspondent Catherine Belton. It describes how the coterie of KGB people with whom Putin worked in East Germany and elsewhere during the 1980s are now running Russia and enriching themselves in the process—they are Russia's new ruling class. You can find *Putin's People* here: https://www.amazon.com/dp/B00X6K0GB4

Another very informative book on Putin and how he has taken control of Russia has been written by Masha Gessen, entitled The Man Without a Face: The Unlikely Rise of Vladimir Putin. You can find it here: https://www.amazon.com/dp/B0078XFTTE

In similar vein is a book entitled *Putin's Kleptocracy: Who Owns Russia?*, by Karen Dawisha, an American academic and writer, who also published several other notable books on Russia.

Dawisha, who sadly passed away in 2018, specialized in Russian politics and especially the background to the small number of oligarchs who between them own most of the major assets within the country. If you're interested in how these oligarchs came to plunder the country, take a look. You can find the book here: https://www.amazon.com/dp/1476795207

There are many good analytical articles out there too that might be a somewhat quicker read than the books above. Some pre-date Russia's invasion of Ukraine, others have come since.

First, on the subject of the Kremlin and Putin, and the role that chess plays in the Russian leadership's broader strategy, a good informative article was published in the Financial Times in 2019, looking back at the election for the presidency of the International Chess Congress, FIDE. Along with the book mentioned above, The KGB Plays Chess, it served as an initial catalyst for the plot in The Queen's Pawn. You can find the article, headlined "How chess became a pawn in the Kremlin's power game," here: https://www.ft.com/content/f4d0dfea-559d-11e9-91f9-b6515a54c5b1

Another interesting article on the same topic appeared on WIRED website, written by Daphne Leprince-Ringuet and

which can be found here: https://www.wired.co.uk/article/
world-chess-championship-2018-london-carlsen-vs-caruana

For those who look at my chess-playing Kremlin character Kira Suslova and think that chess in the Soviet Union
and then Russia has been an entirely male dominated game,
think again. There have been very many top Russian women
chess players, as reported by Jacobin, the American political
magazine. Their excellent article, which references The
Queen's Gambit, the Netflix series featuring a woman chess
player, can be found here: https://jacobin.com/2021/09/netflix-
the-queens-gambit-soviet-chess-grandmaster-nona-
gaprindashvili-sue-lawsuit-champion

Following the invasion of Ukraine, Russia's long-running
presidency of the International Chess Congress—dating to
1995—has not gone unchallenged. In the 2022 election, a
Ukraine-born grandmaster, Andrii Baryshpolets, stood as
candidate alongside two other rivals to the Russian incum-
bent Arkady Dvorkovich.

Baryshpolets highlighted the way in which Russia has
used FIDE as a "soft power to whiten its reputation." The
Financial Times carried a story on this, headed "Ukrainian
grandmaster moves to check Russia's domination of world
chess federation." You can find it here: https://www.ft.com/
content/a399323c-0c9a-4cf3-ae34-e5c6bb82d570

However, Dvorkovich emerged triumphant from the election and remains as president.

On the issue of Germany and other European countries
becoming "hooked" on Russian gas, thus encouraging Putin
to march into Ukraine, and how this addiction came about,
there are many good analytical articles.

The Times scrutinized the Nord Stream gas pipeline
between Russia and Germany in the context of the links
between former German chancellor Gerhard Schröder and
Vladimir Putin, and a former Stasi spy who was managing

director of the Nord Stream project, Matthias Warnig. You can find the story, "Putin's Nord Stream 2 pipeline: the Stasi connection," here: https://www.thetimes.co.uk/article/putins-gas-pipeline-the-stasi-connection-fklvlkk5q

Another feature in The Guardian, "Circles of power: Putin's secret friendship with ex-Stasi officer," tells of the close links between Schröder, Putin, and Warnig. It reports on how Putin and Warnig got to know each other in 1991 in St Petersburg: https://www.theguardian.com/world/2014/aug/13/russia-putin-german-right-hand-man-matthias-warnig

An article in Der Spiegel, "Tasteless Relations Between Gerhard Schröder and Putin," gives more details on Schröder's close relationship with Putin, who celebrated the former German chancellor's seventieth birthday with him: https://www.spiegel.de/international/germany/editorial-on-tasteless-relations-between-gerhard-schroeder-and-putin-a-966718.html

And another piece by Patrick Wintour in The Guardian about Germany's dependence on Russia for gas and oil supplies is also illuminating: https://www.theguardian.com/world/2022/jun/02/germany-dependence-russian-energy-gas-oil-nord-stream

The Washington Post article by Rick Noack mentioned in the Author's Note — "The Russian pipeline to Germany that Trump is so mad about, explained," — about former German chancellor Gerhard Schröder's relationship with Putin and his decision to sign a deal to build the Nord Stream 1 gas pipeline, can be found here: https://www.washingtonpost.com/news/worldviews/wp/2018/07/11/the-russian-pipeline-to-germany-that-trump-is-so-mad-about-explained/?variant=d846d44221ecba95

And there is another in The Wall Street Journal, "How Europe Hopes to Wean Itself From Russian Natural Gas," describing how rather too belatedly, Europe is now trying to

reduce its volumes of Russian gas: https://www.wsj.com/arti
cles/how-europe-hopes-to-wean-itself-from-russian-natural-
gas-11647163803

There is also an article in Politico, "Why Merkel chose Russia over US on Nord Stream 2," that describes how Germany's leadership actively chose to align itself with Russia on natural gas supplies, and how after Gerhard Schroder stepped down as German chancellor in 2005, he almost immediately took a job as chairman of gas pipeline company Nord Stream: https://www.politico.eu/article/vladimir-putin-german-chancellors-nord-stream-russia-energy-angela-merkel/

That's enough of Russia and Germany and gas. On to other matters raised in *The Queen's Pawn*.

The Russian security services, specifically the FSB, have the kind of surveillance powers over Russian citizens that would likely cause outrage in the West.

One example is the work ongoing on technology such as gait recognition systems—which Jayne nearly fell foul of. The technology is linked to the enormous network of surveillance cameras in Moscow and other cities. More information at: https://www.biometricupdate.com/202002/russian-ministry-testing-gait-recognition-as-part-of-national-biometric-surveillance-system

There is no such organization as my fictional Vagnar private paramilitary group for whom Andrey Peskov works. But there is a similar business in real life, called the Wagner Group, believed to be owned or financed by Russian oligarch Yevgeny Prigozhin. Its mercenaries have most recently been seen working in Ukraine on behalf of the Kremlin, and before that in many other conflict zones. Read more at: https://www.news.com.au/world/europe/death-is-our-business-inside-russ
ian-presidents-private-militia-the-wagner-group/news-story/
2fcddo3311eb14e03ffc4635fdaea81c

A significant element of the battle between Russia and the

West has been conducted in cyber space, with a battery of hackers operating out of Moscow, St. Petersburg, and other cities, attacking servers in Ukraine and elsewhere. But the West has been fighting back hard, with a new breed of online keyboard warriors in Ukraine giving as much as they get—a little like Grigori Azarov, head of Kyiv-based Cyber Penetrators, in *The Queen's Pawn*. To read more try this article, "Russia pummelled by pro-Ukrainian hackers following invasion," in the Financial Times: https://www.ft.com/content/3391bf8c-e431-415c-b7c5-9eeee08b3374

Another article, in The Register, describes how a bank account was drained of $60 million by hackers, in similar vein to the way in which Azarov emptied Kira Suslova's account. See: https://www.theregister.com/2016/08/31/swift_reuters/

Another story in similar vein about a hacking attack on a Russian bank can be found here: https://www.reuters.com/article/us-russia-cyber-swift-idUSKCN1Goo0DV

The area around Lake Wannsee, west of Berlin, where my fictional lawyer and chess player Wolfgang Paulsen lives, is well-known for its grand houses and wealthy residents. One of the largest and grandest villas, at 56-58 Am Großen Wannsee, was the location for the so-called Wannsee Conference in 1942. At this conference, Adolf Hitler and his Nazi party colleagues briefed government department heads and others on how to implement the Final Solution—the intended extermination of European Jews. More details can be found in this Wikipedia article: https://en.wikipedia.org/wiki/Wannsee_Conference

I found the investigation carried out by Joe Johnson at the Stasi Records Agency in Berlin an interesting one to research. The building in which the old Stasi files are kept is the same one in which the much-feared East German secret police operated during the Cold War era, albeit now modernized. I have slightly simplified for my plot's purposes the nature of the records that were kept during that period, including the 1980s, but have kept as close to the facts as possible.

You can read more about the Stasi Records Agency and the files kept within it at these links:

"Card systems of the Stasi,": https://owenmundy.com/blog/2017/05/stasi-facebook-big-data-daad-day-10-card-systems-of-the-stasi/

"Access to Stasi files keeps the past in the present – and allows for reconciliation,": https://www.irishtimes.com/news/world/europe/access-to-stasi-files-keeps-the-past-in-the-present-and-allows-for-reconciliation-1.1693950

There is a wealth of interesting background information on the Stasi Records Agency at its website: https://www.stasi-unterlagen-archiv.de/en/

"Germans piece together millions of lives spied on by Stasi,": https://www.theguardian.com/world/2011/mar/13/east-germany-stasi-files-zirndorf

For more background on Vladimir Putin's time in the KGB in East Germany, the following article on the BBC website is worth reading, "Vladimir Putin's formative German years,": https://www.bbc.co.uk/news/magazine-32066222

Similarly with this article on the Russia Beyond website. "Everything you ever wanted to know about Putin's work in East Germany,": https://www.rbth.com/politics_and_society/2017/08/08/everything-you-ever-wanted-to-know-about-putins-work-in-east-germany_818928

Finally, for chess enthusiasts who want to know more about the two famous Berlin chess clubs that feature in The Queen's Pawn, try the following sites. The Kreuzberg club's site, in particular, has a history section that explains how the game was organized in the city during the Cold War era and beyond.

For the Schachverein Berolina Mitte: https://www.svberolinamitte.de/

And for the Schach-Club Kreuzberg: https://www.schachclubkreuzberg.de/

The above details give you at least a flavor of some of the sources and locations I have used in this book. There are, of course, many more, too numerous to mention. I hope it is helpful—I am quite willing to exchange emails if readers have questions about any others not detailed here or if you spot something that you think should be corrected.

ABOUT THE AUTHOR AND CONTACT DETAILS

I have always had a love of writing and a passion for reading good thrillers. I also had a long-standing dream of writing my own novels, and eventually, I got around to achieving that objective.

The Queen's Pawn is the fourth in the **Jayne Robinson** series of thrillers, which follows on from my **Joe Johnson** series (currently comprising six books plus a prequel). These books pull together some of my other interests, particularly history, world news, and travel.

I studied history at Loughborough University and worked for many years as a business and financial journalist before becoming a corporate and financial communications adviser with several large energy companies, specializing in media relations. I am now a full-time writer.

Originally, I came from Grantham, Lincolnshire, and I now live with my family in St. Albans, Hertfordshire, UK.

You can connect with me via these routes:

E-mail: andrew@andrewturpin.com

Website: www.andrewturpin.com.

Facebook: @AndrewTurpinAuthor

Facebook Readers Group: https://www.facebook.com/groups/1202837536552219

Twitter: @AndrewTurpin

Instagram: @andrewturpin.author

Please also follow me on Bookbub and Amazon!

https://www.bookbub.com/authors/andrew-turpin

https://www.amazon.com/Andrew-Turpin/e/B074V87WWL/

Do get in touch with your comments and views on the books, or anything else for that matter. I enjoy hearing from readers and promise to reply.